WHITEHORSE

KATHERINE SUTCLIFFE

JOVE BOOKS, NEW YORK

This is a work of fiction. Names, characters, places, and incidents are either the product of the author's imagination or are used fictitiously, and any resemblance to actual persons, living or dead, business establishments, events or locales is entirely coincidental.

WHITEHORSE

A Jove Book / published by arrangement with
the author

PRINTING HISTORY
Jove edition / November 1999

The Penguin Putnam Inc. World Wide Web site address is
http://www.penguinputnam.com

ISBN: 0-515-12678-0

A JOVE BOOK®
Jove Books are published by The Berkley Publishing Group,
a division of Penguin Putnam Inc.,
375 Hudson Street, New York, New York 10014.
JOVE and the ''J'' design
are trademarks belonging to Penguin Putnam Inc.

PRINTED IN THE UNITED STATES OF AMERICA

10 9 8 7 6 5 4 3 2 1

ONE

"Damn cows. Damn Manord Krups for *owning* cows. Why couldn't he breed dogs or cats, or budgies for that matter? *Anything* that doesn't require a large-animal vet. When is the last time you saw a small-animal vet make a house call for a budgie? I must have been out of my mind to think this is what I wanted to do with the rest of my life. I could be asleep right now in a warm bed, dreaming of pouring coffee for some sexist bastard who thinks copy toner smells like Chanel. Instead, I'm up to my butt in mud, covered in blood, and with a temperature of one hundred and two."

The cell phone crackled with static. Leah Starr, D.V.M., shook it angrily before screaming into the receiver again. "Hello? Can you hear me? Speak up, Shamika. I'm losing you."

". . . I said, you have a message from Roy Moon at Whitehorse Farm . . . a colicky horse or something."

"Do you know what time it is? It's after midnight—"

"Sorry. I guess the horse forgot to check the clock before getting his gut in a twist."

"Tell them to call Dean Crabbet. I've had enough for

tonight. Crabbet is a perfectly reliable vet—''

"Come on, Leah, you knew it was inevitable that they would eventually call. Why shouldn't they, for Pete's sake? You live in their backyard. You lease this farm from them—''

"Forget it!" She punched the End button, cutting off the call, and threw the cell phone onto the truck seat, which was cluttered with a stethoscope, syringes, and shoulder-length rubber gloves. She refused to look at the bloody fetotome on the floorboard. The nausea in her stomach was enough reminder of the fetotomy she had been forced to perform on one of Manord Krups's prized Holsteins. Cutting up a calf in utero that refused to be born was not something she cared to dwell on at the moment. Not when the worst storm to hit Ruidoso, New Mexico, in fifty years was bombarding her truck with hailstones the size of golf balls, turning the already pitiful back road into an ice-skating rink. This was all El Niño's fault. *Again.* This was late May, for God's sake. She should be basking in sunshine and complaining about the heat by now.

God, her throat hurt. She felt as if someone had doused her in kerosene and set her on fire. The fact that she was soaked to the bone wasn't going to help matters one little bit. Neither was the fact that the truck heater was on the blink for the third time this year and there was no longer money in the budget to get it fixed— again. Judging by the way she had begun to shake, she suspected her temperature had just climbed another notch. Thank heavens for Shamika. She would have a honey-laced cup of hot tea waiting for Leah, a warmed blanket to wrap around her shoulders, and a friendly and tolerant ear to listen to Leah's ranting about the pitfalls of being the only woman vet in the area.

Reaching over the steering wheel, Leah scrubbed the condensation from the inside of the windshield and squinted to see through the downpour. With only one good headlight that barely illuminated the way, the dark road might have been an abyss straight to hell. Why she had chosen this route was beyond her—must have been the fever. FM Road 67 was perilous in the best of weather. It twisted and turned like a sidewinder—it had virtually no shoulders and flooded when the skies so much as spit rain. Even now water sucked at her hub-caps. Any deeper and she would stall for certain, and then what? She imagined rescue workers discovering her emaciated, fever-ravaged body somewhere down the river. Good damn deal. At least she would get a decent night's rest for the first time since she'd set foot in the veterinary college at Texas A&M University six years ago.

The hail turned to rain as her headlight reflected off the stop sign at the junction of Highways 249 and 67. Leah took a deep breath and mopped her brow with her shirt sleeve. Almost home. Another fifteen, twenty minutes max and she would climb into a steaming tub of water and then bed. She would not so much as stick her head out of the covers for three days. She might even down a few sedatives to assure that she slept un-disturbed. Not wise, certainly, but occasionally neces-sary when the world became more than she could tolerate. Trouble was, the world was becoming much too intolerable of late.

It would be smooth sailing from here. The road was good. No danger of flooding. She checked the truck clock. It showed ten-ten. "Liar," she said, and thumped the plastic cover over the clock with her finger, as if the action would miraculously remedy the clock's problem.

Pumping the brakes, Leah eased the truck to a stop where FM 67 teed into Highway 249. The light from her headlamp illuminated the hodgepodge of billboards directly ahead. Visit Ruidoso, Land of the Mescalero Apache! Ski the slopes at Sierra Blanca. Relax at the Inn of the Mountain Gods.

Whitehorse Farm. Two miles south on Highway 249.

The truck idled and the window fogged over as Leah focused on the sign pointing toward Whitehorse Farm.

"Forget it," she said. "I won't do it. The last thing I need right now is to deal with a colicky horse—among other things." She slammed her fist against the steering wheel and listened to the rain drum harder on the car roof. Left would take her south, to the imposing entrance of Whitehorse Farm. Right meant home. A hot bath. Hot tea. Warm blankets. And sleep. Oh God, for a mere hour's worth of uninterrupted sleep . . .

She turned left.

The rain drove in spears and the truck shuddered under the impact of the winds. Tree branches somersaulted across the road. Lightning zigzagged across the sky, briefly outlining the mountains in the distance. Visibility dwindled, forcing Leah to slow the truck to a crawl, to lean partially over the steering wheel to search out the yellow no-passing lines dividing the narrow highway. Her hands began to sweat, as did her scalp.

She reached for the volume control on the radio–cassette player, regretting her action even as the first melodious strains drowned out the rhythmic thump of the wipers and the drone of the rain. Tonight of *all* nights was *not* the night for memories. Her obsession with old Neil Diamond tunes and all the history each song stirred up in her mind, not to mention her heart, was just short of masochistic.

Taking a deep breath, Leah relaxed back against the truck seat and did her best to hum along with the tune, despite the rawness of her throat and the sleep that was beginning to tug at her eyelids.

At first there was nothing before her but road and rain. Then the horse leaped out of the dark and into the small halo of light from her headlamp, its hooves skidding on the asphalt and its terrified eyes reflecting the white beam like mirrors.

Leah slammed on the brakes and wrenched the wheel

to the right. The impact and subsequent spin threw her against the door. The world whirred by in slow motion as the truck slid sideways, bumped over the narrow shoulder, then bounced down the embankment before coming to a sudden stop, all four wheels bogged up to their axles in mud.

Someplace in the foggy and confused blankness of her mind, Neil Diamond continued to croon about love, loss, and loneliness amid the pounding rain and thunder.

Leah opened her eyes and stared through the cracked windshield at the stream of light from her headlamp pooling on the black surface of the water-filled ditch. Odd that the only thought to rouse in that moment was the realization that she had not eaten in twenty-four hours.

From the corner of her eye she saw a movement. Carefully lifting her head, she peered through the driver's window, which was criss-crossed with tiny cracks like mullioned glass. A face materialized that was somehow familiar, with black eyes and a wide, masculine brow shielded from the rain by the limp brim of an old cowboy hat.

"Don't move," the face said.

The man grabbed the door handle and wrenched open the door, leaned over Leah, and popped the seatbelt loose. His shirt was soaked and rain streamed from his hat, down the front of her sweater.

"Dr. Starr?" he asked with the slightest hint of Native American accent, gently touching her face. "Are you all right?"

"What happened?" she finally managed.

"The horse—"

"Oh God. I hit it, didn't I?" She shoved the man back and slid from the truck. Her legs buckled. She grabbed the truck door, vaguely aware that she was bogged to her ankles in mud and the rain was fast drenching her hair and clothes. The cold and wet slammed her back to reality as she looked up into Roy Moon's concerned eyes. "Is it dead?"

He shook his head and his jaw clenched. She had seen that look a hundred times in men's faces when they were too damned macho to allow their emotions to show over an animal. "Where is it?" she shouted through the rain.

Roy pointed to the opposite side of the road where a group of men had collected, some with flashlights trained on the ground. She struggled up the embankment, ran toward the gathering, and elbowed the silent onlookers aside. With rain pounding her head and shoulders, she looked down on the injured horse—a gray Arabian mare on her side, lips drawn back in shock, her breath rising in steamy spurts from her contracted nostrils. No matter how many times she had witnessed a downed horse the last years, she still could not get over the sick feeling the sight gave her. But this was worse than she had first imagined. By the looks of the mare she was very much in foal.

"I think her leg is broke," someone said.

Dropping to her knees, Leah checked the mare's pulse and respiration, talking softly, comfortingly as the horse raised her head and made a sound like a groan in her throat.

"Mr. Whitehorse ain't gonna like this," a man said.

Roy bent down beside Leah. "She was colicky. Ramon was walking her until you arrived. She spooked at the thunder and bolted. Went right through the fence before we could stop her."

Leah noted the cuts and abrasions on the mare's chest and forelegs—nothing that could not be remedied with a few stitches. Blood was nominal. Scarring would be minimal.

"She's in foal," Roy said, his brown face distorting in despair. "This one was going to be special."

"When is she due?"

"Any time."

Leah sat down in the mud, legs crossed, elbows on

her knees. She watched steam rise from the mare's trembling body and did her best to think. "We'll need to address the shock first. Then the leg. There are IVs in the back of my truck. We'll get her stabilized, then try to get her to my lab."

"Are you sure you're all right, Doc?" Roy asked. "You're shakin' awful bad."

Was she?

Blinking rain from her eyes, Leah stared down at her hands, which were trembling badly—too badly to attempt inserting a needle into the mare's vein.

A dually truck approached, its diesel engine roaring more loudly than the rain. It pulled off the road and onto the shoulder, its headlights blinding Leah so she was forced to shield her eyes with her hand.

"Here comes trouble," someone whispered.

"I'm outta here," said another.

The truck door opened.

Johnny Whitehorse stepped out, his long legs clad in tight denim. He wore a fringed buckskin jacket and a sweat-stained cowboy hat. He had allowed his black hair to grow long again—Leah remembered the first time he'd cut it those years ago, thinking he would better blend in with the white boys on the football team. The idea seemed as ridiculous now as it had then. A Mescalero Apache standing six foot three at sixteen years old, Johnny Whitehorse had stood as much chance of blending in with the Anglo crowd of Ruidoso High as the Trump Tower would if it were set smack in the middle of the Mescalero reservation.

Roy put his hand on her shoulder and squeezed it reassuringly. "You sure you're up to this?" he asked softly.

"It was going to happen eventually," she snapped more curtly than she intended, then shakily smiled her apology. "Will you help me up? I'm not certain my legs will hold me."

Roy offered his hand. She clung to it almost desper-

ately as she attempted to stand, telling herself that her
reasons for this ridiculous light-headedness had more to
do with her near-disaster, not to mention her exhaustion,
than it did with the fact that after twelve years she was
about to come face to face with the only man she had
ever really loved—and here she stood in the mud after
running down one of his prized mares. Knowing
Johnny's reputation for confrontation, she suspected this
wasn't going to be pleasant.

Adjusting his hat over his brow, Johnny stepped down
the embankment with the same ease of movement that
had fascinated her those years ago. He walked to the
horse, regarding the mare a silent moment before raising
his gaze to Leah.

She held her breath.

Johnny's eyes narrowed. One corner of his mouth
turned under ever so slightly as he regarded her up and
down.

Roy cleared his throat. "You remember Doc Starr,
Johnny. Used to be Leah Foster."

"I know who the hell she is," Johnny drawled, looking back at the horse. "Can she be saved?" he asked in
a monotone.

Leah opened and closed her mouth as her mind scattered over a thousand things she thought he *might* have
said in that moment: Gee, long time no see; I've thought
of you often; Glad you've come back to Ruidoso. Then
again, Johnny had never been one to show *any* feeling
other than anger. Her face burned and she was forced to
remind herself that it was the fever making her feel as
if she were flushed with heat. Not the fact that his brazen
snub had in any way embarrassed her.

"I don't know," she finally replied in a tone as emotionally removed as his. "I'll need to examine her more
closely for broken bones. The fact that she's in foal
doesn't help. Ultimately you may have a choice to make.
Her or the foal."

Looking at her again from beneath the brim of his

hat, he said, "My choices have always left a lot to be desired."

Leah turned away. She struggled up the embankment and headed for her truck. "Self righteous, egotistical bastard," she muttered. "You haven't changed a bit."

Leah stepped into her kitchen at a quarter after five. The room was warm and dim and smelled of the chili Shamika had cooked for supper.

Shamika sat at the kitchen table, arms crossed over her stomach, head slightly tilted to one side as she regarded Leah through the shadows, her full brown lips pressed in agitation, her foot tapping the floor. "Lord, girl, look at you," she said. "You're a mess and dead on your feet."

Leaning back against the door, Leah covered her face with her hands. "I ran over one of Johnny's prized mares."

"I can think of better ways of getting reacquainted."

Leah feigned a smile. "I'm in no mood for anything remotely resembling humor, especially where Johnny Whitehorse is concerned."

"Did you kill her?"

"That remains to be seen. Fortunately, nothing was broken. A miracle in itself. There was a great deal of muscle injury. Could eventually lead to fibrotic myopathy. She's in foal and due at any time. If we can get her through the delivery I'd say she'll make it."

"Yes, but will you? Aside from looking like a drowned mouse, your forehead looks as if someone clubbed you with a bat."

She shrugged and cautiously touched the lump above her left eyebrow. It was going to hurt like hell later. "Tell me again why I do this, Shamika. I could have been a doctor, you know. I could have sat in my sterile office with my degrees plastered over the wall while people grew roots waiting for their appointments. My father would have approved. We might even be friends.''

''It would take a whole lot more than your being an M.D. for you and Senator Foster to be friends.'' Shamika stood and walked to the stove, where a kettle simmered on a burner. She poured hot water into a cup of powdered chocolate and tiny dry marshmallows that looked like pebbles. She stirred it until it was frothy, then carried it to the table and pointed to a chair. ''Sit, girl, and drink. I'll get you a dry sweater before you catch pneumonia—if you haven't already.''

Leah waited until Shamika left the room before removing her muddy boots, then she dragged off her soggy jacket, and leaving it all in a heap by the door, moved to the table. She wrapped her hands around the cup as she sank into the chair and allowed the steam to prickle her cheeks and eyelids, and she thought of Johnny Whitehorse.

Nope, he had not changed a bit. Not since the first time she'd ever set eyes on him—back when his father trained her family's horses. Even then Johnny thumbed his nose at propriety. Shirtless, in fringed buckskin breeches, his black hair in braids, he rode her father's horses bareback around the ranch, and occasionally down Ruidoso's main street, flaunting his Mescalero heritage with an arrogance that belied his poverty. He had carved out a reputation for himself as a rebel, not only with the whites who looked on his antics as an insult and a threat, but also with those of his tribe who considered his actions an open invitation to further trouble with the white man. Had his grandfather not been the tribe's most revered medicine man, things might have gotten ugly.

Shamika returned and wrapped a sweater around Leah's shoulders. With her hands that were as rich brown as the chocolate Leah drank, Shamika massaged the back of Leah's neck, along the tops of her shoulders, and down her spine. Each touch was a glorious agony, and within minutes the tightness that would inevitably leave her feeling as if she had been pummeled by rocks had melted under her friend's adept touch.

"You're burning with fever," Shamika said. "You better get to bed."

"Roy's keeping an eye on the mare for the next few hours. You'll need to wake me by eight."

"Sure. Now get to bed. I'll make you some TheraFlu. That'll help the aches and pains long enough for you to get some sleep." Shamika tapped on her shoulder and said, "Go."

Leah finished off the chocolate and moved toward the door. Looking back, she watched Shamika turn up the burner under the kettle, then reach into the medicine cupboard for the box of flu medicine. "What would I ever do without you?" she asked, and Shamika shrugged.

"You got me," she replied.

"I mean it," Leah said. "If it wasn't for you I would probably be forced to beg help from my father—"

"Leah Starr don't beg help from nobody, hon. You'd find a way. You always do. You're the strongest woman I've ever known."

"Strong? I thought the word was *stubborn*."

"That too."

"I'm not feeling too strong *or* stubborn right now."

" 'Cause you're sick and tired. After a good night's sleep you'll feel different."

"Everything will be the same when I wake up. I'm just on the verge of bankruptcy. I'm two months behind on my rent, not to mention your salary. The ranchers around here think a woman can't possibly have brains enough to be a vet. My truck is bogged up to its axles in mud, and . . . I'm whining. God, I hate whiners."

"Everyone's got the right to feel a little sorry for themselves now and then, especially at five-thirty in the morning. Go to bed, Dr. Starr."

"Right. Bed."

She moved down the short hallway to the closed bed-room door. Gently, she turned the knob and allowed the door to creak open just enough that she could see the sleeping form on the railed bed. Her gaze traveled the room, which was lit by a night-light: a plastic clown with a beam of light shining through its open smiling mouth. In the far corner sat the shadowed hulk of a child's wheelchair. From the ceiling hung a crystal wind chime that would reflect the morning sun into a hundred splashes of light on the wall by the boy's head.

Shamika moved up behind her. "You know you can't go in there. Too risky with that fever."

"I know. I just needed to see him."

"Val sang 'Old MacDonald' nearly all the way through yesterday."

"Not bad for a seven-year-old, huh?"

"Not bad for a seven-year-old with cerebral palsy and light mental retardation," Shamika said gently, and hug-ged her. Then she turned Leah down the hallway and nudged her toward the bedroom.

Shamika had laid clean pajamas out on the bed. The covers were turned back, revealing flowered flannel sheets. Shamika sat the medicine on the bedside table before drawing the curtains closed over the window.

"No," Leah said, dropping onto the bed. "Leave them open. I like to watch the sun come up."

"You want me to draw you a bath?"

"I'm too tired to bathe."

Shamika left the room, closing the door behind her.

It took all of Leah's effort to peel out of her damp jeans, socks, bra, and sweatshirt. Her toes were wrinkled as raisins from standing in water for the last few hours. She put on clean socks, dragged her pajamas on and propped herself up against the pillows, sipped the hot medicine beverage that tasted like apple cider, and waited for the first rays of sunlight to spill in streams through her window overlooking the mountains. The morning sun always turned the cracked, curling, ochre-colored linoleum on the floor into a golden carpet.

Her eyelids growing heavy, she sank back into the pillows and reached for the television remote, hit the power button, and watched the bright, friendly faces of the KRXR Channel 10 news team beam out at her. With neutral expressions and voices, they related the stories of area flooding, robberies, falling interest rates, and an Asian stock market that had crashed for the second time in as many months.

She drifted.

The horse came out of nowhere, ghostly against the rain-drenched darkness, its eyes wild with terror as it skidded into the pool of light in front of her truck. She wrenched the steering wheel hard to the right, sending the truck spinning round and round, closer and closer to the churning, water-swollen ditch. Frantically, she stomped at the brakes, only to spin faster, until the world blurred into an image of Johnny Whitehorse glaring at her icily from beneath the brim of his hat.

Her eyes flew open and fixed on the television screen.

Dolores Rainwater, one of the news anchors, spoke to her audience with the slightest touch of amusement in her voice as a replay of the previous night's news was displayed behind her.

Johnny Whitehorse stood on the capitol steps, surrounded by angry Native Americans, all carrying signs and banners. They chanted in unison, "We want our money back!" to a nonplussed bureaucrat who stood toe to toe with Johnny, as rigorously righteous as the picketers were furious.

"Fed up of waiting for reform, the Native American Rights Fund, spearheaded by Johnny Whitehorse, has filed the largest class-action lawsuit in history against the federal government on behalf of three hundred thousand Indians who have accounts held in trust by the bureau. As we reported some weeks ago, thousands of American Indians have asserted that their money is being mismanaged, even lost, by a Bureau of Indian Affairs trust system that never had an accounts receivable list or a complete audit and has not worked properly since Andrew Jackson was president. The lawsuit seeks a court order directing that the bureau's so-called Individual Indian Money trust account system be fixed. Restitution to those who claimed their savings have mysteriously disappeared could run into the billions of dollars.

"The problems of the New Mexico tribes are as diversified as the state itself. Just last week Mr. Whitehorse again confronted Senator Carl Foster regarding the Senator's role in the bankruptcy of the Apache Casino and Resort development. Whitehorse contends that there is more behind the reversal of the senator's stand against reservation gambling compacts than his sudden desire to accommodate the New Mexico tribes, going so far as to insinuate publicly that there might be more to the senator's relationship with Formation Media, the financier of the casino development, than meets the eye. Senator Foster called Whitehorse's statement a ridiculous accusation bordering on slander, and that Mr. Whitehorse's comments are attributable to his desire to run for Senator Foster's seat in the next election. When we asked Mr. Whitehorse for his response to Senator Foster's remark, he replied: 'No comment.' This is Dolores Rainwater for Channel 10 News.''

TWO

Johnny Whitehorse always slept with his sunglasses on. They blocked the morning sun from his eyes, extending the night a few more precious hours. He liked the dark, the moon, the stars. The blackness brought serenity and soothed the rawness in his chest. The blackness felt cool. It seeped through his pores and put out the fires of his discontent.

He enjoyed sitting atop White Tail Peak at midnight and watching meteorites streak across the endless sky. The Apache believed that each flash of light depicted a new soul in the spirit world. Occasionally, if he listened hard, he could detect the sound of his ancestors singing, their chants whipping through the wind-twisted cedars that clung with exposed, gnarled roots to the sides of the mountain. Sometimes he would even chant with them.

He'd gone to White Tail the previous night despite the lousy weather, hoping to assuage the frustration of that day's meeting with the deputy solicitor for the Bureau of Indian Affairs. He'd been returning home when happening upon the unfortunate accident with his mare and Leah Foster. Leah Starr. *Dr.* Leah Starr, *D.V.M.* She would always be Leah Foster to him. The boss's daughter, voted most beautiful at Ruidoso High. Who graduated first in her class. Untouchable. Too good for the likes of an Apache horse trainer's son. Or so Senator Foster had thought. Leah, for a while anyway, had thought differently.

Lying on his back in bed, Johnny stared at the ceiling. There was great irony in the fact that he now owned what once had been Leah's home. He'd paid a cool two point five million *cash* for the house and eight hundred acres. At the time, Senator Foster had had no idea who was purchasing his farm, and probably would not have cared, not as long as he walked away with enough funds to help finance his reelection to the senate. But he *had* cared when learning the purchaser was Johnny White-horse—the one man who had every intention of making certain Foster would *not* be reelected in the upcoming senatorial race. Who had every intention of proving that Foster was, in some way, involved with the development company that had virtually robbed the New Mexico tribes of their future.

The very bedroom he lay in now had belonged to Senator Foster and his wife, Jane, who had died in 1996 of breast cancer. Leah had slept down the hall in a room facing the stables so the first thing she saw each morning was the horses being worked. More than once he had climbed the rose trellis on the outside wall and sneaked through her window. They had rolled together for hours, arms and legs entwined, bodies feverish with the sort of desire and urgency that came with too many hormones and too little restraint.

He wondered if she still burned with the same sort of passion. He wondered about her husband—the one who had swept her off her feet during her sophomore year at college—who had relocated her to Texas, where she attended A&M University and vet school, during which time she had a child. A son. Born three months early.

Somehow the struggling infant had become infected with meningitis while in intensive care, destroying a portion of his brain. Leah's husband had eventually buckled under the pressure of caring for a disabled child and divorced her. *Jerk.*

The body beside him shifted, drawing his thoughts back to the present. He glanced at the clock. Nearly twelve. He should have trucked over to Leah's hours ago to check on his mare. So why hadn't he? It was not like him to show such apathy toward one of his horses. What was he avoiding?

"Good morning." The warm, moist words whispered against his ear.

"Good afternoon," he replied, grinning.

The woman raised her head and sleepily focused on the clock. She was incredibly beautiful, with eyes shaped like almonds and as dark as espresso. Her chin length hair was glossy black, and she had cheekbones that would make Cindy Crawford envious. As always, she looked poutingly sensual upon awakening. If he kissed her now he would not leave the bed for another hour.

Dolores Rainwater slid her leg over Johnny's hip and nestled against him. Carefully, she removed the glasses from his eyes and tossed them toward the end of the bed. "Did you catch the broadcast this morning? I did a great piece on your meeting with the bureau. I also hinted of your interest in running for office. We were flooded with calls. All women, of course. They want to know how they can volunteer to work on your campaign."

"Getting a little ahead of ourselves, aren't we?"

"Do you still deny you don't want a piece of Senator Foster?"

"Just because I'd like to see that son-of-a-bitch boil in oil doesn't necessarily mean I want his office."

"You're a natural for it."

"I'm a Mescalero Apache. Do you think the white populace is going to put me in a position of power?"

"If a movie star can become president, and a rock singer can become a congressman, a Native American can become a senator." She smiled. "I can see it now. Instead of posters of Uncle Sam declaring 'Vote for Whitehorse,' there will be gigantic images of you, wearing nothing but a loincloth."

Johnny rolled from the bed.

Dolores propped up on one elbow and watched as he grabbed up the damp jeans he had worn the night before and began pulling them up his legs. "Did I say something to offend you?" she asked.

"Yes."

"Sorry. I didn't realize you were still so touchy about those modeling jobs. They paid the rent, didn't they? They paid your tuition through law school and ultimately got you noticed by the leading talent agency in L.A. There's not a woman in America who doesn't cream her panties every time the commercial comes on of you walking shirtless down Fifth Avenue in a pair of low-slung faded jeans. Face it, sweetie. There's not a girl's dorm room in this country that doesn't sport a poster of you on the wall. Should you decide to go back to L.A. and continue your movie career you could name your price."

"I'm not going back, so that's that."

Dolores kicked away the blanket covering her hips. Naked, her skin silky as the sheet between her legs, she patted the bed beside her. "Come on, Johnny, let's discuss the matter. I might change your mind."

He shook his head and searched the selection of laundered and starched shirts in the closet. There were three dozen at least—all expensive, grouped by colors, patterns, dress, and casual.

"There was a message from your agent last night. He has a script he'd like you to read."

"Don't tell me. Someone is doing a remake of *The Lone Ranger* and they want me to play Tonto." He reached beyond the shirts for a frayed football jersey emblazoned with the number thirty-three. "What are you doing listening to my messages?"

"I'm a reporter. It's my business to snoop."

"Oh? I thought you were my girlfriend, trusted confidante, et cetera."

Dolores shrugged. "A ring on my finger will immensely ensure my loyalty."

"Bullshit." He pulled the shirt down over his head and shook his hair free of the collar. "What kind of deal have you made with my agent? He'll represent you if you talk me back into show business? Maybe he teased you with a CNN carrot, or maybe even *Good Morning America*. Why not? They have their token African American and Asian. It's about time for a Native American. Maybe they'll even make you a White House correspondent. Just think of it. Every time the issue of disgruntled and starving Native Americans comes up at 1600 Pennsylvania Avenue they can prop you up in front of panhandling Indians huddled near liquor stores so you can adequately report on the monstrous scale of human suffering on the reservations, and how the government is doing all it can to alleviate their pain."

"Would that be so bad, Johnny?"

"That depends on what you do when the story is over. Do you climb back into your Mercedes and beat it back to your penthouse overlooking the Lincoln Memorial? Or do you picket the liquor store owner who runs specials on the very day the Indians receive their subsidy checks from the government?"

Dolores rolled her eyes. "My, haven't we become righteous. Excuse me, but this house isn't exactly your grandfather's wickiup."

Johnny pulled his boots on, grabbed up his hat, and started for the door.

Scrambling out of bed, Dolores ran after him. "I don't need your agent's help, Johnny. I'm a damned good reporter. If I make it big, I'll make it on my own. I won't do it by riding on your coattails. Do you hear me? I don't *need* you!''

The front door opened suddenly and Roy Moon stepped in. He stopped short at the sight of Dolores standing naked in the foyer, hands fisted, face contorted in rage. He glanced at Johnny. ''Guess I should've knocked.''

''Probably wouldn't have made much difference. How's the mare?''

''She foaled this morning around seven. A real nice colt. You should've seen Doc Starr. Sick and tired as she was she made certain the birthin' went off without a hitch. Looks like both the colt and mare are goin' to make it.''

''Doc Starr?'' Dolores said. ''Do you mean Leah Foster?''

Roy chewed his lip before nodding.

Johnny left the house, stood for a moment on the front porch and looked out over the vast puddles of standing rainwater. The air felt cooler than he had expected. He thought of returning to the house to get a jacket.

''How long has she been back?'' Dolores asked Roy.

''Two, maybe three months.''

''Why didn't you tell me, Johnny?''

''Why should you care?''

''Because of what she once meant to you.''

''That was a long time ago. Forget it.''

''You dumped me in high school for her. How am I supposed to forget that?''

''Yeah, well, I didn't make love to Leah Foster Starr three hours ago, did I?''

''Where are you going?''

''To see my mare.''

''To see your mare or Leah?''

''What do you think?'' He headed for the truck.

''I'm coming with you.''

''Get some clothes on first.''

"Don't you dare leave, Johnny. Give me five minutes."

Johnny stepped up into the truck and settled onto the leather seat while Roy leaned against the open door, arms crossed, his amusement deepening the lines in his Apache face. "You sure she's worth it, boss? You know Dolores. Claws like a cougar's. No way is she lettin' you get away again."

"Just where am I supposed to be going?"

Roy shrugged. "Different truck. Same girl. She's still as pretty as she was back then. Maybe prettier."

"She's still Senator Foster's daughter, Roy. That won't ever change."

"And you hate Senator Foster. That don't make for good pillow talk, does it?"

Johnny turned the ignition key and the truck rumbled like thunder. Roy stepped aside and closed the door. "Once those years ago I thought that you was sniffin' after Leah just to get back at the senator for the way he treated you and your pa. Now here we are twelve years later. Your pa has been dead for ten years and you're still carryin' around a hate for Foster that's more dangerous now than it was then."

"What's your point?"

"Just wonderin' how far you'd go to ruin the senator. That's all."

He did not wait for Dolores, because her five minutes stretched to ten, then fifteen—as usual. The only time she was ever on time was to her job because that was the most important aspect of her life. Seeing herself on the television screen substantiated her existence. As long as Dolores Rainwater looked good on camera, all was right with the world. Besides, he was not in the mood to be second-guessed, interrogated, or nagged about old lovers. Leah Foster Starr was old news. Dusty baggage. What had gone on between them in the back of his father's old Dodge pickup was nothing more than a rite of passage into adulthood for them both.

Easing the truck into second gear, he noted several of his employees repairing the break in the fence. Across the road an enormous black wrecker was struggling to pull Leah's truck from the mud. In the light of day the truck resembled something he'd bought back in the days when he was trying to establish credit and no one would trust an Indian with more than a monthly payment of a hundred dollars. Back in those days a hundred-dollar truck payment was a week's salary pumping gas and scrubbing bug guts off windshields at Conroe's Texaco. Occasionally the customers tipped him, but not often. Not nearly as often as they tipped the white boys.

The turnoff to Leah's place was marked by an unobtrusive sign near the shoulder of the road: "Starr Veterinary Practice." A small red pennant, meant to attract the eye of passersby, fluttered on each corner of the sign. Engine idling, gear in neutral, Johnny sat at the entry of the driveway as memories rolled through his mind like old celluloid grown yellow with time. He had not stepped back into what once was his home since the day he'd buried his father. Not much had changed through the years. The scattering of trees was bigger. The frame house needed painting. The roof could use new shingles. The concrete block that had sufficed as a front porch was still crooked. Someone had, however, at some time, painted it orange, along with the shutters on the house. They had also constructed a path from the drive to the porch using crushed gravel lined with red rocks the size of bread loaves. A sign planted by the walkway requested visitors to kindly not block the drive. Parking was in the rear, thank you.

As he manipulated the dually into a space near the barn, he checked out the office Dr. Starr had converted from a tractor shed. There were several palpation chutes. A two-horse trailer that was showing signs of rust. Stacks of bagged shavings and another of hay bales covered by giant blue tarps. A pair of green, molded plastic lounge chairs resided beside a child's inflated wading pool. Several yellow rubber ducks floated in the water, which was scattered with bits of hay and brown leaves, not to mention sediment that had settled in the bottom of the pool.

The back screen door of the house opened and a black woman appeared. She was tall and thin, with close-cropped hair and features that belonged on the cover of *Ebony* magazine. She carried a cup in one hand, a sandwich on a plate in the other. Her stride was long and determined as she moved toward the office, her thoughts apparently focused on her destination. He was halfway around the truck before she saw him. Her step slowed and her eyebrows lifted. Her gaze took a leisurely trip up and down his person before she spoke in a voice that was huskily sensual.

"You must be Johnny Whitehorse."

"How did you guess?" he replied, and adjusted his hat over his eyes.

"You got to be joking, honey."

"What gave me away?"

"Oh please." She rolled her eyes. "You don't strike me as a man who has to have his ego stroked."

"How's my mare?"

"Do I look like the vet to you?"

"Oh, I don't know. I've seen some vets who were real babes in my day."

"I hope you're not talking about Dean Crabbet. There would be a whole lot of disappointed women if you were."

He laughed and joined her at the barn door.

"I'm Shamika," she said. "And this is Doc Starr's lunch. Long as you're here, why don't you take it to her? She's probably starving by now."

Shamika thrust the plate and coffee into his hands. "Now you make her eat. She won't if you don't." She started to turn, then stopped. "By the way, I think what you're doing with the Native American Rights Fund is right on. On the other hand, the casino issue is going to get sticky as far as Senator Foster is concerned, if you know what I mean. While Leah and her father aren't exactly close, he's still her father. It's that old blood-is-thicker-than-water thing. It's chiseled in granite someplace that the offspring of powerful men are the last to abandon the familial ship—even if that ship *is* the *Titanic*.''

"Warning noted.''

"She's had a tough time of it, Mr. Whitehorse. I'd appreciate it a lot if you take it easy on her.''

"I just came to see my mare, then I'm outta here.''

"That's what I'm afraid of,'' she replied with a thin smile, then turned for the house, allowing the screen door to slam behind her.

A Neil Diamond tune played on a radio cassette player set on a table near the entrance of the barn. Johnny picked up the empty cassette holder and flipped it over. A young Neil Diamond with wild hair and wearing a skin-tight jumpsuit stared up at him just as ''Red Red Wine'' rolled out of the speakers and filled up the silence with memories that he had stored away long ago—he and Leah at Lover's Peak drinking warm sangria straight from the bottle, sitting on the tailgate of his father's truck, this very cassette playing in the background as he educated her on Apache spirituality. She had freely offered him her virginity that night, and he had accepted it like a starving man coveting a crumb of bread. Afterward, they vowed to love one another always—to stay together forever. They would marry soon after graduation and support each other's goals to go to college and attain their degrees—hers as a veterinarian, his as a lawyer.

Fantasies of the young and ignorant, and deliriously in love.

Johnny frowned and gently put aside the cassette box. There was a bull with a grotesquely swollen scrotum

chewing hay in the first stall. A donkey resided in the
next, its back right leg stitched closed from its fetlock
to its hock. A pair of pygmy goats, no more than eighteen inches high, stood like sentinels at the far end of
the barn aisle, regarding him suspiciously and chewing
alfalfa leaves. They twitched their curled tails from side
to side before shaking their horned heads in an apparent
warning—as if anything other than a jackrabbit would
take their threat seriously.

Dr. Starr backed out of a stall in that moment. She
did not see him, but focused instead on the spindly colt
wobbling after her.

The rain the night before had obliterated her features
as she stood in the dark on the side of the road. In his
mind, as he lay in bed hours later, listening to Dolores
breathe deeply in sleep, he had imagined that Leah had
looked just as she had in high school. But seeing her
now, dressed in baggy khaki pants and a man's demim
shirt with sleeves rolled up to her elbows, he realized
that there was little girlishness left in her. Her brown
hair was in disarray, haphazardly secured with a rubber
band at her nape. It was longer than he remembered her
wearing it in high school. The color had not lost its
richness, however. It suited her complexion, which was
fair and prone to burn in the sun. He recalled rubbing
sunblock on her back and breasts when they skinny-
dipped at Copper Springs. With their bodies slick and
smelling like coconut they had made love openly under
the hot sun again and again, only to discover much later
that the sunblock had done nothing to protect the sensitive, tender skin of their naked buttocks. Putting on
their jeans at the end of the day had been excruciating.
She had not been able to sit in hot bathwater for a
week—even after he had sneaked into her bedroom one
night and anointed her butt with ice-cold skin cream.
Her idea, not his. He would have made up a paste of
mescal and aloe. He would have chanted her one of his

grandfather's medicine songs and made her sleep with a
fetish tucked under her pillow.

The mare nickered with worry as the colt unsteadily
rocked on its tiny feet and nearly fell. Leah jumped to
its aid, wrapped her arms around its chest and rump and
laughed as it did its best to buck her away.

She looked up unexpectedly, catching him off guard.
There was a purple knot on her head above her eyebrow
and dark circles under her eyes. The hair around her
temples was slightly damp with sweat, and there was a
smudge of mud on her chin.

"Oh," she said. "I didn't hear you walk up."

"Nice colt."

"Yes." She nodded and nudged the foal back into the
stall. "The mare is going to be stiff for a while. Obviously, I can't give her too much for pain as long as she's
nursing."

"I've brought your lunch."

"No thanks. I'm not hungry."

"No can do, Doc. I've been given explicit orders by
your friend that you are to eat this or else."

She took the cup and plate and walked out of the barn.
Johnny remained standing in the shadowed aisleway,
still regarded by the suspicious goats. His first instinct,
oddly enough, was to follow Leah, but he quickly
checked it (he had not come here to talk over old times
that were best forgotten) and entered the stall with his
mare. Despite the previous night's accident, she looked
none the worse for wear. Doc Starr had done a nice job
suturing the cuts on her chest. There was a nasty swelling on her stifle that obviously caused some pain, as the
mare kept the leg slightly cocked and pinned her ears
whenever the colt stumbled against her in search of a
teat.

He left the stall, adjusted his hat again, and moved
toward the office, glancing toward the wading pool and
then the back door of the house, where he could just

make out Shamika staring out at him through the dark screen, her arms crossed over her chest.

Leah sat at a cluttered desk reading a magazine article. The sandwich had been discarded in the trash, along with balled-up gauze, newspapers, and unopened mail from American Express and MasterCard. He watched her silently through the screen door before knocking.

A moment passed before she looked up. Her face looked flushed and her eyes slightly glassy.

"You don't look so good," he said, stepping into the room.

"You were always a real smooth talker, Johnny." Her hand went up and brushed a tendril of hair back from her brow. "I guess you're wondering when you can take the mare home. I'd give her until the end of the week, just for safety's sake. Since I was partially responsible for the accident I won't charge you daily care."

"I'm not worried about the money."

She gave him a flat smile and sat back in the chair, which creaked like old hinges under her weight. Only then did he recognize the desk and chair as the same one that had belonged to his father. Then it had occupied a tiny office in the house—a cubicle off the kitchen that was more of a pantry than a room. After his father's death, Roy had stored a few furnishings in a warehouse. The others he had donated to Goodwill.

"Looks like you've done a good job fixing up the old place," he said.

"There's a lot to be done. I have no desire to sink any more money in to it than I have to. Hopefully, I won't be here long."

"Moving back to Dallas?"

"Hardly." Sitting forward, she absently looked at the magazine and turned the page. "Once I get my practice up and going I'll get a better place. Something closer to town. I have a meeting with Greg Hunnicutt at the track. I understand there's a need for another on-site vet. I'll take him my résumé and see what happens."

"Tough business vetting at the track. I can't see that you'll like it much."

"Like it? Or do you mean fit in?" She closed the magazine and tossed it aside.

"I mean like it. You know the race business. The horses aren't exactly someone's backyard pet. They're money machines. If they don't earn their keep, they're history, in one way or another. I can't see you putting down a horse because it came in last at a Futurity."

Leah drank her cold coffee, still refusing to look at Johnny directly.

"So why *did* you come back to Ruidoso?" he asked.

"Why not? It's my home. Where I grew up. I still have friends here."

"And family."

Her jaw tensed. Carefully, she set down her coffee cup and finally lifted her blue eyes to his. Hers were bright with anger. "Did you come here to discuss my father, Johnny? Perhaps you have some message you want me to pass on to him? Say, you intend to destroy his reputation by any means possible in order to win the next senatorial election?"

"I have nothing to say to your father that I can't tell him in person, Le."

"Or to every gossip-hungry reporter who's looking to break the back of yet another politician, and don't call me Le. Only my friends call me that, and as I recall, we are no longer friends."

He nodded and shrugged. "Sorry you feel like that. But as I recall, *Doctor*, if anyone has the right to feel pissed about what happened between us, it should be me. You unloaded me, remember? 'Been nice knowing you, Whitehorse, but I have my future to think about and you're not included.' Guess you couldn't handle the heat you would have gotten over showing up at the senior prom with an Indian on your arm. I was good enough to screw in the back of old pickup trucks, but not to be seen with in public."

Leah jumped up and threw the coffee in his face. He did not blink. She, on the other hand, turned white as the gauze in the waste bin. Her body shook. "You're a bastard, Johnny. A real bastard. No one but a cold-hearted bastard would have so proudly and arrogantly told my father to his face that he had been 'screwing' his daughter for nearly a year right under his own roof. But then, maybe that's why you were crawling into my bed in the first place. It was your way of retaliating against my father. How better than to seduce the boss's daughter. Pay him back for what you believed was shabby treatment of your father."

Johnny swiped the dripping coffee off his chin with his hand.

Leah's eyes pooled with tears, and she took a steadying breath. "You were always a hothead, Johnny. So full of anger you couldn't rationalize beyond striking out at anyone you believed wronged you. Fight first, then ask questions. You hated my father for his wealth and power and the fact that your father had to work for a white man in order to survive. Yet look at what you've become. You beat your breast over the stereotyping of Indians. You rant on *20/20* about the mistreatment of Native Americans by the government, and how the whites should strive to better understand the earth's people. Yet, look at how you live, Johnny. Where you live. Not on the reservation. Not among your people—"

"I didn't come here to exchange insults, Le—excuse me, *Doctor*. I just wanted to see my goddamn horse."

"So you've seen it."

They stood in silence, glaring.

"Fine," he finally snapped, then turned on his heels and hit the screen door with the palms of both hands. "See ya around, Doc. I'll have Roy pick up the mare and colt at the end of the week. Just send me a bill. I'm good for it."

THREE

From her bedroom window Leah could lie in bed and watch traffic come and go along Highway 249. There were trucks, mostly, area ranchers traveling to and from the city, some hauling horse or cattle trailers, others hauling flatbed trailers of hay bales stacked as high as a two-story house. Occasionally a tractor lumbered by at a snail's pace, causing impatient drivers to pass on the wrong side of the road into incoming traffic. Just a month before, a teenage boy had driven his car head-on into an oncoming semi, too busy giving the old man on the tractor the finger to notice that he was barreling into death's clutches. Leah had attempted to give the young man CPR while waiting for the paramedics to arrive. But there was too little left of the kid's face and chest for it to do much good. He'd sailed through the windshield of his car and splattered against the truck's grill as if he were a bug.

Not long after Johnny's visit, Leah's fever spiked at one hundred and three. Shamika put her to bed, proceeded to pump her full of orange juice and aspirin, threatened her with physical harm if she so much as thought of answering the phone again before she had kicked the fever. "You're not going to do anyone any good if you're in the hospital," she declared with that telling tone that warned Leah that her friend's patience was long past its limits.

Leah rested against propped-up pillows, her gaze locked on the asphalt highway as the television droned in the background. Shamika had brought her another lunch, chicken noodle soup and Ritz crackers, which Leah had allowed to go untouched. The mail had arrived an hour ago; obviously Shamika had screened it and decided the demands for payment would be too much for Leah to deal with at the moment.

"You're supposed to be sleeping," Shamika whispered from the door.

"That would be nice," she responded wearily. "But I'm beginning to suspect that sleep has been deleted from my memory banks."

Shamika had tied a leopard-print scarf turbanlike around her head and donned a pair of dangling bronze earrings that tinkled when she moved. They were Val's favorites. She regarded the uneaten food with a raised eyebrow. "Your starving yourself isn't going to help build up your strength."

"I was never one who could force myself to eat."

Folding her arms over her chest, Shamika studied Leah closely. "What's going on, sweetie? You haven't been yourself for a while now. That tantrum you threw earlier at Johnny wasn't like you at all."

"You haven't seen me around Johnny before. He's always had a way of driving me crazy. I lose all common sense when he's around."

"I can see how he would do that. He's one good-looking specimen. The photographs I've seen don't do him justice. I imagine getting over a man like that would take some doing."

"I got over Johnny a long time ago. He's arrogant

and shallow. Cher can have him, or whoever that was I saw on his arm in *People* magazine.''

''From what you've said in the past, I got the impression you two were hot and heavy for a long time. You never did tell me what broke you up. Did he cheat on you?''

''Johnny's not a two-timer. With him it's all or nothing.''

''Then he lied to you? Abused you? Took you for granted?''

''We're not talking about my ex-husband here.'' Leah laughed. ''No. Johnny treated me better than anyone has treated me my entire life.''

''I know his race had nothing to do with it. Or did it?''

Leah snatched a Kleenex from a box and proceeded to tear it into shreds. She looked out the window and watched a breeze play with the leaves on a nearby poplar tree. ''I *loved* Johnny for who and what he was. I worshipped his spirit. I applauded his hunger to rise up from his circumstances and succeed. I also loved the fact that he was forbidden to me.''

''By your father, I take it.''

''By everyone. His father didn't approve of me any more than mine approved of Johnny, so our lives were spent meeting on the sly. We were going to come out of the closet, so to speak, and let the world know that we were in love on prom night. What I didn't know was that my father had suspected that something was going on between us. Just minutes before Johnny arrived at the house, Dad confronted me and threatened that if I ever saw Johnny again he would fire Johnny's father and make certain he never worked in New Mexico again.''

Sinking a little deeper into the pillows, Leah took a shallow breath. ''I'll never forget the look in Johnny's eyes. First shock and confusion. Then pain. Then so much anger.''

"You did tell him the truth, didn't you? About your father's ultimatum?"

"Of course not." She shook her head. "Johnny despised my father. Had I told him the truth—dear God, he might have torn Dad in two with his bare hands. The confrontation between them the next day was ugly enough. Johnny spent the night at White Tail Peak, drinking himself into mindless oblivion. He showed up at our door at five the next morning, shirtless and barefoot, drunk and demanding to see me. He'd applied war paint to his face. He and my father stood toe to toe on the front porch. Johnny informed him in shocking detail about our year-long relationship. My father called him a no-account Indian with the morals of a tomcat, and that the only reason he allowed his old man to continue working his horses was because he was the best shit-picker minimum wage could buy. Johnny should kiss his feet for even keeping the old drunk employed. He wasn't worth the three-fifty he paid him an hour to crawl out of bed."

Shamika pursed her lips and whistled softly. "Nasty stuff, huh?"

"Johnny's weak spot was his father. He'd watched Jefferson Whitehorse go from a proud man and one of the finest racehorse trainers in the state to a broken man whose dreams were diluted by whiskey." Leah tossed the tattered Kleenex aside and drew the comforter up to her chin. She had begun to shake and sweat. Obviously the fever had begun to break, thanks to the aspirin she'd taken earlier. "I'm ashamed to say that my father was partly to blame for Mr. Whitehorse's problems, as much as I tried to deny it back then. Jefferson had a special way with horses, as if he could communicate with them. If a horse hurt, he could look into its eyes and determine the problem. If the horse was afraid, he reassured it. I've seen him take the wildest colt and within an hour have it follow him like an adoring puppy."

"So what happened? Did the horses not run well? Didn't they win?"

"Oh yes. They won all right. But not with Jefferson as the trainer of record. Mr. Whitehorse would get them ready for the track, in peak condition, then my father would remove the horses and send them to Jack Jones— a well-known trainer who would run the horses, win, and get the credit for training them. My father's excuse to Mr. Whitehorse was, because of Jack's influence at the track, Jack could request the best jockey, and get them. He could also pull a few strings and ensure he got the best gate positions. There was never a chance of Jefferson Whitehorse getting a reputation in the business for training because there were never any horses running under his name. Johnny often tried to convince his father to go out on his own—start his own training facility— but my father wouldn't have it. He made subtle threats that he would see Jefferson's license revoked. And besides, what chance did an Indian have making a name for himself on the white man's track?

"Johnny wanted desperately to get an education so he could make enough money to back his father's business . . . but when Johnny was a sophomore at the university, he was notified that his father had been found dead from a self-inflicted gunshot wound to his head."

Shamika closed her eyes. "Lord, girl. No wonder Johnny Whitehorse hates your father."

"Can you understand now why it's so difficult to see Johnny?" Leah asked. "My family has done nothing but bring him pain."

"He didn't seem so angry today, at least, not until you booted him out the door with coffee dripping off his nose. I think he's much too smart to think that you had anything to do with his father's problems."

"I'm ashamed to say that through it all I defended my father—right up until the day I learned about Jefferson's suicide. I guess I just didn't want to accept the fact that my own father was the sort of man who could so coldly and calculatingly destroy another human being. My, how times change, huh? If I'd known then what I know now, I would have told my father where he could put his prejudice and walked off into the sunset with Johnny Whitehorse.

"I've thought a lot the last few years about how different my life might have been had Johnny and I got married. Gotta admit that seeing him again stirs up all the old *if onlys.*"

Shamika put her hand on Leah's and gave it a squeeze. "Johnny's not married, you know. Maybe—"

"No. Don't even think it, Shamika. Johnny and I exist in different worlds—different dimensions, for heaven's sake. He can have any woman he wants, and probably has, judging by the tabloids. Besides, you and I both know there are far too many complications to a relationship with me."

"Then why are you going out with Sam Clark again this Friday night? I mean, if you think your life is too complicated to get involved with a man, why are you wasting time on this jerk?"

"Sam is *not* a jerk." Leah sniffed. "He's fun. He likes to dance."

"Excuse me? The man sells used cars—"

"Meaning?"

"Meaning . . . nothing. I just think you could do better."

"I did better, once. I married a petroleum engineer making nearly a hundred grand a year. Look where that got me."

Shamika raised one eyebrow. "Have you told Sam about Val?"

"Not exactly." Leah shook her head and averted her eyes.

"Meaning . . ."

"He knows I have a seven-year-old son."

"And . . . ?"

Leah shrugged. "I'll get around to telling him when

the time is right. I simply haven't seen the necessity of
bringing up Val's disability yet. Our relationship hasn't
advanced to that point. It's really none of his business.''

"I think you'd better *make* it his business just so you
know whether or not you want to waste any more time
on him," Shamika pointed out with an agitated shake of
her head. "We've been down that road before, girlfriend. Don't you be setting yourself up again to get
hurt." She checked her watch, then glanced out the window toward the highway. "Bus will be coming soon.
You need me to pick up anything while I'm in town?"

"Yes. Hostess cupcakes. Chocolate. I feel a craving
coming on."

"Honey, I'll buy you a whole box full if it means
you'll put some food in your stomach." Shamika turned
for the door. "I'm turning the phone ringer off. Stay in
bed. Sleep. We'll be home around six."

"Give Val a kiss for me!" she called. "Hundreds of
'em! And tell him I love him desperately and that as
soon as this damn fever is gone we'll snuggle."

"Yep."

The back screen door slammed. A moment later the
van drove past the house and skidded to a stop at the
end of the driveway. Shamika jumped out and stood by
the highway, hands on her hips, her gaze fixed on the
yellow bus rounding the nearest bend in the road. Sitting
up in bed, Leah watched the bus crawl like some lum-
bersome tortoise along the shoulder, its inhabitants' animated faces peering out at Shamika as the bus stopped
and the door opened with a whoosh that released the
sounds of laughter and garbled noises that were meant
to be words. The driver jumped out, even as the back
door of the bus opened and a ramp automatically slid
from the bus's belly to form a platform, onto which Sandra Howard, the school's occupational therapist, rolled
Val in his wheelchair. As the ramp slowly lowered toward the ground, Sandra, smiling brightly, lifted Val's

arm and waved his hand at Shamika. Val rewarded
Shamika with a brilliant smile.

Leah lay back on the bed and closed her eyes.

At long last, she slept. It was not the drifting-through-
dreamland-like-a-feather-on-air sort of sleep, although
she often dreamed of soaring weightlessly through cu-
mulus clouds while space and time rushed by sound-
lessly below her. Nor was it the frantic, confusing streak
through a jumbled subconscious splashed by strange images that would leave her scratching her head and pon-
dering over their meaning as if they were alien
hieroglyphics. This dream was gut-wrenchingly real.
Fact, not fiction. No cryptic meanings. Just stark as black
print on white paper.

*She chose a place in the very back of the lecture hall,
Room 338, hoping to avoid Professor Carlisle's attention. Since the beginning of her freshman year in vet
school, he had taken great pleasure in zeroing in on her
any time he conjured up a question he was certain would
stump even the most seasoned D.V.M.*

*She'd surmised the first day of class that Professor
Carlisle, like most good old boys at vet schools, did not
much care for women in veterinary medicine—at least,
not large-animal medicine. He felt that women were far
too emotional to make life-and-death decisions concerning animals—especially horses. After displaying a
poster of Elizabeth Taylor in* National Velvet, *he proceeded to explain that anyone who had ever cried over
the movie had no place in veterinary medicine. Likewise
with* Black Beauty.

This class was not *Fairy Tales 101.*

*Leah glanced at her watch. Carlisle was late getting
to class. Good. She would close her eyes for a few
minutes and try her best to will away the spikes of dull
pain prodding at her pregnant belly. Indigestion, no
doubt. Too much Mexican food at lunch—hopefully. Or*

perhaps it was simply stress causing her to feel as if she were in labor.

At six months along she simply would not entertain the idea that the increasing discomfort was due to anything other than the fact that she and Richard had argued again.

Fights over their cornflakes each morning had become as commonplace as her frequent trips to the bathroom. Richard wanted her to drop out of school and devote her time and energy into being a wife and mother—annoyingly chauvinistic considering this was the nineties, especially in light of the fact that they had mutually decided before they married that she would continue with her studies and build a vet practice in the Dallas area after graduation. Only then would they consider children.

But no sooner had they adjusted to the news of her unexpected pregnancy than he began his campaign. He made more than enough money to provide for his family. A child needed the security of knowing he was the most important component of a happy family, and that meant the mother's undivided attention, not to mention loyalty.

With no warning, at exactly the same moment that Professor Carlisle entered the classroom, her water broke. Jumping from her chair, she stood helplessly as fluid ran as if from a faucet out of her pants legs. There were snickers around her—peers believing her problem nothing more serious than a weak bladder. Then the pain—excruciating. Mind-bending. She screamed and doubled over . . .

Valentino Starr weighed one pound three ounces. The doctors gave him a one in one hundred chance of surviving the first forty-eight hours. The nurses put him, naked, in what looked like a plastic coffin, his red, sparrowlike body practically lost amid the tubes and monitors that bleeped his condition every few seconds.

Still hooked to IVs, her lower body feeling as if someone had raked out her insides with a dull spoon, Leah,

*surrounded by stone-faced nurses and cautious special-
ists, sat in a chair beside the incubator, counting the
seconds between her son's heartbeats and singing him
lullabies. She ached to hold him, but they would not
allow it. Not yet. His lungs were far from being developed. His bones were brittle as dry reeds. And his skin—
what there was of it—was as transparent as a moth's
wing. She could see every vein in his tiny body. He
looked like a road map of red and blue highways.*

*Because she had given birth by C-section, the staff
would not allow Leah to remain out of bed for more
than fifteen minutes. They wheeled her back to her room
while Richard walked silent and sullen at her side. He
blamed her for this horrible fiasco. Had she dropped out
of school like he had wanted her to, this probably would
not have happened.*

*Wrong, wrong, wrong! her angry obstetrician argued.
Leah's problem could be summed up easily: an incom-
petent cervix, a condition where the mouth of the cervix
opens prematurely under the weight of the baby. Next
pregnancy, should there be a next pregnancy, they would
know to perform a cerclage procedure by clamping the
cervix closed very early in the pregnancy, thereby elim-
inating the chance of this unfortunate occurrence happening a second time.*

*The hospital smells assaulting her every numb sense
and her uterus knotting like a fist, Leah looked into her
husband's eyes and knew there would never be a next
time—not for them.*

FOUR

The answering machine clicked on at seven-fifteen, waking Leah with a jolt. She listened to her own voice invite the caller to leave a message, then waited for the caller's response. Nothing. The machine cut off with an echoing finality before it reset itself for the next message.

She rolled in bed, aware that her fever had broken. Her pillow felt wet, her pajamas clammy. Lying in the semidark of encroaching twilight, she focused on the silence and wondered why Shamika and Val were running so late returning from his speech therapy.

The answering machine came on again.

Tossing back the covers, Leah slid from the bed and ran barefoot down the hall into the living room, where the illuminated Caller ID glowed in the shadows. WHITEHORSE FARM. Her heart skipped and for what felt like an eternity she stared at the answering machine as if it had turned into a crystal ball. Her recorded voice droned out its monotonous regret for not having been here to take the call, but—

She grabbed up the receiver and hit the Stop button

on the machine. Taking a deep breath, she finally managed a thready hello.

"Doc Starr?"

Leah sank onto the sofa and curled her legs up under her. "Hello, Roy."

"Sorry to disturb you, but I was wondering if we can go ahead and draw blood on that colt? Soon as we can get him blood-typed with the registry, the sooner we can get his papers."

"You have a buyer already?"

"Looks that way. Won't know for sure until next week."

"If you'll drop the blood-typing kit off, I'll do it first thing in the morning."

"You feeling okay?"

"Better. Why do you ask?"

"Johnny says you was seeming a little under the weather today."

"I guess I was a bit out of sorts."

Roy chuckled.

Sinking deeper into the sofa cushions, she twisted the phone cord around her fingers. "Sorry I'm late on the rent again, Roy. You're being very patient."

"Don't worry about it. It ain't as if we're starvin' over here."

"How does Johnny feel about me leasing this place?"

"He ain't said. I guess if he cared he would have told me so by now. Besides, he's too busy tryin' to run the government." Silence, then, "Sorry. Guess I shouldn't have brought up *that* subject."

"It's okay. Really. Confrontation between Johnny and my father isn't exactly news, is it?"

"Glad you don't take it personal. Hey, I got another call comin' in. I'll drop this kit by your place first thing in the mornin'."

The phone went dead and Leah gently replaced the receiver onto the cradle. A clock on the wall ticked. Through the closed windows the distant traffic sounded like the hum of insects as the Caller ID continued to shimmer WHITEHORSE FARM into the dark.

For that instant before grabbing up the phone, she had believed the caller to be Johnny Whitehorse.

But why would he be calling, especially after she had verbally blasted him earlier that day? After she had once vowed to love him forever, to spend her life rejoicing in his spirit and body and children—then, with none of the emotion ripping apart her insides, declared to his wounded eyes that their relationship had been a mistake from the beginning. Their lives were a universe apart. A forever relationship simply would not work—not between them.

Why had her heart tripped at the thought of speaking with him again? She had long since buried her feelings for Johnny in a deep grave of denial. She could not possibly love a man who would intentionally strike out at her father so maliciously. Her father had been right about Johnny. He was a hothead. A troublemaker. A user. His only aim in romancing her had been driven by a nasty need to avenge his father.

Why had apologies over her behavior earlier in the day bombarded her brain like neurotransmitters gone amok?

But most frustrating: Why was she disappointed that the caller had turned out to be Roy Moon, and not Johnny? Why, in those seconds as she raised the receiver to her ear, had anticipation flooded her with a rush of adrenaline that now, in its tide of withdrawal, left her feeling nauseated and irritable . . . not to mention stupid?

The back door opened and Shamika's voice rang out. "Home at last. I got to have a wee-wee and then we are going to chow down on Spaghetti-O's. Is that cool?"

"Cool," came the childish, slightly slurred response, making Leah smile.

She moved to the kitchen where her son sat in his wheelchair, smiling over the prospect of eating Spaghetti-O's for supper. His blue eyes brightened when he saw her. His head wobbled and he struggled to sit up straight. One hand opened and closed in his way of saying, "I want you. Come hug me."

To hold Val now was probably foolish; his immune system was not the greatest. A simple cold could sometimes put him to bed for a week. Leah reminded herself of that as she crossed the kitchen, went down on her knees, and unbuckled the straps and braces that kept him anchored to the back of his chair.

His smile widened and laughter bubbled like spring water through his lips. "Mama hold me?" he asked.

"Yes, Mama is going to hold you," she replied.

"Mama hold Val tight?"

"So tight you're going to squeak."

Wrapping her arms around her son, Leah lifted him out of the chair. She swayed unsteadily, his weight, at sixty pounds, more than half of her own. He rested his head on her shoulder, his lips near her ear as she gripped him fiercely, her eyes closed to allow the swell of feeling in her chest to radiate through her body.

"Mama love?" he asked softly.

"Oh yes. Mama loves." She smiled. "Mama loves you more than life."

Shamika regarded them from the door. "I knew you couldn't stand it for much longer."

"The fever is broken. I'm feeling much better."

"Good. Maybe you'll join us for some Spaghetti-O's."

"I'm not feeling *that* good."

Laughing, Shamika searched through the pantry and exited with a family-sized can. As Shamika rummaged through the cupboard for a saucepan, Leah kissed her son's warm head, enjoying the smell of sunshine that had been absorbed by his skin; then she studied his clothes, which were linted by animal hair.

"Why were you late?" she asked Shamika.

"Got caught by Estelle Wright, and you know what *that* means. She's got to tell everybody everything that's happened since the last time we saw her."

Leah turned Val's hands over and studied his palms, stained by oily dirt—the sort that coats a person's skin when stroking a sweating horse.

"You've taken him to Rockaway Ranch again, Shamika. If you're going to do something behind my back, you might consider cleaning him up afterward. At least you won't get caught lying."

Shamika carefully placed the pan on the countertop before facing Leah. Her shoulders set, she regarded the anger on Leah's features before replying. "Yes, I took him to Rockaway Ranch, to the riding therapy class Equest puts on there every other week."

"I won't have him on a horse. How many times must I repeat myself?"

"The riding is highly beneficial. It's wonderful therapy. Just feel his legs. His entire body, for that matter. Feel how loose he is. When he's up on that horse he's using muscles that I can't possibly work when exercising him. And besides that, he adores riding. It builds his confidence and allows him to experience just a little of normality that he wouldn't experience otherwise."

"And what happens if he falls off? You, of all people, an occupational therapist, should realize the dangers of getting thrown from a horse."

"The horses that are used in this program are very special. And besides that, the children are buckled into the saddle and they are attended every second. The instructors' hands never leave the children for a moment."

"No." Shaking her head, Leah turned away and started for the bedroom.

Following, Shamika said, "Leah, be reasonable."

"No. A thousand times no. If something happened to Val—"

"Nothing will happen. Please, don't deny him his only opportunity to know a little of the freedom that you and I take for granted."

Leah kicked the bedroom door closed between herself

and Shamika. She carried Val to the bed, pulled off his
shoes, and tucked him under the covers. Still smiling,
he gazed up at her, eyes dancing, cheeks awash with
color.

"Mama love?"

She nodded and brushed the hair back from his forehead.

"Mika love?"

"Shamika loves you very much."

"Val love horse."

"I know, my darling." She sighed. "I know."

Greg Hunnicutt, president of the Sierra Blanca Downs
racetrack, rang her the next morning as she was on her
knees removing the stitches from the cantankerous donkey's leg. He wondered if they could move up their job
interview to that afternoon. Apparently another vet had
just turned in his notice at the track, which meant there
were two openings for D.V.M.'s, which, Leah surmised,
largely improved her chances of landing one of the positions.

At two forty-five she pulled Shamika's van into the
Downs parking lot. She checked her face in the rearview
mirror. Makeup minimum, just enough to partially conceal the purple bruise over her eyebrow. A light touch
of mascara to her lashes. A kiss of blush to her cheeks.
Lip gloss, no color. Hair French braided. Clean jeans.
Starched white blouse that buttoned at the throat—annoying, but necessary when she was walking into a
world that functioned strictly on testosterone.

Her papers were in order, tucked neatly into her briefcase. She'd spent the last hour retyping her résumé.
There were letters of recommendation from her former
employer—Dr. John Casey, of Pilot Point, Texas—and
from previous satisfied clients. Her most prized refer-
ence, however, was the one written by Professor Carlisle. He'd presented it to her the day of her graduation,
declaring that anyone who could fight her way through

vet school despite the awful obstacles that had been
thrown in her way obviously had a calling.

At three in the afternoon the parking lot was mostly
empty. The horse owners and trainers parked in lots beyond the offices, near the barns. Soon, however, the influx of traffic would begin. By five o'clock, bettors
would drift in to take their places along the rails, stubs
in hand as they waited for their pick to come racing over
the finish line, hopefully winning them enough to put
down on the next race. By the end of the night there
would be so many losing stubs littering the ground that
one would think the sky had blanketed the ground in
snow.

Immersed in an animated phone conversation, Hunnicutt smiled broadly at Leah and waved her in, pointed
to an empty chair before his desk, and proceeded to tell
the caller that no way in hell was he going to allow a
trainer renowned for drugging horses and blackmailing
jockeys to run on his track . . . but it was nice talking to
him anyway. No hard feelings. Sure, sure, they were still
friends. No problem along that line. His best to the mis-
sus. Good luck in California.

Still smiling, Hunnicutt hung up the phone and sat
back in his chair. His teeth looked like yellowed piano
keys, his nose red as a Christmas bulb. "Trainers, God
love 'em. They shoot up a horse and get caught and
we're supposed to look the other way. Can you imagine
how long the state would let us stay in business if we
allowed shootin' up a horse? 'Bout that long.'' He
snapped his fingers and rocked back and forth in his
chair. "Glad you could make it on such short notice."

Leah crossed her legs and smiled.

His gaze took a slow trip up and down her person.
"So how's your daddy? I ain't seen him since, oh, last
Fourth of July."

"That makes two of us," she said.

"Stays busy, does he?"

"Very."

"Been a lot of controversy lately about his dealin's with the gambling issue and Formation Media."

"Such is life for politicians, I guess."

"I thought of runnin' for office once. Major brain fart." He laughed and scratched his beer belly. "One thing I ain't is stupid. Besides that, I got too damn many skeletons in the closet. Know what I mean?"

She nodded and shifted the briefcase on her lap.

"I don't get it. These dudes in office go around breakin' the law, screwin' interns, et cetera and think they ain't gonna get caught? Major brain fart. Hell, the goddamn press is like a buncha vultures circlin'. If you show a smidgen of weakness they'll swoop down on you and pick your bones clean as toothpicks before you can squawk ouch."

"Silly, isn't it?"

Hunnicutt sat forward, elbows on the desk, his face losing its almost comical animation as he fixed Leah with an intensity that made hot color creep up her neck. "I suppose you've got résumés and references in that briefcase, Dr. Starr. That's all well and good. But I've been in this business a long time, and I'm here to tell you that all the résumés and references in the world won't stop a dirty doctor from shootin' up a horse if the price is right, or puttin' an animal down if a portion of insurance money is dangled like the proverbial carrot in front of his nose."

"I suppose that depends on whether the doctor is in this business for the money, or for the love of the animal, Mr. Hunnicutt."

"Doctors have bills to pay just like everybody else, especially when they're strugglin' to get started."

"If you believe I'm dirty, Mr. Hunnicutt, why did you ask me here?"

"I don't believe anything of the sort. I'm just offerin' you fair warnin'. I don't tolerate shenanigans on my track. We run a clean operation here. If I ever got wind that some asshole owner or trainer has got a vet of mine under his thumb I'd stop at nothing to see his or her license jerked, not just in this state, but in this entire friggin' country."

The phone rang. Hunnicutt grabbed it. A woman's voice buzzed in the silence as he nodded and grunted in response, his sharp gray eyes still focused on Leah. Then he hung up without so much as a goodbye, sat back in his chair and absently adjusted the tie cutting into his fleshy throat. "Tell me somethin', Doc. You married?"

"Divorced."

"How long?"

"Four years."

"Do you like men?"

Leah frowned, then nodded, not certain about his meaning.

"Do you cry easily?"

"That's a very sexist remark, Mr. Hunnicutt. Would you ask that if I were a man?"

He grinned. "Let me rephrase the question. Are you easily hurt or offended by rough language directed at you by an irate trainer or owner? 'Cause sure as you and I are sittin' here right now, there's gonna be some dickhead who is gonna get in your face because he doesn't like the way his million-dollar baby is recoupin' from the sniffles."

"I would expect any caring owner or trainer to question me if his horse isn't responding adequately to treatment."

"What will you do when some good old boy pinches you on the ass? Or calls you Doc Tits? Or worse. Cause I'm here to tell you right now, most men out there think a woman is good for two things. Exercisin' or jockeyin' a horse, or spreadin' her legs so he can jockey her. If you ain't got a hide like an armadillo you won't last a month."

"If I could make it through vet school, Mr. Hunnicutt, I can make it through just about anything."

"Right. You up to a little tête-à-tête with the folks

who'll ultimately decide whether we hire you or not?''

Leah uncrossed her legs and sat forward. "I was under the impression that you—''

"This track is run by a board of trustees, of which I am a member. You have to pass muster with every one of them before we can put you on the payroll.''

"They vote?''

"Yep.'' He chuckled. "Don't look so puny. They pretty much rely on my opinion. For most of them their place on the board is a pastime. They enjoy the horses but do other things to pay the bills. Let's face it, you can count on one hand the number of horse owners out there who can actually make a livin' at this—not since the eighties bust. Damned IRS 'bout buried us all. Sooner we bury them the better.'' Leaving his chair, he moved to the door behind Leah. "Now is as good a time as any to take the plunge, Doc. They're waitin'.''

A few nights ago she had watched a special on *Dateline* about the last moments of a convict on death row. How, just hours before strapping the accused to a table and inserting a lethal dose of knockout into his arm, prison officials moved the doomed from one wing of the prison to another. The cameras had followed the prisoner down long, stark, sterile corridors, focusing luridly on each pitiful drag of the prisoner's foot, the trembling and shaking of his body as the realization set in that there would be no last-minute reprieve from the inevitable.

Leah could relate. As she walked in silence at Hunnicutt's side down long corridors of closed office doors and conference rooms, she thought back on the childish excitement she'd felt when getting his call earlier that day. In her mind as she'd dashed to shower and dress, she'd fantasized over the salary, experience, and connections that working at the track would offer. She'd tallied up said salary and imagined how nice it would be to catch up on her delinquent bills. There might even be enough to put aside each month to eventually buy Val the new wheelchair he so desperately needed. Then there were the Botox shots Val's doctor had recently told her about that were proving vastly successful at limbering tight muscles. But eighteen hundred dollars every six weeks would prove to be impossible for her unless she could count on a decent salary.

Yet, as she and Hunnicutt turned down the last corridor and headed toward the open double doors of the Finish Line conference room, she reasoned that she was as likely to win the approval of twelve men as she was to leap over the Grand Canyon in a single bound. Like the foot-dragging convict headed for his deathbed, she saw her future disperse like an ice cube on a hot plate.

Smoke hung over the conference room like gray smog. The long marble-topped table surrounded by conversing men dressed casually in jeans and T-shirts depicting a horse streaking across a finish line was scattered with remnants of lunch: deli meats, squeeze bottles of mustard and ketchup, empty tea glasses, and discarded napkins. As Hunnicutt introduced Leah, each man stood and offered his hand, smiled broadly, and welcomed her to their "monthly excuse to cut out of the office early." They offered her iced tea, which she gladly accepted. Her throat felt dry as the track she could see through the window.

It did not take long for Leah to relax. Greg Hunnicutt supplied the men with pertinent information regarding her background. The fact that she had graduated from Texas A&M veterinary school brought impressed nods. They spoke in future tense. Vetting at their track would be a tough but satisfying experience for her. She would learn a great deal—sharpen her skills. She would meet some great people. Make lifelong friends. They had great New Year's Eve parties as well, and by the way, the vets were allowed to keep all tips, which could prove to be substantial if the owners and trainers were particularly pleased by her work. Occasionally, Hunnicutt glanced her way and winked, as if to say, No problem. You're in like Flynn.

Giddiness once again settled in the pit of her stomach, infusing her imagination with visions of a nicely padded bank account. Tonight she would take Shamika and Val out to dinner. They would celebrate with a bottle of cheap champagne. She would present Shamika with a money draft for two months' salary with the understanding that she wasn't to deposit it until Leah received her first week's paycheck.

"... Of course we can't affirm the position until you've been approved by all of us. And considering we're one short today, you might have to meet with our missing member one on one."

She counted heads. Eleven. Damn.

Greg checked his watch. "He should've been here by now. Normally he's on time."

"Such is the life of the rich and famous," someone said, and everyone chuckled.

Johnny Whitehorse walked into the room in that moment. The gathering welcomed him boisterously. "Hello!" "What time do you call this, buddy? We were about to give up on you."

Leah sank in her chair and closed her eyes.

Johnny moved to the chair at the opposite end of the table. "Sorry 'bout that. My flight was late leaving Boulder."

"You been harassing the government again, Whitehorse?" someone asked.

He grinned, his only response.

Forcing open her eyes, Leah managed to take a deep breath before looking at Johnny directly. His dark eyes were emotionless as he regarded her, as were his features.

"This is Doctor Starr, Johnny," said Greg. "We're considering her to fill one of the positions—"

"I know who she is," Johnny interrupted. "Senator Foster's daughter."

Silence filled up the room.

Leah gave Johnny a flat smile. "Yes. I am. But I

won't hold that against you, Mr. Whitehorse. Everyone is entitled to his own opinion of a politician—stupid or not. This is a free country, as I recall.''

He relaxed against the back of his chair, his lips taking on a smug curl. ''What makes you think you're cut out to be a track vet, Doctor Starr?''

''I'm good and I'm bright. I care about horses.''

''Ah, but do you care about people, Doctor?''

''Meaning?''

''This is an emotional business. Dreams get crushed. Lives ruined. Do you ever stop to think how your decision can radically alter someone's life?''

Her cheeks began to burn and her throat grew tight. The men lining the table stared down at their food-littered plates and mustard-stained napkins as Leah tried her best to control the surge of emotion rolling over in her chest. Johnny was goading her. He wanted to break her. He might as well have reached across the table and smashed her like a bug with his fist.

''Do you understand exactly what would be expected of you should you get this position?'' he asked, his voice sounding as if it were echoing from a well. ''You would be on call twenty-four hours a day during the meets. You would be expected to work on weekends. On holidays. Your day begins at six in the morning and doesn't end until midnight, or later. I understand that you're divorced. Have you obligations that would get in the way of your duties?''

''I'm more than capable of making certain that any obligations I have are met to my satisfaction.''

His eyes narrowed. ''Do you have children, Doctor Starr?''

She opened and closed her mouth, then nodded. ''A boy.''

He looked down briefly, saying nothing, obviously considering his next words. ''Would you care to tell us about him?'' he invited her in soft monotone.

''He's . . . seven.'' Leah took a deep breath, glancing

the men's pleasant, interested expressions before center-
ing back on Johnny. His eyes looked dark as polished
onyx. And his lips . . . oh, God. "His name is . . . Val.
Short for Valentino."

Valentino. Once he had laughed at the suggestion, as
they lay naked under the summer night sky, young arms
and legs entangled, their hunger for one another sated,
momentarily, planning their future together, the children
they would make together. All boys. She would name
their first son Valentino because she had always had a
passion for old Rudolph Valentino movies. So it had
been decided that night that they would name their first
son Valentino.

Seven years ago, as she pressed her face against the
plastic incubator and gazed down on her son, she'd
thought about Johnny, and about that night they'd
looked at the stars and planned their future together—
of the children they would share. So she'd named her
son Valentino, in memory of the love she had let get
away. In memory of the heart she had broken. In memory of Johnny Whitehorse.

A man in wire-rimmed glasses smiled at Leah. "Have
you adequate child care for him?"

She returned his smile. "I have live-in help."

Silence. An eternal moment passed before Leah raised
her gaze back to Johnny's.

How could you? his eyes asked.

I'm sorry. So sorry.

Greg pushed his chair back. "I think we've covered
all the essentials. I've got your résumé and references.
I'll see that each of the gentlemen here get a copy before
they leave today." He offered his hand to Leah. She
took it and stood, smiled her thanks to everyone at the
table except Johnny, then turned for the door. Greg
walked with her into the hall. "We'll vote next Monday.
I'll give you a call that evening or first thing Tuesday
morning." He patted her shoulder. "Johnny is a good
man. Intelligent, despite his flamboyant and sometimes

controversial reputation. I doubt his feelings for your
father would influence his judgment of you.''

She laughed and looked away, wondering if she
should inform Greg that Johnny's opinion of her father
would have little to do with his voting down her appointment—but because she had broken his heart twelve
years ago and he had every right to despise her, which
he obviously did. Her tantrum yesterday would not help
matters.

She offered her hand and gave Greg as bright a smile
as she could manage. "I'll look forward to your call,
Mr. Hunnicutt. And thanks for your support.''

He returned to the conference room, closing the door
in her face.

FIVE

The emergency call came at just after midnight from Ramona Skunk Cap. At the Mescalero reservation a herd of her goats, spooked by a coyote or wolf, had stampeded through a barbed wire fence, snapping the nasty strands so they coiled like a hungry constrictor around the terrified animals. Dr. Starr should come quick before the animals bled to death.

Leah made herself a cup of strong instant coffee before climbing into her truck and heading down 249. Earlier she had done a passably decent job of shielding the broken window with a square of cardboard, but that did little to stop the wind from whistling in around the masking tape, of sucking at the cardboard so it breathed in and out like some living entity.

She popped a cassette into the player. Diamond's "Beautiful Noise." No memories there. Nothing to stir up the frustration she'd felt earlier in the day when realizing that Johnny Whitehorse held her future, not to mention her livelihood, in the very hands he had once used to drive her mad with desire.

So . . . Johnny knew she had a son.

Why had he waited until the interview to question her about it?

Did he know about the CP?

He couldn't know. Few people did, aside from Val's therapists and his teachers at school. There was her father, of course. No way was he going to discuss the issue with anyone—even her.

The truck veered to the right, then the left. The back end fishtailed as if on ice before a loud hum drowned out the trumpets and violins pumping from the stereo speakers. Leah eased the truck to the shoulder of the road and sat with the engine idling before shifting into Park and killing the engine.

Silence. Darkness, but for the streak of dim light from her headlamp that pooled on the bloated carcass of a raccoon on the road up ahead.

The door creaked and popped as Leah stepped onto the highway. The truck, still covered with crusty mud from two nights before, listed to the left like a sinking boat. The back tire lay in shreds along the asphalt. The wheel appeared bent from her having driven on it God only knew how long before realizing there was a problem. A new tire would set her back a hundred bucks. A wheel would cost several hundred.

"Damn it!" She kicked the wheel. Then kicked the fender. She walked around to the back of the truck and kicked the tailgate. Spying a metal rod lying in weeds littered with beer cans and a Burger King drink cup, she picked it up and proceeded to beat the hood, the roof, the already-broken-out headlamp, the door, then the shredded tire and mangled wheel. She beat it until the rod in her hand snapped in two, one end flying back to miss her face by inches.

"I won't cry," she chanted to herself. "Crying won't do me any good. It won't fix my tire. It won't pay for a wheel. It sure as hell won't buy me a new truck or get me that job at the track." And it would not turn back the clock eight years ago, to the night she and Richard had rented an X-rated video like two naughty and curious kids and became so turned on while watching it that they had unprotected sex.

As she stood on the shoulder of the road, the stink of the rotting raccoon beginning to filter through her senses, Leah rocked back and forth, her arms clamped around her waist, her body shivering from the cool mountain air.

Car lights rounded the bend—two pinpoints at first, looking like little round owl eyes reflecting moonlight, growing larger as the vehicle neared. The old Olds 442 roared by, sounding like a freight train. At the last minute the driver hit the brakes and the taillights lit up like red beacons. The car reversed, rumbling like a Caterpillar 'dozer, stones crunching and spitting as it stopped beside her. A man's face peered out at her, his skinny, unshaven features made eerie by the dim green lights from his dashboard.

He grinned, looking like a jack-o'-lantern. "Need some help?"

Leah hugged herself tighter, the image of her cell phone left lying on the kitchen table popping into her brain like a camera bulb. She had laid it down to fix her coffee and forgot to retrieve it before leaving.

Think. It was ten miles back to the house. It was twelve miles to town, and another eight to the reservation where a half-dozen goats were bleeding to death, chewed up by barbed wire. Chances were Ramona Skunk Cap would call the house when Leah did not show up, but Shamika did not normally answer Leah's business phone, not at this hour.

"Blowout," she finally replied, doing her best to keep her voice steady.

He grinned again and winked. The car crawled over to the shoulder, headlamps trained on the shredded tire and mangled wheel. The man stepped out, hitching up his too-tight jeans before spitting a stream of tobacco onto the road. Despite the cold, he wore a tank top and

a grimy gimme cap that reflected his interest in the
World Champion Denver Broncos. Her initial feeling of
unease streaked up her back and made her scalp prickle.
She glanced down at the broken rod she still held in one
hand, gripped it more tightly and tried to breathe evenly.
Once, she had taken a self-defense course—what women
should do if they found themselves threatened—but she
had always suspected that to be effective in gouging out
eyeballs or cracking testicles with the tip of her boot she
would have to be totally in control of her logic. But how
did one control logic when fear fogged reasoning beyond comprehension?

The stranger walked over, gravel scraping under his
scuffed Red Wing boots. He had the look of a construction worker, skin dried like an old cow hide, lanky body
wiry but strong, arms corded and muscled without the
slightest hint of fat. A tattoo of snakes and skulls entwined both arms from his shoulders to his wrists. He
smelled like beer. And sweat. And rancid Skoal.

Letting loose a low whistle, he regarded the wheel
and shook his head. "Made a mess of it, didn't you?"

"Seems that way."

"I reckon it don't matter if you got a spare or not.
No way in hell you gonna get anywhere on that axle."
He spat again. "If I was you I'd get rid of the whole
damn thing. This baby's 'bout seen its last mile." Looking out at her from beneath the brim of his cap, he said,
"What's a good-lookin' lady like you doin' out on a
highway this late at night?"

"I'm a vet. I was on my way to a call."

"A vet?" He grunted and looked her up and down.
"You mean like an animal doctor?"

She nodded as another car rounded the curve and bar-
reled toward them, blinking its brights to acknowledge
Leah's presence on the shoulder. Perhaps if she jumped
up and down and waved, it would stop. She could tell
the tattooed snuff-sucker to beat it—she did not need

the help of someone who looked as if he were spending his first night out of Attica prison.

Then again, if it did not stop, her actions would indicate exactly how she felt about standing in the dark on an isolated highway with someone who smelled like road kill.

The car roared by, its driver invisible behind tinted windows. Leah watched its taillights dwindle into specks, then disappear completely.

His hands on his hips, the stranger watched the car disappear into the dark, then he looked around slowly, his eyes invisible under the low brim of his gimme cap. Leah focused on his mouth. Lips said a lot about people's thoughts, even more than eyes. She didn't much care for the thoughts running through the Bronco fan's head in that moment.

"Tell you what," he said. "I don't mind givin' you a ride into town."

Leah looked up and down the dark highway again.

"Looks to me like you ain't got much choice, lady. It's me or the road."

"I appreciate the offer, but I really shouldn't leave my truck unattended. There's all of my supplies . . . I can't afford to have them stolen. Why don't you drive into town and send out a tow truck?"

"I'd feel real bad about leavin' you out here alone. A lady was discovered murdered along here just last month. Cops ain't ever found out who done it . . ."

Her scalp began to sweat. And her hands. She was tempted to wave the broken rusty pipe in the man's face as a warning that she would not go down without a fight, but the realization that he just might decide to use the pipe on her made her think again.

"Relax," he said. "You're lookin' a little like a 'possum caught in the lights of an oncoming semi."

"I . . . can't leave my truck."

He took a step closer.

She gripped the pipe more tightly. Go for the throat,

the face, the eyes—the eyes were most vulnerable . . .

A truck rounded the bend, its row of night lights across the top of the cab glowing like orange fireflies, as were the lights on the fenders over the double rear tires. The smart thing to do would be to step out into the road and wave her arms. The driver would be forced to hit her or swerve around her. Either way he could not ignore her. So why wouldn't her legs move?

The truck slowed and blinked its headlights.

The Ford dually emerged gradually from the dark, illuminated with enough white and orange lights to rival a carnival ferris wheel. A *white* dually. Like Johnny's. Only there were probably a thousand such trucks in the area. What were the chances that Johnny Whitehorse would be on this highway at this time of night?

Slower, engine rumbling, ghostly in the dark, a guardian angel sent to rescue her from a man who probably was safe as a priest. Brake lights flashed; the truck stopped. A tinted window buzzed down, revealing Johnny Whitehorse.

Leah sank back against the truck, vaguely aware that the pipe was dropping from her fingers. It hit her boot, then bounced to the asphalt, clattering in the darkness.

"Hi," he said.

"Hi," she mouthed, trying not to look relieved.

Johnny glanced at the stranger. "Is there a problem here?"

"A blowout," Leah replied. "Wheel's wrecked."

"Seems every time I see that truck it's giving you problems."

She nodded and crossed her arms over her stomach. "Seems to be the story of my life recently."

"No joke." Johnny checked the rearview mirror, then did a U-turn in the highway, pulling up behind the 442. Leaving the truck running, he stepped onto the highway, shirttail out of his faded jeans, sleeves rolled up to his elbows. Tonight he was without his hat, allowing his dark hair to flow freely over his shoulders.

The stranger made a sound, not quite a laugh, more like a grunt as Johnny moved toward him. "If it ain't Geronimo. I don't recall the lady sendin' up any smoke signals, chief."

Johnny grinned. "Careful, Bubba. Just cause I haven't scalped anyone this week doesn't mean I can't be tempted."

Leah closed her eyes, telling herself that Bubba would be foolish to pick a fight with a man nearly a head taller than him, with shoulders twice as broad. Johnny had not gotten the scar on his chin and over his right eyebrow by turning the other cheek . . . not during his angry youth.

Bubba wasn't amused. But neither was he a fool, Leah surmised. Without a glance her way, he sauntered to the 442 and sank into its bucket seat. He gunned the engine before flooring the accelerator, tires screaming and stinking of hot rubber as he streaked off into the night, leaving her and Johnny standing in the bright pool of his headlights.

She could not quite make herself look at his eyes, so she focused on the top button that was buttoned on his plaid shirt. A vee of dark skin was exposed to the middle of his chest. "I recall a time when you would have made cottage cheese of that creep's face for what he just said."

"It's called Anger Management 101. Someday I'll probably explode and take out a dozen or more Bubbas with an Uzi."

She smiled at her feet. "After my behavior the other day I wouldn't have blamed you if you had waved and kept on going."

"You know I was always a sucker for a pretty face. Especially when it was yours." He walked around her and stooped to have a better look at the demolished wheel. "Hope you weren't on your way to something important, Doc. This wheel is history."

"Ramona Skunk Cap's goats are dying. They ran through a barbed-wire fence."

"Again?" He laughed. "If it wasn't for Ramona's goats, every coyote around the Sacramento Mountains would starve to death. She might as well change the name of her farm to Cabrito Burrito."

Leah smiled as her gaze reluctantly found its way to Johnny's profile. Thank God he wasn't looking at her. She had never been one to hide her feelings; they radiated like neon in her eyes. Right now there were so many emotions bombarding her insides she felt like a target at a shooting range.

Johnny stood.

Leah looked away.

"I'll run you out to Ramona's if you want," he offered.

"Don't you ever sleep?"

"Don't you?"

"No, actually. I don't think that I do."

"Get what you need from the truck and lock it up. I'll call Triple A and have a tow come out and get it. That way it won't cost you anything."

She started to say something smart-ass, like "I don't accept charity from former lovers," then decided there was no point. She could not afford another towing expense, not when what little budget she had was going to be blown by buying a new wheel and tire. Besides, this camaraderie between her and Johnny felt much better than their earlier hostility.

As Johnny walked back to his truck, Leah collected sutures, scissors, clippers, sterile gloves, syringes, and tetanus medications. Then there were antibiotics, and bantamine for pain. She put them all in a box with gauze and vet wrap, double-locked the drawers of prescription medications, and buried the key deep in her pocket, praying they would all still be there when she got her truck back.

Johnny was on the cell phone to Triple A when she

crawled into the truck. With the box resting on her lap, she sank into the dove-gray leather seats and closed her eyes.

After all these years, Johnny's voice sounded the same. Deep and smooth as a slow-flowing river. Funny how safe she suddenly felt, as if the world could disintegrate around her yet her reality would remain unscathed. Then again, he'd always had that effect on her.

Johnny hung up the phone and tossed it onto the back seat. Glancing over his left shoulder, he eased the truck out onto the highway.

They rode in silence toward the Sacramento Mountains, which were little more than a black silhouette against the star-filled sky. Occasionally, Leah peeked from under her lashes to see Johnny focused on the road ahead, wrist caught on the top of the steering wheel, shoulders cocked just slightly toward the driver's door.

Finally, she sat up, hitting something with her foot. She fished around the floorboard until coming up with a black kid-leather makeup bag that smelled strongly of floral perfume. The zipper had been left open. Inside were tubes of Estée Lauder lipsticks, a compact, nail polish, and a package of condoms—ribbed and lubricated for enhanced pleasure. One was missing.

Leah zipped the bag closed and placed it carefully on the console between her and Johnny. "Coming home from a date, I take it."

He glanced at the bag and shrugged.

"Anyone I know?"

"You know I don't kiss and tell, Leah."

"Still a gentleman where women are concerned." She smiled and fingered the bag. "She has money, I take it. Must have. Only a successful career woman can afford to spend twenty bucks for a tube of lipstick."

Hitting the blinkers, Johnny turned the truck onto Highway 70, bypassing the turnoff to downtown Ruidoso. If they continued to travel east they would ultimately arrive in Roswell—home of crashed UFOs and embalmed aliens. Once upon a time, at least once a month, she and Johnny had driven all the way out to Roswell, parked amid the cactus and tumbleweeds, made love under the night sky, and waited to be abducted by little green men with eyes like dragonflies.

They had not used condoms back then, ribbed or otherwise. She had wanted as much of Johnny Whitehorse inside her as she could get, consequences be damned.

"So . . . is it serious between you?" she asked.

"You're sure asking a lot of questions."

"Am I being too personal?"

"I just wonder why you care."

"I don't. Just trying to make conversation."

He grinned. "I don't know if it's serious."

"Are you in love with her?"

"I don't know."

"Is she Native American?"

"Yes." He nodded.

"Figures."

"What's that supposed to mean?"

"Only that the last few years you've worked to focus the public's attention on the plight of the Native Americans, and most recently to shatter the stereotype of what most people think of Indians. It seems natural that you would settle down with a woman who reflects your ideals and beliefs."

"Jesus, you sound like Dolores."

"Is that her name?"

"No comment."

"Spoken like a fledgling politician."

Silence again, neither of them desiring to traverse the topic of politics, which would lead them to her father, which would ultimately cause a fight.

Johnny made a sudden turn down a gravel-topped road that was little better than a footpath, or so it seemed in the dark of the crowding forest. Had anyone else been driving, she would have questioned his motives. But Johnny Whitehorse knew the region around the reservation better than most people knew their own backyard. After ten minutes of bouncing over rocks and splashing through remnants of previous rains, they came out on Carrizo Canyon Road and headed south, passing signs pointing to Mescalero Lake and the Inn of the Mountain Gods.

Laying her head back against the seat, Leah closed her eyes.

"Where is your husband?" Johnny asked.

"I don't have a husband," she replied sleepily.

"Your ex-husband then."

"I'm not sure. The last I heard he was living in the Florida Keys with some nineteen-year-old swimsuit cutie of the month and trying to write the great American novel. I think he believes he's Hemingway reincarnated. I expect to hear anytime that he's in Spain running with the bulls."

"You married a writer? I thought you had better sense than that."

"I married a petroleum engineer with a master's in business who, at the time, was vice-president of an independent oil company. Just after our son's third birthday he decided life was too short to waste it doing something he didn't enjoy. His dream had always been to live in the Keys and write. So bye-bye marriage and responsibility. I'm outta here for the good life. I'll drop you a line when I get settled. That was four years ago. The only correspondence I've gotten is a sad tale of his inability to pay his child support because 'those fools in New York publishing couldn't see a good book if it leaped up and hit them between the eyes.' "

"So you're getting nothing in the way of child support from the jerk?"

Leah opened one eye and found Johnny frowning, his hands clutching the steering wheel as if he were strangling it. "No," she replied, sounding much too weary for her own liking. "And when he quit his job there was no more insurance . . ." Clearing her throat, Leah sat up again and rubbed her eyes. "I really don't like to talk about it. There isn't any point. I learned a long time ago not to get mired down in *what if*s and *if only*s. You can drive yourself crazy wallowing in self-pity."

"Fucking loser," Johnny mumbled.

"My sentiments exactly," Leah replied, laughing softly.

"So how did you meet such a prize?"

"I hesitate to tell you."

He looked at her with his dark eyes, which were not amused, and something inside her trembled. "My father introduced us. He approved of Richard, so naturally I told myself that I could, eventually, come to love Richard."

"And did you?"

"Hey, for someone whose replies to me were made up of little more than 'no comment,' you sure are getting personal."

"I just want to know if you loved him."

"Why?"

"Because."

"Because why?"

"Just curious, I guess, over how a woman could marry a man she didn't love . . . and have a child with him."

"That's hardly unique in this day and age."

"If you're gonna make a baby you'd damn well better love who you're making it with, don't you think?"

"I goofed, okay? In a moment of lust we got too carried away to stop and take precautions. That, however, has nothing to do with how I feel for my son. He's my reason for living. My universe. I couldn't love him more if he had been planned."

Johnny veered off the road and onto a dirt driveway that wove over cattle guards and around cactus gardens. He hit the brakes hard, skidding toward a small white frame house with a porch crowded with clay flowerpots. Shoving open his door, he said, ''I hope to hell you like goats.'' Then slammed the door so hard the truck rocked.

SIX

As Johnny used wire cutters to peel the rusty strands of tearing teeth out of the dying goats' hides, he could not help but wonder how Leah would have managed the bloody, stomach-turning task on her own. Somehow, he suspected that she would have found a way. As she went about the somber business of euthanizing most of Ramona Skunk Cap's goat herd, her calm, soft-spoken professionalism reminded him of a surgeon—hands gentle and deft, eyes watchful, mind ticking over any and all possibilities of saving the bleating, agonized animals, more for their traumatized owner's sake than for the animals themselves.

The animals whose wounds were not so severe were moved into Ramona's kitchen. Under the yellow glare of a solitary bulb hanging from the ceiling, Leah pumped drugs into the animals' veins and proceeded to sew up their injuries while Johnny held the trembling goats down on the newspaper-covered kitchen table. Ramona stood in the background, talking to herself and smoking one cigarette after another.

At four A.M. Ramona went to bed, leaving Johnny and

Leah to oversee the drugged goats themselves. On paper she found in a kitchen drawer, Leah wrote out explicit instructions on how to care for the animals over the next few days—how to clean the wounds, apply salves, administer antibiotics by crushing them into fine white powder and lacing it with honey in their feed. Leah would come back out in three days to check the goats for infection. She would remove the stitches in ten days. If Ramona had any questions or fears, she was not to hesitate calling Leah any time, day or night.

Leaving Leah to clean up the bloody kitchen, Johnny went outside to wrap up the dead goats in plastic garbage sacks. He found a shovel in the garage and buried the animals in a hole he dug behind the goat shed. To avoid the coyotes from returning and digging up the corpses, he dragged a rusty oil drum over the grave. Then he returned to the kitchen.

Leah sat in a chair, her head on the table, her eyes closed, cheek pressed into the blood-stained newspaper she had apparently failed to remove before falling asleep. She had not even managed to remove the rubber gloves from her hands.

He wanted to turn his back on the scene and walk off into the dark, put the memory of her lips parted in sleep back into his treasure trove of memories that had, over the years, numbed to the pain of losing her. Now here she was again, older, but just as beautiful, more beautiful because of life's hardships. The tiny lines around her eyes accentuated their depth of compassion. And those lips—always so easy to smile, to laugh . . . to kiss. They were bracketed now with slight creases. Not from smiling. No. He suspected that she did not do much smiling any longer.

Johnny walked quietly to the table. He touched Leah's hair with his fingertips, disturbing a coil of golden-brown strands that slid over her cheek.

Laying his hand on her shoulder, he shook her gently. "Leah. Honey, wake up. Leah?"

Her lashes fluttered and she slowly raised her head. She gradually lifted her eyes up to his.

He grinned. "Sleepyhead. Do I gotta carry you outta here?"

Groggy, she looked around, her momentary confusion almost comical. "Sorry," she finally murmured. "I must have dozed off."

"Must have."

She rubbed her eyes, smearing blood across her brow. Johnny caught her hand and removed the glove, tossed it into the sink, then removed the other one, flinging it the way of the first. Then he lifted her out of the chair, his left arm under her knees, the other cradling her back. Her head just naturally dropped to his shoulder, cozied against his neck, her lips slightly pressed against the flesh of his throat where his pulse suddenly raced like the heart of a startled deer.

"I can walk," she whispered.

"Sure you can."

Johnny exited the house, stood for a minute in the bracing air that rushed off the mountain to announce the first stirrings of dawn, then tucked her into the passenger seat of his truck, easing the seat back so she could sleep more comfortably on the trip home.

The point above Brown Bear Lookout had, once upon a time, looked down on the River Road Drive-In, the only drive-in movie theater still standing in the late eighties in the entire southern New Mexico area. Open on Friday and Saturday nights from dusk to dawn, and only during the summer months, it specialized in B-rated movies that portrayed violence and raunchy sex as normal to everyday life, as a Norman Rockwell painting did family togetherness.

Brown Bear Point had been a haven for young lovers. On those summer weekends, pimple-faced adolescent boys and their starry-eyed dates would line their parents' cars up side by side under the pretense of watching the movies below for nothing. But within minutes the windows, rolled up to muffle the sounds of intimacy coming from the backseat, were fogged with condensation. Rumor was three-fourths of the babies born out of wedlock in the area had been conceived at Brown Bear Point.

That had been before the junkies and dope dealers decided the point was secluded enough to carry on their drug trade, sending the lot of hormone-driven teenagers to search out less dangerous rendezvous places.

Johnny had never brought Leah here—would not have dreamed of it. He'd cared too much for her reputation. He had, however, come here alone occasionally, long after the lovers had all gone home, and watched the sun creep over the mountains. With the morning sun warming his face and making him drowsy, he imagined building a house for himself and Leah in a place such as this—where the only noise to disturb the dawn peace was the trilling of birds. He imagined carrying her outside on those sparkling, fresh mornings, laying her on a blanket of green summer moss and making love to her beneath shaded trees.

What had brought him back here today, he could not guess. Maybe because he simply was not ready to take Leah home yet. Maybe because some perverse, masochistic need to watch the pale sun kiss her cheeks one more time had taken hold of his logic.

Leaning back against the driver's door, right leg jackknifed on the console, he sipped hot coffee from a Styrofoam cup and watched as her eyes slowly opened and her head lifted. She stared out at the ball of butter-yellow fire suspended above the distant mountain peaks that were splashed in gold and red streaks.

"Where am I?" Her voice sounded dry and weak.

"Brown Bear Point."

She looked at him, confusion deepening the creases around her eyes. "How long have I been sleeping?"

"An hour." He motioned to the McDonald's sack on the dashboard. "There's coffee if you want it. Cream, no sugar as I recall. There's also a Danish. You still like apple, don't you?''

"You have a memory like an elephant." She reached for the sack. "Mind telling me what we're doing here?"

"Your guess is as good as mine. Sometimes I think this truck has a mind of its own."

She dug like a child into the sack, licking her lips as she pulled out the apple Danish in cellophane.

"Let me." Taking the package from her, he tore it open.

Leah watched, a partial grin on her mouth. "You were always a take-charge kinda guy, Johnny. I could do it myself, you know."

"Just thought you might get tired of doing everything yourself."

"I'm used to it." She tore the bun in two and proceeded to eat, her lids fluttering in pleasure as her tongue slid along her lower lip, capturing slivers of cinnamon and icing. "God, I feel as if I haven't eaten in a month."

"We could go somewhere that serves bacon and eggs if you want."

She shook her head and looked out at the sun. "This really is beautiful, Johnny."

"Aside from White Tail Peak it's my favorite place to kick back and get my thoughts in order."

They remained silent for a while as Leah finished the roll, her gaze locked on the horizon as if she dared not look at Johnny. She was nervous, he could tell. The plain fact of the matter was, so was he. Hell, he'd dated some of the most beautiful models in the world, had bedded a few movie stars who thought it would be cool to screw an Indian, and none of them had stirred the hunger in him as Leah Foster once had. And still did, apparently.

Leah took a deep breath and, without looking at him, said, "Why did you really bring me here, Johnny?"

"Hell if I know," he replied softly.

"I really don't think it's wise."

"Why?"

"We're not the same people we were twelve years ago."

"Yes we are. Maybe our lives have gone different directions, but—"

"Too much water under the bridge. Oh, I forgot. We burned that bridge, didn't we? The fact is, it's still burning. It burns a little hotter every time you slander my father to the press."

"I don't want to talk about your father."

"Why won't you leave him alone, Johnny?"

"I said—"

"How could you go on *20/20* and say what you did about his involvement in the reservation casinos? You're still holding on to your bitterness because he came between us, and what you perceive that he did to your father."

"If you're referring to my father's blowing his head off . . . I don't blame your old man for that. I blame my father. He made that decision. He pulled the trigger. He took the coward's way out. I'm just trying to protect my people. They've been screwed over by a blind system for too long and you know it."

Leah opened the door and jumped from the truck.

Johnny followed. He moved around the truck and caught her arm, pushed her back against the truck, pinning her to the fender. "I didn't bring you here to fight," he told her. "Right now I don't give a damn about your father. Right now all I want to do is lay you over the hood of this truck and make love to you like I used to. Because the memory of my body inside of you has gnawed at my brain ever since I saw you standing there in the rain the other night. Because I want to slide my tongue inside you again. And I want to hear you sigh in pleasure. I want to feel you shiver in ecstasy. Because I've never enjoyed being with a woman like I did with you."

"Stop," she whispered as hot color crept up her

cheeks. "Just . . . stop saying those things. They're cruel."

He slid one hand around her neck, fingertips threading through the fine hair along her nape. His thumb slid along the shell of her ear as he moved his body against hers, the erection in his jeans an unbearable pressure that made his skin sweat.

"Every time I thought of your husband fucking you I wanted to kill him, Leah. I wanted to take all the old anger I had for your father and turn it on a man I didn't even know. I still do. Because I can't get beyond the feeling that you're mine. What's here is mine." He slid one hand between her legs where her jeans were warm and moist. She felt as if she were melting over his fingers. "Ah, Christ," he groaned, then kissed her.

Her mouth quivered. Opened. His tongue danced against hers, inviting, luring, seducing a moan from her throat that made him shake. He clutched at the snap on her jeans; the zipper gave easily from the pressure of his hand sliding beneath her French-cut panties. He knew without looking they would be pink and trimmed with lace. He knew how they would hug the swells of her buttocks and dip slightly into the cleft of her lips, cupping them like a man's gentle but craving palm.

She caught his wrist as she had the first time he'd gotten fresh with her, hungry to experience her inexperienced body, wanting to know her like no other man had known her, knowing even as she tried to deny him the liberty that she wanted and needed it just as much as he did.

The loose jeans slid down her hips as he laid her body back on the truck. He moved in between her legs, his own spread slightly, his free hand plucking at his belt buckle, hearing it tap against the truck as he unzipped his fly. Ah, the memory of their old passion, exploding like fireworks, uncontained, shimmering, and breathtaking. Red and blue and green and gold splashing against a sky of vibrant black—it had never been like that with anyone else. Never. Never.

He laid his body down on hers, kissed her lips, her chin, her nose.

Tears slid from her eyes and down her temples. Her chin quivered.

Johnny frowned as she placed one hand against his cheek, caressing it as she tried to smile bravely. "Please," she said. "We're not kids anymore, Johnny. Consequence means something now. I just don't think I can handle this at this point in my life."

Taking a deep breath, Johnny closed his eyes. The rush of testosterone that belonged more to an eighteen-year-old than a thirty-year-old subsided like water down a drain. Laying his head on her breast, he whispered, *"Sons-ee-ah-ray,* why can't I forget how much I loved you?"

They drove home in silence, Leah gazing out at the awakening countryside that sparkled with morning dew. Dozy drivers on their way to work listened remotely to their car radios and contemplated their day of dealing with tourists with more money than good sense, making the trip back to Leah's more tension fraught than it might have been otherwise.

Johnny pulled into Leah's driveway just after seven.

Shamika stood on the porch, hand cupped over her eyes to shield them from the glare of the sun. Her initial expression of concern melted into relief as Leah jumped from the truck and waved.

Johnny shifted into park and killed the engine, staring after Leah as she moved down the pebbled walkway, the crumpled McDonald's sack in one hand. She did not look back.

He left the truck and followed her.

Shamika regarded them both with an expression somewhere between irritation and bemusement. "You two look like something the cat dragged in."

"Try a pack of hungry coyotes and you've just about hit the nail on the head," Leah replied, tossing her the sack. "I'm dead. I'm getting a shower, then I want to see Val before he's off to school."

"*He* joining you?" Shamika grinned.

Leah flashed Shamika a look that made her eyebrows rise, then she turned on Johnny so suddenly he nearly plowed into her. What little vulnerability had softened her features earlier had vanished.

"I appreciate your help, Johnny. More than you know. And thanks for the breakfast."

"Thanks for the breakfast? That's it?"

"Yeah." She nodded. "That's it."

Turning on her heels, Leah brushed by Shamika and disappeared into the house. Shamika watched her go, shaking her head before looking back at Johnny. "I was just about to cook up some pancakes for Val. Would you like to join us?"

"No, he wouldn't," Leah yelled from the house. Appearing at the door again, her cheeks flaming with color, she said, "I'm exhausted and filthy and . . . I'd like to spend some time *alone* with my son. Perhaps some other time?" She gave Johnny a thin smile before turning away.

"Sorry," Shamika said. "Come to think of it you look as if you could use some sleep yourself."

"Right." He headed for the truck.

"Mr. Whitehorse?" As Johnny looked around, Shamika said, "Don't take it personally."

The reflection in the bathroom mirror resembled something out of a Boris Karloff movie. Her hair looked as if it had not met shampoo in a week. Smudged mascara around her eyes made her look like a raccoon. Not just any raccoon, but the one she'd parked near those hours ago, squashed, bloody, and bloated, and she suspected that she did not smell much better. Newpaper print had been stamped down one side of her face when she'd fallen asleep on Ramona Skunk Cap's kitchen table. If she squinted just right she could make out the words "No arrests have been made" reversed across her right cheekbone.

How could Johnny possibly have found her alluring enough to want to make love to her on the hood of his truck?

Shamika moved up behind her and regarded her reflection before shaking her head. "I'd say any man who was willing to look at you over breakfast has got to have the soul of a saint."

"Johnny is no saint. Believe me."

"Maybe I gave him too much credit. Maybe he's just blind."

Leah moved to the shower and turned on the hot water full blast.

"So what is the real reason you were so rude as to tell Mr. Whitehorse to scram?"

Unbuttoning her shirt, Leah moved into her bedroom, leaving Shamika to regulate the water temperature before steam totally filled the small room. She tossed the shirt onto a pile of dirty clothes near her closet door, then peeled her jeans down her legs, kicking them the way of the shirt.

"You know what I think?" Shamika asked.

"I suspect you're going to tell me."

"I think it's time you start back to your support group. It's been a while, you know."

She unsnapped her bra and flung it on the bed.

"You got a lot stored up in you that you need to get out, girlfriend."

"You're right. I'll go this afternoon."

Shamika's mouth dropped open. She centered her eyes on the ceiling as Leah wiggled out of her panties and returned to the bathroom. " 'Scuse me if I'm speechless," Shamika yelled. "I can't remember a time that I didn't have to strong-arm you to get you to go."

With hot water pounding her shoulders and head, Leah turned her face up into the spray and closed her eyes. Every muscle in her body hurt. So did her heart every time she thought of Johnny's hands on her, the taste of his mouth on hers, like sweet rich coffee. How could she have allowed herself to weaken so?

"You still going out with Sam tonight?" Shamika called.

"Why shouldn't I?"

"Just thought you might change your mind since you and Johnny . . ."

Leah reached for the shampoo and squeezed the apple-essenced soap into her palm. "Me and Johnny what? For your information, Johnny is deeply involved with someone named Dolores. How do I know? Because I found her makeup bag and storehouse of condoms in his truck."

"Are you telling me that there was none of the old spark between you these last few hours?"

"I'm telling you that I intend to continue seeing Sam. I like him. He's a very nice guy."

"He's no Johnny Whitehorse."

Leaning back against the shower wall, shampoo running in streamers over her breasts, Leah closed her eyes and thought:

No, he's no Johnny Whitehorse. But then . . . who is?

SEVEN

Dolores's Mercedes convertible was parked under the big pine near the stone bench Johnny bought back in 1995 during an acting job in Puerto Rico. He situated his truck next to it and sat back in his seat, engine running, his eyes vaguely registering the activity in the distance: Roy Moon climbing up on the big red tractor and preparing to drag the exercise track before the horses were brought out for their morning workouts. Jose Ramirez was leading a rambunctious yearling to a turnout paddock, and a young man named Joe Two Rivers, whom Roy had hired the week before, was pushing a wheelbarrow full of manure and shavings out of the main barn.

The feelings inside Johnny coiled like a spring. He had not experienced desire like he had that morning at Brown Bear Point since the last time he'd been in Leah's presence. The sort that drove a man to act like a fool. To let the base hunger overwhelm judgment. To let the heart shout louder than the whispers of logic in his head.

She did not love him any longer.

It was that simple.

Her response to his kiss had been a physical urge, nothing more. Or an attempt not to totally humiliate him. She had always been very good at avoiding hurt feelings. If there had been a Most Thoughtful category in high school she would have won that too, along with Most Beautiful.

The truck door opened suddenly, snapping Johnny out of his memories. Dolores, in tight starched jeans and an Anne Klein blouse, stared at him as if were Jeffrey Dahmer.

"My God," she gasped. "Is that blood all over you?"

He looked down at his shirt and the front of his jeans, which were stained and crusty with goat blood. "Yeah," he replied. "I guess it is."

The color drained from her face. "Are you all right? What's happened? My God, Johnny, I've been worried out of my mind."

"Not my blood." He smiled to assure her. "Ramona Skunk Cap's goats' blood. Coyotes again."

"What were you doing at Ramona's?" Her gaze fell on an unused syringe and a roll of vet wrap that had fallen on the floor of the passenger seat, and her shoulders squared. "You've been with Leah, haven't you?"

"Her truck broke down. I happened by. Took her out to Ramona's. Took her home." He shrugged. "Here I am."

She studied his face, his eyes, his lips—her look telling him that she did not totally believe him.

Johnny reached for her makeup bag and handed it to her. "Forgot something."

Her fingers reached for the zipper and unzipped it slowly as she peered inside.

"They're all there," he told her, killing the engine and sliding off the seat. "Count 'em. Only one missing. Of course, you know me and condoms. Never could get used to the damn things. Could have screwed a dozen women since I saw you last night and just couldn't be bothered to use them." He slammed the door and walked toward the house.

"You're awfully testy this morning," she said behind
him.

"It's been a long night."

"I tried calling you. I heard from my source. He says
he might have information soon on Senator Foster's link
with Formation Media, and FM's looking more suspicious by the day . . . if you're still interested, of course."

"Why wouldn't I be interested?"

"Why don't *you* tell *me*?"

Entering the house, Johnny unbuttoned his shirt. By
the time he reached the bedroom he'd peeled it off and
proceeded to unbuckle his belt. He walked directly to
the bathroom, to the shower, and turned on the water
full blast and as hot as he could tolerate. By the time
Dolores entered the room he had removed his boots and
socks, and was dragging his jeans down his legs.

"Normally by this time you would be demanding
more information about my source than I could possibly
tell you. You'd be gloating over the fact that you're soon
going to have Foster's ass on a plate."

"I told you, honey—"

"You're tired. Sure. You had a long night."

Dolores leaned her shoulder against the wall and
crossed her arms as Johnny stepped into the glass
shower stall and into the deluge of pounding, steaming
spray. The water felt like a thousand tiny, blistering needles sinking into the tight muscles of his back and shoulders. Propping both hands against the wall, he allowed
his head to fall forward, offering the back of his neck
to the soothing fingers of hot water, holding his breath
as it poured down over his black hair, his brow, his eyes,
his lips.

The stall door opened. Dolores stepped in, still
dressed but barefoot. As Johnny turned his head to look
at her, she grinned and slid between him and the wall.

"You look like a man in desperate need of a little
TLC, Mr. Whitehorse."

"You're going to ruin your Anne Klein, sweetie."

"So I'll buy me another. Or you can buy me another. How's that?" Taking up the soap, she rolled it in her hands, then slid it down his chest, to his belly, then lower.

He caught her wrist, and grinned. "I'm dead. Really. Maybe after I get some sleep."

"Since when have you ever been too tired for a blow-job, Johnny?"

"Since I stayed up all night sewing up goat entrails and burying a woman's pets so mangled up by barbed wire you could hardly tell what they were any longer."

"But you've always said that sex renews your vitality."

Dolores eased down onto her knees, her hands sliding between his thighs. "Did you make love to Leah, Johnny?"

Closing his eyes, he shook his head.

"Not even a kiss, for old time's sake?"

He twisted his fingers into her hair and gritted his teeth.

"Did you? Kiss her?"

Groaning, Johnny fell back against the shower wall, allowing the water to cascade down his chest and belly, onto Dolores's head and shoulders. It poured down her cheeks and into her mouth as her lips parted, sliding like a tight-fitting glove onto his organ, which had become aroused despite himself.

"Yes," he finally replied. "I kissed her. For old time's sake."

"And did you enjoy it?"

"No." He shook his head and turned his face into the hot spray. "No."

"You never had the kind of sex with her that we have, did you, Johnny?" She flicked him with her tongue, fast, like the fluttering of a hummingbird's wing.

"She never gave me a blow job, if that's what you mean. She was too . . . innocent. I would never have asked it of her."

"What about now? Would you ask it of her now? Would she go down on you like I do, do you think?"

He closed his eyes. His fingers, bunched in Dolores's wet hair, gripped her head as his entire body turned hard as stone and his breath caught somewhere in his chest and would not budge. Leah's face shimmered before his mind's eye like a rainbow through the runnels of silver water flowing from his brow, her incredible blue eyes drowsy with passion, lips swollen by his kiss, cheeks flushed with a desire that both mystified and embarrassed her.

With a groan and a pump of his hips, he succumbed like flotsam in a whirlpool to the pull of Dolores's mouth.

A hematoma the size of a tennis ball had sprouted on Johnny's mare's stifle. Leah briefly considered using that as an excuse not to live up to her promise to Shamika to go to her support group that afternoon, but, at the last minute, she climbed into Shamika's van and drove into town. Her attendance of the support meetings had been sporadic the last few weeks. When she felt strong, she braved the challenge. When she felt weak, she holed up in her house and buried her head in animal medicine. But, as Shamika pointed out, it was the times that she felt the weakest that she needed support the most.

And she was feeling pretty damn weak today . . . and all because of Johnny.

Shelley Darmon, a beautiful honey-blonde with sparkling blue eyes and a model's lithe figure, smiled brightly as Leah entered the room. She waved and motioned to the empty chair next to her. Others turned, rewarding Leah with welcomes and outstretched hands whose touches were as firm and assuring as anchors in turbulent water.

Shelley hugged her, holding her close even as Leah tried to pull away. "It's been much too long," she said. "How is Val?"

"Doing great. It's me I'm not so sure about."

"That's why we're here."

Leah eased down into the folding chair that was one of a dozen situated in a circle, spoke and smiled to the women who seemed eager to draw her into conversation. Yes, her vet practice was starting to take off. No, she had not gotten around to reading the James Herriot books yet, but she would, she promised, as soon as she got caught up with all her paperwork, and . . . no, she had not yet received the Special-Needs Parent Bulletin. Was there anything exciting to report? No new medications? Theories?

Certainly, she would be happy to help their fund drive. To say the children needed a new school bus was an understatement. The way it limped up the road, she was surprised that it ever made it to school.

Would Senator Foster consider sponsoring the drive? His influence, and the fact that his own grandson had been afflicted with cerebral palsy, would bring statewide if not nationwide interest to their plight. He could certainly spearhead the drive to get the government to cough up more money for future research.

She would speak to him, of course. But they must understand politicians . . . so much to do and so little time to do it . . .

The meeting came to order. Shelley welcomed the newcomers, then invited them to stand and introduce themselves.

Tom and Betty Thackery were in their early thirties. He was an insurance salesman. She was, or had been, a CPA for a local accounting firm. They had waited ten years to have a child, making certain there was money in savings to handle the costs. They'd bought a nice house with a big backyard because they believed children needed a lot of space to run and play in . . .

Their daughter had been born two months premature. First the baby seemed fine. It wasn't until she was nearly

eight months old before they realized there was a problem. It began with seizures . . .

The doctors could not tell them for sure how the damage had been caused. Could have been due to the early
birth, as was most cases of CP.

Betty blamed herself. Obviously she had not done
something right during her pregnancy . . .

They didn't know if they could cope with the aspect
of caring for a handicapped child for the rest of their
lives. They were struggling with guilt over the fact that
they did not want to—why were they being punished?
What had they done in their lives to warrant God's bur-
dening them with such a catastrophe?

Why, dear God, could the child not have died in delivery and saved them all from this nightmare? Betty
wept into her hands, fingers hiding her shamed face,
shoulders shaking as her husband hugged her, consoled
her, and cried himself.

Shelley went to Betty and took her in her arms.
"We've all thought the same thing. Why us? What could
we have done differently? And there are times still,
when we look out on a normal world full of normal
children and ache to see our own chase kites, and play
ball, and tap dance in tutus on a stage before proud giddy
parents. We would love to go out in public with our
children and not be stared at with pity and morbid curiosity. We would love to go into a restaurant or a movie
without fearing the reaction of others. We would love to
grow deaf to the taunts and jeers of healthy children
whose cruelty stems from ignorance and not meanness.
We would love to know the feel of our own sons' and
daughters' arms around our necks, of their warm, wet
kisses on our cheeks, of their squeals of pleasure on
Christmas morning.

"But those pleasures are so minor compared to the
moment your little girl finally manages to say 'mama,'
to reach for your hand, to read her first word. Or the
sparkle in her eyes when she knows she's pleased you.

She may never walk, or run, or gather daisies in a meadow and present them to you on your birthday, but she *will* love you—never doubt that for a moment. Her brain may be damaged, but not her soul. It is as vibrant and strong as a thousand healthy bodies. Let it carry you, and you both will learn to soar with eagles.''

Dana Carpenter sat forward in her chair, elbows on her knees, hands clasped loosely together. ''I remember when my son was born prematurely. I told my best friend, 'I don't think I can cope if something goes wrong with my baby.' And she said, 'Yes you will. You will because you have to. God never gives us more to bear than we can handle.' Now I like to think that God gifted me with my son because *He* thought *I* was special.''

Shelley took her chair and crossed her legs. ''My husband left me when Michael was still a baby. Hell, I hadn't worked in several years. The only job I could expect to get was answering phones. That salary wouldn't even cover paying for private day care for my son, much less his therapy and medications, which were running nearly three thousand dollars a month. Fortunately my husband might have been stingy with his emotional responsibilities, but he has lived up to his financial ones. He carried all the expenses while I went back to school and got my teaching degree. Now I get to work and enjoy the same holidays as Michael. I can afford to hire a nanny who comes in and gets Michael ready for school, and is there in the afternoon when he gets home. And to top that off . . . are you ready for this, ladies? I met a man.''

The group whooped and high-fived one another as Shelley beamed. ''Yep. Just when I thought I'd grow old and gray before ever finding a man who wanted to shoulder the responsibility of a special-needs child, I meet this incredible man when I took Michael up to Rockaway Ranch. He volunteers twice a week at the ranch, helping with the horses and children. He and Michael hit if off immediately. We started seeing one another and ... I'm feeling really good about this relationship. I don't have to be terrified of some joker finding out about my son and dumping me like a hot potato." She wiggled her eyebrows and added, "Did I mention he's a hunk?"

Laughter around her as Leah looked from one face to another, smiling herself, feeling any moment as if she would implode.

"Leah?"

She looked around at Shelley.

"You look as if you'd like to say something."

She opened and closed her mouth, shrugged, bit her lip.

"Are you still seeing Sam?" Dana asked.

"We have a date tonight."

"Have you introduced him yet to Val?"

"No." She shook her head.

Shelley smiled. "Have you told Sam yet about Val?"

Leah lowered her eyes. "No," she replied more softly.

"Because ... ?"

"Because the last time I grew fond of a man, the moment I introduced him to Val he split."

"Then obviously you've grown fond of Sam or you wouldn't worry about him taking a hike," Shelley said.

"No. Not really. He's a nice guy. It's just that ... it's nice to be with a man sometimes. To go out. See a movie. Get dinner."

"Yes, but eventually you're going to want to commit yourself. To get serious."

"Not with Sam. He doesn't do that for me."

"Are you sure? Maybe you're simply afraid of falling for him too deeply. You're not going to allow yourself such freedom until you know exactly how he's going to respond to Val."

"Maybe." She shrugged. "I just think, at this stage, I haven't bothered introducing them because I don't see a future for us, regardless of Val."

Someone changed the subject, and with a sense of relief, Leah relaxed back in her chair, aware that she had refused to speak up and say what she'd come here to say. That a man she once loved with all her heart had stumbled back into her life, stirring up all the old yearnings of desire and fantasies, all the old anger and confusion over his feud with her father and how Johnny ripped her heart, not to mention her loyalties, in two and oh God she could so easily allow herself to fall for him again, despite her father, but there was Val, always Val, and while she could handle any other man turning his back on her and her son she could not handle Johnny doing it and because of that she wanted to hide Val, tuck him out of sight so for the first time in years she could grasp that fragile glass rope of happiness before she drowned drowned drowned in loneliness and self-pity.

The two hours flew by. Session over, the group met at a table cluttered with punch and cookies and brochures about coping with special-needs problems and products for special-needs children, including wheelchairs, walkers, and silverware that was crooked to facilitate eating. Leah picked up the pamphlet about the wheelchairs and studied the four-thousand-dollar price, frowning.

"Ridiculous, isn't it?" Shelley said, handing her a cookie. "When you're ready I have a friend who can get the same chair twenty percent cheaper. Will your insurance cover any of it?"

"There isn't any insurance."

Shelley rolled her eyes. "My God, how do you manage?"

"I don't." Leah smiled. "Val's outgrowing his chair like crazy. I simply can't afford four thousand dollars, not unless I take him out of physical therapy. And that's out of the question."

"There are a number of financial aid programs out there that could help."

"I've contacted them. Hopefully I'll hear something

soon. But you know how it is; the waiting lists for these organizations are astronomical. It may take up to a year just to make our way onto the list.''

"Would you like to talk about Sam?''

Leah broke the cookie apart, amazed and amused at Shelley's ability to read people's emotions. "It's not Sam I'm afraid of. Someone has come back into my life and I'm terrified of my feelings for him.''

"The one who got away, huh?''

"My fault. I'm surprised he even speaks to me.''

"Is he still in love with you?''

"I . . . don't know. He kissed me. I'm not sure why. Maybe he was just all wrapped up in *used-to-be*s. I'm afraid he thinks I'm still the same person I once was. That I'm the same girl who thumbed her nose at consequences, rebelled against the demands and expectations of my father. The free spirit who, in her love for him, would have defied the world to protect him.''

"He sounds very special.''

"He was. And is.''

"Then if he's so special, he should have no problem with Val. Should he?''

Leah tossed the crumbling cookie onto the table and sighed. "I'm just too damned frightened of finding out.''

Sam Clark bought his clothes straight out of the Sears catalog. He did not care for shopping malls at all, though he would break down at Christmastime and shop at J. C. Penney and Dillard's for his mother's and sister's presents. That way he could put them on his charge cards and pay them out over time. He always managed to make the last payment before the next Christmas rush, at which time he would start all over again.

Sam stood five-eight in his bare feet. Same as Leah. She was always careful to wear shoes with little or no heel because she felt uncomfortable looking down at her date. Shamika once pointed out that Nicole Kidman was several inches taller than Tom Cruise, and Leah had pointed out that she wasn't Nicole Kidman, and Sam sure as hell wasn't Tom Cruise. Not even close. Sam outweighed gorgeous Tom by at least a hundred pounds. His scalp was showing through his thinning brown hair, and he had fingers like little Polish sausages. His breath always smelled like the wintergreen Certs he carried in his shirt pocket.

Leah waited for Sam on the front porch, sweater draped around her bare shoulders. She'd deliberated half an hour over what to wear. Not that she had a big choice. Her biggest decision had been over how much skin to reveal.

She'd finally opted for a halter-style sundress that exposed her shoulders and most of her back. This was the third date with Sam, after all. She was allowed to relax a little. She'd swept up her hair in a banana clip, dabbed a touch of an Elizabeth Taylor knock-off perfume behind each ear and borrowed Shamika's pearl drop earrings. She'd dragged out makeup she had not used since the last time she'd gone out with Sam. A spot of Pearlized Warm Copper on her eyelids, Mocha Mist on her cheeks, and Brun Rose on her lips—all from the clearance table at the local five-and-dime.

Sam pulled up to Leah's house at seven-thirty sharp, driving a 1980 El Dorado Cadillac sporting dealer tags. Last date he'd shown up in a maroon Lincoln Continental with an interior permeated by cigar smoke. The time before that an Olds Cutlass boasting two hundred thousand miles and a crunched left bumper that was to be banged out at the local body shop the following Monday—before the car was put on the lot for sale, of course.

He bounced from the car with his usual enthusiasm, hair slicked to one side to better cover the thin spot on top of his head. His coat was brown-and-gray plaid over an ochre-colored shirt and green trousers. His tie was red and blue pinstripes stamped with bucking horses.

Leah smiled as Shamika began laughing somewhere in
the house behind her.

Randy's Bar and Grill on Cedar Creek Road served
the best steaks in town. Sam could afford the best tonight, he informed Leah; he'd sold three cars that afternoon and was ready to celebrate. He'd called ahead for
reservations, requesting a table outside on the patio overlooking the valley and the outdoor dance floor where a
group specializing in '60s and '70s music were warming
up their instruments.

As usual, the place was packed with tourists, most in
town for the races. Texans in ostrich boots and cowboy
hats flashed wads of money and ordered beer and margaritas by the pitcher. A group of New Yorkers took up
a table for twenty, all having disembarked the chartered
bus parked across the road. By the looks of them they
had stripped the local souvenir shops of every tacky
made-in-Taiwan Native American relic within a fifty-
mile radius. One man wore a headdress of painted
chicken feathers and wielded a rubber tomahawk, causing his companions to hoot in laughter every few
minutes.

"Looks like the old place is rumbling tonight," Sam
said, showing Leah to her chair. "We can go someplace
else if you'd like."

"Wouldn't think of it. Besides, it's Friday night in
Tourist Town. Every place will be packed."

Sam took his chair next to Leah, flashing his *This-
car-has-never-been-driven-over-thirty-miles-an-hour-
and-was-owned-by-a-little-old-octogenarian-who-only-
drove-it-on-Sundays* smile at the teenage waitress
dressed in a flamingo-pink can-can dress short enough
to show off her frilly black petticoat.

"I called in earlier," he told her. "Name's Sam
Clark. You got an order back there for me."

Without a word she turned on her spiked heels and
elbowed her way toward the kitchen.

Lacing his fingers on the table, Sam looked around

the patio. The trees twinkled with firefly-sized white
lights. Candles burned under globe chimneys on each
table, giving the area a fairy-tale appearance.

"You're looking especially nice tonight," he told her.
"I like your earrings."

"And I like your . . . tie."

Sam looked pleased. "Good. It's got horses on it.
See?" He flapped the thing at her. "I wore it just for
you. Thought you'd appreciate the equestrian motif."

"Where on earth did you find it?" she asked, still
smiling.

"Wal-Mart. They'd marked it down from seven dollars to three-fifty. Leftovers from their Easter sale, I
think. Anyway, I found several I liked. Stocked up.
Can't pass up a deal like that."

They nodded in unison.

"Hope you like this kinda music. I seen in the paper
that this group was going to be here tonight. I saw them
once before down at the convention center and thought,
what the heck. Why not?"

"I like the oldies very much. They're my favorite."

"Yeah?" He fluttered his tie again. "Somehow you
looked like the kinda gal who would enjoy a blast from
the past. So who is your favorite?"

"Neil Diamond."

"Yeah." He nodded. "Ever seen him in concert? Puts
on a helluva show. Least he used to. Haven't seen him
in oh, probably twenty years or so."

"I have every album he ever did. His early ones are
my favorites, though."

The waitress returned, wheeling an ice bucket stocked
with a chilled bottle of champagne: Mums Extra Dry.
Not Dom Perignon, certainly, but neither was it André's.
Sam's face lit up like a Christmas tree as he looked at
Leah with an expression that made a knot form in her
throat. Something was up, and she wasn't certain she
was going to like it.

EIGHT

After much cajoling on Dolores's part, Johnny finally agreed to a night out, despite his lack of sleep and the fact that he was supposed to fly his Cessna up to Boulder in the morning and catch a flight to D.C., where he was to speak first thing Monday morning before a congressional committee regarding the situation with the Indian Trust Fund.

With the top down on her Mercedes SL, Dolores's short black hair whipped freely in the night wind, as did Johnny's. The drive from Whitehorse Farm to Cedar Creek Road had been exhilarating, the mountain air biting their faces and taking their breath away. Johnny needed all the help he could get. His mind felt like mush. The idea of dancing away the next few hours was not high on his list of things he'd rather be doing. But, as usual, Dolores got her way. She always did. Which, he surmised, is what made her one of the finest reporters in the state. She simply did not know when to say no. Besides, she'd flogged him with enough guilt over his dalliance with Leah that he supposed he owed it to her.

And maybe a few beers and some light music would

get his mind off the memory of Leah's mouth opening under his that morning, the way it had the very first time he'd kissed her. Timid. Hesitant. Experimenting with passion.

The valet hurried from his perch near the restaurant door, obviously enthused over the prospect of driving Dolores's car. The young man recognized Johnny and Dolores immediately, thrust a pen and scrap paper at them and pleaded for their autographs. Dolores glowed as he gushed over her reporting—she was the only reason he watched the news that early—she deserved a network spot—best-looking babe on television. Had she ever thought about acting? Posing for Playboy?

And Johnny Whitehorse—who would have thought it. Saw Johnny's jeans billboard on the Las Vegas strip near the Mirage Hotel—Johnny standing three stories tall wearing unzipped jeans and no shirt—shit, man—awesome. My girlfriend gets turned on every time she sees it. Would Johnny sign the autograph to Karen, with lust? No? With love, then. That would do. Oh, by the way, heard a rumor Johnny was going to do a movie up in Arizona with Robert Redford and Kevin Costner. Any truth to it? A sequel to *Dances with Wolves*? No? Too bad. Was he really thinking about running for Senator Foster's seat in the next election? Wow, mind-blowing karma, huh? Get pissed at the Senate and take a few scalps, huh? Just think of it—Indian dude finally gets even for all the injustices put on his people by the white populace. Far out!

"Hello, I'm Candy. I'm your hostess tonight and . . . oh my God. You're Johnny Whitehorse, aren't you? Oh my God. Sarah! Sarah look who's here. *Johnny Whitehorse!*"

"Oh my God. Mr. Whitehorse, we were talking about you just this afternoon."

"I just bought your poster—"

"I've had it hanging up on my bedroom wall for the last three months—"

"I loved you in that *ER* episode. Oh, geez, you know, the one where you were shot during that demonstration—"

"Is it true you're dating Cher?"

"Doofus. He's with a date."

"Oops. Sorry. Hey, aren't you . . ."

"Doofus. That's Dolores Rainwater. God, don't you know anything? She does the morning news, on Channel 10."

"Sor-*ry*. I don't watch the news."

"Mr. Whitehorse, would you *please* sign this menu? You will? Oh my God. I'm going to faint. Oh my God, I'm going to frame this and hang it over my bed so it's the first thing I see when I wake up in the morning."

"God, you're even more gorgeous in person than you are on your poster. And you're *sooo* tall. Oh my God, Sarah, isn't he tall?"

"I made my boyfriend buy those jeans you wear in that commercial where you're waking down Fifth Avenue and traffic is crashing all around you and the women are hanging out of the office windows and whistling? Duh. Not even. He looks like a dork in them compared to you."

"Someone told me at school they'd read in *People* magazine that you've been offered a cola commercial, that they're going to use that same jeans commercial, only at the very end you're going to pop the tab off the cola and drink it—"

"And all the drooling women rush to their soda machines to buy that drink—"

"Shhh. Randy is staring at us."

"Give them table eight on the veranda near the band. Oh my God, Judy, your waitress, is going to die when she sees you. Thank you so much for the autograph, Mr. Whitehorse. Oh my God, I can't believe I actually met him! Oh my God."

Sarah turned on her high heels and flounced away,

menus tucked under her arm, blond ponytail swinging side to side like windshield-wiper blades.

Dolores looked up at Johnny, her mouth curved in something just short of sarcasm. "I'm surprised they didn't have an orgasm right there."

Johnny grinned. "You're just jealous because they didn't know who the hell you are."

"Need I remind you that the valet thinks I should be in *Playboy*?"

"I'll give Hugh a call for you if you'd like."

"That's right. He tried to get you to do a layout with Miss October, didn't he?"

"No that was the publisher of *Playgirl*. Wanted me to *be Mr.* October."

"And you turned his offer down. Johnny, Johnny, Johnny. What you could have done with two million dollars."

"You know what they say, sweetheart. It's better to leave 'em guessing. Fantasy is usually more satisfying than reality."

"You're joking, right? One could hardly say that about you."

"Thank you."

"You're welcome."

By the time they had crossed the main dining room, every patron, plus those at the adjacent bar, had noted Johnny's presence. Women squirmed in their chairs for a better look. Men rolled their eyes and glared at their wives and girlfriends, obviously annoyed at their blatant appreciation for another man.

The band's rendition of John Denver's "Sunshine on my Shoulders" reverberated from the half-dozen speakers suspended in the clusters of trees scattered over the restaurant's well-manicured and landscaped grounds. A lone middle-aged couple, holding one another tightly, slid across the dance floor, oblivious to the tables of people watching them, too wrapped up in one another to care.

Sarah scanned the crowd and the few empty tables Randy always kept set aside for his special friends who dropped by on the spur of the moment. "You can sit near the band, but that's pretty loud. There's a more secluded table just back of that wall. You can still see the band from there but you're sorta hid from gawkers, ya know?" She smiled and batted her eyelashes at Johnny.

Dolores checked out the crowd. She would choose the most conspicuous table in the place, Johnny surmised. She always did. She liked attention. She liked being seen with him. It was damn good promotion. The more her photo showed up in the gossip rags, the better chance she had of landing a job with a more prestigious network affiliate. And he knew for a fact that her contract was up for renegotiation soon, which was the major reason she was so eager to sniff out dirt on Senator Foster. Breaking the story would get her worldwide recognition.

"Well, well, look who's here," she said.

Johnny followed her gaze, to a table where a waitress was pouring champagne and a pudgy man with a receding hairline was reaching for his date's hand and—

Dolores took off through the crowd, heading straight for Leah's table. Sarah fell in behind her. Johnny wondered if he could get away with murder in front of so many witnesses.

"My God, if it's not Leah Foster," Dolores said, sweeping around the table to grab Leah in a hug. "How long has it been, Leah? Twelve, thirteen years? You remember me, don't you? Dolores Rainwater?"

The smile froze on Leah's face as Johnny walked up. The flush that had accentuated her blue eyes moments before drained down her neck. But for a spot of hot color glowing just above her cleavage, she suddenly looked white as paper.

"Dolores," Leah repeated, forcing herself to focus on Dolores and not on Johnny. *So, you're that Dolores,* her tight smile said—*the one who uses Estée Lauder lipstick and condoms ribbed for your enjoyment.* "Sure, I remember you. I watch you every morning."

Dolores caught Johnny's arm and dragged him up beside her. "You and Johnny have already gotten reacquainted, I understand."

"Our paths have crossed, yes." Leah reached for her glass of champagne and smiled at her date. The man stared at Johnny and Dolores with his mouth open, obviously star-struck and speechless. "Sam, these are old friends of mine. We grew up together, sort of."

Sam sprang out of his chair, dropping his napkin to the floor and knocking the table so hard the glasses tottered precariously. "Yes, ma'am, Ms. Rainwater. Mr. Whitehorse. I know who y'all are. Geez Louise, I'm pleased to meet you both. Real honored. Leah never told me y'all were acquainted."

Leah sipped her drink, still smiling, still refusing to look at Johnny. Her color was returning little by little, creeping up her shoulders, her throat, and fingering across her rigid jaw.

"Y'all here for dinner?" Sam asked.

"Why, yes we are," Dolores replied.

"Well, you're welcome to join us if you want. Course, I can understand if you'd rather be alone—"

"Why, Sam. What a wonderful idea. Wouldn't that be fun, Johnny?" Dolores flashed him her most brilliant smile. "We can kick back a few margaritas for old time's sake."

"Sure," he replied, aware he sounded sullen and pissed. Not sure he felt sullen and pissed because Dolores was making an ass of herself and embarrassing him, not to mention Leah, or because the moron who was Leah's date had been holding Leah's hand those moments before Dolores insinuated herself into their privacy.

He pulled out Dolores's chair for her, whispering in her ear as she sat down, "Cute. Very cute, sweetheart. We're going to discuss this later. Aren't we?"

Smiling, Dolores whispered back, "I'm counting on it."

Johnny took the chair next to Leah. His knee brushed hers under the table. Without so much as a glance at him, Leah shifted in her chair, moving her legs out of his way.

"Ummm, champagne," Dolores said. "Are we celebrating something?"

Sam motioned to the waitress, who stared at Johnny in a sort of daze. "Hon, could you bring us two more glasses? Yoo-hoo. Ma'am?" He chuckled and nodded toward Johnny. "I reckon she's a fan."

The waitress blinked and focused on Sam.

"Two more champagne glasses if you will, darlin'."

"Sure." She nodded and moved like a robot toward the kitchen.

Dolores laughed. "God, you can't take Johnny anywhere that he doesn't cause a scene. You get used to it after a while. The women simply love him."

"I have to admit, I got two daughters back in Austin who think you're God's gift to women," Sam declared, shaking his head. "They ain't ever gonna believe this."

"I'll bet Johnny would be more than happy to give you a couple of autographs to send them."

"That would be super." He searched his coat pocket and found a pen, but no paper, so he grabbed a couple of napkins. "Just sign one to Debbie, and one to Lynda. That's Debbie with an *ie* and Lynda with a *y*. Hell, my ex is going to be green with envy. She met Willie Nelson once. Ran into him on the street in downtown Austin. She's got his autograph framed and hung over the mantel in the living room. Just something else she got in the divorce."

Johnny scrawled his name on the paper napkins as Leah continued to sip her champagne and Sam fidgeted like a nervous kid in his chair. Finished, Johnny shoved the napkins at Sam and said, "So what were you celebrating . . . Sam?"

"Celebrating? Oh. Ah. Well." His face flushed and he glanced at Leah. "Our third date."

"How sweet," Dolores offered. "I can see you're a real charmer, Sam."

Sam reached for his glass, tipping it toward Leah before drinking it down in one long quaff.

As the waitress returned with two glasses, the band struck up "Heard It through the Grapevine." The scraping of chairs was followed by a half-dozen couples heading for the dance floor.

The waitress took Dolores's order for a pitcher of margaritas for the table, then their food order, so flustered by Johnny's presence that she was forced to start over twice before getting it right.

Dolores and Sam chatted through the margaritas and fajitas while Leah and Johnny stared into their drinks and did their best to listen to the music that was fast becoming diluted by the growing din of conversation and the clattering of dishes.

Johnny did not have an appetite after all. Obviously Leah didn't either. She poked at her food and nibbled on greasy tortilla chips, pretending to be immersed in Dolores's and Sam's conversation, which focused entirely on Dolores's career. At one point, Johnny found his foot nestled against Leah's. He waited for her to move it; she didn't, and for a moment her eyes became distant, her expression dreamy. Was she thinking about yesteryears, when they would meet on the sly at Mojo's Truck Stop way out on Highway 70, halfway to Roswell, sit in the back booth with their legs pressed together and plan how she would sneak out of her room that night and meet him behind the stables? Or were the champagne and margaritas simply catching up with her? She'd never been one who could handle her liquor. It made her sleepy, and romantic.

A beeper sounded. Sam dug through his pocket and withdrew the credit card–sized machine. "Looks like the boss needs me. You ladies excuse me while I use the phone?''

As Sam made his way toward the pay phone, Dolores poured herself and Leah another margarita. ''What a pleasant man. He seems to adore you, Leah.''

Leah moved her foot away from Johnny's. ''Sam's a good guy.''

''Is it serious?''

''Define serious.'' Leah sipped her drink.

''Think you two will . . . you know. Get married?''

''This is only our third date.''

''So? There are a great many people out there who know the moment they meet someone that they're destined to be together forever.''

''That's not the case with Sam. He's a . . . friend. Nothing more.''

Smiling, Dolores looked at Leah sternly. ''I get the idea that Sam feels differently. He positively beams when he looks at you. Of course, who can blame him? You're still as lovely as you were in high school. Isn't she, Johnny?''

Johnny tossed down the chip he'd been eating and gave her a flat smile. ''Prettier. Much prettier. In fact I'd say she was the best-looking woman in this room. And probably the brightest. At least she knows when to keep her mouth shut.''

''Goodness. Seems I've hit a nerve.'' Picking up her glass, Dolores toasted Leah. ''Here's to old friends and lovers. To pasts, and futures.''

Johnny looked at Leah. ''I'd like to dance with you. As I recall you always enjoyed this song.''

Leah tipped her head, listening to the band's version of the Righteous Brothers' ''Soul and Inspiration.''

Pushing back his chair, Johnny reached for Leah's hand. ''If you say no I'll probably make a scene. I'd hate that because it would wind up on the front page of the paper tomorrow, making me look like the ass I'm feeling like right now.'' He flashed a glaring Dolores a bright smile. "Just for old time's sake. Right, sweetheart?"

With his fingers wrapped around Leah's wrist, he threaded their way through the tables and onto the dance floor. Pressed and jostled by swaying dancers, Johnny slid his arm around Leah's waist, entwined his fingers with hers, and drew her up against him, close.

She felt rigid, her movements clumsy as they settled into the slide-and-sway rhythm that Johnny set for them. So far, she had not said a word, just set her focus on the wall of bodies around her and appeared to tune Johnny out.

"Relax," he whispered. "You feel as if you're going to shatter. I don't bite—unless you want me to." He grinned.

"Why do I get the feeling things are a little tense between you and Dolores tonight? It wouldn't have anything to do with our spending last night together, would it?"

"Probably."

Her head fell back as she looked up at him, her blue eyes serious. "You told her?"

"It's not like we have something to hide."

"I hardly call your practically undressing me on the hood of your truck innocent conversation."

"Just a kiss for old time's sake."

"You didn't tell her *that*."

"You know I don't lie, Leah. She asked me. I told her."

"No wonder she looks as if she'd like to scratch my eyes out. I don't blame her."

He pulled her closer. "Remember the first time we danced to this song? I'd bought that collection of old 45s at a flea market. I think I paid a whopping five bucks for the entire box."

"And we used your father's old phonograph to play them."

"The record kept skipping and I'd have to kick the player—"

"And you broke the needle—"

"My father got pissed—"

"And you drove all the way to Alamogordo trying to find a needle to replace it."

"Yeah, well, the old man was pretty fond of that phonograph." He spun her around and drew her in again, this time close enough that he could lay his cheek against the top of her head. "Still using the same shampoo, I see. Apple. No wonder I was always hungry around you."

He felt her laugh, and she relaxed, allowing her body to melt slightly into his. Turning his lips against her brow, he closed his eyes and allowed the essence of apple to filter through his senses until the heat of close bodies became a cocoon of memories of her and him dancing under a spray of pine trees to a tune he hummed in her ear.

The song ended. The couples parted and shuffled back to their tables.

Reluctantly, Johnny stepped away, releasing her hand only after she turned and moved back toward their table. He watched her walk, remnants of her childhood ballerina days still evident in her graceful stride, shoulders back, arms loose. She glided smoothly as a swan on water.

Sam had returned. Dolores, however, was missing.

Smiling as he moved around the table to join Johnny and Leah, Sam said, "Dolores stepped away to speak to a friend. She'll be back directly. Mind if I dance with my date?"

Stepping aside, Johnny watched Sam take Leah's arm and escort her back to the dance floor.

He thought, *Yes I do mind. If you hold her too close I'll pound out your brains, Sam old boy. You won't ever get the chance to sell another of the rolling crap cars you foist on unsuspecting customers.*

Leah and Sam were immediately swallowed by the couples sliding and spinning to the rhythm of "A Whiter Shade of Pale."

"Mr. Whitehorse, would you care for another drink?"

He looked around. The waitress smiled and stepped a little closer. "A drink?" she repeated, pointing to the empty margarita pitcher.

"Better not. I'm driving."

She handed him a piece of paper. "My phone number. Just in case, you know. If you got nothing better to do."

Johnny smiled and tucked the paper into his pocket. Her eyes widened; her cheeks flushed. As she walked away, he dropped down into his chair, thinking about all the phone numbers women had shoved into his hands. No doubt they had waited by their phones for hours, days, believing he would call them on a whim and sweep them off to fantasyland. He often wondered what was worse for them: to sit around waiting for a call that never came, or to know that the minute they were out of sight he would toss their numbers into the nearest trash bin.

The song ended. Another began.

Where the hell was Dolores?

Where the hell were Sam and Leah?

He searched the dance floor, so packed with bodies that couples were forced to dance between the tables.

"Hey. Buddy."

An overweight, bald man wearing a dyed chicken-feather Indian headdress tapped Johnny on the shoulder, his jowls flushed by too many drinks, his eyes bloodshot.

Where the hell was Dolores?

"How," the man said, grinning.

"How what?" Johnny replied.

"You know. How." The man lifted his hand, palm out. "How."

Where the hell was Dolores?

"Don't you speak Injun?" the man slurred.

Johnny glanced at the table of snorting, chuckling

tourists from which the drunken moron must have come. Another man got out of a chair, an instant camera clutched in both hands as he headed across the room, bouncing off diners and a waitress who nearly dropped her tray of empty glasses.

The idiot in the headdress bent over Johnny so his breath rushed over his face, smelling like gasoline. "You don't dress like no damn Injun. Where's your loincloth and wolf teeth? You do speak white man's English, don't you? Wanna say somethin', Cochise? Ug?"

"Hey, Howard," the cameraman yelled. "Put your headdress on him and I'll get a picture of you two together."

Howard dragged the bonnet from his head, prepared to do just that. Johnny grabbed it, crushing the fragile feathers in his fingers as he slowly stood up, towering over the squat man who stumbled back, his grin sliding from his face.

"Hey, you broke my . . ." Howard licked his lips and glanced around. The room had become suddenly silent as the patrons all stared, anticipating Johnny's reaction. "What's ever'body staring at? Geez, we're just having a little fun here. That's why we came here, ain't it? To look at the Injuns?"

Randy Moorhouse appeared from nowhere, sliding in between Johnny and the tourist. "Do we have a problem here, Mr. Whitehorse?"

"Seems one of your customers has had a little too much to drink, Randy."

"Sorry about that, Johnny." Randy shot a look at the nervous tour guide, who had frozen in her shoes the moment Johnny got out of his chair. "Carrie, you want to do something about the gentleman? And you, no photos, please." He pointed to Howard's friend.

The man looked at his camera, then back at Johnny. "I'll pay him ten bucks for a picture with my wife so we've got a snapshot of her with a real Indian."

"I don't think so," Randy replied, wagging his finger at the camera.

"Twenty bucks, but he's got to wear the war bonnet."

"Johnny?" Leah laid her hand on Johnny's arm. "There is something to be said for tolerating ignorance. Your grandfather once said that such tolerance helps to make you wiser and stronger."

He turned his back on Randy and the tourists, trying his best to ignore the explosive stab of anger and intolerance gouging at his raw mood. Like those years before, Leah's calmness slid around him like a cool blanket of crystalline water. How many times had he grasped that gentleness, that understanding, that acceptance she offered in a touch of her hand or a smile of her lips, and clung to it while his anger and frustration sent him on an emotional riptide. Had it not been for Leah those years ago he would have wound up in prison—a confused and furious young Native American like so many of his peers—fighting against a white man's establishment and prejudice that had destroyed their pride and future so many generations ago.

Her hand still on his arm, Leah smiled. "Think of who and what you are. What you've become. What you can and will stand for. Is punching him in the nose worth losing all of that? Besides, we both know you'll hate yourself in the morning."

He took her hand from his arm, folding his fingers around it. "Come home with me," he said.

Her eyes widened, her lips parted. For an instant he was again looking down into a girl's eyes full of intense love, and the wing beats of memories fanned his anger into a much hotter flame, an inferno compared to his desire to pulverize a white man's face. But then . . .

She stepped away, taking her hand and burying it in the folds of her sundress skirt. "Can't." She lowered her eyes. "Sam . . ."

Johnny raised his gaze to the used-car salesman with his tacky tie and sweating scalp, standing in the background with his pudgy hands on his pudgy hips, his pocket full of napkins Johnny had signed for his no doubt pudgy daughters back in Austin.

Randy slapped a hand on Johnny's shoulder. "Sorry about all this, Johnny. You know what they're like sometimes. They don't mean anything by it. He'll wake up with a hangover tomorrow and feel like a jerk. Look, I'm picking up the tab for this party—"

"I don't want your fucking charity," Johnny snapped, and dragged his wallet out of his back jeans pocket, fingered out a stack of hundred-dollar bills and tossed them on the table.

He needed air. Desperately.

Where the hell was Dolores?

Turning his back on Leah, Johnny made his way out of the restaurant and stood for a moment on the front porch, allowing the night air to chill the heat from his face.

A group of eight young Native American boys, barely into their teens, gathered in the parking lot beneath a vapor streetlight, dancing in a circle while another pounded on a drum and chanted. Their young faces were painted in stripes of colors. They wore cloaks of eagle feathers over their shoulders and down their arms, which did little to conceal their tee shirts, jeans, and Nikes.

Around them gathered smiling tourists, cameras popping with light and whirring videocams zooming in on the children's faces, which looked older than they should.

The dance ended. The boys bowed, heads down, eyes down, shoulders bent, and fists hidden beneath their feathers as the onlookers tossed coins at their feet. The boys fell to their knees, scrambling to grab the glittering nickels and dimes and quarters, causing the tourists to laugh louder.

"Hey, Mr. Whitehorse." The valet moved out of the shadows, his hands in his pockets. "If you're looking for Ms. Rainwater, she's out in her car."

Johnny moved down the steps, shoved his way through the tourists, and grabbed a boy by the scruff of the neck, jerking him to his feet so hard the coins in the boy's hands sprayed across the asphalt.

"What the fu—"

"Shut up and listen to me." Johnny shook the boy and looked around at the others, all frozen in the process of stuffing their pockets with change. "Don't ever go on your knees for a nickel or a dime or a quarter. Don't ever go on your knees for nothing or no one. Remember who you are and what you stand for."

The boy twisted away and stumbled back, his look of anger exaggerated by the paint on his cheeks and brow. "Look who's talking. *Johnny Whitehorse.* Big man who lives in big houses away from his people. You're nothing but an apple. Red man on the outside, white man on the inside. What do *you* stand for? What *are* you? No Apache, that's for sure. You walk in the white man's world now. *Tu no vale nada*—you are good for nothing." He spat on the ground, then motioned to the others. Silently, they turned their backs on Johnny and walked off into the dark.

The tourists filed into the restaurant, leaving Johnny standing alone beneath the buzzing vapor light, coins shimmering around his feet.

NINE

Dolores sat in the passenger seat of the Mercedes, the car door open as Johnny moved across the parking lot, focusing more on the sick feeling of disgust in his stomach than the fact that a man was swiftly walking away from the car, dissolving into the shadows beyond the deserted highway.

Music from the band drifted along the parked cars, the bass drum like a heartbeat tapping at the night as Johnny moved up to the SL where Dolores was hunkered over, so intent on what she was doing she did not hear him.

A mirror compact lay open on her lap, several threads of white powder lined up side by side on the glass. With a clear glass straw she snorted the cocaine up one nostril, then the other, her groan of pleasure like a sigh of sexual gratification.

Johnny closed his eyes. No, no, he wasn't going to jump to any conclusions here. He was not seeing Dolores Rainwater snorting powder into her brain—

"What the hell are you doing?" he heard himself ask. Her head flew around and she stared up at him, her nose dusted with powder and her eyes like glass reflecting the distant streetlight. "Oh. This . . . this isn't what it looks like—"

"You idiot. You stupid—" He grabbed the straw from her hand and knocked the compact from her lap. It landed on the asphalt, scattering the remainder of powder over the mirror. He ground his boot heel into the glass, pulverizing it as he crushed the straw in his hand, slivers of glass biting into his flesh like stinging ants.

Dolores stared at the scattering of white powder and glass on the ground. "Look what you've done. How dare you. Do you know how much that cost?"

Grabbing her purse, open by her legs, Johnny dumped it on the ground, spilling makeup, credit cards, chewing gum, and a tiny plastic bag of more powder. Dolores flung herself onto it, snatching it up and clutching it to her stomach as she turned on him, face twisted, teeth showing behind her smeared lipstick.

"You self-righteous son of a bitch. How dare you come strutting out here and proceed to demean me when I just left you in there wrapped up with Miss Goody Two-shoes like you were a couple of teenagers with the hots for one another. You're a hypocrite, Whitehorse. A two-timing egomaniac who thinks he was put on this earth to save the whole Indian nation. Well I've got news for you. You're nothing. You're not an Indian and you're not a white man. You're an . . . *it* with a dick between your legs."

"Keep your voice down, dammit, and get in the car."

"Get your hands off me." She kicked at his shins and struck at his face as he shoved her back into the car and threw her purse in her lap. Slamming the door, Johnny dug the keys from his pocket and moved around the car, glancing at the restaurant where the valet was still standing, hands in his pockets, looking out at them as if not knowing, exactly, how to deal with the fact that Dolores Rainwater was screaming profanities like a drunken sailor.

Johnny gunned the accelerator and the Mercedes jumped like a cat onto the highway, spitting gravel, tires squealing, back end fishtailing onto the opposite lane, causing a trucker to swerve onto the shoulder and blow his horn. The cold night wind hit them with a blast that made Johnny catch his breath, but no way was he going to stop and put up the ragtop, not now.

Dolores crawled onto her knees, face in the wind. He grabbed at her arm. "Sit down, Dolores, and put on your seatbelt."

She stared at him, her hair plastered against one side of her face. "You're still in love with her, aren't you?" she yelled.

"Sit down—"

"I knew it the moment you saw her tonight. It was written all over your face. You want her. You want to be with her. Despite the fact that you intend to destroy her father." She threw back her head in laughter. "I hope I'm around to see her face when you prove that her father is up to his ass in casino corruption. I wonder how eager she'll be *then* to dance with you, much less fuck you."

He grabbed for her arm; the car swerved, right tires slithering off the shoulder then back on again.

Dolores reached under the seat and withdrew an envelope. She waved it at him. "Just how badly do you want to prove that Senator Foster is corrupt, Johnny, honey? What's it worth to you?"

"What's that?"

"Information from my source. Proof that Foster is linked to Formation Media."

He stared at the envelope, forgetting, momentarily, the winding road ahead. Was this some sort of perverted joke?

Dolores slid down into the seat, her smile turning smug. "Well? What's it worth to you, Johnny?"

"That depends on the price," he shouted.

"That you never see or speak to Leah again. That you

announce to the papers tomorrow that you and I are going to get married. And then you're going to call your agent and ask that he take me on as a client—as a personal favor to you, of course.''

The car came out of nowhere, its bright lights suddenly reflecting off the rearview mirror, into Johnny's eyes. He hit the mirror with the butt of his palm, a sign to the inconsiderate driver to dim his lights. No chance. The car moved up behind him, inches from his bumper.

Both hands on the wheel, Johnny glanced at Dolores. She had turned to look back at the car, her expression less dazed and angry now than suspicious.

''Put on your seatbelt,'' he yelled. ''Now.''

''What the hell do they think they're doing?''

''Put it on!''

She fumbled with the belt, yanking on it as it locked at her shoulder.

The car rammed them, slamming Dolores against the passenger door. Johnny fought with the wheel, keeping the car from weaving into oncoming traffic.

He checked his speed. Sixty. Sixty-five—

He knew every bend in the road, how fast he could take the curves—lots of practice in his father's old truck, pushing it to its endurance until it shuddered so hard he thought it would fall apart around him.

Seventy—couldn't push it much more than that, not with the sharp bend coming up—no way he could make it at seventy—the lights flooded the SL as the car roared up behind them again, slamming into them, filling the night and the close forest with the sounds of crunching metal—no warning this time, the son-of-a-bitch meant business—Dolores still fighting with the goddamn seatbelt—

The car moved up beside him—a bulky, black thing with black windows—it careened against him, bouncing the Mercedes sideways, toward the shoulder that dropped off into nothingness.

He hit the brakes just as the demon car slammed him

again, metal grating against metal with a shriek like fingernails on a blackboard, whining like an animal in pain. Then it hit him, the reality, that they were going over the side, airborne, floating momentarily like an eagle, car slowly rotating, rolling like a lazy old cat that might have tumbled from a tree limb while napping. Dolores screamed, her hands outstretched toward him—

The night gyrated with firelight and shadows, flames sluicing along trails of gasoline, shimming up the trunks of trees, lapping hungrily at the thick brown pine needles carpeting the ground.

Horn blaring, the Mercedes lay like some dead armored armadillo on its back, burning wheels resembling bonfires sending up acrid black smoke that formed a cloud close to the ground. The crumpled metal groaned and popped with the escalating heat. There came a hissing, like a snake, as if the machine were breathing its last—

The explosion shook the ground. Sparks streaked into the sky and trees, drifting like dandelion fluff over the thatches of weeds and thistle before dying out. Hot waves radiated across the ground in a rush like heat from a suddenly opened oven.

Shamika had left the front door of the house open. Light and music from a *Sesame Street* CD spilled through the old screen door, forming a dim yellow box on the orange front porch where Leah and Sam stood, thanking each other for a wonderful evening.

"It's early yet," Sam said, checking his watch. "We could still make that movie if we hurry."

"Perhaps another time." Leah smiled and tugged her sweater more closely around her shoulders. "Besides, I need to spend a little time tonight with my son."

Sam looked around her, into the house. "I'm real good with kids, you know."

"Are you?"

"Heck, I got this way of communicating with them. Guess 'cause I'm nothing but a big kid myself at heart. Your boy play sports?"

"No." She shook her head.

"One of those intellectual types, huh? Probably spends his time on a computer."

Leah looked around, into the house. She could hear water running. Shamika walked out of Val's bedroom, his pajamas tossed across her shoulder as she moved toward the bathroom, singing along with Bert and Ernie.

"I really should go, Sam. Shamika is getting Val ready for his bath."

"I'm real good at giving kids baths." He smiled into her eyes, and Leah realized that the aspect of returning to his efficiency apartment to watch television on this Friday evening when the rest of the single world was humming with activity was as appealing to him as a stomachache. She knew the feeling all too well. The emptiness. The sounds of clocks ticking in the silence. The hours that dragged on, measured by late movies and reruns of *Andy Griffith* and *I Love Lucy*.

Leah smiled back. "All right, Sam. Maybe it's time for you to meet my son."

He hitched up his pants and slapped his hands together as Leah reached for the screen door.

Shamika came out of the bathroom, drying her fingers on a towel emblazoned with Cookie Monster. She stopped in her tracks when seeing Leah and Sam, hands falling still amid the terry folds of the towel. "Hi," she said. "You're back early." She looked around Leah, and smiled at Sam. "I was just getting Val ready for bed."

"Then we're just in time," Leah replied, removing her sweater and tossing it over the back of a chair. She kicked off her shoes and walked barefoot toward Val's bedroom. "Coming, Sam?"

Sam, the used-car salesman with two normal teenage kids back in Austin fell in behind her, rolling up his sleeves, relaying his girls' escapades in the bathtub—

how Debbie once poured so much Mr. Bubble into the
water she'd filled up the entire bathroom with suds, and
Lynda, the little minx, locked herself in the bathroom
when she was only two and the water was running in
the tub. They'd been forced to replace the carpet, not to
mention remove the lock from the door.

Valentino Starr lay on his bed, naked but for his diaper, his legs twisted into odd curvatures due to the rigidity of his muscles. He let out a squeal when he saw
her, and his arms floundered helplessly in an attempt to
reach out to her. His blue eyes twinkled and he smiled
with only one side of his face.

"Mama home!" he yelled.

"Yes, mama is home!" She grabbed his face and
kissed his cheek.

He squealed again, and managed to turn his head,
pressing his lips against her cheek. "Mama hold me?"

"Mama's going to bathe you."

"Val no bathe. Val rather stink."

"No Val of mine is going to stink." She tweaked his
nose, then blew a raspberry against his stomach. He
squirmed and bucked, filling the tiny room with laughter.

Leah slid her arms under his shoulders and lifted his
upper body slowly, giving his rigid muscles time to
gradually relax so he could bend at the waist and sit up.
His head fell back onto her shoulder as she wrapped her
arms around his chest for support. Only then did she
look up at Sam.

Standing in the door, he stared at her with a look of
shock and despair.

"Sam, this is my son, Val. Val, can you say hello to
Sam?"

Without moving his head, Val peered at Sam from the
corners of his eyes. "Sam," he repeated, smiling
broadly.

Sam opened and closed his mouth, looking like one

who had just discovered that the trapdoor beneath him had dropped open with no warning.

"Would you mind taking his feet for me, Sam? We'll carry him into the bathroom before removing his diaper."

Nodding, Sam moved cautiously to the bed, eyes roaming the room, refusing now to focus on Leah or Val. He took Val's feet and they lifted him from the bed, made their way out into the hall where Shamika was leaning against a wall, arms crossed, towel draped over one wrist.

"Had I known I was going to get the night off, I'da got myself a date," she said.

Leah laughed. "I'm sure it's not too late. Randy's place is really humming tonight."

"Randy's nothing. I've got a good mind to head out to Mojo's, where the truckers are good-looking and the jukebox is rocking."

"Be my guest. I can hold down the fort here."

Leah and Sam shuffled Val into the bathroom, where Shamika removed his diaper and tickled his tummy, causing him to shout and laugh.

Last year Leah had saved enough money to purchase a tub chair—a thousand-dollar plastic seat that allowed Val to sit reclined in the water, strapped for security into its curvatures, which had been formed specifically for his body. She buckled Val in and reached for a washcloth and soap, glancing around at Sam where he sat on the closed lid of the toilet, staring at her with hound-dog eyes.

"Thanks. I can take it from here. Why don't you go get to know Shamika while I finish up bathing Val. I'll call you when it's time to get him out."

He nodded. Then nodded again. Slowly standing, he walked from the room.

A collection of rubber ducks bobbed in the warm bathwater as Leah gently washed her son's body, crooning to him, smiling as his eyelids grew heavy, as they always did in the tub. The warm water relaxed him and eased the rigidity somewhat in his muscles, allowing him to more easily mold to the chair.

From the living room came sounds of adult conversation, an oddity that somewhat unnerved her. Closing her eyes, she floated on the tones as easily as Val's ducks did on the water. Laughter. Footsteps. The tunes from *Sesame Street* cut off abruptly, replaced by television chatter.

Her mind drifted back to earlier that evening, and she was again drawn close to Johnny's body, so familiar after so many years. He'd held her the same, like a treasured possession, their bodies swaying to music, their faces painted by candlelight.

"Come home with me," he'd whispered.

Come home with me.

"Mama sad?" Val asked.

Leah blinked, spilling tears down her cheeks. She quickly blotted them away with the washcloth, smiling into her son's concerned eyes, which seemed a thousand lifetimes wise. "No, Mama's not sad. Val makes Mama very, very happy."

Bath done, Shamika and Sam returned, bundled Val up in towels, hoisted him to his bed and proceeded to vigorously dry him. As Leah tugged his pajama bottoms up his legs, Shamika buttoned his top, discussing hers and Val's plan for tomorrow. No school meant fun day. Perhaps they would go to the park, or down to the fish hatchery. If Mama had no emergency calls, maybe she would join them. Would Val like pizza for supper tomorrow night? If he was good and cooperated with his exercises in the morning, she might even make homemade pizza, because that was his favorite, with diced-up pieces of pepperoni and sprinkled with M&M's.

Leah tucked Val into bed while Shamika and Sam returned to the living room. Sam had relaxed enough to ask questions: what, exactly, was the extent of Val's cerebral palsy and mental retardation? What had caused it? Turning out the overhead light, Leah sat on the edge of Val's bed, watching his eyes grow drowsy in the pale beam of the smiling plastic clown on the wall. With shadows kissing his face and his blanket tucked under his chin, she could almost imagine he was as normal as a million other seven-year-old boys, dreaming of Saturday freedom, of parks and playgrounds, of gathering daisies . . .

She kissed his brow and tiptoed from the room, closing the door silently behind her.

Sam had taken the rocking chair near the window. Shamika sprawled on the sofa, feet propped on the coffee table cluttered with magazines, an empty cola can or two, and a stack of Val's folded clothes, fresh from the dryer and smelling like fabric softener.

"How about coffee?" Leah asked, smiling at Sam.

His old cheeriness had returned and he waved one hand in the air. "Decaf if you have it, hon."

"Not me," Shamika yelled. "Give me the real thing. I'm just liable to cruise on out to Mojo's here in a little while and I'm gonna need all the pick-me-up I can get."

"Just what the heck is a Mojo's?" Sam asked Shamika as Leah turned back to the kitchen.

After putting the kettle on and locating the two jars of instant coffee, Leah dove into the refrigerator, shoving aside leftover Spaghetti-O's and Saran-wrapped peanut butter sandwiches until locating the last of the cheesecake she had purchased four days ago at an Albertson's deli.

"Leah?" Shamika called.

"Just a minute. I've just found dessert—"

"Leah, I think you'd better come here, sweetie."

Something in Shamika's tone made Leah frown. Leaving the fridge door open, the plate of cheesecake wedges in her hand, she walked to the living-room door. Shamika and Sam were standing still as scarecrows, staring down at the television, where a reporter stood before the blackened wreckage of a burned-out automobile, doing her best to talk over the shrieks of fire engines and the roar of helicopters.

"It appears the accident took place around two hours ago. As you can see, the bend in the road is extremely sharp, and the investigators on the scene are guessing that they were simply traveling too fast to handle the curve safely."

"Connie, can you tell us if alcohol could have been involved."

"Police won't speculate, Jan. We do know that Dolores and Johnny had earlier spent the evening with friends at Randy's Bar and Grill. From our understanding they left the bar around nine o'clock, which would put the time of the accident around nine-fifteen, nine-thirty at the latest."

"Thank you, Connie. We'll go now to the hospital, where Carl Simpson is standing by. Carl, have you any word yet on the condition of Johnny Whitehorse and Dolores Rainwater?"

"Jan, the doctors and nurses here at the hospital are keeping a pretty tight lip regarding Johnny and Dolores's condition. Shortly after the ambulance arrived here there was some speculation that one, or both, had been killed instantly, but that rumor has not been confirmed or denied by anyone so far. We do have some witnesses, however; two young ladies who happened upon the accident and called 911 on their car phone. Ladies, did you observe if, in fact, there were survivors of this terrible crash?"

"We really couldn't see much of anything other than the fire. We had no idea who it was even, not until we heard the police telling the paramedics. Oh God, I can't believe it's Johnny."

The girl turned away, her hands covering her face.

Carl looked back at the camera. "There you have it, Jan. I suspect that soon as word of this tragedy gets out there will be a great many more like her showing up here. As for myself, the thought of losing such a fine colleague as Dolores breaks my heart.''

"Leah?''

Leah turned her head, did her best to focus on Shamika's face, only vaguely aware that the cheesecake and plate lay in a heap on her feet. "What are they saying?'' she asked. "Are they saying that Johnny is dead? Is that what they're saying?''

"They don't know—''

"Yes they do. They're just not telling us.''

Sam moved up beside her and put his arm around her shoulder. "Would you like to go to the hospital, hon?''

Leah nodded, her eyes still fixed on Shamika. "Johnny can't be dead. Not *my* Johnny. I just danced with him. He said my hair made him hungry.'' She laughed. "And he said I was the prettiest girl in the room. He asked me to go home with him, Shamika. Had I agreed then, he wouldn't—''

"Sam is going to drive you to the hospital. I'll stay here with Val. Soon as you hear anything, you call me.'' Looking at Sam, she reiterated, *"Call* me.''

TEN

The car radio imparted nothing but music. Why music, when Johnny Whitehorse might well be fighting for his life, or worse? Perhaps the deejay's silence was an omen, or a conspiracy to keep the world from knowing that another of its idols had been snuffed out too early. Like James Dean and Elvis and Princess Diana—beautiful, adored, misunderstood, isolated in a frenzy of a hungry, demanding populace whose own worries were eased by the trials and tribulations of their idols— Johnny's death would ultimately make him an icon to be worshipped. There would be movies about his life, books spewing rumors and innuendos he would be unable to refute.

Leah turned the radio off.

"Johnny isn't dead," she said aloud, staring out the passenger window. "I would know it if he was. I would know it here." She pressed her hand to her heart.

Sam said nothing.

The hospital parking lot was a blockade of police cars, television crews, and teenage girls clutching posters and magazine photos of Johnny to their hearts, tears streaming down their faces, holding one another in their arms, bodies shaking with grief. Sam wedged the Cadillac into a space behind a Channel 10 van, then looked at her with a gentle smile.

"You want me to go up first? You know, see what's happened? If they know anything yet?"

"No." She shook her head and shoved open the door, leaving it open as she ran toward the emergency room entrance. The same reporter she had watched earlier, Carl something, stood in a wash of bright lights, staring into a mini-cam as he spoke into a microphone.

"We've just received confirmation of one fatality . . ."

Leah plowed through a pack of yelling news hounds, all thrusting microphones toward an obviously nervous physician whose responses to them were drowned out by shouts and more questions.

As she sprinted toward the automatic door, someone caught her from behind. "Whoa, lady. Not so fast. Back behind the barricade—"

She twisted around, shoving at the officer's chest. "I have to see Johnny—"

"You're a little old for a groupie, aren't you?"

"I'm a friend—"

"Yeah, that's what they're all saying."

"Please—"

"Look, lady, are you a member of the family?" He looked her up and down, grinning. "I don't think so."

"The lady is a close friend," a voice said. "She can go up with me."

Leah turned. Roy Moon stood just outside the door, his hands in his pockets, his cowboy hat shoved back on his head. "Roy," she whispered, her voice breaking.

"If you say so, Mr. Moon." The officer released her and returned to the barricade, where a dozen screaming girls were waving photos of Johnny in the air.

Roy reached out his hand to her. She grabbed it, refusing to take her eyes from his.

He said nothing, as usual, just escorted her into the hospital, where she was drowned by bright lights and the smell of disinfectant. Police loitered in the hallways, as did women in white uniforms and men in long white coats.

A pair of men stood side by side at the end of the corridor, their jackets stamped *Coroner's Office.* Her step slowed and for an instant the peripheral world became a gray haze.

"In here," Roy said, directing her toward a door flanked by police with walkie-talkies strapped to one hip, a gun on the other. He shoved the door open and stepped aside, waiting for her to enter.

Despite the noise in the corridor, the room was quiet. And cold. A group of doctors and nurses clustered around a body on a bed, speaking softly, jotting notes on clipboards.

"We'll continue the IV through the night. Check his stats every two hours. If he wakes up and needs something for pain I've noted his medication on his chart. I suspect he'll be out for a while, though. I gave him enough sedation earlier to put down an elephant."

The group laughed quietly and turned for the door, filing past Leah and Roy as the physician with a somewhat twisted sense of humor smiled at Roy and motioned him toward the bed. "You can come in now, Mr. Moon. I think we've about done all the damage we can do to Mr. Whitehorse, at least for the time being."

Roy smiled at Leah. "Go on. You first."

The glare of the lights made Johnny's skin look pale. His face showed signs of bruises and abrasions. Cuts on his brow and chin had been closed with a few stitches. There were bandages securing an IV needle into the back of his hand, and there was grass in his hair, along with dry blood.

"Does he know about Dolores yet?" Roy asked the doctor.

"He knows. He was awake when the paramedics

brought him in. He took it pretty hard, which is one of the reasons I sedated him so heavily.''

"I don't know how he managed to survive that wreck. I've seen it on the news. There's nothing left of the car.''

"He was thrown clear. One of those rare times it paid not to have his seatbelt on. Miss Rainwater wasn't so lucky. Even if she had survived the impact by some miracle, the explosion would have killed her.''

"It don't make sense, Doc. Johnny's a real good driver. He wouldn't do anything to jeopardize their lives.''

"We're running blood tests for alcohol—''

"He wasn't drunk," Leah said, reaching for Johnny's hand, frowning at how cold it felt, and unresponsive. "We had dinner together. The four of us. He had two drinks. You have to know, Johnny, Doctor. It takes a great deal more than a glass of champagne and a margarita to buzz him. Whatever caused that accident, it wasn't due to his driving drunk.''

The doctor put his chart aside. "We're also running tests for drugs.''

Leah looked around. "Don't bother. Johnny would never do drugs. He despises them and everything they stand for.''

"Cocaine was found near the car, in the lady's purse." The doctor lowered his eyes. "There will be an investigation, of course. If his tests show positive . . . he could be looking at a manslaughter charge. I suggest, Mr. Moon, that you contact his attorney as soon as possible. I can keep those cops out of here only so long. Come morning, when he wakes up, he's going to have a lot of answering to do.''

Roy nodded. "I'll call him now.''

The doctor left the room. Roy stood at the end of the bed, hands slid into his back pockets as he watched Johnny sleep.

"You don't believe it, do you?" Leah asked. "You

know Johnny would never touch drugs. Roy? Look at me.''

"There was a bad time, after you left Ruidoso. He wasn't himself. He lost his pride, and his soul was angry. He had much pain in his heart. His spirit became his enemy. He turned to drugs and alcohol. I think he wanted to die. I found him one night, unconscious, a needle in his arm. I took him to his grandfather, and his grandfather called on the Great Spirit to repair and comfort his wounded soul. When Johnny returned to us, he was healed. But the emptiness of loss remained. He became like the eagle with one wing. He could no longer fly.''

The door opened and a nurse peered in. "You'll have to go now. We'll be moving Mr. Whitehorse up to a room for the night.''

Leah bent over Johnny, searching his face. "I'm here,'' she whispered. "We'll get through this together. I won't leave you again, Johnny. I swear it.''

Sam waited in the hall, smiling as Leah left Johnny's room. He took her aside as a group of nurses and aides hustled into the room, followed by several police officers. "He's going to be fine, Leah. I spoke with the doctor. They did extensive X rays; nothing internal to cause problems. He'll be good as new in a few days. I'll drive you home. You can get some sleep and come back first thing in the morning.''

The door opened again. Johnny was rolled out into the hallway, flanked by nurses carrying IV bags. Officers closed in around him, their walkie-talkies squawking and buzzing with static. Two peeled away and moved to the end of the corridor, assuring that no overeager reporters would find their way beyond the outer barricade and zero in on Johnny's whereabouts.

Elevator doors slid open, and Johnny disappeared from view.

• • •

The fear and adrenaline rush that had vibrated Leah's nerves on the way to the hospital having subsided, she felt as if every inkling of energy, not to mention bone and muscle, had been drained from her body. As Sam drove them back to her house, she rode with her eyes closed, mind blank, sleep pulling at her consciousness like the moon on tide.

Dolores Rainwater was dead. But Johnny was alive. In that moment that was all that mattered. Johnny was alive. She would see him tomorrow, and comfort him, assure him that all would be fine. She would again be his port in a storm. His Rock of Gibraltar.

Sam shook her.

Raising her head, she blinked sleepily at the house, its windows blazing with light. Shamika stood in the door, arms crossed, staring out at the car.

The Cadillac running and the radio turned low, Sam reached for Leah's hand and kissed it. "Some night, huh? I'm awful sorry about Dolores. But at least Johnny is going to be okay. We can thank God for that."

She smiled and curled her fingers around his. "Thanks for helping me with Val earlier."

He squeezed her hand. "I'd say that I'd be more than happy to lend you a hand any time you need it, but I suspect, judging by watching you and Johnny together tonight, that there is more going on between you than simple friendship. Heck, I'm an overweight, balding used-car salesman. I can hardly compete with Johnny Whitehorse." He laughed, sounding sad. "Still, if things don't work out, I'll be around. You give me a call if you need anything at all—a shoulder to lean on. Someone to help you bathe Val if Shamika wants to cruise up to Mojo's."

"You're very special, Sam."

Smiling, he leaned over the console and kissed her cheek. "Get some rest. I'll give you a call tomorrow, see how Johnny is doing. Give Val a kiss for me."

Leah nodded and left the car. She stood on the graveled path, watching as Sam backed down the drive. He honked the horn before pulling out onto the highway and driving off into the dark.

Shamika opened the screen door for Leah as she mounted the porch. "Nice guy, is Sam. Sorry that I laughed at him earlier."

"Johnny's going to be fine."

"I know. They finally broke the news of Dolores's death about an hour ago. The reporter said something about the police finding cocaine in her purse. This could get very ugly, Leah."

"I'm certain the results of the blood tests will clear Johnny."

"Let's hope so. It's not going to look very good for him, considering he's been so outspoken about the use of drugs. God, he just did that anti-drug commercial—"

"I don't want to talk about it, Shamika."

Leah kicked off her shoes and tossed her sweater on the floor. She entered Val's bedroom, quietly lowered the bedside rail, and eased back his blanket.

Val opened his eyes as Leah shimmied under the covers and nestled her head on the pillow next to his. "Mama lonely?" he asked.

"Not when I'm with you," she whispered, smiling into his eyes.

An emergency call awoke her at six-thirty A.M., just as Clyde's Automotive Repair pulled into the driveway with her truck in tow. As Leah climbed out of her rumpled sundress and reached for her jeans, she listened to the tow driver explain to Shamika that all charges had been taken care of by Mr. Whitehorse. There were four new tires and a new wheel, the driver's window had been replaced, and the vehicle had been washed. The doctor might want to change the oil soon, however, and the spark plugs weren't looking so hot. If she cared to have it done at Clyde's they would make her a real deal, considering she was such a good friend of Johnny's.

Returning to the house, keys dangling from her finger, Shamika grinned at Leah as she pulled on a tee shirt and tucked it into her jeans. "My, my, it does pay to have friends in high places. Charges taken care of by Mr. Whitehorse, huh?"

"I'll pay him back." Leah snatched the keys from Shamika. "Have you heard anything—"

"Just that funeral arrangements for Dolores are pending. So what's the emergency?"

"A horse with choke."

"Lovely. Will you want breakfast when you get back?"

Grabbing up her purse and cell phone, Leah started out the door. "I'm going to the hospital afterward. If I get any more calls, direct them to Dean Crabbet. And give Val a big kiss for me when he wakes up."

By the time she reached Dan Braden's Quarter Horses, a half-hour drive from Leah's, the horse's impaction had cleared itself. Just to be on the safe side, she hung around for another twenty minutes, making certain there were no more heaves or spewing, draining nostrils. She collected her forty-five-dollar trip fee and headed for the hospital.

There were no police cars and barricades. No weeping, screaming young women, no television crews. Something was up.

The woman behind the registration desk peered at Leah over her bifocals. "Mr. Whitehorse is no longer at this hospital."

Leah checked her watch. "It's only eight-thirty. Surely he hasn't—"

"Left the hospital sometime last night, or early this morning. He was gone when I came on duty at five-thirty." She smiled and shrugged. "Sorry."

Sitting in the truck at a red light, Leah called home. Shamika answered on the second ring.

"Has Roy Moon or Johnny called?"

"Nope."

"Johnny's not at the hospital."

"That's good. It means he was well enough to leave."

"But the doctor said it was imperative that he stay the night for observation."

"Hon, from what you've told me about Mr. White-horse, I suspect he is going to do exactly what he wants to do. I doubt he's going to lay around in bed waiting for the vultures to land. He's going to find him a placc to hole up for a while, keep out of the public eye while he gets his life back in order."

"I thought he might have called, is all."

Silence.

"I guess there's no reason for him to call, is there? I mean unless Roy told him I was at the hospital last night."

"I'm sure Roy told him."

The light changed and traffic surged around her.

"Sure you don't want some breakfast?" Shamika asked.

"Why not." Disconnecting the call, Leah then threw the phone on the seat.

There were two black cars parked in the driveway when Leah arrived home. Truck idling, she sat behind the steering wheel, staring at the government-issue license plates, feeling her stomach form a fist-sized knot. She thought of making an about-face and heading back to Braden's, just to make positively certain his horse was not still choking, but then a man in a brown sports coat got out of one of the cars and stood staring at her. She could hardly make an unnoticed getaway now.

She drove around the cars, ignoring the watchful driver, and parked by the barn. There was no use in stalling the inevitable, so she headed for the house, then peered through the screen door with her hands cupped around her eyes. Shamika sat at the kitchen table, softly encouraging Val to feed himself from the pile of scrambled eggs on his plate.

Leah, quietly as possible, stepped into the kitchen. Shamika looked around, eyebrows raised.

"Where is he?" Leah whispered.

"Waiting in the living room. Watching CNN, of course. I'll warn you, he's not happy."

"What have I done now?"

"Better have a look at that." Shamika thumbed toward a newspaper on the table.

Picking up the paper, Leah opened it to the headlines and a color photo of Dolores's smashed, blackened car. Dolores's and Johnny's pictures were side by side, the caption reading, "News Correspondent Killed Instantly in Fiery Crash. Whitehorse Under Investigation."

Frowning, Leah shook her head. "What's this got to do with my father and me?"

"Turn the page. Wait. Maybe you should sit down first."

Leah opened the paper.

There was a photo center page.

She and Johnny dancing together at Randy's Bar and Grill, smiling into one another's eyes, bodies close, a portrait of lovers.

"When the hell did they take that?" she said to herself.

"To summarize the story, you and Johnny are an item—a very juicy tidbit considering Johnny is out to destroy the senator. According to the valet at Randy's, Dolores left the restaurant in a huff of jealousy after finding you two 'wrapped in one another's arms on the dance floor.' She and Johnny had a terrible fight in the parking lot. Things got really ugly. Lots of screaming, crying, and profanity. They even scuffled. Johnny drove away from the restaurant like a bat out of hell."

"Shit."

"I'd say that was putting it mildly." Shamika gave Val a big smile and popped a piece of egg in his mouth.

"Would you like me to take Val for a drive?"

She shook her head and tossed the paper onto the table. "I'll handle it. Besides, I may need some backup."

Rubbing her hands on her jeans, Leah moved to the living room where her father, Senator Foster, sat on the sofa, his gaze fixed on a CNN correspondent reporting on some catastrophe in India—a barge sinking and drowning two hundred passengers. She stared at the back of his gray head, wishing she had taken the time to grab a glass of water. Her mouth always went dry as sand in his presence.

"Hi," she said, trying to sound cheery and failing miserably. "This is a surprise."

"Have you read the morning paper?" he replied.

"Just like you, Dad. Get right to the point. Forget about trivialities like 'Hello, sweetheart, long time no see, how are you, and, most importantly, how is my grandson?' If you're referring to the story of me and Johnny, I only just saw it as I came in the door."

"Come around here so I can see you."

She walked around the sofa, then stopped between the Senator and the television.

He looked her up and down, shaking his head. "You look like shit. You're a goddamn bag of bones. Don't you eat?"

"When I have time."

"Thank God your mother isn't alive to see what you've become. Living in this dump like some poor white trash, looking like a scarecrow, smelling like a pile of horse shit. I cringe everytime I think of what you gave up when divorcing Richard."

"Richard walked out on me, Dad. Remember?"

He made a noise and shook his head. "Can you blame him? Who the hell wants a wife who smells like horse shit all the time, who can't be bothered to wear a dress now and again, or put on makeup, or brush her hair for that matter? The man was a saint to stay with you as long as he did."

There came a clatter of dishes from the kitchen, a slamming of a cupboard door.

Leah crossed her arms and took a deep breath. "Get to the point, Dad."

"The point is, you're back with that goddamned Indian again."

"I'm not back with Johnny."

"You were photographed together last night. By now the Associated Press has picked up that story and plastered it from California to Istanbul. Jesus H. Christ, Leah. The man has been trying to torch my ass for the last two years. He has all but publicly said that I'm a crook, and here you are dancing cheek to cheek with the son-of-a-bitch. Do you realize how that looks? Just where the hell is your loyalty?"

Leah cleared her throat. "I danced once with Johnny. *Once.* I was at Randy's with a date—not Johnny. You can ask anyone there. Besides, it's really none of your business who I date. I'm not a child any longer, Senator. I'm a grown woman, and if I want to date Saddam Hussein I'll date him."

Foster left the sofa, and Leah stepped back. His face flushed red, his lips pressed so tightly against his teeth they looked white. "You can tell your Indian heartthrob that if he thinks he's going to ruin me, he's got another think coming."

Straightening his tie and buttoning his coat, Foster laughed to himself. "Of course, who the hell is going to believe a druggie? Soon as those drug test results come back, proving he was strung out on cocaine when he went off that road, he's history. The district attorney will bury him so far in prison he'll be an old man before he ever sees daylight again."

Foster walked from the room. Leah listened to his footsteps as he moved down the hall. The screen door slammed.

She ran to the door, her throat tight with all the words she wanted to scream at him.

As the driver opened the rear car door he dropped into the seat, glancing back at the house as the man in the brown sports coat shut the door, obliterating her father's face behind the tinted glass. The second black car backed down the drive and waited for her father's sedan to pull out onto the highway before falling in behind it.

"Seems he was in one of his better moods today," Shamika said behind her.

"He's such an ass. If the voters only knew . . ."

"You okay?"

"He'll call tonight and apologize. He always does. He might even send flowers. Monday he'll send Val a present, maybe some money. And I'll forgive him, again. Because each time he apologizes and says he'll never lose his temper at me again like that, I'll hope like hell that *maybe* this time he means it and there might be a smidgen of a chance that he'll turn out to be human after all."

"Do you really think that's going to happen, Leah?"

"No." She shook her head. "Not a chance."

ELEVEN

The Sunday papers were ablaze with photos, innuendos, speculations, and condemnations of Johnny Whitehorse. Was he simply another icon too good to be true? Had he managed to dupe his adoring public? And what about his people, the Native Americans whom he represented as an example of what they were capable of becoming?

The interview on the local news with her father did not help. He gloated over the fact that Johnny had publicly insinuated that the senator was involved in corruption of the reservation casinos—and here he was obviously involved in drugs. The public could be assured that the senator would be encouraging an all-out investigation of Mr. Whitehorse. When asked what he thought of his daughter's relationship with Whitehorse, the senator looked directly into the camera, and replied:

"I adamantly deny that my daughter is involved with Johnny Whitehorse. They are acquaintances. Nothing more. My daughter and I have an incredibly close relationship. She would never associate with a man like Whitehorse, especially knowing how he has publicly massacred my reputation the last few months.''

By Sunday afternoon Leah had called Johnny's house no less than a dozen times, always getting his answering service. The first few times she left a message: *Urgent. Call Leah.* Later, her frustration mounting, she'd simply hung up in the service's ear.

"Why don't you just get in the truck and go see him?" Shamika asked.

"I don't want to seem pushy."

"Since when were you ever concerned about that?"

"He must be going through incredible worry."

"Maybe he needs a shoulder to lean on."

"Considering what my father's been saying, I'm probably the *last* person he'd want to lean on."

"Might be nice to assure him that your father doesn't speak for you. As I recall, he never did."

"What if he rejects me, Shamika?"

"He might. But I doubt it. Go, girl. You're not going to have a moment's peace until you do."

Leah made the drive over to Johnny's house in less than two minutes. The front iron gates were shut and locked against the curious and concerned fans milling around the entrance, hoping to get a glance of Johnny. The dozen bodyguards positioned along the entry and the stretch of fence lining the highway made certain that the women's attempts to shimmy over the barricade were unsuccessful. Engine idling, her fingers tapping the steering wheel as she collected her thoughts and watched a guard tackle an enthusiastic fan who attempted to climb the gates, Leah assessed the situation until a truck pulled up behind her and blasted its horn.

She drove south down the highway until she came to a barely visible track between a cluster of pines. By the looks of the weeds growing amid the tire marks, a few years had passed since the road had been used. No telling what she might run into along the way.

Leah eased the truck off the highway and onto the sandy track. As brush scraped along the undercarriage, the truck bounced like a buckboard wagon into and out of the old ruts.

The forest closed in around her, a wall of pines and cedars and wild berry bushes. The air became tangy with their scents, rousing memories of lazy picnics in pine-needle-covered hiding places, her mind drowsy with love, desire, and warm red wine. She and Johnny had discussed building a home in these trees, hidden away, wrapped up in nature and thumbing their noses at the hectic, prejudiced world.

She almost missed the fence opening. Over the years weeds and bushes had almost swallowed it. Leaving the truck, Leah waded through the overgrowth, jimmied with the gate latch that had become rusty over the years, and finally gave it a hard kick that sent the corroded metal flying through the air in two pieces. She was forced to pick up the gate end and shove it through the high grass to make room for the truck to pass through, onto Whitehorse Farm property.

The trail leading back to the house had long since grown over. Following the fence line, her memory leading the way, Leah wove through the rises and gullies that she had once ridden horseback over—long before she had fallen in love with Johnny Whitehorse—back when her world was made up of make-believe, her companions those only in her imagination. Her mother had been alive then, and sometimes joined her. They would spend hours exploring their domain. Her mother would take dozens of photographs and return home to paint them on canvas, selling them in shops that specialized in supporting local artists.

Topping a hill, Leah hit the brakes. Before her stretched the compound, glistening like a scattering of polished white stones under the afternoon sun: the house, the barns, the offices. The mile-long exercise track formed an oval of rich brown dirt, starting gates at one end, observation booth at the other where Johnny's father would wait, stopwatch in hand, for her father's horses to streak across the finish line. She had never been able to judge Jefferson Whitehorse's thoughts by his expressions—whether he was pleased or unhappy over a horse's running time. That was simply the way it was with the Apache. Only their eyes gave away their thoughts and feelings. They either embraced you, or cut you to the bone.

She drove to the house, parking beside Johnny's truck near a bench under a tree. There were several cars scattered along the drive: a BMW, a Jaguar XJS with the convertible top down, a Jeep Cherokee.

The door opened at her knock. A tall man with broad shoulders and no hair, wearing an extremely well-cut and expensive suit, peered down at her through his John Lennon–style glasses.

"How the hell did you get in here?" he demanded. "Jeez, where is that security?" He stepped around her, onto the porch, searching the grounds. Leah slipped into the house and was halfway across the foyer before the man turned and shouted, "Hey, come back here. Dammit! Where is security?"

"I'm a friend of Johnny's," she said without looking back. There were voices coming from the study. She headed there.

A collection of suited men sat in chairs, a couple smoking cigars that clouded the room in a dingy haze. Leah knew immediately that Johnny would not be among them. He did not allow smoking in his company. In fact, had he been anywhere on the premises, the cigars would be tucked away in the men's briefcases.

Their talk came to an abrupt stop as they stared at her. The bald man she'd left at the front door moved up behind her. "We have company, gentlemen. Does anyone know where security has gone? What am I paying those sons-of-bitches for?"

"Where is Johnny?" Leah asked, making eye contact with an older gentleman who did not seem so perturbed by her entrance.

"I hoped you could tell us, Ms. *Foster*. Sorry. I meant Mrs. Starr." He rolled the cigar between his lips before adding, "Gentlemen, this is Senator Foster's daughter. The young lady in the paper dancing with Johnny? I believe they're old friends."

"Jesus," the bald man muttered, stepping around her. "That's all we need."

"I assure you, gentlemen, I'm here strictly on my behalf. Not my father's. I haven't heard from Johnny since the accident. He hasn't returned my phone calls. I'm concerned."

"That makes four of us." The man with no hair adjusted his glasses. "I'm Edwin Fullerman. Johnny's agent. We were just discussing you. We'd hoped you might have spoken with Johnny."

"No." She shook her head.

The gentleman she'd addressed first left his chair and extended one hand. "I'm Robert Anderson, Johnny's legal advisor. This gentleman over here is Roger Darnalli, Johnny's business manager, and this is Jack Hall, public relations advisor. We all flew in last night, for whatever good it's done us. No one seems to know where the hell our client is."

"Not even Roy Moon?"

Edwin rolled his eyes. "Trying to get anything out of *that* man is impossible."

"He'll talk to me."

Johnny's agent dropped onto a leather sofa and crossed his legs. "Great. Terrific. Go to it. You might tell him to pass on to my client that his silence and sudden disappearance are not exactly going to endear him to the advertisers who have spent millions on ad campaigns plastered with his face and body. Jesus!" He leaped from the sofa, arms thrown open as he stared at the ceiling and yelled, "We're talking frigging ten million dollars in endorsements here!"

"Not to mention the impact this will have on his own companies," Darnalli interjected as he flipped open a file and ran his finger down a compilation of numbers. ''Whitehorse Jeans had the third highest sales profits for jeans for the first quarter of this year, both in this country and Japan. Christ.'' He shook his head. ''Johnny's bigger than Buddha in Japan. One hint of scandal and he's cooked.''

''You can imagine how my conversation went with Craig Morris at the Celebrities for a Drug-Free America this morning. Just last week we finalized a deal with NBC and the National Football League to air a thirty-second commercial of Johnny's anti-drug rhetoric during the next Super Bowl. Johnny would have made the cover of *Newsweek* again. Oh, and did I fail to mention what that little coup would have meant if we got around to negotiating the Costner-Redford deal? We're talking fifteen million easy.''

Jack Hall studied the tip of his cigar. ''We'll simply get him into Betty Ford—explain that the pressures of his success became too much—I'll point out to Craig Morris that this slip of Johnny's could make one hell of a point. See what disasters befall you when you succumb to drugs . . .'' He grinned. ''Brilliant. Think about it. All this publicity. Rainwater's death—his beloved fiancée— I'll call the *Enquirer,* promise them an exclusive if they really make an issue of Johnny's grief. I'll slip them a few photos of the funeral—''

''Great.'' Ed shook his head. ''While you're at it, slip them a few photos of Johnny in prison for manslaughter and possession. He's hardly going to be able to do the Costner-Redford deal when he's serving ten to twenty, is he?''

''He should have thought about that—''

''Wait a minute,'' Leah shouted, causing the men to shut up and look at her as if forgetting she had been there in the first place. ''You're all talking about Johnny as if he's already been tried and found guilty of something. Listen to yourselves. Not one of you has shown any concern whatsoever for anything other than what

this may or may not do to his ability to make money—
excuse me, make *you* money. Have you stopped to consider *his* feelings? What he must be suffering, and I
don't mean because he might lose an endorsement or
won't get his picture on the front of *Newsweek* again.
Dolores Rainwater is dead, and if any of you jerks had
ever taken the time to get to know Johnny, you'd realize
that he must be dealing with incredible guilt, not to mention his sorrow over losing a friend.''

They stared.

Fullerman sat on the desk edge and crossed his arms.
''His up and disappearing doesn't exactly paint a positive picture, Miss Foster.''

''The name is Starr, Mr. Fullerman. And if your ref-
erence to my maiden name is somehow a means of link-
ing me with my father, then you can stuff it. What
problems may exist between Johnny and my father have
absolutely nothing to do with me. I have no intention of
taking sides on their issues.''

''You may be forced to,'' Anderson said. ''As
Johnny's legal counsel I must say that the allegations
your father is publicly making about Johnny border on
slander . . . if Johnny is found to be clear of drugs, of
course. Should Johnny decide to sue, I suspect your father will be hard-pressed to collect enough money to
satisfy us, much less finance his upcoming election.''

''Is that a threat?'' she said through her teeth.

''Simply a fact, Mrs. . . . Starr. If you have any influence with your father whatsoever, I suggest that you
relay this little conversation to him, pointing out that a
lawsuit slapped on a man of his prominence will have
major consequences down the line . . . should he ever decide to run for a higher office.''

Leah backed toward the door, shaking her head.
''You're all a lot of hyenas.''

''Just businessmen, Mrs. Starr,'' Hall said, tapping cigar ashes into a container the shape of the state of New
Mexico. ''With a very lucrative commodity at stake.

Johnny Whitehorse is worth a cool hundred million in
endorsements and television and movie projects, not to
mention Whitehorse, Inc., revenue. In short, should
Johnny decide to, he has the financial capability of
squashing your father's bank account like a cockroach.''

Turning on her heels, Leah left the room, stalked from
the house, and stood beneath the tree near her truck,
doing her best to control her anger before getting behind
the wheel.

Leah pulled the truck onto the highway shoulder and
shut off the engine. Ahead of her, on the side of the
road, were two cars, windows rolled down as the oc-
cupants focused their long-lens cameras on the crash site
and snapped away. Souvenirs of death. Leah wondered
if the photos would take their place inside someone's
picture album or find their way to the tabloids, for a
hefty reward, of course. Obviously, anything to do with
Johnny was worth a tidy sum, even if it depicted tragedy—*especially* if it depicted tragedy.

A half-dozen or so flower wreaths had been placed
amid the blackened and scarred earth where Dolores's
car had collided with the ground and burst into flames.
There was evidence of the police investigation. Strips of
yellow ribbon fluttered from charred tree trunks, their
lower limbs, stripped of their needles, looking skeletal.
The grass—what had been spared from the inferno—
had been flattened by numerous car tracks.

Finally, the cars pulled away.

Leah left the truck and stood on the hot asphalt, feeling the heat of the day seep up through the soles of her
boots as she scanned the area. A stench of gasoline and
ashes hung in the air, as did the unusual and discomfiting
silence.

A double stretch of black rubber lay imprinted along
the road's surface, stretching perhaps fifty feet before
disappearing off the shoulder. Leah followed the tire
marks, toe to heel, balancing on the strip as if she were

a tightrope walker until coming to the end, where the marks took an abrupt jag to the right—almost a perfect ninety-degree angle. Very odd. Hands on her hips, she stared down the embankment, to the place where the car had hit first, rolling back the earth, then again, further, where it had come to rest, wheels up.

Where, she wondered, had Johnny fallen? Had he witnessed the horrible explosion, knowing that Dolores was still strapped in the car, knowing there was no way of helping her? Or had he been unconscious?

Please, God, let him have been unconscious.

A crow cawed from above, circling the clearing, floating on outstretched black wings before diving into the trees. Cupping her hand over her eyes, Leah searched the treeline beyond the accident site. Some niggling disquietude tapped at her, as if there were something there she should be seeing, but couldn't. Sort of like the *Where's Waldo* pictures that always made her crazy with frustration. She knew it was there, laid out for her to recognize, though what *it* was was a total mystery.

This particular bend in the road had been a major source of despondency for a number of people through the years. During her senior year in high school the curve had claimed three lives, each going too fast to make the curve safely. How many times had she and Johnny so foolishly pushed the limits of safety in his father's old truck, racing ninety to nothing to get her home and back in bed before sunup—before her father realized that she'd spent the night making love to an Indian. Funny, but she'd never been frightened of the drive with Johnny. He'd handled the bends in the road as gracefully and competently as he made love—a man in total control of his actions.

The place where the car had come to rest was a flat hollow some fifty yards from the road. There were shreds of metal strewn over the ground. The larger rocks scattered around the clearing showed evidence of metallic blue paint.

What was she doing here? Leah thought. She was feeling a lot like a rubbernecker at a particularly grisly accident, slowing down to catch a glimpse of gore.

"I wondered how long it would take you to come here," came a voice near the treeline. She spun around, her heart pounding. Roy Moon stepped from the shadows. "You're looking for Johnny?"

She nodded.

"You won't find him here," Roy said.

"Why are you here?" she asked.

"I am here for Johnny. Searching."

"For what?"

Roy stepped over a rotting tree branch, his footsteps cautious and silent. His cowboy hat had been replaced by a bandanna tied around his wide, brown brow. He wore knee-high moccasins instead of boots. By the looks of his sweat-damp shirt he had been nosing around the site for some time.

It became apparent that Roy had no intention of answering her question, so she did not bother asking again. "Will you tell me where Johnny is?"

"What good will you do him?" he replied, stopping beside her.

"He shouldn't be alone, Roy."

"It is his choice, I think."

"But do you think it's wise, considering what you told me at the hospital?"

He studied the area with sharp eyes.

"He must be suffering," she said.

Roy nodded. "If I take you there, you must promise to keep his secret."

"I swear."

"I risk his trust by doing so."

"He'll be glad I've come."

Without another word, Roy turned back to the forest. Leah fell in behind him.

They walked a long while until coming out on a dirt road where Roy had parked his truck—well hidden from view from the highway. Leah climbed in and they made the ride in silence through the trees, finally coming out on a blacktop road that wound north toward the reservation.

After a half-hour's ride, Roy pulled up in front of a tiny adobe hut. An old man sat in a ladderback chair on the porch, fanning himself in the heat. The engine still running, Roy looked over at Leah. "You know Johnny's grandfather."

She nodded, feeling a flutter of nervousness in her stomach. The old màn had been totally opposed to his grandson's relationship with Leah those many years ago. Like Johnny's father, he looked at her as one more object to lure Johnny's loyalties away from his people. She was very certain they had celebrated her and Johnny's breakup with much pleasure.

Killing the engine, Roy left the truck. "Wait here. I'll speak to the old man alone. It will be up to him whether you see Johnny."

She nodded and watched as Roy mounted the porch and sat on an overturned crate next to Johnny's grandfather. As Roy spoke too softly for Leah to hear, the old man stared out at her, his expression inscrutable.

God, it was hot. The first really hot day of the summer. The sun beat down on the line of hovels, shimmered in waves off the roofs and weed-thatched gardens, reflected off the barren ground so the glare made Leah squint.

Closing her eyes and doing her best to ignore the sweat forming under her clothes, Leah leaned her head back against the seat, allowing memories to rise like threads of hazy smoke in her mind.

The first time she'd ever noticed Johnny Whitehorse had been the spring of her sophomore year in high school. She supposed that he'd been around for nearly a year, since his father had come to work at the farm, but she'd been too wrapped up in cheerleading, student council, and keeping her grades up to realize there was actually a life around her own house. Her steady at the time had been the quarterback for the football team—blond, blue-eyed Larry Norman. He drove a black Corvette convertible and lived in the second-finest house in Ruidoso, hers having been the finest, of course. Larry was dumb as a box of rocks, but it didn't matter, not with his throwing arm. Half the colleges in the country were trying to lure Larry Norman with scholarships. She'd always thought it rather sad that someone with his father's money could get his education paid for entirely just because he could throw a football.

Larry had brought her home from school one day after cheerleading and football practice. Gunning the 'Vette up the drive, he'd come within feet of plowing into Johnny and the horse he was riding. The animal reared straight up on its back legs, yet Johnny handled the situation with all the adeptness of his ancestors, whispering to the horse in Apache, his expression saying nothing of what he was really thinking.

Larry laid into his horn and shouted, "Hey, Geronimo, wanna watch where you're goin'?"

Leah slapped him on the arm. "Dingbat. Watch where *you're* going, why don't you?"

As Larry eased the car by the skittish horse, she looked up into Johnny's eyes, and smiled. "Sorry," she called. He did not reply, just watched her, perhaps hypnotizing her a little, causing her existence to hone to a pinpoint that made her heart ache. It had been all she could do to turn away from him, and for the remainder of the night she'd tossed and turned in her bed, thinking of the Indian with haunting eyes.

TWELVE

May, 1985

The alarm clicked on and music filled the bedroom. Five
A.M. Without turning on the lamp on the bedside table,
Leah slid out of bed, grabbed her shorts off the floor
and tugged them up her long legs. She dug through a
drawer and chose a pale-blue crop top with just enough
elastic to conform to her breasts and exposing her midriff to just below her navel.

The excitement she felt had little to do with the fact
that there were only two more weeks of school, although
the idea that she would soon be a junior in high school,
therefore coming one year closer to graduation, was
enough to make her giddy. No, her anticipation stemmed
from the fact that she had every intention of introducing
herself to Johnny Whitehorse.

Barefoot, hairbrush in hand, she made her way down
the back stairs, stopped long enough in the dim kitchen
to search out a Dr. Pepper and a Snickers bar from the
fridge, then exited the house. The grass felt cool and
damp, the air brisk enough to bring goosebumps to her

arms. That would change however, just as soon as the
sun crept up over the mountains.

Lights blazed in the barns. Hands hurried about their
chores, graining the eager horses, mucking the stalls,
scrubbing buckets they would fill with fresh water.
Though daylight was still a half-hour away, there were
horses on the track already, full of energy, their light-
weight riders carefully going through the ritual of walking the animals out before putting them through their
runs. The animals' breath rushed from their flaring nostrils into the cold air like steam from a locomotive's
smokestack.

If the grooms thought Leah's appearance in the barn
so early unusual, they didn't show it. They nodded re-
spectfully, some being so bold as to smile. She moved
down the concrete aisle, flanked by stalls of horses with
their heads in the feed buckets. Ah, how she loved the
sounds of horses eating in the morning, their contented
sighs, the grinding of teeth upon fragrant oats, the occasional blow if they happened to inhale too much dust
from the grain. Top that off with sweet-smelling, fresh-
cut alfalfa and she felt as if she were in heaven.

She found Johnny in the rehab barn.

On his knees, he carefully wound an elastic bandage
around the horse's cannon bone, his long dark fingers
gently situating the pressure so as not to hamper the
circulation.

Funny how she forgot to breathe. And how the sight
of him, bent over, his threadbare shirt pulled tight across
his broad back, black hair spilling over his shoulders,
made her feel upended and thinking she was really dumb
for doing this. After all, what if he turned out to be a
creep? Or to have an attitude toward whites like so many
Native Americans did.

''Hi,'' she said.

Johnny looked up. His eyes narrowed, his only show
of surprise to find her standing barefoot in the barn be-

fore dawn, a Dr. Pepper in one hand, a partially eaten Snickers bar in the other.

"Bowed tendon?" she asked, pointing the candy at the horse's cannon bone.

He looked at her feet. "Nice toes. If you want to keep them you'd better put on some shoes."

Leah wiggled her toes and smiled. "Thanks. I do have nice toes, don't I? Do you like the color on the nails? It's called Flamingo Fruit Passion. It's supposed to smell like papaya. Wanna sniff?" Sticking her foot up by Johnny's nose, she wiggled her toes again, swallowing back her need to giggle at her own outrageousness, but there was something so serious in his face and eyes that she felt obligated to relieve it, if for no other reason than to see him smile.

"Well? What does it smell like?"

"Fruit."

"What kind? Papaya? I think it smells more like peaches. My mom said strawberries."

He looked at her toes, waving just below his nose. "Watermelon."

"Umm. Yummy. I can live with watermelon." Dropping to her knees beside him, Leah forced herself to focus on the horse's leg, and not Johnny Whitehorse's dark eyes. They were beginning to scatter her thoughts and make her realize just how silly she was acting. Normally guys were attracted to ditsy, but not this guy. He was probably thinking now that she was a major doofus.

"So what's wrong with the leg?" she asked seriously.

"A bow, I think."

Leah bent over a bucket of foul-looking goop and sniffed. "Oh my gosh. What is that?"

"Bigel oil, lard, honey, and rosin. It's my grandfather's remedy for bows. You plaster the inside of the cannon bone from knee to fetlock and bind it with warm wraps. It takes away the swelling and soreness and strengthens the tendon."

"Have you called a vet?"

"No need to. The poultice works every time."

"There's talk of magnetic therapy soon. Something about positive and negative ions or something that's supposed to generate heat and better blood circulation to the traumatized area."

Wiping his hands on the knees of his jeans, Johnny shook his head. "Sounds like bad medicine to me. My father won't like it." He stood, grabbed up his pail of goop, and walked away.

His jeans were old and thin and fraying a little along the inseams over his thighs. There was a hoof pick and a comb jutting out of the left rear pocket. His shirt had seen much better days and was just on the verge of being too small. He wore Justin boots. Not the pointed-toe sort, thank goodness. Not rattlesnake hide or ostrich. Just plain brown leather that was scuffed and gouged, the sole nearly worn through and the heels in desperate need of replacing.

Johnny disappeared down another barn aisle, obviously uninterested in her ploys to get to know him. That didn't surprise her, really. The Apaches were known for showing great caution toward strangers, especially whites. They did not trust easily, and friendship was something to be earned.

Johnny sat on a bench in the supply room, elbows on his knees, forehead propped upon the palms of his hands as he stared at the floor between his feet. Leah leaned against the door frame and watched him a long moment before speaking.

He looked up, as he had before, face expressionless. Yet there was something in his eyes that had not been there before.

"I suppose I should introduce myself." Smiling, she crossed the small room that smelled like liniment and pine tar and Leather New, and extended her hand. "I'm Leah Foster."

Ignoring her hand, he stood and, turning his back to her, began collecting an assortment of vet wraps, rice brushes, and hoof dressings. "I know who you are," he said, dropping a wash mitt into a bucket, along with shampoo and a bottle of baby oil. "You're the boss's daughter. And you shouldn't be out here dressed like that. The men talk among themselves and say things that are less than honorable."

Hot color rushed to her cheeks as she stared at his back, her hand still extended. She could put anyone in his place, should she decide to, and had been known to get in an employee's face if she didn't like his manner or attitude or his treatment of a horse. She could cut Johnny Whitehorse off at the knees with a slice of her tongue for his rudeness and blatant honesty, but she wouldn't because he was right. She had dressed like this to catch his attention. To flirt. To . . . tease, which was totally unlike her. She had never been an airheaded bimbo, so why was she acting like one?

Johnny turned and looked down at her with a gentleness in his face that had not been there before. "You're a very pretty young woman, Miss Foster. Your heart is good, and your eyes honest. If your face looked like that of a horn toad you would still be attractive to me."

"Should I take that as a compliment?" She grinned.

"A very big compliment. There are few things as ugly as the face of a horn toad."

Leah laughed and shook her head. "Gosh. Beneath that somber if not outright grim demeanor, Mr. Whitehorse, I suspect there is a sense of humor lurking."

"Don't count on it." He moved around her toward the door.

Stepping in front of him, Leah offered the Dr. Pepper and candy bar. "A peace offering. Wanna bite?"

"Could be dangerous. You might catch Apache fever." As Leah frowned, Johnny took the candy from her hand and bit into it, then replaced it between her fingers as she continued to stare up at him, waiting for an explanation. "Your skin will gradually turn dark and you'll develop a craving for mescal."

"I could think of worse things than my skin turning dark."

"I'm not so sure your father could."

Johnny left the supply room and Leah fell in beside him. "I guess you're wondering why I'm here," Leah said, virtually running to keep up with Johnny's long stride.

"It's your barn. You need no explanations."

"I wanted to see you for several reasons. First, to apologize for Larry's rudeness last week. He knows nothing about horses. I'm sure he didn't realize that honking like he did was very dangerous."

"Then my assessment of him was right. He's an idiot."

"Secondly, I was very impressed by your handling of the situation. You managed to control the horse beautifully, and you were riding bareback. My gosh, most people would have hit the ground—"

"I'm an Indian, Miss Foster. My father is a trainer. It stands to reason that I'd know how to ride a horse bareback."

"Exactly. Which is why I'm here. I'd like you to give me lessons."

Johnny dropped the bucket next to an empty wash stall. His hands on his hips, he finally looked down at her. "I've seen you ride. You don't need any lessons from me."

"But I don't normally ride bareback. And when have you ever seen me ride?"

"You ride with your mother a lot. Out there." He nodded toward the distant pastures. "You're a decent rider. You have good hands, and a good seat. The horse is happy with you. Besides, what with school and helping my father, I really don't have time. Sorry."

He walked away, toward a rider and horse that had just entered the barn. Steam rose off the heated animal and lather dripped off its belly and ran down its legs. The jockey removed his protective glasses that were spotted with dirt and tossed them to Johnny.

"Fine," Leah said to herself. "Be that way."

She headed for the back barn, where the pleasure horses were stabled.

Genesis nickered as Leah slid open the stall door and looped a lead rope around the stallion's neck. As always, he lowered his head, nuzzled it against her and waited for her to stroke him.

"Big baby," she murmured, sliding her hand down his silken muzzle. His eyes grew drowsy and he released a sigh of contentment that made Leah smile. "You'll be a good boy for me this morning, won't you, Pooh? You'll keep your mind on me and not the babes? I've already made a big enough fool of myself this morning. We don't need to add insult to injury."

After securing the big bay between cross ties, Leah curried his dark coat until it shone, brushed out his black mane and tail, then wrapped his lower legs with polos— the ones she kept for special occasions—then located her bridle in the tack room.

No saddle today.

She mounted by way of a step stool.

The sky was just beginning to gray as Genesis pranced out of the barn, neck arched and ears erect, Leah playing with the reins just enough to remind the hot-blooded Arabian that this was not to be his usual dawn frolic around the turnout paddock. They headed for the breaking pen, a hundred-foot-diameter round pen not far from the stables.

Leah had not lied about her bareback capabilities. She was good, but not great. As long as the stallion behaved she could handle the situation. Her father would explode, of course. He preferred her to look the part of the senator's daughter—all refined and ladylike, a role model for young women who aspired to represent the very best of Uncle Sam, apple pie, and money.

The horse easily gave to the bit as she set him into a collected canter around the arena, glancing occasionally toward the stables where she had last seen Johnny Whitehorse. The horse warmed between her legs, and its easy rocking motion fingered a slow, oozing sensation through her, one that she had come to recognize and appreciate over the last couple of years. She wasn't ignorant of what it was, and meant. She and Larry weren't exactly angels, not that they had gone all the way. No way was she giving her virginity to such a moron, but they had, on occasion, enjoyed some fairly heavy petting.

Johnny leaned against the wall and watched her.

Leah brought the horse down to a slow, collected trot, a more difficult gait to sit with no saddle.

So Johnny wasn't as disinterested in her as he'd pretended.

She sank her heels hard into the stallion's side. He jumped forward, front feet leaving the ground as he pushed powerfully off his rear end. The reins slid through her loose fingers and she slipped sideways, hitting the ground and rolling face down in the sand. Eyes closed, she waited.

Footsteps running. The gate thrown open.

Leah smiled.

Johnny sank to his knees beside her, took her gently in his hands and turned her carefully. "Leah?" he said softly, but urgently. "Speak to me, Leah."

Her eyelids fluttered and opened.

His face was no longer expressionless. His eyes looked turbulent. Cradling her cheek with one hand he eased his thumb along her lower lip and asked, "Are you all right?"

"Yes." She nodded.

He raised one eyebrow and sat back on his heels. "Then the next time you bail off a horse to try and impress me you should try harder to land on your head. A little blood would go a long way to inspiring my pity."

"What are you insinuating? That I purposefully fell off that horse—"

"Exactly." Standing, Johnny turned on his heels and walked toward the horse that was nervously watching from the far side of the round pen.

"You're crazy," she shouted, sitting up and dusting sand from her arms and legs. "Why would I bother doing such a stupid thing?"

"Because you're rich and spoiled and accustomed to getting your way."

"I am *not* spoiled."

Johnny took the reins and led the horse to her as Leah got up, slapping dirt off her rear. He extended the reins. "One thing you must learn about the Apache, Miss Foster. We tolerate nothing but honesty from any man or woman. As my mother always said, 'Say what you mean, and mean what you say.' "

Leah rolled her eyes as Johnny started back toward the gate. "Fine," she yelled. "I fell off the horse on purpose. I thought you might be more receptive to giving me lessons if you thought I was a klutz. Look, I just want to get to know you. What's wrong with that?"

He stopped and slowly turned back. "Why are you so interested in getting to know me? I'm only an Indian."

"You're a guy first, aren't you?"

"No." He shook his head. "I'm Indian first. And you aren't. That's reason number one why you shouldn't bother getting to know me. Reason number two is your father. He doesn't like Indians, remember?"

"That's just stupid." She laughed. "He hired your father, didn't he?"

"If my father was from the moon and had eight eyes and seventeen arms, your father would have hired him because he's the finest trainer in this state. That doesn't mean he has to like him."

Shaking her head and crossing her arms, Leah said, "That's just not true."

"No?" Johnny walked toward her. "When is the last time your father asked my father into his house? Never. When has he ever asked about my father's health? Never. When has he given my father the credit he deserves for training his horses? Never. Instead, he takes these horses and gives them to Jack Jones to run because he doesn't want it known that an Indian trains his horses. And while my father drowns his disgrace in mescal, Jack pockets thousands of dollars in bonuses and commissions that should be my father's."

Taking the reins from her, Johnny tossed them over the stallion's withers. "Get on your horse, Miss Foster, and I'll give you one lesson only." He turned her toward the horse and gave her a leg up. With his dark hand lying upon her thigh, he lifted his black eyes up to hers. "You must become one with your animal. Your body is his body, from here—" He slid his hand to the top of her leg, where her crotch nestled into the animal's flesh, then down, slowly, along her leg, to just below her knee. "—to here. You hold his heart between your knees. Be gentle but firm and there's nothing he won't do for you. His heart and spirit are yours, *Sons-ee-ah-ray.*"

"Sons-ee . . . ?"

"*Sons-ee-ah-ray.* Morning Star." He pointed to the solitary star that continued to shine in the dwindling gray of the bluing sky. "You shine like fire in the mist, Miss Foster."

Leah smiled, aware that Johnny's hand remained on her leg, like shadow upon sunlight. Even more aware that she liked it in a way that she had never liked Larry Norman's touch.

Johnny's father exited the barn, his step slowing as he saw Leah and Johnny. "*Ish-kay-nay!*" he shouted angrily, striding toward the round pen, fists clenched and jaw bulging.

"He looks pissed," Leah whispered. "What does *ish-kay-nay* mean?"

"Boy." Removing his hand from her leg, Johnny backed away, lowering his head. "In my father's eyes I haven't yet achieved an act worthy of an Apache name."

Jefferson Whitehorse shouted again at Johnny, his language as foreign to Leah as Japanese. But his anger was undeniable. He did not look at Leah directly, but turned his profile to her, and with hands on his hips, waited until Johnny left the arena. They exchanged words before Johnny turned his back on his father and walked toward the barn. Only then did Jefferson Whitehorse look at her—briefly, the whites of his eyes red as fire.

That night after dinner, Leah sat on the porch with her mother. The whir of insects filled the air and the first bite of chill settled around her shoulders, making her glad that she had put on jeans and a long-sleeved tee shirt before curling up in the chaise. This was her favorite time to spend with her mother. Jane Foster was usually more relaxed after her evening meal and several strong drinks she called her dessert. When she was totally sober she was far too concerned with living up to her husband's expectations.

Jane held a partially full glass of Jack Daniel's on the rocks as she gazed out over the sprawling front gardens. At eighteen she had won the coveted title of Miss Louisiana and had gone on to become a top five runner-up for Miss Universe. She'd met Leah's father the following year. Their marriage had been the joining of two of the most prestigious families in the country—arranged by their fathers, of course. Even modern aristocracy made certain their bloodlines ran with nothing but the bluest blood money could buy.

"I met Johnny Whitehorse today," Leah said.

"Did you?" Jane replied.

"He's very nice."

Jane sipped her Jack Daniel's.

"Not bad on the eyes either."

"Like father, like son, I guess."

"He called me *Sons-ee-ah-ray*. That means 'Morning Star.' "

"Pretty." She drank again.

"Did Daddy ever have a nickname for you?"

Her lips thinned into something less than a smile. "I'm occasionally surprised your father even knows my *real* name. Then again, he has his staff to remind him." The ice in the glass tinkled as she raised the drink to her lips. "His winning this election should suit him nicely. He can now legitimately spend all his time in Washington rubbing elbows with men as power hungry as he is."

Leah sighed and sank back in the chair. She'd never been comfortable with her mother's cutting remarks about her husband—Leah's father—but only from the standpoint that it forced Leah to face the fact that there was no love between them. Not that she need worry that they would divorce. Foster made certain his wife was kept financially satisfied.

"You could always move to Washington," Leah said.

"You're joking, right?" Jane laughed. "I would suffocate within a week. Nope. This is my home. My Shangri-La. I have the freedom here to do what I want, and be whom I want. If I want to climb on a horse buck naked and ride howling under the moon, I can do just that."

Grinning, Leah said, "As if you would."

Turning her blue eyes on Leah, Jane raised her glass as if in toast and said, "Wanna see me? Another couple of these and I'll be ready to parasail off the fucking Sierra Blanca."

"What if I told you that I have a crush on Johnny Whitehorse?"

"I'd say that I wouldn't blame you. He's a hunk. Just like his old man. They're walking, talking testosterone in blue jeans. They're enough to make a woman come just looking at them." Glancing at Leah, Jane grinned.

"Oops. My little girl probably doesn't know what that means yet. Or do you?"

"I'm sixteen, Mom."

"Sixteen going on thirty. Jesus, Leah, you're too damned mature for your age. But then again, you always were. You have an old soul. A girl your age and with your looks should be out partying every night, getting laid by the football team before you marry some jerk who'll ultimately make you feel as sexually dead as an android."

"There are names for the girls who sleep with entire football teams."

"So what difference will it make when you're forty-two years old? At least you'll have your memories."

"So you're giving me your permission to sleep with the football team?"

Jane finished her drink and set the glass of ice on the floor by her chair. "Over my dead body," she finally replied.

THIRTEEN

Even as Johnny killed the engine to his father's truck he knew that the minute he stepped into the house there was going to be big trouble. The music blasting through the open front door was a reminder of Johnny's mother. When his father listened to the records he and Johnny's mother had collected over the years, all the old hurt boiled to the surface. He would drink to dull the pain, but each song brought on a flurry of memories. He would grow angrier with each drink, then he would have to take it out on something, or someone.

Johnny buried the truck keys deep in his pocket.

Frank Sinatra crooned on the old phonograph, hiccuping each time the needle scraped across a scratch on the 45. Jefferson sprawled in a chair, one hand holding a bottle, the other a gun, a Magnum he'd bought out of the trunk of someone's car a few days after Johnny's mother had run off with a white man from Kilgore, Texas. He'd had every intention of finding them and killing them both, then decided his killing himself by degrees would prove more satisfying.

Johnny walked to the phonograph and turned down

the volume. Jefferson looked up, narrowed his eyes, and belched. He spoke in Apache, refusing to allow anyone to speak English in his house. "Where have you been? The sun set hours ago."

"I was seeing to the horses like you told me to."

"I think you lie. I think you are fucking the man's daughter."

"No." Johnny moved to his father and reached for the bottle. Jefferson yanked it away and stumbled to his feet.

"I saw you with her today."

"She fell from her horse."

"I think you like white pussy. Like your mother likes the white man's cock." Jefferson shoved his face up to Johnny's. "You are like your mother. Your eyes look at that girl with the same fire I saw in your mother's when she looked at the white man. You want to *be* a white man."

Johnny grabbed for the bottle and missed. "I don't blame my mother for leaving you. You're crazy mean and drink too much."

Jefferson slammed the grip of the gun against Johnny's cheek. Pain splintered through his face as he hurled back against the wall, stumbling into a table loaded with the collection of miniature china thimbles his mother had left behind when running off with her white man. He slid down the wall, landing in tiny shards of broken glass that dug into the palms of his hands.

Shoving the barrel of the gun against Johnny's head, Jefferson said, "I think I will kill you so I no longer have to look into your mother's eyes."

"You have no bullets in that gun," Johnny said through his bleeding teeth.

"Are you sure?" Jefferson drew back the hammer with his thumb. "Perhaps I bought bullets today. Perhaps this is the day I have chosen for us to die."

Johnny glanced at the gun cylinder, but there was sweat in his eyes and he could not see clearly.

Jefferson pulled the trigger and the hammer cracked against the empty chamber. Johnny jumped and his heart climbed his throat, choking off his breath and making him forget, briefly, about the intense ache spreading over the right side of his head.

He knocked the gun from his temple and shoved his father away. Climbing to his feet, he said, "Do me a favor, old man. Next time load the gun before pulling the trigger."

Unsteady, he made his way to the kitchen, spat a mouthful of blood into the sink, thought of puking, then decided against it. There really was nothing in his stomach to puke up anyway since he had not eaten since breakfast, and that had been nearly fifteen hours ago.

Throwing open the freezer door, he reached for an ice tray and cracked it against the countertop to dislodge the cubes just as Connie Francis began singing "Where the Boys Are." Holding a square of ice against his throbbing cheek, Johnny closed his eyes and did his best to ignore his escalating fury. He wanted to return to the living room and beat the shit out of his father for being the kind of man who would mistreat his wife so badly she would turn her back on her only son to rid herself of her misery. He wanted to drive his fist through his father's teeth for taking his anger out on the only human being left who gave a damn whether he lived or died.

Tossing the remaining sliver of ice into the sink, he reached into the fridge for a six-pack of Budweiser, slammed the door as hard as he could and left the house through the back entrance, digging the keys from his pocket and hurling the beer through the open passenger window of the truck before climbing in himself and fumbling with the starter. At last, the engine turned over. He slammed the gear in reverse and backed down the gravel drive, spitting rocks and sand into the night air.

Dolores Rainwater peeled her panties down her legs and tossed them on the floor where her clothes and bra lay in a heap by Johnny's boots and jeans and shirt, and four empty Budweiser cans. As sounds of drunken laughter and the whoops and hollers of gambling boys reverberated against the walls, she fell back on the bed and spread her legs.

"Hurry up. God, a girl would die from waiting on you to finish that damn beer. How many does that make, anyhow?"

"Eight. But who's counting?" He crushed the can in his hand and tossed it to the floor.

"Your old man did a number on you tonight. You never get this bad unless you're pissed at him."

"Shut up. I don't want to talk about my old man."

"He let you have it good—"

"I said to shut up!" Grabbing up another beer, he peeled back the pop-top and tossed it to the floor. The beer was warm and bitter and made him shudder. Glancing around at Dolores, her legs spread and her fingers caressing her nipples, he said, "Exactly how many of those guys out there have you already been with tonight?"

"That's a creepy thing to say."

"You came here with *somebody*. And considering you're the only girl here—"

"You know I don't care for anybody else like I do you, Johnny."

"You're a whore, Dolores. And a liar."

"It just so happens that I enjoy the finer things in life. Sex happens to be one of them."

"You *are* on the pill, right?"

"*Yes.*"

He drank the beer so fast his eyes watered. But his cheek didn't hurt any longer and the image of his father shoving a gun muzzle against his temple became as blurred around the edges as the vision of Dolores lying spread-eagled in front of him, massaging her breasts and pumping her hips in invitation. "You look like a porno chick," he murmured, allowing the can to roll out of his hand and off the bed.

"Well it doesn't seem to be getting me anywhere," she replied, exasperated. Propping up on her elbows, she stared at him. "Don't tell me you're too drunk now to get it up."

"I'm gonna make you wish you hadn't said that."

"Promises, promises. You know what your problem is, Johnny? You haven't ever looked upon sex as like . . . recreational. You think it's supposed to *mean* something. Until you decide just to let yourself go and have fun with it you're never going to reap the benefits."

He climbed over her, rocking back and forth on his hands and knees; the bed felt as if it were rolling like a canoe on waves. Grinning, Dolores slid her hand down his belly and wrapped her fingers around him.

"You know I love you, Johnny. We're a team. We're gonna make it out of this hellhole, you just wait. You won't have to let your father beat you up any more and I won't have to live in that hovel on the reservation. Tell me you love me, Johnny. Just once."

He kissed her as he slid inside her, sank deep, drawn deep as she lifted her legs around his waist and clutched him close. "I don't love you," he whispered as she squirmed against him, making little whimpering noises in her throat. She didn't seem to hear him. Or maybe she simply did not care. He was not the only boy who used her body; there were plenty, and probably most of them were more than willing to tell her what she wanted to hear even if it was a lie. But he had never used those three words to anyone. Not to his mother or father. Not Dolores or the few girls he had made it with since turning fourteen. There had never been a person worthy of them . . . until he happened one day to see Leah Foster riding her stallion along a creek bed that skirted her father's property. He had known for certain the day she smiled up at him from Norman's convertible.

* * *

As the traffic light turned green, Johnny eased his foot off the clutch, gave the truck a little gas, then felt it shiver, sputter, tremble like an animal in death throes before dying. He pumped the clutch and turned the ignition. Nothing.

The car behind him blasted its horn. Johnny glanced up into the rearview mirror, frowning as the car's bright lights reflected back into his eyes. He tried the ignition a second time, then slammed his fist against the steering wheel and shoved open the door.

He was too damn drunk for this. He should have gone home immediately after leaving Dolores, but the idea of facing his father when he had had this much to drink was not a good idea. He had never lifted a hand against his father and he wanted to keep it that way.

With horns blaring behind him, Johnny at last managed to lift the hood of the old Dodge. The traffic light cast an orange glow over the engine parts before turning red.

"Hey, buddy, you gonna move this heap tonight or what?"

Johnny looked up. A middle-aged man with a beer belly straining at his shirt buttons stared at him, hands on his hips, a Stetson shoved back on his head. He wore a gaudy Rolex watch encrusted with gold nuggets and diamonds, and his belt buckle, or what Johnny could see of it below the man's belly, was a gold-and-silver replica of Texas. Johnny had seen a thousand of him—a Texas oil man with a stable full of quarterhorses. They moved into Ruidoso like locusts every year to run their animals on the track, acting as if they owned the place.

"Well?" the man shouted. "You habla ingles?"

Johnny gave him a flat grin. "You habla Apache?"

"You movin' this piece of crap or what, smart-ass?"

"No." Johnny slammed the hood, leaned against the truck and crossed his arms. "I think I'm going to let *you* move it since you want it moved so bad."

The light turned green and the cacophony began again

from the dozen cars backed up down the highway.

"Look, punk, I gotta be at the track in five minutes. Now I'm tellin' you, get this junk pile outta the highway before I get really pissed."

Shrugging, Johnny got in the truck, shifted the gear into neutral, and got out again. The Texan continued to glare at him as Johnny walked toward his car, a sparkling new top-of-the-line Cadillac—black with gold trim—with dealer tags still stuck in the back window. A young woman with bleached hair and fake eyelashes, wearing a rhinestone halter top that exposed most of her tanned breasts, and a leather miniskirt that hardly covered her crotch, stared at Johnny as he dropped into the seat beside her and flashed her a smile.

"Holy crap," she said, looking him up and down, her painted mouth curling and her tweezed eyebrows rising. "You an Indian, honey?"

"In the flesh." He slammed the door and locked it.

The Texan slowly moved toward his car, his jaw sagging and his beady eyes becoming round as pennies.

"You gonna kidnap me or something?" the woman asked, starting to breathe hard.

"You want me to?" He shifted the transmission into Drive. "Ever made it with an Indian, lady?"

"Uh-uh. But lookin' at you I'm beginning to wonder what I've been missing."

"That fat old man your father?"

"Hardly."

"Your husband?"

She shook her head, smiling.

"You a hooker?"

"Not unless you want me to be." She winked.

Johnny looked out at the Texan, who continued to stand in the middle of the street, jaw sagging, expression dazed. Johnny flipped him the finger, then eased the car against the rear fender of the truck and pushed it out into the intersection, bringing traffic to a screeching halt.

"Hang on, lady," Johnny said, then stomped the accelerator as hard as he could.

Rubber screamed and smoke flew as Johnny steered around the truck and wove through the traffic. He headed down the highway at seventy miles an hour while the woman beside him squealed and bounced in her seat.

"God almighty, the girls back in Dallas ain't even gonna believe this! I've been kidnapped by a damned Apache!" She reached under the seat and dug out a pint of Jack Daniel's. "Time to party, baby. This is the most fun I've had since I got to Ruidoso with that old fart." Tossing the cap out the window, she turned the liquor up to her lips and drank deeply, shuddered, then handed him the bottle.

He shook his head. "I'm drunk enough already."

"Come on. Just a drink. It's not every day you steal a car and kidnap a white woman, is it?"

"Whiskey makes me crazy."

She drank again, laughed, and hung her head out the car window, allowing the wind to whip back her blond hair.

He pulled off the highway onto a gravel-topped road and headed toward White Sands. The earlier drunken buzz in his head was settling into a throb behind his eyes, and the huge anger that had driven him to get into the situation he was in began to diminish.

"Come on, Injun Joe. Have a drink. Just one. I hate to drink alone." She waved the bottle at him.

Grabbing it from her, he tipped it up to his mouth and drank while keeping his eyes on the dark road ahead. The liquor hit his stomach and ricocheted like a bullet straight to his head. He squeezed his eyes closed briefly; the car swerved, skirted the road shoulder, then wove back over the center yellow stripe.

He took his foot off the gas. To his right was a dirt road. Braking, he eased the car off the highway, onto the side road, and stopped.

The woman reached over and shifted the car into Park,

then killed the engine. Removing the pint bottle from his hand, she lifted it to his lips and tipped it up. The whiskey ran smooth as hot honey down the back of his throat.

"How old are you, sweetie?" came the woman's voice, soft and husky near his ear.

"Seventeen," he heard himself say.

"Ooh. Just hitting your prime, huh? All those raging hormones. My name is Janice, by the way." She kissed his ear. "Love the hair. It's so . . . savage." Her fingers slid over his chest, threaded through the openings between the buttons on his shirt, massaged his nipples, then eased down his belly to his crotch. "So . . . you wanna? You know, do it?"

He looked at her, trying to focus on her face. Her hair stood out wildly from her head. Her lipstick had smeared and one breast had almost come out of her halter, exposing most of her nipple. Now that she was up close he could see that she wasn't young at all. There were wrinkles under her heavy makeup and her breath smelled like stale cigarettes.

"Ever made it with a white woman?" She grinned and rubbed her breasts against him. "Young strong buck like you, bet the girls just can't say no, huh?" Her fingers unsnapped the button on his jeans, then the zipper. Johnny caught his breath as her cool fingers slid through the Y front on his Jockey underwear.

"Ever had a woman go down on you, sweetie?"

He swallowed and shook his head.

Her mouth smiled and her lips parted. "Imagine that." Easing the bottle into his hand, Janice lowered her head toward his lap.

"Hey," he slurred. "Lady. What the hell . . . Oh, man. I'm too drunk for this." He groaned and stared down at her with fascination, what she was doing to him with her lips and tongue and teeth. His eyes rolling, his head falling against the back of the seat, he said, "I'm gonna get in real trouble for this."

She reached across his lap and hit a button on the door. Johnny's seat eased back. He grabbed the steering wheel, hit the horn accidentally. Where the hell was he supposed to put his hands?

God, oh God, what was she doing?

He took another hit of Jack Daniel's, groaned and gritted his teeth as it seemed she would draw the very life of him out through his organ. Geez, he was going to come. "Lady, you'd better . . ." Too late.

Not that it mattered to her, obviously.

He heard himself cry out once, then again.

Finally, the woman lifted her head, and licked her lips. "Not bad, huh? There's more where that came from if you're interested."

The red-and-blue lights from a squad car on the road behind them suddenly swirled in the rearview mirror. Johnny dropped the whiskey and zipped up his pants. As Janice sat up and looked out the back window, he grabbed for the door handle.

"Hey," Janice cried. "Where the hell do you think you're going? Don't be stupid, kid. You can't outrun them."

He jumped from the car just as the police skidded to a stop behind the Cadillac, siren whooping and lights whirling. He took off across the rocky terrain, jumping rocks and cactus and low-growing prickly shrubs.

"Stop, Johnny!" an officer shouted.

Rocks and sand tumbled as he clawed his way up the side of a steep hill, slipping, stumbling. Normally he would not have had any problem outdistancing the pair of pudgy cops chasing him—he'd done it a dozen times before—but then he hadn't been loaded with Budweiser and Jack Daniel's, which was making the ground tip from side to side like an out-of-control seesaw.

A cop hit him from behind. Hard. Drove him to his knees and then his belly, slamming his face into the rocks and dirt. "Damn you, Johnny, get down and stay down. Hey, Chuck, I got him!"

Johnny drove his elbow into the cop's rib and did his best to pitch him off, causing the cop to curse and slam his knee into Johnny's back. Then a second pair of hands buried in his hair and snapped back his head.

"You're just one breath away from assaulting an officer, kid. If I was you I'd lay real still and think about what I was doing."

"God," came Janice's voice. "You gotta be so rough with him? He's just a kid, for gosh sakes."

"Evading arrest, ma'am. You want to get back in the car?"

Johnny's arms were wrenched around his back and cuffs were slapped on his wrists. "You've done it now, Johnny. Jesus, what were you thinking to steal a car and kidnap a woman? You gonna behave now? You gonna get up and walk back to the squad car without me having to call in another unit? 'Cause if I got to call in another unit somebody is going to want to get nasty and I wouldn't like to see that with you. Johnny? You listening to me?"

He nodded.

The cop dragged Johnny to his knees, then helped him to his feet. His partner, officer Chuck Parker, shined his flashlight into Johnny's face and shook his head. "You and your old man been at it again, Johnny? He do that to your face? If he did, you can press charges against him. You don't have to take that kind of bullshit from him. When you gonna stop protecting the son-of-a-bitch?"

"Save your breath, Chuck," Officer Delaport said, shoving Johnny toward the squad car. "They're all alike. They're not gonna tell you jack shit."

Janice stood by the Cadillac, hugging herself against the cold as Johnny walked by.

Officer Parker opened the rear door of the squad car, and Johnny dropped in. The door slammed and automatically locked. Through the grilled windows he watched the cops walk back to the Cadillac; one spoke to Janice while the other dug through the car, exiting with the bottle of Jack Daniel's.

Closing his eyes, he laid his head back against the seat. His face throbbed. His stomach churned, not simply from the booze and beer he'd imbibed, but from the far-too-familiar smell of the car. It stank of sweat and vomit and the barbecue the officers had eaten for dinner.

The car doors opened and the officers climbed in. Officer Parker looked back and stared at Johnny from beneath the brim of his hat. "You okay?" he asked.

Johnny nodded.

"Not gonna puke all over our car, are you?"

He shook his head.

"You know what kinda time you can get for car theft and kidnapping, Johnny?"

"I'm a juvenile. I won't get forty-eight hours and you know it."

"I want you to think real hard about pressing charges of abuse on your old man, Johnny. You can't let him keep beatin' you up like this every time he has too much to drink and gets pissed off."

"Go to hell," he mumbled.

By the time the cell door slid open and Officer Parker shouted Johnny's name, Johnny had slept off most of his drunk. Opening his eyes, he squinted toward the bright light overhead and tried to remember where he was.

"Whitehorse, you're up and outta here."

Raising his head, he focused on Parker's face.

"You're free to go," the officer said.

Johnny sat up slowly. His head felt like hell and his mouth tasted little better.

"Get the lead out, kid. My shift is over and I wanna go home."

"What about the charges?" He ran one hand over his eyes and down his face, lightly touching the swelling on his cheek.

"Folks are not pressing charges. Lady says she invited you to take her for a ride."

Standing unsteadily, Johnny then moved toward the door. "You call my old man?" he asked.

"Yep. He didn't answer."

"My grandfather?"

"No luck." Parker slid the door shut and followed Johnny down the corridor, toward the office with large plate-glass windows, where an officer in charge of juveniles sat on the edge of his desk, talking with a woman with her back to Johnny. He slowed as the woman turned in her chair, her blue eyes connecting with his.

"What the hell is *she* doing here?" he asked.

"She's who I call to bail out your father."

In jeans and a purple sweatshirt, Leah's mother stood and tucked her clutch purse under her arm. Parker stepped around Johnny and opened the door, allowing Johnny to enter the office before him.

Jane Foster smiled unsteadily. "You don't look so good, Johnny."

"I'm not feeling so good." He shoved his hands into his back pockets and stared at the floor.

Flashing a look at Officer Parker, she said, "What about the charges?"

"No charges this time. He's lucky. Grand theft auto isn't exactly a misdemeanor. Obviously he made quite an impression on the lady."

"Like father, like son," Jane said. "Can we go now, officer?"

"I suggest you find him a place to sober up before taking him home. He could probably use some food by the looks of him, not to mention a bath."

Jane pointed toward the door and Johnny turned, moved out of the office and through the station lobby, to the door marked Exit, out into the parking lot of black-and-white squad cars. "Get in," she said, pointing to a baby-blue Lincoln by the curb.

Sinking into the beige leather seat, he watched Jane

Foster round the car, her long dark hair not unlike her daughter's.

Sheesh. Her daughter. The last person in the world he wanted to know about this stupidity was Leah Foster.

Jane slid in beside him. The musky scent of her cologne in the confined space made his stomach queasy.

The engine purred and the heater automatically kicked on as Jane backed the Town Car out of the parking space and headed down Main Street. Flipping open her purse, she dug out a pack of cigarettes, then punched in the car lighter. "You smoke, Johnny?"

He shook his head no.

"Good. It's bad for you. I've tried to quit a hundred times at least, but I've had to face the fact that I like the crap. Guess it's a little like your drinking. You know you shouldn't do it. It's going to make you sick, but you do it anyway." The lighter clicked and she reached for it, pressing its glowing end to the tip of the cigarette in her mouth. She inhaled deeply, closing her eyes.

Johnny pressed the window down button, allowing fresh air into the car.

"You don't say much, do you, Johnny?"

He looked out the passenger window at the dark countryside and wondered what time it was.

"It's that Apache mystique, huh? What's that belief? By talking too much, or telling too much, you—"

"Give away your soul."

"Right." She laughed, then coughed, then inhaled again.

They continued to ride in silence for a while, then Jane said, "Must have been a bad one tonight. What did he hit you with?"

"Doesn't matter."

"What set him off?"

"What else? Jack Daniel's."

"It makes him crazy. Makes you a little crazy too, huh?"

"Life makes me crazy."

"It makes us all crazy, Johnny. We could all be out there boozing and fighting and raising hell, but some of us find less violent and self-destructive means to work out our problems."

Turning his eyes on her, he said, "That why you're screwing my old man?"

She hit the brakes hard, causing the Lincoln to fishtail before sliding to a stop in the middle of the black, deserted highway. Reaching across his lap, she yanked on the door handle and shoved open the door. "Get out. Get out of my car, you ungrateful young shit."

Johnny stepped out onto the asphalt, then looked back. The overhead light made Jane look sallow, the skin around her eyes dark as soot. "You're a nice lady," he said. "And nice-looking. I just think you can do better than him."

Tires squealing, the Lincoln shot away, leaving Johnny standing in the road, head pounding and stomach churning, watching the red taillights grow small in the distance. Then the brake lights flashed and the car backed toward him, weaving from side to side before sliding to a stop beside him.

"Get in," she said.

He opened the door and got in.

Again they rode in silence. As they sped past the driveway entrance to his house, he looked at her.

"I can hardly take you back there considering your condition. The last thing you need is to get into another brawl tonight. Besides, that cut on your cheek needs seeing to. If you're worried about Leah, you needn't be. She already knows about their hauling you in. She was still up when Officer Parker called."

"Great." He slouched into the seat.

The house glowed from every window. Leah stood in the open front doorway, fingers tucked into her jeans pockets as she watched the car pull up to the porch and stop. Jane got out. Johnny took his time, watching Jane bound up the steps and speak to Leah before disappearing into the house.

He closed the car door and leaned against it.

Leah moved down the steps, shoulders slightly hunched as she stopped at the edge of the light, bare toes with their polished nails slightly hanging over the lip of the stair. Flamingo Fruit Passion, he thought. Had it only been that morning when she'd shown up at the barn looking like a bouquet of fresh-cut flowers? And smelling just as sweet? Making him hate his life more than he ever thought possible?

"I made sandwiches," she said softly. "Sometimes it helps to put something in your stomach."

"How would you know?"

"My mom has a little too much sometimes. I fix her peanut butter on crackers. But you don't look like the peanut-butter-and-crackers sort, so I made ham and cheese." She rubbed her arms and curled her toes under. "It's really chilly. Let's go in, okay?" She turned and bounded up the steps, her hair dancing around her shoulders.

Taking a resigned breath, Johnny followed as far as the door, then paused, allowing his eyes to adjust to the bright lights flooding down from the massive chandelier over the foyer. There were fresh-cut flowers on every table, and portraits on the walls.

"Are you coming?" Leah shouted from a hallway leading off the foyer.

He walked carefully over the black-and-white marble-tiled floor, his gaze fixed on Leah where she stood in the shadows, her smile encouraging him onward; then she slipped through another illuminated doorway that turned out to be the kitchen, nearly as big as his father's entire house. There were pots and pans hanging on hooks from the ceiling. Glistening countertops and sparkling glass cupboard doors. A stone fireplace on one wall, bookcases on another, loaded with cookbooks that looked as though they had never been opened.

Leah opened the refrigerator and reached for two sodas, along with an apple and orange and a bowl of grapes. "Sit." She pointed with her foot toward a three-legged stool next to a counter bar.

Johnny glanced around. "Where's your father?"

"Washington. Where else?" Grinning, she laid out the food next to his plate. "You can relax. He isn't going to come roaring through the door like the cavalry or something."

"I don't think he'd like me here."

"Like I said. He isn't here. When he isn't here I do what I want and see who I want."

"And when he is?" He picked up a grape and rolled it in his fingers. "Are you Daddy's good little girl when he's home? See who Daddy wants you to see? Go where Daddy wants you to go?"

Leah slid onto a stool and reached for her soda. "I pretty much do what I want to do. How's your face? When we're done here I'll clean it for you."

He shrugged. "I've had worse."

"Do *you* like *your* father?" Leah asked.

Tossing down the grape, he reached for the sandwich, not sure he wanted it, thinking he probably should eat it, feeling very strange standing in such a grandiose kitchen and talking so nonchalantly with the girl he'd had a crush on for months—who, until this morning, had not even acknowledged his existence.

"I like him sometimes. When he's sober."

"Then you acknowledge that he's stupid when he drinks."

Johnny removed the lettuce from the sandwich and set it aside. "Your point?" He flashed her a look, suspecting already what her point was going to be.

"Just that you see what drinking does to your father. What he becomes. Why do you want to be that way?"

"I don't."

"Johnny, stealing a car and a woman isn't exactly smart. And I don't think you would have done it if you hadn't been drinking. You're very lucky that the lady took pity on you.''

"Is that what she took on me?'' He shook his head, remembering Janice's head in his lap. "Let's just say we hit it off and leave it at that.''

Leah frowned and stared at him hard. There was a tiny crumb of bread on her lip, and he wondered with an odd sort of spitefulness what she would do if he leaned over and licked it off.

"Well.'' She cleared her throat. "Have you given any thought to what you're going to do with your life?''

"What are you? A social worker?''

"No. Just someone who sees a tragedy in the making when I look at you. To say you're good-looking is an understatement. But I think you know that already. I asked Mr. Dilbert, the principal at school, about you last week. He told me you're a straight B student but your attitude sucks. You fight too much. You're consistently late for class and you enjoy getting in the teacher's face. He said you drove Mr. Dubach so far over the edge last year that the two of you wound up in a fistfight.''

"He called me a stinking Indian.''

"I know Mr. Dubach. He's a good guy. For him to get nasty he must have been pushed to the edge. Why do you get so angry at being called an Indian? It's what you are.''

"It's the *stinking* that pissed me off. I happen to be proud that I'm Apache.''

"Great. Then if Apache is something to be proud of, why don't you act it? Represent your heritage in a shining example. Educate us. Teach us what it means to be a Native American.''

"I think I've done a good job of that tonight,'' he said angrily, throwing down the sandwich. "You want to know what being Native American is, *Pindah-Lickoyee?* It is living in poverty. It is existing like animals in a zoo, where people stick their cameras in our face and take pictures of us like we're oddities. It is dealing with a government that goes back on its promises to us. We listen to the horror of Hitler and the Holocaust, of a government that wiped out millions of innocent men, women, and children, and the world weeps for them, Leah. But who weeps for us? Who remembers that the white man swept over our country and slaughtered us, left our children's corpses to feed the coyotes, and those who remained were gathered like cattle onto parcels of shitty land and left there to die of starvation and white man's diseases, and the loss of our dignity?''

Leah reached over and laid her hand on Johnny's, and she smiled. ''Then you should know by now that it will do you no good whatsoever to fight with your fists. Anger only begets anger. Use your brain, Johnny. Show us all what it *could* mean to be Johnny Whitehorse.''

Her hand squeezed his, then drew away, yet her gaze remained on his, the blueness of it a tranquility that made him feel weightless. ''So,'' she said, her lips still smiling, ''ever played football? You look like you would make a great tight end.''

FOURTEEN

"Leah? Are you okay?"

Leah opened her eyes. The inside of Roy's truck felt like an oven. She couldn't breathe. "I must have dozed." She cleared her throat and sat up, looking beyond Roy to the porch where Johnny's grandfather had been sitting. He was gone.

"The old man has agreed to let you see Johnny," Roy said. "But you must swear to tell no one of his location. He only does this because he knows what you mean to Johnny." Roy opened the door and stepped back. "It's a long journey. You'd better start now if you want to get there by dark."

She followed Roy toward the corral at the back of the old man's property. Ben Whitehorse, whose face looked as aged as the dilapidated barn, stood by a swaybacked paint horse with one brown eye and one blue. Ben had bridled the horse, if one could call the rope braid wrapped over the horse's muzzle and looped around its withers a bridle. There was no saddle.

Roy helped Leah to mount, then smiled up at her. "Let the horse take you. He knows the way." He pointed to the low mountain that seemed to Leah in that moment as tall as the Sierra Blanca. "The mountain spirit rides with you. *Yalan.*"

Stepping back, Roy slapped the horse on the rump and the animal moved down the path toward the trees. Leah looked back as Ben Whitehorse lifted his arms toward the sky and began chanting softly in Apache. Roy raised his hand briefly, then turned and walked toward his truck.

The path climbed sharply up the hillside, forcing Leah to lean slightly over the horse's withers and grasp its mane with both hands to steady herself. Occasionally fir and piñon and cedar trees formed a low canopy overhead, so she had to lie low or risk getting scraped from the animal's back.

The rocky thread of ground curved like a snake's back through crevices of boulders that rose up to form cathedral-like pitches over her head. More and more the path inclined until the horse was forced to scramble for footing, lunging itself upward while Leah closed her eyes and gripped her legs tightly as possible, remembering what Johnny had told her once about riding bareback. *Hold his heart between your knees. Become one with the animal and he with you. Trust him and he will take care of you.*

The earth to her right disappeared, dropping sharply out of sight so it seemed to her that the horse balanced on thin air. Crows and eagles soared level with her and the trees below blurred into a green, indistinct cloud, interrupted only by the diminutive gray lines of highways and the clusters of buildings that represented Mescalero and Ruidoso. But even that disappeared as they wound around the far side of the mountain.

The horse's flesh turned hot and sweaty, soaking her jeans so they rubbed the insides of her thighs raw. The sun burned down on her and the reflection of it off the rocks made her eyes sting. The horse stumbled, going down on both front knees. She clutched its neck and looked over the lip of the ledge as stones bounced like rubber balls down the side.

They climbed for another hour. Then another. Until the sun disappeared over the western mountains and shadows of rocks painted strange shapes on the trail. Her legs cramped, as did her shoulders. Having clutched the reins and mane so fiercely for so long, her hands ached with a numbness that shot hot pain up her arms.

A moment passed before she realized they had stopped climbing. Its head down, the horse made a grunting sound and blew through its nostrils.

The mountaintop formed a mesa of sand and rocks and scrubby wind-twisted trees. Before her burned a campfire, and just beyond that stood a small inipi covered with heavy colorful blankets to allow no light and air inside the brush structure.

Leah slid off the horse, wincing as her feet hit the ground. Carefully as possible she straightened, massaged the small of her back and took a couple of unsteady steps before being certain her legs would hold her.

The wind whipped over the mesa edge, scattering brown grass and kicking dirt around her ankles as she moved toward the primitive structure. "Johnny?" she called softly, glancing toward the campfire, where glowing coals were mounded around rocks the size of tennis balls.

The opening of the inipi had been covered with a blanket. Going down on her knees, Leah drew the flap aside and did her best to peer into the dark room. Steam rushed over her face, robbing her of breath.

"Johnny?" she whispered, crawling through the opening and into the dark, wet heat.

Naked, his skin beaded with water and sweat, Johnny sat near the glowing, steaming stones in the center of the sweat lodge, his back to her, his head fallen forward so his hair partially covered his face. He did not acknowledge Leah's presence. His eyes closed, he rocked back and forth, silently chanting.

Leah moved around the confined space until she was sitting across from him. The steam rose up from the stones so thickly that she felt suffocated. Her eyes stung and her clothes clung to her skin as she did her best to see Johnny's face in the fog.

"Johnny?"

He continued to sway. His lips moved.

"Johnny?" Leah touched his scraped and bruised cheek and his swaying stopped. Slowly, his head came up and his eyes opened. He stared at her, emotionless, as if his soul were someplace else. A niggling of uneasiness centered in her chest, causing her voice to tremble. "Are you okay? God, Johnny, I've been worried out of my mind."

He said nothing. Did nothing. Not so much as a blink of his dark eyes to acknowledge her.

Leah moved closer, around the pit of stones, sank into the sand beside him so his wet gritty skin pressed against her own. She took his face between her hands and forced him to look at her. "Have you taken something?" she asked. "Johnny, are you on drugs? Please, answer me."

"Dolores is dead," he whispered.

"I know. I'm sorry. But hiding away here won't change the fact that she's gone."

At last some life came to his eyes and he focused hard on her face as sweat beaded on the tips of his lashes, then ran down his cheeks. His jaw became rock solid. His expression became fierce and savage as he wrapped his hand around her nape and roughly pulled her closer. "Johnny Whitehorse runs from nothing, *Sons-ee-ah-ray.* I'm more than ready to face the consequences of Dolores's death, and to tell all that I know. I came here because of you. To sweat *you* from my soul, and my heart. To sweat away the pain that I feel every time I think of you. To sweat away the love that has eaten away at my heart since the first moment I saw you those years ago riding your father's stallion, the wind in your hair and the sun dancing on your face. Foolish, isn't it, to think I could suddenly stop loving and needing you now when I couldn't do it the last twelve years.''

Twisting his fingers in her hair, he drew her face up to his. ''Now here you are, breathing life again into my spirit, and a hunger as hot as the desert wind. I want you. I *don't* want you. I need you. I *don't* need you. You are more complication than I need in my life. You're a ghost that haunts me, and if I could I would exorcise you back to your sky world and make you take your memory with you.''

''I never stopped loving you,'' she said, and began unbuttoning her blouse. ''There hasn't been a day that I haven't regretted what I did. The decision I made. I felt your pain every night that I lay in my bed and thought of you, and the life we might have had together. But I had no choice, Johnny. When my father learned of our relationship, he vowed to destroy your father if I continued to see you. I broke up with you to protect you—''

''You murdered me, Leah.''

He cupped his hand over her breast, slidding his fingertips along the edge of her bra before flipping the strap off her shoulder. The masculine, musky scent of his sweating body roused a hunger in her that, over the last many years, had inspired vast fantasics, yet none had felt as overwhelming as this moment. How many nights had she nestled in her husband's arms thinking of Johnny Whitehorse, and what she would do if ever she lay with him again.

''For a very long time I wanted to destroy you, but in hating you so I destroyed myself.''

''I'm sorry,'' she whispered, her voice sounding rough and low as she allowed the blouse to slide down her arms. The steam slid over her skin like hot velvet as she watched Johnny unhook the bra closure between her breasts and peel away the filmy material. Her head falling back and her eyes drifting closed, Leah caught her breath as Johnny lowered his head and took a taut, throbbing nipple between his teeth, gently at first, then almost painfully, sucking it hard, cruelly, causing her to gasp and whimper in her throat, at the same time acknowledging the sensation of heat igniting between her legs and mounting as he lay her back on the ground and stretched his big body out on hers.

He pressed kisses against her heated flesh, swirled his tongue upon the ridge of her ribs, grazed her skin with his teeth and breathed hotly against it until she writhed in both pleasure and pain and made soft keening sounds in her throat, until she lifted her hips and invited him to unsnap her jeans.

For a moment they clung insistently to her, until he tore them down her legs and tossed them aside. Wearing only the briefest panties, she lay sprawled before him, sweat and steam turning her pale skin as red as the embers heating the stones outside. On his knees between her legs, his black hair falling over his shoulders, he allowed her to look at his body, to acknowledge his massive erection that she had once been much too shy to openly admire.

Johnny Whitehorse was no longer a boy. The memory of his younger body did not do him justice—that body had not been honed of long bone and defined muscle that came from hours of working out—and though she once had felt the cravings of adolescent desire while in his arms, the hunger that streaked through her in that moment was beyond anything she had ever experienced.

"What are you waiting for?" she asked.

His black eyes narrowed and his lips curved sensually. He ran one hand down the length of his erection and she watched with caught breath as it swelled even more, causing Johnny's face to tense, his teeth to clench, and a low groan to rattle in his throat.

"Twelve years," he murmured, sliding the tips of his fingers up her thigh, to the elastic edge of her panties, dipping beneath to search out the sensitive place between her legs that had turned as hot and liquid as the steam pressing down on her. "For twelve years I thought of other men holding you, of touching you, of teaching you things I wanted to teach you. Of smelling you. And tasting you, and making your body desperate to be fucked. I've been with a lot of women, Leah. Some of them nice. Most of them not so nice. I'm not the same boy who got drunk on sangria and took your virginity with clumsy recklessness. But then, you're no longer a virgin."

Twisting his fingers in the crotch of her panties, he ripped them in two and shoved the silk remnant up around her waist, exposing the fading scar of her Caesarian surgery across her abdomen. He traced it with one finger before bending and kissing it, following the slightly puckered skin with the tip of his tongue.

Closing her eyes, feeling the slight tickle of his tongue and the ends of his hair over her sensitive skin, she reached to bury her hands in his hair. He caught her wrists in his hard fingers, and as he rose up once again to cover her body with his, he stretched her arms out to her side and pinned them to the ground.

"Don't touch me," he told her, sliding his knees between her thighs and shoving them apart. "I'm going to give you exactly what you deserve, Leah. What I've wanted to do since the night I showed up at your door with my heart in my hand and my idiotic dreams of happily ever after branded in my brain. Remember what you said to me that night, Leah?"

"I don't love you," she said, turning her face away as he slid his body into hers, stretching it painfully, causing her to gasp at the shocking pressure that lifted her hips briefly from the ground and wrung a short startled cry from her. "Oh God, Johnny. I didn't mean it."

"What else, Leah?" He looked down her body, to the place where his own disappeared into hers. "Do you recall what else you said that night?" He moved deeper, opened her legs further to better accommodate him while his fingers tightened on her wrists and ground them harder into the dirt.

"That I had never loved you. It was all a mistake. Foolishness. I must have been crazy to even think I could have been attracted to you."

"And?"

"You didn't and never would fit into my life, not being what you are." She shook her head as her chest tightened and the tears began to stream. "I didn't mean it. I didn't mean it. Please believe that I didn't mean it. I only said those things because my father was there. I couldn't allow him to hurt you."

"Hurt me?" He grinned. "The son-of-a-bitch has destroyed everything I have ever loved. I won't allow it to continue, Leah. I can't. Damn you for coming here. For reminding me that no matter how I try I can't get you out of my system."

His hips pumped hard, grinding her buttocks into the dirt, yet she refused to take her eyes from his, just gave her body in supplication like one happily sacrificing her soul.

She awoke, shivering, despite the shirt Johnny had laid across her, her knees drawn up to her chest and her head resting on her rolled-up jeans. Where was she? And why in God's name did she feel as if she'd been stampeded over by a herd of horses?

The stones in the center of the inipi had grown cold and the brisk air bit at her skin as Leah sat up, her eyes heavy, body aching and shivering as she carefully slid her arms into Johnny's shirt sleeves and wrapped the garment around her. The darkness inside the inipi felt suffocating, and the throbbing between her legs made even breathing an effort. Then she remembered . . .

There had been nothing remotely resembling love in what Johnny had done to her. He had treated her like a whore—worse, she suspected, than he treated the women who, over the last several years, had so eagerly spread their legs for no other reason than to be screwed by the famous, and infamous, Johnny Whitehorse. He had fucked her with all the pent-up hurt and anger that had eaten at him over the years. All the fear and sorrow that must have incapacitated him in the days since Dolores's death. Did he blame her for that as well? Was that why he had come here, as he said, to sweat her out of his system? To be done with her emotionally once and for all?

Leah laughed to herself. What irony that at long last she had acknowledged her feelings to him and now he wanted no part of her.

As she reached for her jeans the sound of chanting came to her. Tossing back the flap over the opening, Leah looked out through the predawn gray haze, to the yellow light cast up by the campfire flames.

Dressed only in his jeans and a mantle of brown and gray eagle feathers that had been attached to his arms, all the way to his wrists, Johnny moved in carefully choreographed steps around the halo of flickering light, his head fallen forward and his hands stretched toward the sky. He had painted white dots on his cheeks and zigzag lines resembling lightning bolts down the backs of his hands, and segments of his long hair had been plaited and decorated with colorful beads. He took her breath away. This was the part of Johnny Whitehorse that she had never experienced. Frightening. Mystical. Savage. Yes, savage. Wild. Free. Dangerous. And arousing despite what he had done to her in the last few hours.

He danced. And danced. Spun. Dipped. Leaped. His voice rose and fell, odd choppy words that made no sense to Leah. Grunts, cries, shouts. His arms outstretched like eagle wings as his bare feet kicked up dust, making him appear as if he were soaring through clouds. And as he chanted and danced, it seemed to Leah that the beat of drums and the birdlike warbling of flutes rang out a rhythm as steady as a heartbeat from the dark sky, along with the singsong rise and fall of ghostly voices that chanted along with him.

Ghosts. Spirits—*Gans,* as the Apache called them.

Leah believed in neither. It was only the play of firelight and dust and the first streaks of daylight creeping in scarlet waves over the eastern mountain peaks that formed the shapes of dancing men in fierce headdresses and buckskin masks, their dark eyes peering out at her through the slits in the colorful hides as they moved in unison around the firelight. No doubt if she looked back into the black inipi she would see herself asleep still, her head lying on her jeans, her body curled up under Johnny's shirt and shivering with cold, and she would realize that she was dreaming. Just dreaming.

Johnny chanted to the awakening sky, his arms outstretched, the eagle feathers fluttering in the clash of cold and warm air as the sun rose higher. Blood-red and burning it filled up the sky, dwarfing the earth, turning the mountains into hills and the sky into a scarlet mirror. He became a black silhouette against the fiery shield, a speck of dust upon the universe, yet his voice rose as clear as bells on a soundless Sunday morning.

Then it was over. As the last of the sun's red flood drained into yellow, Johnny stopped dancing and his voice fell silent. Wearily, facing the sun, his head fallen back, he dropped his arms to his sides and slowly fell to his knees.

Leah dragged her jeans on, then, tossing Johnny's shirt aside, slid her blouse on and clumsily buttoned it. She felt around for her shoes, then crawled from the inipi into the sunlight that was fast becoming brilliant enough to blind her. She was forced to squint in order to determine that Johnny was no longer there.

"It's time to go," came his voice.

She looked around.

Astride the painted horse, he looked down at her, his face gaunt, his eyes hollow. Beneath the white paint on his cheeks, his skin looked ashen.

Johnny held his hand out to her. She moved stiffly to the horse and took his hand. He swung her up behind

him, and as he turned the animal down the trail Leah
wrapped her arms around him and laid her head against
his back, the vision of his dancing before the burning
red sun still vivid in her mind.

FIFTEEN

The funeral service for Dolores was held at the reservation's Catholic church, erected a century before by Father Albert Raun, who had hoped to flush heathenism from the Apache spirit. However, the only Apache to grace the small congregation on that day was Dolores herself, closed inside her rosewood coffin that Johnny's agent had picked out at Dickenson's Funeral Home the day before.

The scattering of attendees were from the television station where she worked. Johnny suspected they were there out of duty more than real grief and respect for a colleague. Dolores had stepped on a lot of toes while establishing her name and reputation as a top-notch reporter. He suspected there were more than a few of her peers who would leave the service and celebrate with Dom Perignon.

"So where the hell is her family?" Edwin whispered as Johnny moved up the church aisle, toward the open doors where the sounds of excited reporters and fans sounded like revelers awaiting the passing of floats during Mardi Gras.

Johnny put on his dark glasses and glanced around the church. ''The Apache believe in burying their dead at night. They'll come for her later.''

''Maybe we should leave through the back entrance.''

''And make me look guiltier than I already do? I don't think so.''

The bodyguards moved in around Johnny as he stepped from the church. The sea of faces and cameras surged like an incoming tide toward the steps, shouts, and the buzz and click of cameras drowning out Edwin's comments and the orders he barked at the bodyguards as he elbowed his way through a line of police and a group of teenage girls who had managed to get beyond the barricade.

As the limo door swung open, Johnny got into the dark car and sank into the seats as the outside noise became muted by the insulated steel wrapped around him.

Ted Weir, the assistant district attorney, had remained in the limo throughout the services. Sitting next to Johnny, he gazed out at the pushing, shoving crowd and shook his head, grinning. ''Damn. Who would have thought it, huh? When the two of us played football in school I figured you'd go on to college on a football scholarship and then come back to work on the slopes if you didn't make it in the pros. Me? I figured I might make it through school by the skin of my teeth and come back to Doso and work at my old man's auto parts shop. Now here we are: you the hottest hunk in the country and me humping to bust crackheads and child molesters.''

The car eased through the crowd as Johnny continued to search the faces that peered back at him, eager for a glimpse of their idol but unable to see anything but the reflection of their own hopeful expressions.

''You know, Johnny, keeping shut mouth about this investigation is only gonna get harder. And frankly, I'm surprised that the boss is even going along with it.''

"Phil Singer is thinking about his own ass, Ted. If he comes out and informs the media that Senator Foster is being investigated for murdering Dolores and attempting to murder me, he's going to feel more heat than the O. J. Simpson jury."

"Let's face it. Not every day a state senator is accused of murder. This could be just another of your ploys to cover your butt and at the same time bring the man down for what he's done regarding the reservation's resort and casino issue."

"Dolores had proof of Foster's involvement with Formation Media. Foster found out about it and tried to have us both killed."

"Dolores *had* proof. Whatever proof she had burned up in that car wreck, Johnny. If Senator Foster was somehow involved in your accident he got exactly what he wanted. He destroyed your evidence and has made you look like a reckless crackhead."

"My blood tests will prove otherwise."

"So what? Hell, you could just as easily have been Dolores's supplier." Ted shrugged. "One very positive side note. You have no history of drug usage. Right?"

Johnny looked back out the window, at the businesses crowded with tourists, men wearing Bermuda shorts with cameras hanging from long straps around their necks and women whose faces were partially hidden under straw-brimmed hats or visors. They glanced curiously at the limo as it crept through the traffic.

"Right, Johnny?" Ted repeated.

"Right," he finally replied.

Inspector Chuck Parker had put on forty pounds since the night he'd tackled Johnny out near White Sands. Johnny had always suspected that Officer Parker had done much to dissuade the irate Texan, whose Cadillac and girlfriend Johnny had hijacked on a whim, from pressing charges of auto theft against him. Parker's hair had thinned and grayed and he'd grown a substantial mustache that exaggerated the puffiness of his cheeks. By the looks of his red eyes and flushed face, Johnny suspected high blood pressure. His weight wouldn't help matters.

Parker put a cup of hot black coffee in front of Johnny, then took a seat across the table, next to Robert Anderson, Johnny's attorney.

Johnny sipped at the steaming java, and winced. "Still tastes like old gym socks, Parker."

"I thought you'd appreciate it, Johnny. Brings back old memories, huh?"

"There were times I thought you were going to feed me this stuff intravenously."

"Anything to get your head straight." Parker sat back in his chair and laced his fat fingers over his belly. "I hoped we'd never see you back in this place."

"Thirteen years is a long time to go without getting in trouble, you gotta admit."

"This is hardly petty stuff, is it?"

"Hardly," Anderson joined in. He tapped the table with one finger as he studied Parker's face. "Are you arresting my client, Inspector? If not, why are we here?"

"Thought you'd like to know that forensics has possible proof that someone ran you off of that road, like you said. They've located gouge marks and scrapes on the driver's side of the car that would indicate a collision of some sort with another automobile. There are also dents in the back fender, as well as broken taillights. They'll take paint samples—"

"The car was black. You don't need paint samples to determine that," Johnny pointed out.

"Okay. You want to tell me again why you think Foster is behind this?"

"Who the hell else has reason to shut me and Dolores up?"

"Granted, you've been pretty vocal about your displeasure of his handling the gambling issue. But, hell,

Johnny. That's an ongoing argument that, while hot, is hardly enough to warrant murder."

"Since Foster took office he's been an opponent of reservation casino gambling in this state. He feels it gives the Native Americans too much power. God forbid the sickening unemployment on these reservations gets wiped out. God forbid families have the money to feed and clothe their children properly. Educate the Indians and they're liable to vote him out of office and shut down his aspirations of running for president."

Johnny shoved his coffee away. "A little too convenient that he suddenly does an about-face after the resort went belly up and reverted to Formation Media. Now he's supposed to invite statewide gambling because he thinks it's a *good* thing for the people?" He shook his head. "There's not much hope of the Native Americans becoming involved considering we all lost our butts on the Apache Casino and Resort."

"Lot of folks feel that gambling corrupts."

"So do poverty and ignorance and sickness."

Parker sat forward, his elbows propped on the table. He toyed with a book of matches and remained silent for a while. Finally, he said, "Let me get this straight. You think Foster took a bribe from Formation Media to stall the construction completion on the resort long enough so the resort was unable to open in time; therefore, the resort consortium was unable to make their loan payment to Formation, who then acted on the loan default and took control of the development. Somehow Dolores found the proof that she needed to link Foster to Formation; he learned about it and attempted to kill you both—or had someone do it for him."

Parker looked skeptical. "That makes no sense. With the shutdown of construction on that project, Formation has lost its ass. Why would Formation shoot itself in the foot?"

"Insurance," Anderson provided.

"Not good enough." Johnny shook his head. "Insurance wouldn't provide a profit. They would be lucky to get back what they had already spent.'' Johnny pushed back his chair and stood up. He proceeded to pace. "Formation is a giant in resort development. Eight of the last six mega-resorts have been developed and financed by Formation: Toronto, Vegas, Atlantic City. Over the last five years they've gobbled up the competition by buying out the New York–New York and the Bellagio before it even completed construction. In Atlantic City they moved in on the Trump Taj Mahal and Harrah's. There were rumors that they attempted to bully their way into Branson, but it didn't happen. They want tight control over major competition. Maybe they thought that the Apache resort would ultimately cut into the Vegas traffic. Or maybe they decided the resort was too ripe a plum not to own it one hundred percent. Either way, they got to Foster. Maybe they promised to finance his next election. Or, more important, his bid for the presidency. I know for a fact that there is only one thing Foster worships more than money, and that's power. He'd sell his soul to eternal damnation if he thought it would buy him the White House.''

"We have to find Dolores's contact," Anderson said.

"That might be tough," Parker replied. "If he suspects that the cause of the wreck was intentional . . . he's not likely to put himself in jeopardy again."

Johnny looked around, frowning. "If he's smart he's left the country. If Foster was aware that Dolores had discovered he's dirty by way of a snitch, then he must also know who the snitch is. All the more reason we sit on this information a while longer. No way we should allow the press to think this incident was anything more than an accident."

Parker drank his coffee and continued to watch Johnny. "Dolores never hinted about her contact? Never gave you any indication who was feeding her information?"

"She wanted all the glory to herself. She saw it as a

way to get her out of Ruidoso and into the big time. I also think she was protecting her source." Johnny gave Parker a thin smile. "Which makes me think her source was someone closer to her than I ever suspected. Dolores wasn't above tossing a baby to lions if she thought it would protect her own interests."

Parker took a weary breath and shook his head. "She sure got her wish, didn't she? She found a way to get the hell out of Ruidoso . . . for good."

Her eyes closed and every muscle in her body aching, Leah soaked for an hour in hot water and gardenia-scented bubbles, a sweating bottle of white Zinfandel on the floor by the tub, and Neil Diamond crooning to her from the tape deck perched on the dressing table in her bedroom.

The phone rang and Shamika ran from the kitchen to answer it, her voice drowned out by Diamond's "Brooklyn Roads."

Shamika tapped on the door.

"I'm not home," Leah replied, reaching for her glass of wine and sinking deeper into the tub. "Especially if it's Johnny. I don't want to talk to him, Shamika. I don't want to see him. Tell him to go away!"

"It's not Johnny."

Frowning, Leah downed the wine.

"It's Greg Hunnicutt from the track. Remember, he was going to call you today about the vet job—"

God, she'd totally forgotten!

With bubbles dripping off her legs, Leah wrapped a towel around her and ran from the bathroom, leaving a trail of soapy water down the hallway. Val sat in his wheelchair before the television, his face brightening with pleasure as Leah grabbed up the receiver and planted a kiss on his forehead. "This is it, puddin'," she whispered. "Wish me luck."

Taking a steadying breath, Leah raised the receiver to her ear. "Hello?"

"Doc Starr? Greg Hunnicutt here. How you doin', darlin'? Have yourself a good weekend?"

She rolled her eyes and rubbed her sore buttocks. "Great, Greg. And you?"

"Not bad, not bad. Guess you've heard of Johnny's problems. Hell, it's probably made the news in Bangladesh. Too bad about Miss Rainwater. Shit, when God decides it's time to go he don't fool around, does he?"

"Tragic," she said, her gaze falling on the television screen, where images of Dolores's crushed and burned car were followed by those of a funeral procession arriving at the Catholic church on the Mescalero reservation.

"We got a message from Johnny about an hour ago. He was the last holdout on your appointment, but he's given us the go-ahead to bring you on."

Leah sank to the sofa in relief.

"Course you know you'll need to get your state license before you can actually practice on the track. But if you want to come on out tomorrow morning first thing, I'll get you introduced to the trainers and your co-worker, Jake Graham."

She nodded. "I'll be there, Mr. Hunnicutt."

"Greg, darlin'. We don't stand on formalities here. See you at six sharp."

"Thank you."

"Hell, don't thank me yet, Leah. A month from now you might be cussin' my ass for ever gettin' you in this situation."

"I won't let you down, Greg."

He was silent for a moment, then, "I know you won't, hon. If I'd thought that I never would have pitched you to the lot of hyenas. Now get you some rest, 'cuz you're gonna need it. Bye."

Leah hung up the phone and sat back on the sofa. Val watched her with bright, sparkling eyes and a smile.

"Mama happy?"

She nodded. "Very happy."

"Mama give Val a hug?"

Grinning, she crossed to her son and lifted him out of his chair, returned to the sofa and cradled him in her lap. Stroking his hair, she focused again on the television at the reporter who stared into the camera and relayed the day's news from the prompter.

"The media turned up in full force to see Johnny Whitehorse attend the funeral of his fiancée, Dolores Rainwater. Whitehorse was surrounded by bodyguards and legal representatives as he made his way into the church, where the services were attended by Dolores's friends and co-workers here at Channel 10.

"It is our understanding that Whitehorse spent the hours after the service being questioned by investigators as to the cause of the accident and the drugs that were found in Miss Rainwater's system at the time of her death. According to the DA, Phil Singer, Whitehorse has agreed to a polygraph. The DA's office is still waiting on the outcome of the drug tests taken on Whitehorse's blood immediately after the accident.

"Law enforcement officials as well as the DA's office are keeping tight-lipped about this investigation. They are unprepared at this time to discuss any part of their interview with Whitehorse, and have announced that there will be no forthcoming information until all aspects of his interview have been investigated."

Leah watched as Johnny left the church surrounded by bodyguards. Wearing dark glasses and a black suit, he avoided looking directly at the lineup of fans, television camera crews, and the ever-present paparazzi. Reaching for the remote, Leah pointed it at the screen and hit the Power button.

Standing at the kitchen door, Shamika studied Leah as she cuddled Val close. "Dinner is about ready. You *are* going to eat, aren't you?"

"I'm really not hungry. But thanks anyway."

"Just what went on with you and Johnny, Leah? You come home this morning looking like you'd been dragged behind a rogue horse, saying nothing, spending the next hours holed up in your room crying your eyes out.''

Leah stood and swayed, Val's weight throwing her off-balance slightly as she moved toward the kitchen. ''I got the job at the track. I begin assisting Jake Graham in the morning. Isn't that great? With a decent paycheck coming in here twice a month, maybe we can eat something more substantial than macaroni and cheese four nights a week.''

''Val and I happen to like macaroni and cheese. Don't we, pal?'' Shamika pinched Val's cheek as Leah walked by.

Leah situated Val in the specially built highchair next to the table and strapped him in. ''I understand Jake is a real hunk. Thirty-eight years old. Divorced. No kids. Great sense of humor.''

Shamika picked up a plate of fried pork chops and a bowl of mashed potatoes from the stove and set them on the table between a platter of hot-water cornbread and a pitcher of tea. ''I don't care about Jake Graham. I want to know what's up with you and Johnny.''

Leah headed for the bedroom, dragging the damp towel off and tossing it in the vicinity of the bathroom door. As she dug through her lingerie drawer for her cotton pajamas, Shamika entered the room, stopping short at the sight of Leah's scraped and bruised back.

''Good God, girl, you fall off that damned horse or what?''

''Which one?'' She grinned and stepped into the pajama bottoms. ''The Whitehorse or the paint?''

''This isn't funny, Leah. Just what went on between you two?''

Jerking the cotton top out of the drawer and tugging it over her head, Leah turned on Shamika so suddenly that Shamika stepped back in surprise.

''He fucked me, girlfriend. That's it in black and white. I went to him to offer comfort and reassurance. I naïvely thought that my giving him my body would alleviate his pain over Dolores and all the hurt he experienced over my breaking his heart those many years ago. Can you believe I was so arrogant to think that such a sacrifice would appease his turmoil? Guess he showed me. I simply got a little taste of what it's like to be humiliated by the one you so desperately love."

She returned to the kitchen, dropped into a chair next to Val's and reached for a patty of hot, crisp cornbread, which she covered in butter then broke into tiny pieces and put on a plate before her son, who watched her with serious eyes.

Shamika took the chair across from her and picked up the bowl of potatoes. "So when are you seeing him again?"

"Probably never. Since he—" She glanced at Val and shrugged. "He didn't speak to me the entire journey back to his grandfather's."

"He had a lot on his mind," Shamika pointed out.

"He hasn't called."

"There was his meeting with the police and the district attorney, not to mention Dolores's funeral. The man is probably wrung out. God only knows what his lawyers and agents have been heaping on him the last several hours as well."

"He always called. Always. Just to make certain I was okay and to tell me how much he loved me."

"He's not a starry-eyed love-struck kid any longer, Leah. There's a lot to consider. Same with you." She smiled and looked at Val as she popped a piece of cornbread into his mouth. "You told him about Val yet?"

She shook her head.

"Why not?"

"No reason to. Not yet. The way things ended I'll probably never see Johnny again. Maybe that's just as well."

"Then you wouldn't have to tell him about Val's disability, hm?"

"Don't start." She stabbed a pork chop and began tearing at it with a dull knife.

"Yep. Better it end this way, Leah. Then you don't have to face the fear of him dumping you because he doesn't want the responsibility of becoming involved with a woman with a handicapped child. Of course, you could always give Sam a call. It's obvious the man adores you, and he has no problem with Val. Maybe you could learn to love him in time. I mean, if you have no intention of allowing the one you *really* love into your life because you're just too big a coward to risk his reaction, what alternative do you have other than to spend the rest of your life alone?"

Leah shoved back from the table, unbuckled Val's straps, and lifted him out of his chair. She kicked open the back screen door and left the house, entered the barn and allowed the smells of rich hay and manure to slide through her system like a sedative.

The pair of pygmy goats trotted out of a stall and let loose a noisy squalling of bleats that made Val raise his head and grin. "Val see goats?"

"Sure." She smiled and sat down in the barn aisle, resting Val on her crossed legs. The goats waddled toward them, curled tails flickering from side to side in pleasure, each shaking their little horned heads and skipping sideways in their excitement to be petted. Val squealed and squirmed, causing Leah to laugh as the black-and-white spotted billy climbed into Val's lap and proceeded to lick his cheek.

Taking Val's hand, Leah gently stroked it across the goat's back, inviting the little beast to peer at Val with a kind of adoration that caused her son to sigh in pleasure.

"Goat likes Val?"

"Of course. See? He's smiling."

The goat *baahed* and nestled closer, pawed at Val's chest and peered with its odd yellow eyes with their thin, horizontal pupils into the child's face.

"He's saying he loves you," Leah whispered and scratched the billy under his chin. "He says he's your friend."

Val laughed again as the goat tugged on his shirt, demanding more strokes. His laughter sounded sweet as birdsong, like that of any normal seven-year-old.

Hugging him close and laying her cheek against the top of his head, she said more to herself than to Val, "I got a job today that's going to pay me real money. We'll be able to buy you a bigger wheelchair, maybe a powered one that you can learn to drive yourself. But most important, we can try out the injections of Botox. Sometimes they help to supple your muscles. Then petting the old billy here wouldn't be so hard. You could even give him a hug. I'm sure he would love that . . . to feel your arms around him."

"Mama hug Val?"

She turned Val to face her and wrapped her arms around him tightly as his head rested on her shoulder. She felt his body stiffen as he tried desperately to raise his arms around her neck, knowing even as he struggled it was not going to happen.

The foal in the stall at the far end of the barn nickered and Val's smile widened. "Horse, please," he said.

Leah stood and moved to the stall where Johnny's mare and foal both whinnied in greeting. The swelling on the mare's stifle had improved tremendously. She would be sure to call Roy first thing in the morning and remind him that he could take the pair back to Whitehorse Farm, and she would suggest that he find another vet.

She simply would not have time for private practice when she began working at the track.

"Val pet?"

Leah shoved open the stall door and stepped in. Val's body strained and swayed, his flesh turning warm from his exertion as he attempted to lift his hand toward the mare.

"Val fly . . ."

Smiling, Leah moved to the mare's side. The horse turned its beautiful dished head and nuzzled Val's hand, her big brown eyes regarding him with a softness that made Leah's throat tighten.

Turning his eyes up to Leah's, Val repeated, "Val fly?"

"I don't understand," she said. "You want to pet—"

"No! Val fly!" He squirmed his body closer to the mare and his hands opened just enough to grab fistfuls of mane. "Val fly," he cried.

Leah peeled his fingers out of the horse's mane and struggled to hold him as he bucked and flailed his body against her. She stumbled from the stall as he wailed, looking around frantically as Shamika ran down the aisle.

Shamika grabbed his hands and held them firmly. "Hush. Hush now."

"Val want fly! Val want horse!"

"You are not to scream," Shamika said firmly, looking into his face. "Be nice, Val, or you'll go to your corner."

He closed his eyes tightly and wailed again, the sound intensified by the metal barn.

Shamika took him from Leah, her strong arms entrapping his. "Okay, buddy. You know the price for tantrums. Off we go." Shamika marched out of the barn as Val peered back at Leah over Shamika's shoulder, his big blue eyes brimming with tears.

By the time Leah entered the house, Shamika had situated Val in his wheelchair and sat him facing a blank wall. Shamika returned to the kitchen table and pointed to Leah's plate of cold chops and potatoes. "Sit and eat. Don't look at me like that. You cannot allow him to throw fits—"

"He's just a child—"

"Just because he's disabled doesn't mean he's allowed to act any differently than any other seven-year-old who throws temper tantrums. Let him get away with that kind of behavior and you'll soon have a problem on your hands. Try wrestling a hundred-pounder who gets pissed because he doesn't get his way.''

Leah sank into the chair, glancing again into the living room where Val sat silently, head fallen to one side as he stared at the wall. ''He must be hungry.''

''He'll eat just as soon as he's had time to think about his behavior.''

''I don't understand what set him off—''

''I'll tell you what set him off.'' Shamika spread butter on her fried cornmeal patty. ''He wants to ride.''

Leah sank back in the chair.

''Don't get that stubborn look on your face, Doc Starr. Your son wants to ride. Simple as that. He enjoys it. I don't blame him for being angry. It's the one thing he does that rewards him with a sense of freedom and accomplishment. He said it himself. To ride is to fly.''

As Shamika ate her cornbread she studied Leah's face. ''Just what are you so frightened of?''

''He's too damn vulnerable, Shamika. He can't catch a cold without suffering for it. A fall from a horse—''

''He's not going to fall.''

''You can't guarantee that.''

''You can't guarantee that he's not going to fall out of his bed or his wheelchair or choke on a noodle, for heaven's sake.'' Shamika reached for her iced tea. ''It's the guilt thing, isn't it? You still blame yourself for his condition. If you allowed him to ride and something happened you'd blame yourself—again. You think by smothering him with safety you're going to somehow make up for giving birth to him three months early. How many times do the doctors have to assure you that his condition is no fault of yours? It was the hospital staff who brought in that germ, Leah. You sued them. They admitted fault and paid you a million dollars. The annuity check you receive each month should be a reminder that you are in no way to blame for Val's brain damage.''

Shamika left her chair and rummaged through a kitchen drawer. She tossed a stack of papers and brochures on the table next to Leah's plate. ''At least read the stuff with an open mind. Come out to Rockaway and watch the children ride. The instructors and volunteers are incredible. Their highest priority is safety.'' Smiling, Shamika added, ''Do it for Val.''

Leah sat cross-legged in the middle of her bed, the stack of information on one side, her plate of food on the other. She nibbled on the pork chop and flipped through the papers until finding one titled:

ADVANTAGES OF RIDING FOR THE DISABLED

Riding, like swimming, can be done with crutches discarded. Confidence is achieved or strengthened by the discipline of learning to ride and control a horse. Particularly in the case of children with spastic muscles, riding is an extension of physiotherapy treatment. Symmetry of the body is helped by the necessity to sit evenly on the horse. Trunk rotation is facilitated.

The rhythmical motions of the horse help relax spastic muscles, and improvement in hand function is motivated by the need to acquire the skill of using the reins. The command "Look between the horse's ears" is a marvelous exercise for head control.

Riding can improve posture and trunk balance.

The smells and sights and sounds of the outdoors are made available to these children, who would find it difficult or impossible to negotiate a trail with crutches or a wheelchair. For once they are looking down on people instead of looking up. They are doing something only a few of their peers have an opportunity to do.

A warm relationship with and an appreciation of the horse help a child emotionally, and sometimes speech is stimulated by this novel experience. The contact with volunteer helpers is a further plus and also gives those who have had little to do with the handicapped an appreciation of their abilities as well as their needs.

Most of all, it is fun! We all need outdoor recreation, and riding is one of the few suitable to the disabled.

She tossed the chop onto the plate and flipped through several more brochures.

Falls are very rare, but can and do happen. . . . Do not panic if there is a fall. These children fall frequently in all types of situations. They fall on sidewalks, off swings, etc. The fall off the horse is really not any worse than any they could get at home. . . .

The job of the side walker is to maintain the balance of the rider when he cannot maintain it himself. Some students, especially in the beginning stages, have a definite balance problem off the horse as well as on. Depending on the degree of difficulty, there will be either one or two side walkers assigned to the student. The instructors will inform you as to the requirements of the particular student. For an example, some students will not have to be held all the time, but just have to have someone walking beside them for emergencies. Others will be held onto by means of the safety belt attached around their waists with a handhold at the back.

Wearily, Leah lay back on her pillows and gazed out her open window, into the dark. The night sounds were a hypnotic drone that made her lids grow heavy and her sore muscles relax. A lifetime ago she would have climbed out of her bed and roamed the barns in bare feet and pajamas, allowing the contented sighs of resting horses to fill her with a magic that inspired her to dream. The barns had been her escape even then, a place of refuge, safety, and sanity, away from the unhappiness that vibrated the air between her parents.

Leah rolled out of bed and moved down the corridor toward the back door, passing Val's room, pausing long enough to hear Shamika reading aloud and Val struggling to repeat the words after her. Occasionally Leah read to Val herself, but never with the success that Shamika had. To Val, Mama meant playtime: kisses and cuddle time, fairy tales and laughter. Shamika meant business. Concentration. Effort. By the time she finished *The Poky Little Puppy,* Val would be more than happy to shut his eyes and sleep.

Closing the screen door quietly behind her, Leah eased down the steps and headed for the barn. A single light burned at the far end, mostly for the goats' sake. They didn't care for the dark. Lying on a bale of hay, they jumped up at first sight of her and came prancing down the aisle, bleating their vociferous greetings and side-kicking in excitement. She dropped to her knees and held out her arms.

They licked her face and chattered in pleasure as she scratched between their horns, causing their upper lips to roll back in ecstasy, revealing their toothless upper gums and black-spotted pink tongues. Leah laughed and buried her face into the billy's woolly coat, laughing harder as he took a mouthful of her hair and began to chew.

Suddenly they jumped away and skittered down the aisle, bleating loudly enough to make Leah cover her ears. Then she realized: Someone was standing behind her.

SIXTEEN

"Johnny." Leah nudged aside the insistent billy and stood. "What are you doing here?"

"I came to see my girl. What do you *think* I'm doing here?"

Self-consciously, Leah glanced down at her pajamas, imprinted with tiny red prancing horses as well as goat footprints and hay.

Leaning against the open barn door, hands in his trouser pockets and his black suit coat caught behind his wrists, Johnny gave her a lazy grin. "I always imagined slipping you out of lingerie. But I had something a little more risqué in mind than PJs stenciled with little horses."

"Sorry to blow your fantasy."

"I doubt you could look any sexier if you were dressed in Frederick's of Hollywood." He eased down the aisle in that slow walk of his that had always made her feel hypnotized.

"I didn't expect to see you," she said breathlessly.

"Because I didn't call?"

"You always called."

"I had a lot to think about."

"I saw the news—about the funeral—"

"I didn't come here to discuss funerals. I've seen and heard enough about death the last few days. I came here to apologize for my behavior last night. I was angry and I took it out on you."

Johnny reached for her. She stepped away, more out of instinct than nervousness, then reminded herself that this was Johnny Whitehorse. She had nothing to fear from him. He reached again, catching her arm and tugging her close. The expensive cloth of his suit brushed her skin as softly as a breath. His cloud of black hair, spilling over his black suit and shirt, made his skin look rich as mahogany and his eyes dark as onyx. The tender yet insistent pressure of his fingers on her arm made her knees go weak, and she sank against him as if every bone and muscle in her body had become water.

"I was prepared to never see you again," she confessed, her head against his shoulder, her eyes drifting closed as he wrapped his long arms around her and gently rubbed her back. "At least I thought I was. Now that you're here I realize that I would probably have gone to you, even if you told me that you never wanted to see me again."

"You were always too stubborn for your own good, Leah." He kissed her temple and breathed in her ear.

"Wanna make love in the feed room?" she grinned.

"The next time we make love, sweetheart, it's going to be in a bed with champagne and caviar—"

"Oh, dear. I don't like caviar."

"Fine. Then champagne and Ritz crackers with Squeeze-It cheese spread."

Laughing, Leah looked up into his intense eyes. "You remembered."

"How can a guy forget something as romantic as Squeeze-It cheese spread, for God's sake? Except . . ." He ran his hand under the waistband of her pajama bottoms, over her buttock, cupping it firmly with his fingers. ''The next time we share Squeeze-It I'm gonna educate you on the finer things you can do with it. You'll never look at a can of that stuff the same way again.''

Leah laughed, lifted her arms around his neck, and went to her tiptoes to brush his lips with a kiss. Only he turned his face away slightly and eased her arms down, setting her back on her heels. His expression appeared strained, the lines around his eyes more evidence of the stress and emotional turmoil he had experienced the last few days.

''There's something wrong.'' She touched his cheek.

''Life sucks.'' He grinned wearily.

''What's the old saying? Life's a bitch and then you die. But we're together again. How can that be bad?'' Stepping away, she studied the slant of his mouth and the odd dullness of his eyes. ''Is there something you're not telling me, Johnny?''

''Nothing we need to discuss tonight.'' He turned away and walked to the barn door. Before him, in the distance, stretched Whitehorse Farm. The distant lights of the house twinkled like golden stars against the black night. ''Funny how things change with time,'' he mused thoughtfully. ''Once I stood in this same place and looked out at your house, wishing I could hold you. Now here we are. I'm here and you're here and . . . I'm too damn afraid to hold you.''

Partially turning, he looked back at her, and his eyes were sharp, his lips curled in something less than a smile. ''I'm going in the house now to meet your son.''

She felt the blood drain from her face, and her mouth went dry. Johnny walked from the barn, leaving Leah standing in the glare of the barn's yellow bug lights, the goats tugging at her pajama legs, her heart pounding in her throat like a jackhammer. The overwhelming urge to run after him, to postpone the inevitable, made tears sting her eyes—not from nervousness, but from shame. She felt sickened by the very thought that she was embarrassed for him to know that her son was less than perfect.

The screen door slammed. Shamika's voice wormed its way through Leah's haze, then Johnny's, deeper, words that distance turned into a drone of indistinct syllables, then silence.

At last, she followed, goats at her heels, her body shaking as she mounted the steps and reached for the door.

Shamika opened it for her and smiled into her eyes. "I'm getting everyone ice cream. Want some?"

The goats darted past Leah, into the house. She watched them trot through the kitchen and down the hallway straight to Val's room. "No." She shook her head.

Shamika walked to the refrigerator, opened the freezer and dug through the frozen dinners and ice trays before extracting the half-gallon tub of Cookies and Cream. She laid out two bowls and proceeded to fill them. "You look like someone just cracked you over the head with a tire rod, Leah. Relax. They're going to hit if off just fine."

"But he doesn't know."

Shamika glanced at her with a smugness that made Leah frown. "Of course he knows, Leah. He's known all along."

Leah slowly blinked and shook her head. "What are you saying? That's impossible. I never—"

"He called here one day last week to speak to you. You were out at the barn or something. We talked."

"You told him?" Her voice quivered.

"Nope." She licked her fingers and replaced the lid on the tub. "Your mother told him. Seems they kept in touch right up until she died." Shamika returned the ice cream to the freezer, picked up a bowl and extended it to Leah. "He knew everything, Leah. About your marriage, the birth of your son, your divorce. He also understands your fear."

"He never said . . ."

"He wanted you to tell him."

Her hands shook as she took the bowl and moved to Val's room, pausing at the door to watch Johnny sit in the rocking chair next to the window, her son in his lap. Val's face beamed with pleasure, and it occurred to Leah in that instant that the precious child whose face was rosy with excitement probably could not remember the last time a man had held him.

Johnny looked up. Whatever intensity had hardened his eyes earlier was gone, replaced with a twinkling mischievousness that made him appear childlike himself. "Look who's here, Val. Mom. Wearing pajamas with horses on them. She's brought me some ice cream."

Val's smile widened and he rolled his head to look up at Johnny. "Val's ice cream," he said.

Frowning, Johnny shook his head. "No. My ice cream, pal. Cookies and Cream happens to be my favorite."

"Val's ice cream, pal." Val laughed as Johnny gave him an exasperated expression. "Val share?"

"I'm not sure we'll have anything to share if your mom doesn't stop standing there staring at us."

Johnny and Val looked at her expectantly, and Leah moved into the room that seemed in that moment to be surreal—the dim light playing on the posters of Rudolph Valentino on the wall, the goats curled up and comfortable on the end of Val's bed, Johnny Whitehorse and her son wrapped up together in her grandmother's old chair before an open window where night wind billowed *Sesame Street* curtains.

Handing over the bowl, her gaze locked on Johnny's, Leah gave him a trembling smile. "I think I'm going to cry."

"Don't cry," he replied softly. "Just get yourself a bowl of ice cream and join us."

"Coming right up," Shamika said from the door. She entered the room with two bowls and handed one to

Leah. "As for me, I'm off to bed. Keep the party noise down and remember that Val has school tomorrow and Leah starts her new job."

Leah sat on the bed, rested the bowl on her lap, and watched Johnny spoon ice cream into her grinning son's mouth; then *he* took a bite, making Val's smile grow even broader. Emotion swelled in her chest. It buzzed in her head and burned like nettles behind her eyes. At last, the two people she loved most in the world were together in one room, some palpable connection vibrating the air between them so strongly it turned the space around them a soft glowing white.

Ice cream finished, Johnny set the bowl aside and left the chair, easily handling Val's weight as he carried the boy to the bed and tucked him under the covers, poked a Big Bird doll in beside him and kissed him on the cheek.

"Johnny stay?" Val asked, the hope in his voice undeniable.

"No."

"Johnny come back, see Val?"

"Yes."

"When."

"Soon."

"When."

"Tomorrow."

Val grinned. "Not soon enough."

Johnny laughed and tousled Val's brown hair. "You sound like your mother. I'll call you."

"Promise."

"I promise, Val. Now go to sleep. You have school tomorrow."

Still smiling, Val closed his eyes, pretending sleep, but peering at Johnny and Leah as Johnny turned away from the bed and took the bowl from Leah's hand, directing her toward the bedroom door and out into the hall.

"He's fibbing, you know. He isn't asleep." Leah said.

"I know."

He escorted her to her own bedroom, over to her bed.

"Does this mean I'm about to get lucky?" she asked, dropping down onto the edge of the mattress as Johnny pulled a chair over in front of her and sat down. The ice cream had mostly melted. He stirred it around until the chocolate chunks began to dissolve into rivulets of rich brown streaks, then he raised a spoonful of it to her mouth. "Eat," he ordered her. "And while you do I'm going to say something.

"I like your son. He looks like you. I'm sorry about his situation, but it doesn't mean I think less of either of you, or pity you, or am turned off by the idea of having a relationship with you—either of you. We're all handicapped in a way. I'm an Indian. I know what prejudice and ostracism is. I know what it feels like to not fit in. You, on the other hand, are handicapped by your fear of rejection because of Val's problems. Did you honestly think I could love you less because of Val?"

"What's a woman supposed to think when even Val's own father couldn't cope—"

"The man's an immature ass, and if you're judging all men beside him then you do us one hell of an injustice—especially me, considering our past together. Richard Starr should be castrated, or at the least given a good punch in the nose. When is the last time he saw Val?"

"Two-and-a-half years ago."

"Does he send you child support?"

"No."

"Want me to find him and break his legs?" He grinned.

"I don't think so." She grinned back.

Johnny put the bowl aside and took Leah's face between his hands. "I wish he were mine," he told her softly, and lightly kissed her mouth, making her quiver with feelings that scattered through her like dandelion fluff in a wind: weightless, spiraling, dancing to all corners of the universe.

Then he pulled away, left the chair and moved toward the door. "Will you stay?" she called out a little desperately.

"I can't, Leah. I have something to do."

Leah followed him to the front door, moving onto the porch as he jumped off the steps and headed for his truck. "What could be so important this late at night?"

"I have to see Dolores's family. They're holding her burial ceremony tonight."

"Can I come?" she asked, stopping him in his tracks. Obscured by the dark, Johnny looked around.

"You would do that?"

"I can be ready in five minutes."

"Yes, then." His voice sounded weary but relieved. "I'd like that, Leah."

A bonfire roared on the front lawn of Dolores's mother's four-room frame house. A scattering of relatives sat cross-legged around the fire, faces somber as they spoke together softly. Dolores's mother, Bernice, sat alone by a pile of Dolores's neatly folded clothes, which would be burned soon after Dolores was buried. At her back was her daughter's open coffin—a simple pine box, not the expensive mahogany casket lined with pale blue silk that Johnny had purchased—containing Dolores's body now completely wrapped in bright blankets.

Upon leaving the truck, Johnny removed his suit coat and tossed it into the backseat. He loosened his tie, flipped open the top button of his black shirt, and rolled the sleeves up his forearms. He glanced at Leah, where she stood in the dark. "You can stay in the truck if you want," he told her.

"I'm here for support, remember?" She tried to smile. "The Rock of Gibraltar can hardly do its job if it's cowering in the background, can it?"

"This could get ugly. The family never approved of me much, especially after I moved off the reservation. They saw me as a bad example and believed I influenced

Dolores to turn her back on her people and pursue life
in the white man's world."

"Then maybe you shouldn't."

"I have a responsibility." Johnny moved toward the
light. Leah fell in beside him.

Silence fell over the group as Johnny moved into the
firelight. Leah dropped back as he approached Bernice
Rainwater, his head slightly bowed, his eyes averted.
Bernice stood.

Stopping before her, his eyes still not meeting hers,
he spoke softly in Apache. "I've come here to offer you
my condolences. My sorrow is deep for the loss of your
daughter. I cared for her very much."

Bernice drew back her hand, then slapped his cheek
hard enough to rock him back. Then she slapped the
other, and spat on his chest. "You have murdered my
girl, Whitehorse, and brought the ruin of this family.
How am I to live now that she is gone and can no longer
give me money?"

"I'm obligated to provide for you," he replied in a
sharp tone, his eyes still not meeting hers. Bernice was
an elder, after all, and to look at her directly, considering
he was involved in Dolores's death, would have been a
greater insult than slapping her.

"This family deserves more from Johnny than
money," came an angry voice. Johnny looked around as
Billy Rainwater, Dolores's brother, stepped between
Johnny and Bernice. The younger man had painted his
face for war, and he held a knife in each hand. "I demand retribution," Billy slurred through his teeth, his
breath smelling heavily of whiskey. "As Dolores's
brother it's my right to fight you."

"I won't fight you, Billy. The old laws no longer
apply—"

"Then you're no Apache." He kicked dirt over
Johnny's shoes and sneered. "But you've not been
Apache in a very long time."

"Your interest in your sister comes too late for me to

take you seriously,'' Johnny replied. ''As does your apparent grief. I find it ironic that you and your mother wouldn't see her or speak to her for the last several years because you didn't approve of her lifestyle, yet you happily took her money when she offered it.''

''It was the least she could do for breaking my mother's heart.''

''Would you have her remain here and languish in this poverty?''

''She was an Apache.''

''Apache was something to be proud of, once, when this land was ours and our homes were wherever our hearts led us—when we were warriors to be respected and feared. Do you take pride in this?'' He pointed to the line of shabby, cookie-cutter houses built fifty years ago, with yards cluttered with rusting automobiles that lay shadowed in the dark like the bones of long-dead buffalo.

''You drink yourself to oblivion every night and are too damned hung over in the morning to work. Dolores gave you money to go to college, and what did you do with it? Spent it on whores and Chivas. You could have gone to medical school like you once wanted, but you allowed the old ones to convince you to stay for the sake of keeping the tradition and culture alive. How can you keep a culture alive when it's squirming in malaise and Jack Daniel's? For that matter, who the hell wants to keep such a culture alive? Where is the pride and dignity in dying before you're forty of cirrhosis of the liver— or suicide? Do you really think the world out there is going to listen to an uneducated drunk when he stands up to decry this reservation's situation? They won't respect you, Billy. They'll pity you. Since when did the Apache crave the pity instead of the respect of a white man?''

Billy swung at Johnny; Johnny jumped back as the knife blade sliced within inches of his face.

''Stop this!'' A tall, slim-hipped woman in faded

jeans and a plaid cowboy shirt tied at her midriff planted
her hands against Billy's chest and shoved him back. He
tripped and fell, sprawling heavily into the dirt at his
mother's feet.

"Idiot," she hissed, and kicked his leg. "What do
you think you're doing? You shame me for your stupidity, not to mention your drunkenness. If you truly cared
about showing respect for our sister, you would have
laid off the Jack Daniel's tonight."

The woman turned on Johnny, her dark eyes snapping
with emotion, her waist-length black hair swirling
around her shoulders. "As for *you* . . ." She glanced
past Johnny to Leah, who remained nervously in the
distance. "What the hell are you doing bringing *her*
here?"

His eyes narrowing, Johnny looked her up and down.
"Savanah?"

"What's wrong, Whitehorse? You look like you've
just seen a mountain spirit up close and personal." She
propped her fists on her hips. "Long time no see, you
arrogant son-of-a-bitch. So much for dropping me a
postcard from the Big Apple."

He opened and closed his mouth, refusing to believe
that the shapely, beautiful young woman before him was
Savanah Rainwater, Dolores's sister. "The last time I
saw you you were thirty pounds overweight, four inches
shorter, and were fighting a bad case of puberty acne."

"That was ten years ago. I've grown up. And you
haven't answered my question. What is Leah doing
here?"

"She was a friend of Dolores's—"

"Don't bullshit me, Whitehorse. Dolores hated Leah
Foster with an Apache passion. And to top that off,
you've been plastered all over the news trying to castrate
her father. Don't tell me you and the senator are in bed
together now."

"Hardly." He grabbed her arm and pulled her to one
side, ignoring Billy's rambling. He glanced again at

2226   *Katherine Sutcliffe*

Leah, doing his best to reassure her with a smile as she stared at him and frowned.

"So it's true." Savanah yanked her arm away. "Dolores was right. You're back together with Leah. You dumped my sister—"

"I didn't dump your sister, Vanah. The fact is I had no intention of it—at least not at the time. Leah and I have just . . . after Dolores died—"

"She moved in on you like a copperhead on a lazy field mouse." She shook her head. "Dee was always afraid this would happen. She knew you had never gotten over Leah. She told me just a few days ago that she suspected something was going on between you."

"I wasn't aware you two were even in contact. Where the hell have you been the last few years?"

"Here and there. I came home when I heard about the accident."

"From . . . ?"

Savanah crossed her arms and again looked past Johnny. He turned as Leah moved up beside him, her gaze locked on Dolores's sister.

"Savanah?" Leah smiled and extended her hand. "My gosh, I hardly recognize you. It's wonderful to see you again."

Savanah stared, ignoring her hand.

"I'm sorry about Dolores." Leah lowered her arm.

"I'll bet. Just like you were sorry when you stole Johnny away from Dee in high school."

Leah set her jaw and raised one eyebrow. "I see you're still cursed with an attitude. I thought you might have mellowed over the years."

"And I didn't come here to see two women get in a goddamn catfight," Johnny interrupted, grabbing them each by an arm and hauling them toward his truck. "In the last five minutes I've had my face slapped twice, been spat upon, and had my nose nearly cut off by a drunken Indian. My temper is slightly on edge so I suggest the two of you draw back your claws and shut up."

Reaching the back of the truck, he lowered the tailgate and set Leah and Savanah on it side by side. Then he paced, dragging one hand through his hair. "We're all here for the same reason, for God's sake. Dolores is dead." Pointing one finger at Savanah, he added, "And don't sit there and pretend you and she were tight again. Dolores herself told me you haven't spoken in years. She didn't even know where the hell you were. The last time the two of you were in the same room you about clawed each other's eyes out, according to Dolores."

Savanah looked off into the dark.

Leah took a weary breath and released it. "I knew I shouldn't have come. I start a job at six in the morning and it's nearly midnight now. I've only provoked more anger—"

"It's not your fault," Savanah said more softly, yet still refusing to look at Leah or Johnny. "Dolores never stood a chance in hell of landing Johnny Whitehorse. No one did except you. She knew it. She accepted it, I think. With Dee it was more of the chase, trying to prove herself by outdoing someone else. By being the best, not just in everyone else's eyes, but in her own. She simply couldn't get beyond the fact that she was an Indian. She never felt . . . equal. It made her take stupid risks . . ."

She turned her big eyes up to Johnny's. "Whatever caused that accident . . . I'm sure it had nothing to do with your carelessness. Or because you were drinking or taking drugs. My God, you're the finest role model we've ever hoped to have, Johnny. Since you've become a household name people have actually appraised us as a people with potential. The problem is, they're now asking, if you can do it, get educated and successful, why can't they all? Your achievements only make the rest of these people look like sluggards and exaggerates their own sense of failure."

Laughing, she shook her head and thumbed over her shoulder. "Take Billy for instance. He would never admit that he envies you. With his looks and his smarts he could have become a fine doctor. But he allowed my mother's cloying demands that he remain here and take care of her after our father died to drain him of his dreams and aspirations. He hates you now because you're a reminder of what he could have been.''

"It's not too late," Leah said. "It's never too late to change your life for the better. He could still go to school.''

"He's a borderline alcoholic. He'll end up dying just like our father, his insides rotted by whiskey and his mind eaten away by ignorance.'' She looked at Johnny. "We need to talk. *Privately*,'' she stressed, sliding off the tailgate. "I'm leaving tomorrow night. Will you call me in the morning?''

Johnny nodded and Savanah walked away.

SEVENTEEN

Jake Graham didn't bother to look up as Leah stepped into his neat, sterile-smelling office with charts of horse anatomies on the walls, framed degrees from universities and veterinary schools, his state license to practice medicine on the track, and photographs of horses streaking across finish lines. With a stethoscope hanging around his neck and his long brown hair falling in a wave over his brow, he was focused on a clipboard of papers, scratching notes on one before flipping through others and writing something else.

"You're late, Doctor." He turned to a metal filing cabinet and yanked open the drawer. "Rounds start at six sharp. It's now six thirty-five. Your tardiness has put us half an hour behind schedule."

Leah opened her mouth to apologize—

He slammed the drawer shut and turned on her, jaw unshaven that morning, eyes as clear blue as a mountain spring, and just as icy. She'd heard he wasn't bad to look at—true, in a rugged sort of way, if one liked the Foreign Legion mercenary sort who appeared as if he would rather run you through with a bayonet than say good morning. Whatever qualities might have made him appealing were canceled out by the intimidation of his scowl and the downward slant of his mouth.

Graham shoved the clipboard at her as he walked around her toward the door. ''I just got a call from Lorian Farm. Their stakes winner, Cool Me Down, has a gut problem. Get your ass in gear and follow me.''

Her face beginning to burn, Leah glanced toward the coffee maker on a table near a water cooler that sported a label from a distillery just outside of town. Graham had every right to be angry, she reminded herself. She'd fallen back to sleep when her alarm went off. If it hadn't been for Shamika dragging her out of bed, she would no doubt still be sleeping or thinking of Johnny and the ridiculous fear she'd experienced over his reaction to Val. She'd spent the better part of the night tossing and turning, not out of worry but over the memory of watching Johnny hold her son, and hearing his words, ''I wish he were mine.''

She hadn't bothered with coffee after her shower to revive her, and without coffee her mind would continue to feel like cotton for another two hours.

''Starr!'' Jake shouted, causing her to jump and turn away from the coffeepot, toss her purse into a corner, and hurry out the door, into the bracing morning that was barely an hour old.

Business was bustling throughout the facility's vast barns. Electric horse walkers hummed as they went round and round with horses walking or jogging on the end of ropes. The high-spirited, muscular animals wore leg wraps around their cannon bones, their glossy bodies sending steam into the cool air. In the distance animals sprinted around the track with jockeys checking them back or driving them on, trainers standing on the sidelines with stopwatches in hand shaking their heads, cursing and shouting directives to the slender young men riding the horses.

Leah ran to catch up with Jake Graham, whose long

legs made quick time of crossing one barn lot after another. She did her best to read the material Graham had
shoved into her hands—not easy considering she was
forced to jog just to keep up with Graham.

"Clinical Diagnosis," she read aloud. "Gastric ul-
ceration hyperkeratosis. The horse is suffering from
stomach ulcers."

"The gastric mucosa looks as if it's been sprayed with
buckshot. You'll see the endoscopic evaluation there in
the file. He's been on twenty-four hundred milligrams
of Ranitidine tablets two times a day for the last week.
He gets nothing more to eat than alfalfa and timothy hay
four times a day. Until this morning the abdominal discomfort had abated. We were due to rescope tomorrow."

"Signs of discomfort this morning?"

"Pawing, lying out flat, looking at his side, camping
in back."

"Colic."

"Maybe."

By the time they reached barn six, Leah was struggling to breathe. She paused at the door long enough to
take a much-needed breath as Graham moved down the
barn aisle, glancing back at her with a smugness on his
face that made her want to take his stethoscope and pal-
pate him with it.

Finally she followed, catching up with him just as he
reached the string of stalls belonging to Lorian Farm. A
tall, lanky man with faded orange hair that had thinned
to a half-dozen strands wrapped over his bald head stood
by a sleek black thoroughbred stallion with drawn-in
flanks and heaving sides, its head down with nostrils
wide and muzzle pinched.

His step slowing, Jake looked down at Leah and said
quietly but firmly, "Watch. Listen. Do what I tell you
to do and nothing more. Don't give Lorian an opinion.
Don't even open your mouth. You have no license yet
to practice here. If you were to diagnose wrong, that

son-of-a-bitch could sue us and the state could close us down quicker than you could wiggle that cute little ass. Understand me?''

She nodded, understanding thoroughly.

Leah stood back, remaining silent as Graham checked the animal's vital signs: respiration, heart rate, gut sounds, the color of its gums, its temperature. He checked the stall: kicked around the shavings, toed a pile of dung, then glanced into the water bucket, hay and feed bin, then told Lorian to move the horse to the clinic to be palpated.

Lorian shook his head. ''I'm gonna have to hock my truck to pay this bill, Jake. Shit, man, that Ranitidine alone is costing me two hundred bucks a week. Hell, I could go down to Wal-Mart and buy up a buncha Tums to give this bag of bones.''

Jake turned on Lorian so fast that Lorian nearly tripped on himself. ''Fine, Lorian, you do that. Go buy you some Tums, and while you're at it a plot to bury the goddamn horse in because that's what's going to happen if you don't start following my directions in the care of this animal. Is that it? You trying to kill the horse? You got plenty of insurance on him or what?''

Lorian's face went beet red. ''What the hell are you accusing me of, Graham?''

''I told you not to be giving that horse grain for a week. There's molasses on his breath and oats in his droppings. You've been graining him, you stupid bastard.''

''He was losing weight. I can't run no damn horse if he's fifty pounds underweight. He won't make it around the goddamn track.''

''He sure as hell isn't going to make it if he's dead, is he?'' Jake shouted back, then turned on his heels and stormed from the barn, leaving Leah to take the lead rope from Lorian. He glared at her with sweat running down his temples.

"Who the hell are you?" he said through his tobacco-stained teeth.

"I'll be assisting Doctor Graham for a while. I'm Doctor Starr." She extended her hand and tried to give him a steady smile. "I'm sure your horse will be fine, Mr. Lorian."

"I don't give a shit, lady. He ain't won a goddamn dollar since last year and if you ask me I'd just as soon put the sombitch down. Je—sus. Get the nag outta here, why don't ya?"

Lorian walked off, shouting orders to a pair of Hispanic grooms, who scuttled like crabs out of his way. Leah ran her hand along the horse's withers and down its massive shoulder bone, smiling as Cool Me Down raised his head and turned his big dark eyes, reflecting intense pain, on hers. "No wonder you have ulcers," she said, then headed back to the clinic.

"There is a swelling on the left that might be a gas pocket, but I don't think so." Leah leaned further into the horse, her eyes closed as she visualized the interior walls of the colon and the location of the spleen and kidneys. The pressure and heat around her arm, all the way to her shoulder, felt uncomfortable if not outright crushing. "The gastric ulcerations are probably contributing to his discomfort, but in my opinion I think we're dealing with a nephrosplenic entrapment. The large colon has somehow gotten tossed over the ligament, probably while he was rolling." Leah gently withdrew her arm from the stallion's rectum, peeled the examination sleeve off and tossed it in the trash. Turning to Graham, she said, "You can run another CBC fibrinogen and PCV for total protein but I suspect they're not going to tell you anything you don't already know. He's anemic and dehydrated, which means this has been going on a while. I suggest a good shot of calcium and a thirty-minute turn out on the walker at a trot. The calcium will shrink the colon and the exercise will allow it to shift back into place.''

''Unless the entrapped area is distended by the god-damn grain Lorian has been feeding him.''

''Then you sedate the horse and manipulate the colon rectally.''

Jake reached into his medicine cabinet for a vial of clear liquid and a syringe, then proceeded to ease the needle into the horse's vein, first drawing back blood to check his efficiency. Tossing the syringe into a canister labeled Hazardous Waste, he glanced at Leah.

''You may as well know I think your working here is a bad idea.''

''I don't have to be psychic to figure that out.''

''It's no reflection on your abilities as a fine veterinarian. I've asked around about you. You've got a decent rep. But it's a tough job. You deal with a lot of assholes that could make Hitler cry. Aside from that, there's no place here for feminine emotionalism.''

She gave him a flat smile. ''Is that another term for PMS, Doctor Graham?''

''Not at all, Doctor Starr.'' Jake poured himself a cup of coffee and reached for a stack of files. ''We're asked to make some tough decisions, not just occasionally, but every day we come to work. And you'd better believe there is going to be somebody in your face at all times. Take Lorian. He trains his own horses, races them, lives in the feed room because he doesn't have the money for rent. He's got half a dozen kids off in Oklahoma or Arkansas that may or may not all be his—he doesn't really care, just as long as there's a wife to give him some sense of purpose. Cool Me Down was a stakes winner last year. Lorian's first to win a major purse. The horse showed every promise of becoming a superstar, blew the hell out of the record books in the following several races. Then it was over. He quit running.''

''There has to be a reason.''

''Aside from the gastric ulcerations, we've found no

evidence of anything else. He's just shut down."

Leah moved to the horse's head and allowed him to nuzzle her hand. "Maybe it's time to turn him out to pasture and let him be a horse for a while."

"Try telling that to Randy Lorian. Go on. I dare you. That bastard would rather bury the animal than allow it the pleasure of running free in green pastures. After all, what good is having a horse that can't pay for itself."

As Leah frowned, Jake laughed and shook his head. "Get used to it. This isn't the world of women infatuated with pet horses or some good old boy named Bubba who likes to rope off his favorite quarter on the weekends. Those animals could hop around on three legs and as long as they eat carrots and apples and molasses cookies out of hand and halfway tolerate their owners they'll live out their lives in comfort until they die of old age.

"Not here. Not these machines. If they don't pay for themselves, they're useless. The owners can sell them to Alpo for ninety cents a pound and get a small return on their investment. Or if the horse is lucky he gets put in an auction and maybe someone other than Alpo will find him interesting enough to take a chance on him. That is if he's not already lame or his brains aren't fried by steroids and stress."

Jake shouted to an assistant to put Cool Me Down on the walker for fifteen minutes. "Coming?" he asked Leah, then walked out the door.

With the radio on low and the deejay suggesting that thanks to El Niño the area was in for the hottest summer on record, Johnny pulled the dually up to the curb outside Bernice Rainwater's house and, reaching across the passenger seat, shoved open the door, allowing the June heat to wash through the cab in a simmering wave. He glanced up at the temp gauge on the rearview mirror, not surprised to see it registering ninety-two degrees—damn hot for so early in the season. He made a mental note to run the truck by the auto shop to make certain there was plenty of coolant in the engine, and also to check out the air-conditioning system at Leah's house. He knew from experience that the small house baked like an oven in this sort of heat.

Savanah Rainwater, shielding her eyes from the sun, looked up and down the quiet narrow street before slinging her suitcase into the truck bed, then more gently laying the collection of cameras she had hanging from each shoulder onto the backseat. She climbed up into the truck and slammed and locked the door before reaching for the seatbelt.

In the light of day there was something about her appearance that affected Johnny. Not in the way she was dressed, certainly, in faded jeans and a turquoise cotton blouse, but in her energy and will that seemed to both absorb and reflect the light around her. Her skin was dusky with the slightest hint of copper and her huge, almond-shaped eyes were the darkest plum purple, which she accentuated with the merest touch of purple shadow on her lids. Her hair had been feathered around her face, the cut drawing the observer's eye to the high cheekbones and a nose so perfectly formed that, had he not known her better, might have been the result of a very fine plastic surgeon.

"I could have rented a car," she told him, grinning. "Driving me to Albuquerque seems excessive, even if we are old friends."

He shrugged and turned off the radio. "You said we needed to talk. So I'm here to talk."

"Good ol' Johnny on the spot. Mr. Reliable." She laughed and adjusted her seat back, stretched out her long, denim-clad legs and released a weary sigh. "I should never have come home. It was a mistake. Seeing Billy and Mother accomplished nothing more than making me feel guilty again for walking away, especially now that Dee is gone."

They drove for a while without talking, until Ruidoso was behind them and the highway stretched like a silver ribbon before them, waves of heat rising from the asphalt, making the oncoming cars resemble mirages. Johnny glanced at Savanah occasionally, thinking to himself that if he had bumped into her on the street he would not have known her. The ugly ducking had certainly turned into a swan, yet there was still that edge of tomboyishness that made him think that she could hold her own against any man who thought he could best her physically in a wrestling match—not to mention romance. This one would not fall in love easily. There was a chip on her shoulder the size of the Sierra Blanca, and he wondered to himself what sort of relationship she had experienced that had stamped wariness and distrust so indelibly over her features.

"Ever thought of modeling?" he asked, drawing her attention from the scenery back to him.

She shook her head. "Been there and done that. Unlike Dolores, I prefer to be in back of the camera, thank you."

"You're into photography, I take it."

"Dabble in it a bit." She grinned. "Next time you want a partially nude shot of you taken on Fifth Avenue, give me a call. I do my best work photographing wild animals."

"Does it pay the bills?"

"Hardly, I work at a casino outside of Toronto. I'm a dealer sometimes. A waitress sometimes. And occasionally I'm one of those annoying photographers who skulk about dark romantic corners of the hotel and snap cozy couples in the throes of hormonal upheavals. The old geezers with young girls are the best. It's fun watching them squirm when they think the wives back home might somehow get their hands on the pictures."

Johnny laughed. "So, you're into blackmail."

Savanah wiggled her eyebrows. "The philandering old coots pay handsomely for any snapshot that could be used as evidence against them."

"You and Dolores have more in common than you think."

"*Had.*" She looked out the window. "So tell me. You and Leah getting married? Or is that a stupid question?"

"I haven't thought that far ahead."

"What about her father? If you go fooling around with Daddy's little girl he's liable to get angry. He's a lot more powerful now than he was when you were eighteen. Not to mention corrupt." Shifting in the seat, Savanah looked at Johnny directly. "I mean it, Whitehorse. Senator Foster isn't someone to take lightly. He isn't going to stand still for long while you brutalize his reputation. And now Leah's back in the picture. What, exactly, will that do to your fight with him regarding the Formation issue?"

"I won't back down, Vanah."

"Then I assume you'll be forced to make a choice. The love of your life, or your people. The question is, who needs you more? Just how much is Johnny Whitehorse willing to sacrifice?"

"I won't back down," he repeated more firmly. "I'm too damn close, Savanah. I had proof in my hand until . . ."

"Until the accident?" Savanah's voice quivered a little, yet she did not take her gaze from Johnny. "What happened the night Dolores was killed? Don't tell me you were reckless. You're not a reckless man. What sent you off that highway, Johnny? What really caused Dolores's death?"

Johnny rode in silence as Savanah watched him, her expression expectant and worried. "She had dirt on Foster," he admitted. "Proof that there was more behind his involvement in closing down the Apache gambling resort than just his great crusade to stop gambling corruption on the reservation and save the Indian from himself. That night after leaving the restaurant, we were forced off the road by another car. Whatever proof she had about the senator burned up in the crash." He said more to himself than to Savanah, "I suspected she was getting pretty damn close to discovering something. She hinted occasionally that after she broke the story there wouldn't be a network in this country that wouldn't beg her to work for them."

"She told you nothing?"

Johnny shook his head. "No way. She wasn't about to risk the information leaking out before she could break it herself. Whatever evidence she got the night of the accident would have, in her own words, blown the lid off the gambling industry as well as Washington."

Savanah sank back in the seat and closed her eyes. "I was afraid it was something like that. Damn, oh damn." She began to cry.

Johnny hit the brakes and eased the truck onto the shoulder of the highway, then shoved the gearshift into neutral before turning to Savanah and taking her face in one hand. "You didn't come back to Ruidoso just to pay your condolences to Dolores, did you, Savanah? Let's face it. You and she weren't exactly friendly the last few years."

Savanah shook her head, crying harder. "I had to know. I didn't want to think that I . . ." She tried to pull away. "I have to get out of here. I can't breathe."

Shoving open the truck door, Savanah jumped out, stumbling down the shoulder as Johnny killed the engine and left the truck. He slid partially down the grassy slope before finding his footing and catching up to her. Grabbing her arm, he spun her around, caught her with both hands and held her in place as tears streamed from her eyes.

"It's all my fault," she cried, refusing to look at him. "What the hell was I thinking, Johnny? I should have realized. They somehow found out . . ."

"What are you saying, Savanah?" He shook her gently, insisting that she regain composure. "Look at me, sweetheart."

At last she raised her dark eyes up to his. "This is all my fault. I shouldn't have listened to her. I only wanted to help you. To help the resort and put the people back to work. Had I for one minute realized she was doing all this for the sake of her career—"

"What the hell are you saying?" Johnny demanded, holding her tighter as her body began to shake uncontrollably.

"Oh, God, Johnny." She sank into his arms. "I think I killed my sister."

EIGHTEEN

The wading pool had been filled with fresh water, and by the looks of the muddy sand around the base of the blue-and-green molded plastic there had been a great deal of recent activity. There were several yellow rubber ducks gliding on the water's surface, scooted along by the occasional gust of hot wind whipping down the mountains.

Throughout the hours of boiling sun, swarming flies, colicky horses, and trainers who questioned and cursed Jake over every decision he made, Leah had found her mind drifting to days long past when she and Johnny would sneak away into the mountains to swim in the cold water of crystal-clear streams, then lie like basking seals on massive boulders, naked, counting hawks and eagles that soared high overhead. Back then their only worry in life had been over their being discovered together. Not that she really cared, much. But Johnny did, not for himself, but for his father.

With the windows rolled down on the truck and sweat inching down her sides under her manure- and blood-stained clothes, Leah stared vacantly through the bug-spotted windshield at the ducks that, scooted by the wind, bumped and nudged one another, and she thought how nice it would be to take Val to those streams, to see the pleasure on his face as the brisk water rushed around his tight legs, and trout, easily seen through the clear-as-glass water, swam round and round his ankles before nibbling at his toes. But those places were for children who could walk, who could pull themselves up over ledges that were little more than footholds for birds.

As the engine shuddered and died, she blinked salty sweat from her eyes and glanced down at the clock.

"Seven-thirty," she read aloud, then tapped the plastic over the clock face, certain there must be some mistake. For the last week she had not left the track before ten at the earliest. Yet the sun just creeping behind the western horizon was proof enough that she was, indeed, home. It was daylight, for a while anyway. She would get to see her son awake for a change. Perhaps he could even entice her to run down to the local Dairy Duchess for a hot-fudge sundae, his favorite, topped with two fat cherries.

She stepped from the truck to be greeted by the pygmy goats, grabbing her jeans and tugging for attention. She scratched them between the horns and allowed them to give her a wet kiss on the cheek before heading for the kitchen screen door. Only then did she discover the collection of cars and trucks parked on the north side of the barn, out of the sun—one of them Johnny's truck, she noted with a flutter of excitement in her stomach.

A Weber barbecue grill sat beside the steps, coals glowing hot and the smell of cooking grease making her stomach growl. When had she last eaten anything that had not come out of a vending machine in the jockeys' lounge?

A shout of masculine voices erupted through the door, stopping Leah short. There were whoops followed by, "Kick his ass! Oh, man, that kinda play should be il-

legal. You guys get ready to pay up. Yo' money is his—
tory!''

''Damn game isn't over till the fat lady sings, you
baldheaded bastard. Gonzales is gonna knock that ball
into the next county.''

Leah eased open the screen door.

The kitchen table was crowded with platters of crispy
hamburger patties, blackened wieners, bowls of chips
and tubs of dips. A washtub full of ice and stuffed with
beer, wine coolers, and a sweating bottle of Chardonnay
sat on the floor near a pile of wet towels and muddy
rubber flip-flops.

Shirtless and barefoot, Johnny walked into the
kitchen, a ketchup-stained dish towel thrown over his
shoulder, a hot dog oozing mustard and relish in one
hand. His eyes widened when he saw her, and he gave
her a lazy smile.

''Wanna a beer? Never mind. You like strawberry
wine coolers, as I recall.'' He reached into the tub and
withdrew an icy cooler, tossed it to her, then grabbed
up a Budweiser and pointed toward the living room.
''We're watching the game.''

''We?''

''Me and the guys.''

''The guys?''

''Edwin. Bobby, Roy. Oh, and Sam Clark.''

''Sam?''

''He dropped by to say hello. So I invited him to stay.
It's Friday and he didn't have anything else to do.''

Leah allowed the screen door to close behind her, allowing Johnny a good look at her at last. His eyes narrowed and the amusement that had twinkled in his eyes
became serious. ''Looks like you had a rough day,
baby.''

''Not the best. Jake thought I'd had enough and sent
me home early.'' She grinned. ''Wanna tell me what's
going on? Where is Shamika?''

''I gave her the night off. She said something about

Mojo's Truck Stop and kicking up her heels.''

"And Val?"

He grinned again and crooked his finger at her. Leah moved to the living-room door. Ed, Roy, Sam, and Robert Anderson were huddled around the television. Situated among them in his wheelchair, smiling, was her son, hair still wet from his pool time, shirtless like the rest of the gang, his face and shoulders red from the sun.

The men shouted again, their enthusiasm punctuated by Val yelling, "Kick his ass!"

Edwin extended his flattened hand to Val. "My man, give me five."

Val struggled hard, then slapped Edwin's hand.

The image brought moisture to Leah's eyes.

Laying both hands on Leah's shoulders, Johnny directed her toward her bedroom. "Where am I going?" She laughed with a lightness that made her feel giddy.

"To sit in a hot bath with lots of bubbles, drink your cooler, maybe listen to a little Neil Diamond, and when you've relaxed thoroughly, you can join us."

He escorted her to the bathroom, where a full tub of steaming honeysuckle-scented water awaited her. He kicked the door shut behind them, turned her around to face him, and began to unbutton her blouse.

"I called the track and talked to Jake. He said you were headed home and that you were exhausted."

"That's putting it mildly." Leah closed her eyes, enjoying the feel of Johnny's hands working the tiny buttons of her blouse. His knuckles brushed her breasts, then his fingertips. He unbuttoned and unzipped her jeans, allowing them to fall open while he eased the blouse off her shoulders and let it drift to the floor.

As Johnny sat her down on the closed toilet seat and proceeded to remove her boots, Leah twisted the cap off the cooler, somewhat bemused that she was sitting on a toilet, half dressed, drinking a warmish wine cooler in front of Johnny Whitehorse.

"I wonder what your legion of adoring fans would

think if they saw you now,'' she said, then took a swig
of the drink.

"I'm not the one sitting on a toilet in my bra and
drinking wine coolers,'' he retorted, flashing her a smile.
"Hell, they've seen more of me exposed than my
chest.''

"Oh, yeah. That *NYPD Blue* show you did, showing
your naked butt off to the entire country. As I recall, it
was the highest-rated show of the season.'' She sipped
again and rested back against the tank as Johnny slid the
jeans down her legs and tossed them the way of her
blouse, boots, and socks. "When I watched the show I
thought, Aha, they've used makeup on his butt. I happen
to know you have a birthmark on your right cheek. As
I recall it looks like rabbit ears. Wonder what the *Globe*
would pay for that juicy bit of information?''

He tweaked her nose, then reached for the bra hook
between her breasts. "Not much, I think, unless you
suggest to them that an alien bit me.''

The bra fell away from her breasts, and Johnny's eyes
turned smoky. "I remember the first time you actually
allowed me to touch your breasts. You were so shy. And
when I kissed them you would turn your face away and
close your eyes.'' His fingers slid under the elastic of
her panties and eased them down her hips to her knees
and then her ankles.

"We've both grown up a lot,'' she replied softly.

"Learned a lot, have you?'' He lowered his head and
gently eased his lips and teeth over the tip of her nipple.
The touch of his tongue sluiced like hot honey to the
juncture of her thighs. Reaching for his hand, she slid it
between her legs, groaning at the luscious intrusion of
his fingers.

Then he pulled away, his flesh moist from the steam
that was fast turning the room hazy and hot. "Don't
tempt me, Leah. This house is too damn small for us to
get too carried away. The guys like their sports, but
given the opportunity to listen to a lot of fast breathing

and moans of ecstasy they would choose the ecstasy part every time. Get in the tub and soak for a while. If you need someone to wash your back, let me know.''

Standing, he turned for the door, hesitating as he took a couple of long breaths, the obvious ridge in his jeans making Leah giggle like a naughty schoolgirl.

The water felt unbearably hot at first, and she eased into it cautiously, allowing her skin to become accustomed to the silken heat before sinking up to her armpits in it. She didn't bother with Neil Diamond; the masculine sounds coming from the other room were music enough to her ears—especially those of her son: laughing, talking, being treated like any normal boy of seven years.

The all-too-familiar lump rose to her throat, and Leah turned the cooler up to her lips and drank deeply, the instant lethargy it produced making her sink into the mounds of white bubbles and lay her head back against the tub.

She thought of Shamika out at Mojo's Truck Stop, laughing and dancing with lonely truckers, listening to their sob stories of frigid wives and empty marriages— all ploys to entice her back to their cubbyhole cots for hire. She would not go, of course. Shamika enjoyed the laughs and an occasional free meal, but that was as far as it went. She was so level-headed and dedicated to Val that she often made Leah feel guilty for devoting so much time to her job.

Then Shamika would remind her that Leah had little choice. While the annuity check she received from the lawsuit was enough to pay for Val's medications—Tegretol for his seizures and Baclofen for his muscle stiffness—there were the costs for therapy and the scores of specialists who poked and prodded at Val in hopes of somehow helping his situation. Then there were the extras: AFO boots that cost seven hundred dollars. Wheelchairs that ran four thousand—unless she decided on the electric one, which would run her an easy ten thousand. Occasionally the annuity simply would not stretch far enough to pay Shamika's salary, any unexpected doctor visits, or food, clothing, and lodging.

Leah closed her eyes. When she opened them again she found Johnny looking down at her, his dark eyes soft, his lips curved ever so slightly.

"Water's cold," he said gently, reaching for the towel and offering her one hand. "The guys are gone. I read Val a story and put him to bed. If you don't get out of there soon there won't be anything left of you to make love to."

Blinking the sleep from her eyes, Leah glanced at her water-wrinkled hands. God, how long had she dozed? The water felt uncomfortably chilly, the bubbles all gone flat. Its label partially off and disintegrating, the wine cooler bottle floated on its side, resembling debris from a sinking ship.

Johnny eased the towel around her as she stepped from the tub, then swept her up in his arms and carried her to the semi dark bedroom lit only by the light of the bathroom behind them, to the bed where he had already turned back the blanket and sheets and fluffed the pillows. She sank with a sigh onto the mattress, her eyes drifting closed with pleasure as he gently dried her body, then tossed the damp towel on the floor.

He unzipped his jeans and eased them down his hips.

Leah gave him a sleepy smile. "Where's your underwear, Mr. Whitehorse?"

"I don't usually wear them. Remember?" Kicking the jeans aside, he eased onto the bed, sliding one knee between her thighs, rolling her to her side, her stomach against his, her breasts against him, his hard arms holding her fiercely as he whispered in her ear:

"I love you."

"Is that the Budweiser talking, or you?" She laughed, feeling ridiculously breathless. She wasn't a kid anymore, she reminded herself, yet the expansion in her chest felt no less thrilling than it had the first time he murmured those words in her ear.

"Both." He nuzzled her ear, teased it with his tongue, lightly nipped it with his teeth. "I'm drunk and crazy as hell about you."

"You always get a little loose-tongued when you've had too much," she teased, wrapping her leg over his hip and drawing him closer, so close that his penis felt like an iron rod against her belly, hard and hot, a throbbing velvet-skinned erection that made her ache unbearably.

"Would you like to see just how loose my tongue can get?" Grinning wickedly, he squeezed her buttocks then slid his hand between her legs, cupping her mons, easing his long fingers between the folds of her flesh, making her groan and arch against him.

Sliding down her body, he lifted her knees over his shoulders, surprising her at first, then rousing in her a shameless pleasure that made her bite her lip to keep from crying out as the first flick of his tongue inside her streaked like jagged lightning down her legs. Her hands flailed, twisted into the sheets, then grabbed the headboard; her body arched into him; his hands slid up her body to caress her breasts as his mouth moved on her, tongue swirling, diving, dipping, teasing until she felt mindless and a scream clawed at her throat that she feared would explode at any moment.

She writhed, twisted.

His body sweating, he fought his need to drive himself into her—deep into her: he'd been too caught up in his grief and anger those nights before to enjoy what once, so many years ago, had brought him such emotional and physical pleasure. The taste of her in his mouth sluiced through his raw senses like a sweet, floral fire and he was caught between his need to make slow, passionate love to her and his raging lust to fuck her harder and faster than she had ever been fucked. To show her that he wasn't a timid boy any more too afraid of hurting her to really enjoy her.

As the first quivering of climax made her grasp his shoulders, her nails digging into his skin, Johnny pulled

back, leaving her gasping, her teeth clenched, her body
hurting with the desperate need for him to finish pleasing
her. He considered taking his time, drawing out the pleasure . . .

"To hell with that," he murmured, then slid his body
up hers, sliding inside her, to a place once dark that
erupted suddenly like bright colorful Roman candles.

The midnight wind whipped the window curtains back
and spilled over Leah's and Johnny's damp bodies as
they lay with arms and legs tangled, her head resting on
his chest, his heart a racing murmur against her ear. Her
eyes closed, Leah nuzzled him with her cheek.

"I think every woman alive, at one point in her life,
dreams of reuniting with her first love, hoping to capture
the magic again that once swept her away, wondering if
the reality could ever live up to the memory."

He hugged her close, but said nothing.

"I'm happy to say you more than lived up to the
memory." Raising her head, her lips smiling, she said,
"Hey, do you realize this is actually the first time we've
made love and didn't worry about getting caught? Unless, of course, there is a photographer from the *Enquirer* hidden under the bed. I wonder what's worse?
My father or the paparazzi."

Still, he did not reply, just stared at the ceiling, his
body relaxed, his hand stroking her back absently. Finally, he looked down at her.

"I want to marry you, Leah."

A look of surprise crossed her face but she did not
look away, as she might have many years ago, when
even his slightest compliment unnerved her. "Is that a
proposal?"

"You and Val and Shamika should move in with me
immediately. That way my people can control the situation, the fans, the media, et cetera. I'll have my agents
handle all the arrangements for the marriage. It'll have
to be done quietly. I don't want a circus—not so soon

after Dolores's death. We'll fly my plane to Las Vegas and get married there. Later, if you want, we'll have a formal ceremony with your friends and family in attendance.''

''You're serious.''

''I don't intend to lose you, Leah.''

''You're not going to lose me, Johnny.''

Gently taking her face between his hands, he looked into her eyes that reflected the moonlight spilling through the window. ''That's what you promised me last time . . . just before you told me to get lost. I don't intend to let that happen again, Leah. I won't let you walk away from me again.''

Word arrived at the Inn of the Mountain Gods, where Johnny's agents and attorney had been staying during their sojourn to Ruidoso, to meet Johnny at ten sharp at Whitehorse Ranch. Always punctual, Edwin Fullerman arrived ten minutes early, looking sharp in his Armani suit, constantly checking his watch as he paced the foyer, mind worrying over the phone conferences he had been forced to postpone due to the impromptu get-together. Jack Hall pulled up five minutes later, his face concerned as he mounted the steps and waved a copy of the *Enquirer* under Ed's nose.

''Read it and weep, Fullerman. If this is true our client is up you-know-what creek without a paddle.''

Ed focused on the headline:

JOHNNY WHITEHORSE COKE ADDICT
DA OFFERS ULTIMATUM
Admit Himself to Betty Ford or Go Straight to Prison

Rolling his eyes and groaning, Ed shook his head.

''I'm not finished,'' Jack announced, and unrolled another tabloid showing a blurry photograph of Johnny holding Leah Starr on the dance floor at Randy's Bar and Grill.

NEW LOVE DRIVES WHITEHORSE FIANCÉE TO FIERY
DEATH RAINWATER WAS HEARD TO CRY ONLY
MOMENTS BEFORE TRAGIC ACCIDENT:
*"I'd Rather Die Than Lose Him to Another
Woman!"*

"What a lot of hooey." Edwin slapped the tabloid
aside.

"Yeah? Then how about this one." Jack held up the
Washington Post and recited, " 'Will scandal foil Foster's plans for reelection? It will if Johnny Whitehorse
has anything to say about it.' Seems there is a leak in
the DA's office. Word is out that Johnny has proof of
Foster's involvement with Formation Media."

Ed adjusted his glasses and took the *Post* from Johnny's
PR manager. He scanned the article. "*Had* proof. We all
know that whatever proof Dolores dug up about Foster
burned up in that crash, along with Dolores."

Robert Anderson arrived. Joining Edwin and Jack, he
slapped them both on the back and smiled. "Good news.
I just got a call from the assistant DA. Ted Weir informs
me that Johnny's blood tests just came back. No trace
of drugs, and his alcohol level was well below limit."

"Great," Edwin groaned. "Now the only thing they
can charge him with is manslaughter due to reckless
driving."

"Fullerman, you're such a pessimist."

"Easy for you to say. If Johnny gets charges slapped
against him, you double your fees and spend the next
year charging him a thousand bucks an hour to defend
him. What the hell do we get?" He looked pointedly at
Anderson. "A big fat zero because no producer or di-
rector or advertising firm will touch him with a ten-foot
pole until he wins his case."

"I'm glad to know you have my best interests at
heart, Fullerman." Johnny stepped out of the library, a
cup of hot coffee in one hand, a copy of the *Washington
Post* in the other.

Edwin shrugged and spread his arms. "You know I love you, Johnny, but let's face it. You're worth a million bucks a year to me."

Johnny stepped aside as the men filed by him into the library, where a table with coffee, juice, and danishes awaited. Edwin made for the refreshments immediately, loading his coffee with three spoons of sugar, while Jack grabbed up two sweet rolls and headed for a chair near the window. Anderson walked directly to a chair and sat down, placing his briefcase by his feet, his shrewd eyes watching Johnny as Johnny closed the library door, then headed for a chair next to his.

His mouth partially full of raspberry danish, Edwin said, "Wanna tell us now why you dragged our asses out of bed at six this morning and why this meeting couldn't wait until this afternoon? I do have other clients, you know."

"You wouldn't know it, hearing you talk a few minutes ago," Johnny replied.

"Don't get cocky, Whitehorse. I'm having lunch with Brad Pitt next week. If I'm lucky I could be representing him soon."

"Tell me you're going to have lunch with DiCaprio and then I'll be impressed."

"Swine. Should I remind you that before you signed on with me you were actually considering modeling for romance-book covers?"

"As I recall, *you* came knocking on *my* door, Ed. You knew a good thing when you saw it."

"Right. If you'd stayed with that other agent you'd be doing nothing but cheap butter commercials like Fabio, wiggling your ass at romance-book conventions and giving a lot of horny old women postmenopausal orgasms."

"You're just jealous, Ed." Jack laughed and blew into his hot coffee.

"What have I got to be jealous about?" Edwin rubbed his bald head as if it were Aladdin's golden lamp.

"Some of the sexiest men in history have been bald. Yul Brynner—"

"Savalas," Jack added, laughing harder.

"That *Star Trek* captain, what's his name. Patrick something. Face it. Bald is in, gentlemen. Eat your hearts out."

Johnny listened to his companions spar a while longer as he sipped his hot coffee and thought just how to delicately break the news that he intended to marry Leah Starr. They wouldn't be pleased, he surmised, glancing from one to the other.

But they wouldn't be the only ones. Not by a long shot.

He set his coffee aside, rubbed his sleepy, burning eyes, and took a deep breath. Raising his voice to be heard over the men's cajoling, he announced:

"Gentleman, I'm getting married."

Sudden silence, then they all asked in a woeful tone: "To whom?"

"Leah, of course. Who else? If she agrees, we're flying to Vegas day after tomorrow."

Ed's eyes widened behind his wire-rimmed glasses and his face flushed with hot color. There were flecks of white icing on his lips that fell like little snowflakes onto the front of his suit as he stared down at Johnny. "Shit," he groaned. "I was afraid you were going to say that."

Jack, balancing his rolls on one knee, stared off into space, as he always did when he was attempting to contain his mortification over a sudden turn of events.

Anderson, on the other hand, reached for the pocket tape recorder he always kept within grabbing distance and began to murmur directives for his secretary into it.

"Let me understand this precisely." Edwin attempted to swallow his partially chewed pastry. "You've just sauntered into this room and announced that you are marrying Senator Foster's daughter. Or perhaps I misunderstood. Dammit, Johnny, please tell me I've misunderstood."

Jack shook his head. "You didn't misunderstand our client, Edwin. The son-of-a-bitch said he's getting married day after tomorrow. To the senator's daughter, no less. Where are my nitroglycerin tablets. Shit, I feel a coronary coming on."

Pushing the Pause button on the recorder, Anderson scribbled notes on a pad and said, "This doesn't give me much time to write up a pre-nup."

"There won't be a pre-nup," Johnny replied.

They all glared at him and said in unison, "No pre-nup? What are you, crazy?"

"Have you any idea what you're worth, White-horse?"

"I believe you said close to a hundred million a few days ago."

"That's a conservative number. Whitehorse Jeans alone—"

"There will be no pre-nup."

Edwin tossed the danish and coffee into the trash, removed his glasses, and nervously cleaned them with his silk tie. "You need your head examined. That's it, isn't it? The wreck jarred something loose."

Jack dragged his chair in front of Johnny, sat and propped his elbows on his knees. "We have to talk, Johnny. A man in your position just doesn't up and get married like that." He snapped his fingers under Johnny's nose. "Have you any idea what this could do to your career? You're the most eligible and desired bachelor in this country. Your Fifth Avenue posters alone rake in two million a year. Every damned adolescent girl in this country and Europe has got that frigging photograph over her bed. Women will be throwing themselves off of buildings."

Johnny laughed and crossed his legs.

"Don't laugh." Jack shook his head. "I'm serious. They buy your jeans for their boyfriends just so they can imagine they are peeling them off of you."

"Marriage didn't hurt Elvis or McCartney. Hasn't tarnished Cruise."

"They will build effigies in Leah's image and burn them. Every wacko fan out there will be after her."

"Besides all of that," Edwin interjected. "You spring this a week after Dolores is killed. How is that going to look? You bury one fiancée, then turn right around and marry someone else?"

"I wasn't in love with Dolores. That bullshit that she was my fiancée was her doing, not mine. It would have been a cold day in hell before I married her."

Laying aside his notepad and tape recorder, Robert asked, "Have you informed Doctor Starr that you intend to accuse her father of attempted murder, and that you had in your hands the proof that you needed that he's heavily involved with Formation Media? Just how and when do you intend to break the news to her that you have every intention of putting her father in prison? On your wedding night?"

"That's it." Edwin shook his head and rubbed the lenses a second time. "You're going to marry the woman before the shit hits the fan, aren't you? Because you know that as soon as you accuse her father of corruption—"

"Don't forget murder," Jack said.

"—she's history. For God's sake, Johnny, what are you doing? All these years you've kept your nose clean; you move back to Ruidoso and all hell breaks loose. The most desirable women in the world are banging on your door and you up and marry some woman who smells like horse shit and has a retarded kid."

Johnny left the chair so fast Edwin had no time to react. Johnny grabbed him by the collar of his shirt and flung him partially over a desk, sending Edwin's glasses flying against the wall and scattering paperweights and magazines over the floor.

"I don't think I like your attitude, Ed. Need I remind you that I pay you fifteen percent of every cent I make to kiss my ass?"

Jack and Robert moved up behind him, their faces almost as white as Edwin's.

"Sorry," Ed managed, doing his best to remain calm.

"You're about to be even sorrier, you greedy son-of-a-bitch. Now take your goddamn BMW and Rolex watch that I bought you and get the hell out of my sight. You're fired."

His green eyes widening and his face totally colorless, Edwin gave Johnny a weak smile. "You don't mean that, J. W. Sheesh, I didn't mean—"

Johnny dragged him off the desk and shoved him toward the door. "You're finished. Get out."

Edwin swept up his glasses and, hands trembling, situated them on his face. He stared at Johnny through two broken lenses. "We'll talk later, after you've calmed down a little."

"Out!"

As Ed pivoted on his heels and left the room, Johnny turned back to the others. "Either of you have anything else to say about my decision?"

Anderson picked up his briefcase and popped open the locks, tucked the yellow legal pads into a side pouch, situated his recorder into a pocket, then gently closed the case, locking it with a double snap and a click of the combination dial. Only then did he look at Johnny.

"It's your call, Johnny. It's none of my business who you marry. I will, however, have my associate contact you as soon as possible. His name is Joe Conrad. He's smart and as lethal in a courtroom as they come. He's handled some of the nastiest divorce cases in L.A. I suspect that as soon as Leah discovers what you intend to do to her father, you're going to need the likes of Joe, because by the time the new Mrs. Whitehorse gets through with you you'll be lucky to have your worshipped testicles intact."

NINETEEN

Dressed in a white terry bathrobe, a towel wrapped around her wet hair, Shamika shook her head as if clearing it of cobwebs. "Obviously I'm still hung over from last night and didn't hear you correctly. Johnny Whitehorse asked you to marry him and you said you'd think about it?" Dragging a chair back from the kitchen table, Shamika sat down and watched Leah steady Val's hand as he attempted to feed himself a spoonful of Cheerios. "Hello, girlfriend? I think you've spent too much time with your arm up horses' butts. Or is it your head? The one love of your life, the most eligible bachelor in this country wants to marry you, and you have to think about it?"

Val looked up and smiled. "Johnny come see me today?"

Leah grinned. "Yes."

"Put down that spoon of Cheerios and talk to me," Shamika pleaded, then lowering her voice, added, "What is there to think about? You're in love with him, right? The man was the third-highest-grossing entertainer in the industry last year; you wouldn't have to work another day of your life, and best of all, you wouldn't have to worry about where you're going to get the money to buy Val a new wheelchair . . . and you have to think about it?''

Gently wiping Val's face with a damp cloth, Leah shook her head. ''It's not as simple as it sounds, Shamika. There's a lot of baggage that comes along with marrying Johnny.''

''Excuse me?'' Shamika wagged her head back and forth and rolled her eyes. ''I think I could handle that kind of baggage no problem.''

''There's his career to consider.''

''You telling me you couldn't handle a few million women throwing themselves at his feet? Rubbing elbows with the rich and famous? Yachting with royalty? Ooh, honey, I can see us now, basking in the sun on the Riviera. Me coating this beautiful brown body in cocoa butter and flirting with Denzel Washington—''

''Part of Johnny's appeal to women is because he's *not* married. You know what women are like. Once their idol marries, the women's fantasies go up in smoke. They move on to the next hunk they can fantasize sweeping them off their feet and into the nearest bed.''

''So what. So let them. Fact is, honey, Johnny Whitehorse could never pose half-naked again on Fifth Avenue or flash his cute butt on *NYPD Blue* and *still* be filthy rich. He's a smart man. He invests wisely. I get the impression that he's ready to move out of show business anyway and into . . .''

A look of realization crossed Shamika's face, and she slowly sat back in the chair, laced her fingers together on the table, and took a weary breath. ''Senator Foster wouldn't have anything to do with your hesitancy, would he?''

''I can hardly ignore the fact that there are major problems between Johnny and my father.''

''There are a lot of fathers-in-law who don't like their daughters' husbands. It all boils down to who you want to spend the rest of your life with: your father or Johnny.''

''I think the problems go a bit deeper than simply their liking one another.''

''I can't believe you'd let him come between you and Johnny again. For heaven's sake, Leah. The man virtually ignores your existence.'' She glanced down at Val meaningfully, then shook her head. ''If Johnny's able to get past it, you should be able to as well. And who knows, if you two were to marry, maybe Johnny would lay off your father. For *your* sake.''

''Wrong. Johnny would never go against his own principles, not if he feels very strongly on an issue. It isn't in his character. Who knows, maybe Johnny simply looks at me as a way to get even with my father.''

Shamika's jaw dropped. ''You don't mean that. The man is crazy in love with you. And Val, too.''

Her face warming, Leah moved to the kitchen sink and turned on the cold water. She rinsed the milk and Cheerios out of the dishcloth and stared out the window, to the distant horizon where the highest peaks and chimneys of what once had been her home thrust up behind the rolling green pasture dotted with grazing brood mares.

Shamika moved up behind her. ''You *are* in love with him, aren't you? You haven't suddenly discovered that what you two shared those years ago was nothing more than infatuation? Because if you're not in love with Johnny, then this whole conversation is moot. The *last* thing you want to do is marry some jackass again just for security.''

Leah pressed the damp cloth to her cheeks, doing her best to block from her mind the hours of mindless passion she had spent in Johnny's arms the night before. ''Johnny loves kids,'' she said wearily, unfolding and refolding the soggy rag.

''That's obvious,'' Shamika replied softly. ''He's crazy about Val, and Val's crazy about him.''

Leah smiled dreamily as she recalled the many hours they had lain together, too much in love to think of anything beyond the merging of their bodies and souls. "When we were young we vowed to have several children."

Moving around her, Shamika crossed her arms, leaned one hip against the counter, and waited for Leah to continue.

Leah shrugged and avoided looking at her concerned friend. "He'll want more children, Shamika."

"And that's what's got you worried?"

Looking over her shoulder at Val, watching him struggle to pluck Cheerios off the table, struggling even harder to put them in his mouth, Leah shook her head. "The doctors have already said that I'll always have problems carrying a child full term."

"And you're frightened that this will happen again." Shamika took Leah's hand in hers. "The doctors have assured you there are remedies for the problem. There's no reason why you shouldn't be capable of carrying a baby for nine months. Besides, it wasn't the premature issue that caused Val's problem. It was the meningitis."

"But we both know that extreme premature babies are at high risk for CP."

"It won't happen again, Leah."

"I just don't think I'm strong enough to go through this again, Shamika."

"So what does that mean? You're going to spend the rest of your life alone, refusing to marry any man who wants children?"

The phone rang and Shamika left the room. Leah followed, hoping Jake had not decided to renege on his decision to give her the day off. She'd promised Val a picnic lunch at the park, Johnny to join them as soon as he finished his business meeting.

Shamika laid the receiver down and looked around. "It's your father," she said in an exasperated tone.

•   •   •

"Leah, darling. Have I caught you at a bad time?"

Leah glanced at Shamika where she stood in the doorway, hands on her hips and terry robe fallen open, revealing her pink flannel nightgown. "No, Dad. Not at
all. What a surprise to hear from you this morning."

"I'm in town for a few days and would love to meet
you for lunch."

"Gee. I would have liked that, with a little notice. I'm
afraid I have plans for lunch."

"Now what, or who, could be more important than
your old man?"

"My son," she replied pointedly. "I promised him a
picnic at the park."

"I see." A familiar silence ensued. Leah could imagine her father sitting behind a desk in some posh hotel
room, surrounded by his fawning aides, stiff as a poker
in his dull gray suit, mouth pressed in an effort to contain his irritation over not getting his way. It was that
same look that had made her, as a child, dig her heels
into the carpet to keep from running from the room—
but that would have given him far too much satisfaction.

"What about dinner?" he finally said.

"What's the occasion?"

"Do I need an occasion to share some time with my
daughter?"

"Normally."

He laughed, ignoring her sarcasm. "Shall we meet at
La Hacienda, say sevenish? That *is* still your favorite
restaurant, isn't it?"

She nodded, aware that Shamika was watching her
like the proverbial hawk and not liking what she was
hearing one little bit. "Fine," she finally responded.

"I'll have a car pick you up at six-thirty sharp. And
by the way, we'll discuss that funding idea for the
special-needs issue that was recently proposed by your
friend—what's her name? Darmon?"

The phone clicked in her ear before she could recover
from her surprise enough to respond.

"Leah, if I didn't know better I'd think that man had bugs planted in this house. It's just a little too coincidental that he shows up out of nowhere to see you the very morning after Johnny proposed."

Leah dropped the receiver onto the hook. "You're actually starting to sound like Johnny, as if there is some conspiracy behind my father wanting to have dinner with me."

"Well? Don't you think it's a *little* coincidental?"

She scanned the room, feeling a niggling of unease raise the hairs on her arms. There were dozens of photographs scattered over the tables and on the walls: smiling images of Leah and her mother, her grandparents, and Val. A few sickly Boston ferns lightened up dark corners; the sadly sagging sofa and matching chair with ottoman had been the first household items she and Richard had purchased from a garage sale shortly before their marriage. All appeared so normal and safe and familiar: no listening device buried like a reclusive spider within the leaves of ferns or behind heartwarming photographs.

"You've been reading too many Robert Ludlum and John Grisham novels, Shamika. He said he has some time off."

"When is the last time he did that, Leah? I'm telling you, he's come to town for a reason and that reason is you and Johnny."

"Why would he spy on me? I'm his daughter, for heaven's sake."

"It's not you he's worried about, Leah. Is it? It's Johnny that's got him jumpy, and you'd better believe he's going to do whatever he can to make certain Johnny doesn't cause him any more grief than necessary."

"So what has all that got to do with me?"

"If he can't get to Johnny through Johnny, he'll get to Johnny through you."

Leah turned her back on Shamika and retreated to her bedroom, closed the door behind her and leaned against

it, her gaze fixed on the unmade bed, sheets and blanket
a tangle, the pillow Johnny had slept on still showing
the indentation of his head. Even the smell of him lin-
gered in the room, the slightly musky, spicy scent of his
cologne, his sweat, the odor of the hot fierce sex they
had shared throughout the night.

"No way," she said aloud, shaking her head. "He's
my father, for God's sake. No way could he know about
me and Johnny." Closing her eyes, she repeated, "No
way."

The idea of picnicking at the park had been a good one:
a blanket spread under a tree overlooking the meandering river, enjoying fried chicken, potato salad from the
local deli, and Twinkies, Val's choice for dessert, with
strawberry Kool-Aid for a beverage. A time to relax,
forget about the mounting pressures in their lives, rem-
inisce about the old days, and plan for the new ones,
should Leah allow herself to consider Johnny's proposal.

But Leah had no more spread the red-and-white
checked blanket out over the trimmed grass, and Johnny
had no more situated Val in his brace on the blanket
when a group of teenage girls in brief bikinis and piña-
colada-scented suntan oil recognized Johnny, despite his
dark glasses and Roy's old sweat-stained cowboy hat
that he had pulled down over his brow, and screamed
loud enough to bring every woman with or without a
camera running as fast as they could.

Within minutes they were swamped. Women thrust
pen and paper at Johnny, and if they had no paper they
offered miscellaneous body parts. Leah was forced to
collect Val and rush him back to the truck, where they
sat in the front seat and watched Johnny fight his way
toward them as if he were swimming through piranhas.
The blanket and picnic lunch did not fare any better.
The blanket was torn into souvenirs and the food was
scattered for the ants and lurking squirrels.

By the time Johnny climbed into the truck, slammed

the door and locked it, his hat was gone and so were his glasses. The black-and-orange T-shirt boasting "Apache Rodeo Championship June 1–5" had been ripped in two places. There were fingernail scratches on his arms and one across his cheek.

He reached for the ignition just as a girl climbed onto the hood of his truck and flattened her naked breasts against the windshield.

Johnny looked at Leah, his dark eyebrows raised.

Leah covered Val's eyes with her hands and began to laugh.

"This isn't funny," Johnny said, motioning to the girl to get off his truck, then hitting the windshield wipers, causing the blades to swipe at the girl's nipples. Still, she didn't budge, just pressed her lips against the window and proceeded to tell him exactly what she was willing to give him if he'd just autograph her crotch.

Leah laughed harder as Johnny's face turned red. Her eyes watered and her ribs ached, and the idea occurred to her that she couldn't remember the last time she had laughed so hard.

He shifted the truck into first gear and revved the engine, then popped the clutch, causing the truck to buck like a pissed mule. The girl tumbled off the side and Johnny floored the accelerator. The tires spun momentarily on the asphalt, spitting gravel before the truck careened toward the highway, leaving the waving, jiggling, squealing women behind.

Johnny glanced down at Val, who grinned back at him. "You okay, pal?"

"Okay, pal."

He looked at Leah as she bit her lip to keep from laughing again. "What's so funny about getting torn limb from limb?"

"I was just remembering how shy you were in school. You blushed every time a girl looked at you."

"I hate it. What makes women behave like that?"

"That's what you get for posing half-naked on Fifth

Avenue and exposing your cute ass on *NYPD Blue*."

"Thanks for your support."

"Hey, you studmuffins make yourselves into gods to these women, then you whine because you can't saunter through life with some semblance of privacy. If they weren't tearing your clothes off you'd be whining about their indifference. There's no pleasing you."

"You don't write for tabloids, do you?"

She pursed her lips and looked thoughtful. "I just might if you're not nice to me. I think they'd pay a pretty sum for the juicy details of our meeting last night."

"Just as long as you tell them I'm the best you ever had. I have my reputation to think about."

"Best what?" Val asked, looking from Leah to Johnny, making Leah grimace and Johnny grin like the Cheshire cat.

"Friend," Leah declared, tweaking his nose. "Best friend I ever had."

"Val is Mama's best friend," Val announced, giving Johnny a stern look, then smiling. "Johnny can be Val's best friend."

Smiling, Johnny slid his arm around Val's shoulder, and his tone became conspiratorial. "I'll be more than your best friend soon if your mom will stop being so stubborn."

"I'm not stubborn," Leah argued, shaking her head. "I'm simply being . . . cautious."

"You've never been cautious. Stubborn, yes. Cautious, no."

"I just don't want to throw open some Pandora's box, Johnny. There's a lot to consider. And if you deny *that*, then you're not thinking with your head."

"You sound like my agents."

Leah raised her eyebrows. "Oh? Then I take it they aren't exactly jumping with joy over the possibility of our . . ." She glanced down at Val who watched her intently. "I just think we need to discuss the situations

that might arise. We should take our time. Get to know
one another again. We're not the same people we were
twelve years ago.''

"I know I never stopped loving you," he said softly,
and reached for her hand. "Will you sit there and deny
to me that you feel the same?"

"No." She shook her head and wrapped her fingers
around his.

They rode in silence as Johnny wove the truck
through traffic, heavy due to the influx of weekend tourists. He pulled through a Jack in the Box and ordered
hamburgers and French fries to go, piled the warm, fragrant sacks of food on Val's lap so the boy could filch
himself some fries, then directed the truck down the
highway and onto the Mescalero reservation.

Leah said nothing, just watched the mountainous
scenery flash by, hardly questioning in her own mind
why Johnny would head for the reservation. Like so
many years ago, it was the one place he could lose himself. There wasn't a trail, a river, a valley, or a mountain
for that matter, that he had not explored thoroughly,
mostly to escape his father's drunken rages. Just as he
had done after Dolores's death, he would search for and
find a place that would provide them emotional comfort
and physical security. He needed to be on *his* ground to
deal with her so-called stubbornness.

The actual town of Mescalero was a compilation of
modern buildings and rock-and-frame structures. Heat
radiated off the street and the cracked, meandering sidewalks, bleaching color from the surroundings. A scattering of small stores boasted barriers across their
windows, and signs: FOR SALE. OUT OF BUSINESS.
CLOSED. Johnny drove by them slowly and pointed to
an adobe building with dull red shutters and a bright
orange door, the windows broken out despite the lumber
that had been nailed over them.

"Bill Crow's place. He sank every dime into it five
years ago. His wife made baskets and pottery in back.

They netted twenty five thousand last year, enough to send their daughter to college out east. Anna made the finest baskets in New Mexico. They were bought by tourists from all over the world.''

Frowning, Leah looked over the weed-infested, trash-littered building. "What happened?"

He pointed to a small grocery across the street—the mom-and-pop sort that roused images of creaky wood floors and penny bubble gum. Ragged, faded GOING OUT OF BUSINESS banners flapped like tattered flags from their moorings on the dusty windows. "Last year Hank and Helen Crookneck finally saved enough money from the store to build them a nice house on the mountain. They sank their savings into the house, but no sooner did they move in than they were forced to close the store. They went bankrupt and are now subsidized by the government.''

Turning off the main street, he moved by a parking lot jammed with Native American men, women, and children, all idling under whatever shade they could find, fanning themselves with anything that might provide them a breeze. There were young men with dark, angry faces, old men with haggard expressions, and women who stared blankly out over the countryside, ignoring the crying children who tugged on their skirts that were as faded of color as the GOING OUT OF BUSINESS banners.

The sign posted on the employment office behind them read: Closed until Further Notice By Order of the United States Government.

"The . . . government felt that since there really are no jobs to provide these people it would do no good to staff the office. So the office was closed four months ago. These people congregate here waiting for the occasional contractor or builder to come looking for a worker for a few hours or a few days.

"The old men work cheap, usually half of minimum wage. Anything to put food on the table, but the work is hard on them, so the builders are forced to hire the younger men who demand a higher wage. The women will scrub floors and toilets for food for their children. Some of the restaurants in the area will bring them in after closing and pay them with food that was left over from the day's business.

"Two years ago these people looked very different. Their faces weren't hollow and their eyes were bright. The children laughed instead of cried. Two years ago you would not have found these people loitering around parking lots. They had jobs then, working for the businesses that are now closed."

He directed the truck north, following the highway into the hills, through expanses of towering trees where the heat became a cool, dim relief. As the air conditioner hummed and the tires droned, Val's eyes closed and his head nodded. Only then did Leah look directly at Johnny, who stared straight ahead, one wrist hooked over the steering wheel, one hand lying on Val's knee.

Upon exiting the tunnel of trees, Johnny slowed the truck and pulled off the road, onto a vast empty parking lot that wrapped around an expanse of partially constructed buildings, their frames and beams fast being overtaken by wildflowers, weeds, and thistle trees.

Johnny stopped the truck and killed the engine. Without looking at Leah, he reached for the door and said, "Get out."

Leah did not get out. It had occurred to her as she'd studied the weary faces of the unemployed Mescaleros just what Johnny was getting at; the point he would try to make concerning the welfare of his people and their future. A sickness settled in her stomach. The greasy French fries in the sack on Val's lap didn't help, any more than the vision of the Mescalero dream gone bad. The corroding steel ribs of the buildings rising up behind weeds as tall as a man resembled a dinosaur graveyard.

Johnny walked around the truck and opened the door. He offered his hand.

"Why are you doing this?" she asked in a dry voice.
"What are you afraid of?"

"I have no intention of listening to you character-bash
my father."

"I don't intend to. I simply intend to show you what
a people's failed dream looks like."

She left the truck, easing the door closed so as not to
disturb Val. Johnny walked away from her, toward the
stretches of partially constructed walls made all the more
bleak by the flocks of birds that rose up in a cloud of
caws and popping wings from the stark steel structures
high over Johnny's head. Shivering, Leah hugged herself
and glanced at the dark blue sky with its feathering of
thin clouds, and the conversation she had shared that
morning with Shamika came back to her. No matter how
much she wanted to ignore or deny that there were problems between Johnny and her father, the evidence
sprawled out before her now was a reminder that there
were more reasons than Johnny's career to avoid any
talk of marriage.

A fallen billboard lay on the ground. "Future Home
of Apache Casino and Resort. Financing by Formation
Media."

"What do you think, Leah? This is all that's left of
the people's dream."

Johnny jumped onto a pile of rubble, spread his arms
and slowly turned. "The casino alone would have offered twenty-five hundred slot machines and two hundred tables: roulette, blackjack, big six, poker. Six
restaurants would have offered guests everything from
Native American fare to French cuisine—open twenty-
four hours a day."

He pointed to an arch of steel beams some distance
away. "That was to be the theater where major concerts
and gaming tournaments would have been held. It could
have seated fifteen thousand. There would have been
forty shops selling everything from pottery, baskets, and
beadwork, all made by the New Mexico tribes, to de-

signer originals from Paris. The hotel would have had fifteen hundred rooms. An eighteen-hole golf course was planned, as well as a riding stable, a theme park for kids, and an outdoor theater where the People would perform their dances in a setting that represented the different Apache villages of a hundred years ago.''

Turning his face into the breeze, Johnny looked down on the crystal-clear lake in the valley below. Sun danced upon the surface like silver glitter. ''The lake would have offered swimming, boating, fishing, water skiing. And in the winter we would have provided trams to the slopes for a day of snow skiing.''

He remained silent after that, lost in thought, his dark hair reflecting the sun. Finally, he turned back to Leah and jumped from his perch. Almost angrily, he swept his hand toward the stretch of highway that disappeared around a sharp bend in the road. ''By the year 2020 this area would have rivaled Branson, Missouri, Atlantic City, or Vegas with casinos, hotels, and theaters. Every family residing on this reservation would have known employment and financial stability for themselves and their children, and their children's children.''

Finally, he met Leah's eyes. ''Sixty percent of the financing for this initial casino and hotel project was to come from the Apache Consortium, not just the Mescalero but from all the New Mexico tribes. Therefore they would hold the majority control of the running of the business. They mortgaged their homes and businesses. They took what little life savings they had and invested in this dream. Formation Media would invest the other forty percent, plus act as the private money lender to those who mortgaged their homes and businesses or used their homes, businesses, or personal effects as collateral. If, for some reason, the majority failed, one hundred percent of the control and ownership reverted to Formation Media.

''Had everything gone as planned, the building of the resort would have been completed last year. By now this place would have been filled with tourists gambling, enjoying the theme park, swimming, browsing the shops for souvenirs that *weren't* made in Taiwan. Instead of loitering on parking lots hoping for some white man to toss a few coins their way, the People would be here, employed, productive, proud of their accomplishments and, most of all, realizing their dreams of prosperity for the first time since they were corralled on this land like cattle and forced to become something they aren't.

"In 1995 the governor signed gambling compacts allowing the tribes to begin the construction of the resort. What you see here is how far the construction got before your father brought it to the attention of the state and federal courts that the compacts the governor signed were void because he did not get approval for the gambling from the legislature. Under federal Indian gaming law, a tribe cannot legally run a casino without an agreement with the state legislature."

"You can't fault my father for following the law, Johnny."

"I don't fault your father for following the law, Leah. I fault him for continually thwarting our attempts to get the legislature to alter the state's gambling laws. He fought us on every avenue, pointing out how gambling will introduce corruption, exacerbate alcoholism, weaken the Apaches' character further by allowing them an opportunity to gamble away what little money they have, therefore disintegrating the dignity of an already diminished people. He pointed out that the People, as a whole, are lacking the education necessary to successfully manage and maintain such a broad endeavor as we proposed in the building of this casino and resort."

Leah turned away, shaking her head. "You're not making sense, Johnny. My father eventually compromised on the issue and the state, not six months ago, negotiated new compacts allowing gambling—"

"Better late than never?" He shook his head. "Not in this case, Leah. Not when the ownership of the casino and resort reverted to Formation Media when the People could not make their payments when due. Formation now owns this resort, lock, stock, and barrel. They can either build it or walk away and leave it to the coyotes and jackrabbits. If they build they are under no obligation to employ a Native American anywhere on the premises and most likely won't. They'll move in their employees from other resorts and casinos, as they've done in the past.''

As Leah frowned and started to speak, Johnny cut her off. ''Formation Media is owned by a group of international investors. We're not certain who they are. They go by numbers, not names. They've developed some of the largest and most successful hotel casinos in the world. Most recently they built the Shanghai Vista in Reno. It takes up twenty complete city blocks.''

''I've read about the Shanghai Vista, that there's no other casino hotel like it in the world, and to visit is like actually visiting Shanghai in person; every minute detail is authentic. I had no idea it was developed by Formation.''

''It's authentic all right, down to the Fuzhau Road that's lined with book shops, gift shops and the Xin Hua Bakery, to Zhongshan'dong Avenue, which looks out over a manmade reproduction of the Huangpu River. There are the same number of slot machines as there are rooms in the hotel. Five thousand. The only thing missing is the mosquitoes and the monsoons.''

''So what are you insinuating, Johnny? That my father manipulated this entire fiasco so that Formation could get their hands on this project? My God, this is small potatoes compared to the Shanghai Vista.''

''Not if you look at the big picture, Leah. The only thing that kept Branson, Missouri, from hurting Vegas or Atlantic City was the fact that they don't have gambling.''

''And what, exactly, would my father get out of it?''

''That's pretty damn obvious, isn't it? Money. Lots

of it. Enough to finance his next campaign. Or maybe he simply wants a bite of the action.''

As usual, the senator had acquired the best table La Hacienda had to offer. Situated on a private balcony, it offered a panoramic view of the entire valley and the river that reflected the sky and clouds like a flawless mirror. There had been times during her childhood when the three of them—her mother, father, and herself—had come here to celebrate certain occasions. Her birthday, Mother's Day, graduation. She always ordered Enchiladas Mexicana. Her mother varied: Tacos el Carbon, fajitas, sometimes nothing but a vodka and tonic, depending on how the conversation had gone in the car on the way over.

Leah's father raised his glass of wine to her, drawing her attention back to the present. ''To my beautiful, brilliant daughter. Here's hoping that the future will bring us much closer.''

She touched her glass to his, but did not drink. Instead, she placed it aside and sat back in her chair. ''What's this all about, Dad? The last time we had dinner together, Mom was still alive. Gee, that must have been four years ago, when the two of you flew down to College Station for my graduation.''

''You're my daughter, for God's sake. I have a right to see you occasionally.'' He laughed. ''Is there some law against it?''

''Senator, you never do anything without a motive. Remember? You're too busy to fit such normalities as having dinner with your family into your hectic schedule.''

''Good Lord. You sound like your mother.'' He gave her a thin smile and a slight narrowing of his eyes. ''The two of you were always blessed with a razor-sharp wit, not to mention an equally destructive tongue. But tonight

I bow to you. I did not, regretfully, spend enough time at home with my family.''

Foster finished off his glass of wine. "So how is the new job going?"

"I haven't actually started practicing yet. Simply assisting Jake. Until my state license comes through I don't dare even take a horse's temperature."

"But the money is good?"

"It's steady and reliable. The work is hard and occasionally heartbreaking. That, however, is nothing new."

"Which brings me to the basic reason for asking you here tonight."

"Ah. I knew there had to be some ulterior motive. What do you want from me, Senator? Don't tell me you've decided to get back into the horse business. Perhaps you want me to do a prepurchase exam on an incredible Arabian stallion you found in Cairo? I warn you, I'm not cheap. And I don't lie. I'm known in the business, at least in Dallas, for being brutally honest."

"No horses, Leah. I'm done with that. Besides, your mother was far crazier about the horses than I ever was. This time I'm going to do something for *you*. What would you think about working for me, in Washington? I need someone trustworthy and dedicated, someone willing to look out for her old man's tail when it gets in a crack. I could start you off at fifty thousand a year, living accommodations included. Of course, it would mean your moving permanently to Washington, rubbing elbows with men in high places."

"I've heard there is a lot more getting rubbed in Washington than elbows these days."

"I'll point out that D.C. offers certain advantages for your son."

"His name is Valentino, Dad; just in case you forgot."

"Of course I haven't forgot. For God's sake, Leah,

why must you always get so defensive every time I bring up the boy?"

"The fact that you haven't asked about his welfare since I sat down here thirty minutes ago might have something to do with it."

"Sorry. I've not been blessed with the gift of idle chitchat. You know that."

"I never considered asking about the welfare of your only grandchild nothing more than mere chitchat." She reached for her wine, her throat growing tight with emotion. "Let me save you the trouble. Val is doing beautifully. He's beginning to read. His speech has improved tremendously. He'll never walk, of course, but the therapy he receives every day helps his hand coordination tremendously. We finally managed to get the seizures under control; the medication for that is astronomical, but necessary. There are medications available now that help to relieve the rigidity of the muscles. They're still in a somewhat experimental stage . . ." She drank again, more deeply, before adding, "The series of shots is given every three months: seven shots in each arm and leg, directly into the muscles, at a cost of two thousand dollars a series. And there's no guarantee that they'll work for every case. But when they do, the results allow the individual a much greater range of movement and balance, not to mention comfort.

"Val enjoys school very much. He's the teacher's pet. He's attending summer school now, where the emphasis is more on social activities rather than studies. There are swimming activities and games that help with coordination and sportsmanship. What's most important is the time he spends with other children like himself. It assures him that he's not alone in the world. That there are others, like him, who are . . . special. Of course, the program isn't subsidized by the government, but by private donations. Which is why Shelley Darmon contacted you, in hopes you would propose to the state legislature the possibility of the state footing the bill for the pro-

gram. The rattletrap bus they are forced to ride is in-
adequate, to say the least. It's continually breaking
down. It's not air-conditioned. And while there have
been alterations in the bus to accommodate the special
needs of the children, it's still lacking the appropriate
appointments to guarantee their safety one hundred percent.''

''I'll look into it,'' he said in his typical dismissive
tone that told her he would not look into it, that as soon
as they walked out the door the subject would be buried
in his mind.

The waitress appeared to take their order. As her father quickly perused the menu one last time, Leah sat
back in her chair and watched him, the same way she
had often observed her mother studying him: with a
sense of curiosity and confusion, disappointment and
frustration settling like stone in her chest. When, she
wondered, had her father become the cold, remote, and
indifferent man who now sat before her? Had he always
been so emotionally unattached to everything but
power? Surely not. Knowing her mother, who thrived
on attention, Leah could not imagine the woman marrying for any other reason but love.

''What happened between you and Mother?'' she
asked when the waitress retreated. ''When, exactly, did
you fall out of love?''

If he was surprised by the suddenness of her unusual
question, he didn't show it, just wiped his mouth with
the white linen napkin and laid it in his lap. ''Your
mother and I had different interests. That didn't necessarily mean we didn't care for one another.''

''I never saw you touch her. You slept in separate
bedrooms since I was ten.''

''I lived a very hectic and intrusive life, Leah. Always
getting calls in the middle of the night. I simply didn't
wish to disturb her. Besides, it afforded both of us much
greater freedom.''

''Did it matter to you that she took lovers?''

He laughed. "Sweetheart, your mother was welcome
to entertain herself any way she wanted . . . as long as it
kept her pacified and sober and away from the American
Express card."

She supposed she should have been surprised by his
blasé attitude. But she wasn't. Just irritated that he didn't
have the decency to indicate even the slightest annoy-
ance over the fact that his wife had been unfaithful,
which only proved all the more that he had not cared a
whit about her.

"You were never jealous? Not even a little?" she
pressed.

"I simply expected her to be discreet, and to exhibit
a modicum of selectivity in the men she chose to sleep
with."

"Is that why you hated Jefferson Whitehorse so
much? Because you didn't like Mother fucking an Indian?"

For the first time in her life Leah watched her father's
face flood with dark color. He sat back in his chair,
shoulders squared, jaw bulging. Even the whites of his
eyes turned blood red as he fixed her with so smoldering
a look she wondered if he would actually explode in this
room full of prospective voters.

Bingo! she thought. At long last she had finally discovered his Achilles' heel. A spiteful satisfaction surged
like a bubble in her chest.

"For the love of God, Leah, is that any way to talk?
I thought your mother had taught you better etiquette."

"My mother taught me several four-letter words,
some of which would make your blood pressure go up
even more. Would you like to hear them? They were
mostly directed at you anyway."

"Fine," he snapped. "As long as you want to bring
up the Foster women's penchant for screwing Indians,
why don't you enlighten me as to your plans with
Johnny Whitehorse?"

"I wondered how long it would take you to get around to Johnny."

"You've been seen with him."

Her eyebrows lifted. "Maybe Shamika is right. Maybe you *have* planted a bug under my bed."

"How could you," he said through his teeth, glancing around to make certain his tone had not caught anyone's attention. "You know what that son-of-a-bitch is trying to do to me, and yet you still . . ."

"What is he trying to do that any activist who truly cares about a cause wouldn't do? You screwed over his people, Senator. You bankrupted an entire populace. Why?"

"What the hell are you talking about, Leah?"

"I'm talking about the game you played with the gambling issue. Your stalling the legislature's legalizing state gambling until the tribal investors of the Apache Casino and Resort rolled over, giving Formation Media full ownership of the development."

Foster tossed his napkin on the table, and, for an instant, looked as if he would spring from his chair and make a quick exit from the restaurant. "How dare you," he uttered under his breath, pinning her with his blue eyes that, despite the fire of anger in his face, looked frigid. The look set her back and made her heart skip with disconcertment. A chill as cold as icemelt sluiced through every vein and bone and muscle.

"Fine, sweetheart. If that's the way you want to play this, fine. Give your boyfriend a message for me. I won't stand for his slandering me. I won't tolerate the charges he's made about collusion. If he thinks he's going to unseat me the next election he'd better be prepared to lock up his closets, because I don't intend to leave any rock unturned in my efforts to smash his character and reputation—starting with the death of Dolores Rainwater."

As steadily as possible, she said, "You still haven't answered my question, Senator. Exactly what was your motive behind stalling the gambling issue?''

He pointed one trembling finger in her face. "I've offered you a job, Leah. A new beginning. Financial stability. If I were you I would consider it. On the other hand, if you take a stand with Whitehorse against me, in fact, if you continue to see him at all, I sever all ties between us. You are no longer my daughter. Think about that while you enjoy your dinner.''

Scraping back his chair, Foster stood and exited the restaurant.

TWENTY

TaliazDancinDarlin was the favorite for the night's big-gest race, offering the highest purse of the season so far: Forty-five thousand, the winner taking sixty percent. A groom had found her on her side that morning in her stall, obviously having been rolling; not a good sign. That meant colic. By the looks of her beat-up hocks and the bruising on her head, she'd been floundering in her stall for the better part of the night.

They had pumped enough mineral oil through her gut to grease a Boeing 747. Had there been an obstruction it should have passed by now. Instead of showing signs of improvement, the mare appeared to be growing worse. Respiration, heartbeat, temperature were climb-ing.

Both Jake and Leah suspected a gut twist, which meant surgery. But even that outcome was iffy, certainly no guarantee that they could save the suffering mare. Especially if the gut had been twisted for a long period of time.

Jake shook his head. ''I can't do anything else for her without opening her up, Mr. Davison. Or we can put her down. That's your call, of course. Either way, this mare isn't running tonight or anytime in the foreseeable future.''

Bill Davison closed his eyes briefly, and his shoulders slumped. Behind him, his wife Betty began to cry. Both in their late fifties, they had spent their lives breeding for the horse that would make their farm respected in the business. TaliazDancinDarlin, named after their granddaughter, Talia, had shown every promise of doing just that. She had broken her maiden the first time out, going on to win five of the next seven races.

''Will she ever run again?'' Bill asked.

''Maybe. Maybe not. Founder usually follows this kind of colic, and that means lameness. If she survives, she might make you one hell of a brood mare.'' Jake ran his hand along the mare's sweating neck. ''She's a nice horse. She's made you some decent money. If she was mine, I'd open her up. Give her every chance.''

''Easy for you to say. It ain't as if I've got five grand ready to toss down the crapper if she dies.''

The mare's trainer laid his hand on Davison's shoulder. ''You gotta do what you gotta do, Bill. There will be other horses. Don't beat yourself up over this.''

Davison turned his gaze to Leah where she stood at Jake's side, her heart in her throat as she wondered to herself if she would ever get used to witnessing the pain on her clients' faces when confronted with life-and-death decisions regarding their animals, and, more often than not, the end of their dreams.

''It's a hell of a thing, isn't it?'' Bill said. ''You pour your heart and soul into raising these beauties. You pamper them like they was the Queen of England, invest half a lifetime of money and dreams. One minute they're fine, on top of the world, the next they're useless for anything other than Jell-O.'' He ran one hand through his hair and cleared his throat. ''I'll call my brother, see if he can loan me the money.''

Davison, his wife, and the trainer headed for the door,

and Jake gave his assistants orders to prepare the mare
for surgery.

"Shouldn't you wait until Mr. Davison returns?"
Leah asked, raising her voice to be heard over the roaring of the lifts that would move the anesthetized horse
onto the operating table. She followed Jake into the
scrub room, grabbed up a surgical gown that was ster-
ilized in plastic bags and began to slide the garment on
over her clothes.

Jake turned on the water and began to brush his hands
with disinfectant. "There isn't time to wait," he said as
she moved up beside him and began to scrub. "I suspect
we'll be lucky to save her as it is."

"But the money—"

"We'll cross that bridge when we come to it, Doctor.
I've known Bill a long time. He'll come across with the
money. It might take a while, but he'll pay me."

Within fifteen minutes the mare was on the table, flat
on her back, tubes running out her nose and mouth, her
feet supported by chains from the overhead lift. Leah
prepped the mare's belly, shaved away the hair with a
#40 surgical clipper blade, and swabbed the skin down
with Betadine scrub. Then Jake stepped in and opened
her up.

Leah gagged and turned her face away.

Jake cursed, flinging the scalpel to the far side of the
room.

Leah had not wanted to be present when Jake broke the
news to Bill and Betty Davison that their horse was
dead, that the colon had been twisted so long it had
ruptured, spilling poisons throughout her body cavity.
Sitting in a lawn chair outside the clinic, the sun hot on
her face, Leah closed her eyes and did her best to will
away the stench of peritonitis that permeated even her
hair. She wanted to go home and spend a long, lazy
Sunday afternoon with Val. They would cuddle in the
hammock hanging from the pine trees out back of the

house until the heat got too unbearable, then they would put on their swimsuit and play in the blue wading pool until their shoulders became sensitive to the sun. They would nap, snack on microwave popcorn, watch old Godzilla movies and laugh until their sides hurt.

Or she could march into the clinic and tell Jake that she was taking tomorrow off because she was flying to Las Vegas with Johnny Whitehorse—yes, Johnny Whitehorse—and they were going to get married in some tacky little chapel with a justice of the peace who looked, talked, and dressed like Elvis. In all probability she would not return to work because she would no longer *need* to work to pay for her son's therapy, medications, wheelchairs, and thousand-dollar bathtub seats that were nothing more than molded plastic and which Val would outgrow in another three months.

Jake would say in his typical dry manner: "You're joking, right? Allow a man to take care of you? I thought you were a millennium kind of girl, too independent to rely on a man." Then he would remark: "What about the senator? How is he going to take the news that his only daughter has gone over to the enemy?"

Her father the enemy. Even after their meeting last night she couldn't bring herself to believe Johnny's innuendos that her father was in bed with Formation Media. That he had, in some way, played a part in the bankruptcy of the Apache Casino and Resort.

Then she reminded herself that the fallout of the bankruptcy didn't affect just the resort, but an entire state of people who had sunk their entire lives into a dream that had left thousands destitute.

Granted, Senator Foster might never win Husband or Father of the Year, but she refused to believe that he was the kind of man who would destroy another for financial gain.

"Mind if I join you?"

She looked around as Jake sat down beside her, a diet cola in one hand, his stethoscope in the other. He had

changed out of his surgical smock. His shirt was pale
blue and his jeans were faded to the point of being white.
He needed to shave. His eyes looked weary and sad.

"How did they take it?" she asked.

"Better than I expected. He's lucky to have a wife
like Betty. She'll get him through it. They'll be back
next year with another contender. Bill raises good
horses." He swigged the cola and regarded her closely.
"Why do I get the impression you'd rather be someplace
else today?"

"Wouldn't you?"

He shrugged. "Not really."

"Don't you have a social life?"

"Are you asking me if I have a girlfriend?" He
grinned.

"Yeah." Leah laughed. "I guess I am."

"If I didn't read the papers I'd think you were flirting
with me." As Leah frowned, Jake got up and walked
back into the office. He reappeared with a newspaper
that he tossed into her lap. She stared down at an image
of herself, Val, and Johnny, taken the day before at the
park, just moments before they were forced to run for
their lives from Johnny's fans. Below that was a photograph of her father attending a Clinton White House
function.

WHITEHORSE TO MARRY SENATOR'S DAUGHTER

*Sources close to Johnny Whitehorse have indi-
cated that wedding bells will soon be ringing for
America's most eligible bachelor. Identified as
Leah Foster Starr, only daughter of Senator Carl
Foster, the two have been seen together frequently,
despite the tragic accident that recently took the
life of Whitehorse's fiancée, Dolores Rainwater,
news anchor for KRXR Channel 10. Starr, who
practices veterinary medicine, recently returned to*

Ruidoso after a twelve-year absence, during which time she married Richard Starr, graduated from Texas A&M University, and practiced medicine in Pilot Point, Texas. Dr. Starr and her husband were divorced four years ago.

Problems between Whitehorse and Senator Foster have been ongoing since Foster stood hard against the compact reformation allowing gambling on the New Mexico reservations. Whitehorse, representing the New Mexico tribes, subsequently sued the state of New Mexico for its refusal to negotiate in good faith, and to force it to work out a compact. However, the U.S. Supreme Court reaffirmed the state's sovereign immunity to lawsuits by Indian tribes in gambling compact matters. Six months later Foster, in an act of good will toward the state's Native Americans, reversed his stand and spearheaded the legalization of casino gambling on the state's reservations. "Too little, too late," Whitehorse was quoted. "Foster's sudden turnaround, coming eight months after the Apache Casino and Resort development faced bankruptcy and rolled over to Formation Media, smacks of corruption and collusion. I intend to launch a full-scale investigation of the senator and his dealings with Formation Media. I assure the people of this state that Foster has not heard the last of this issue."

Comments from the Whitehorse camp neither confirm nor deny that Whitehorse and Starr are to be married this week at an undisclosed location. When contacted late last night for his comments on the rumor, Senator Foster replied only, "Over my dead body."

Leah tossed the paper aside just as her pager went off. She glanced at Jake as she reached for it. "For your information, I haven't agreed yet to marry Johnny. And furthermore, any decision I come to will in no way be determined by my father's feelings on the matter.''

"Spoken like a true future politician's wife."

She stuck her tongue out at him.

He laughed.

The pager read: *Call home asap.* Leah returned to the office and grabbed the phone. It rang only once before Shamika picked it up.

"Is Val okay?" Leah asked.

"Val is fine. I'm not so sure about me. Listen to this, girlfriend."

A racket came over the phone, making Leah remove it from her ear momentarily.

Shamika returned. "Thirty minutes ago at least fifty newspaper and television reporters appeared on our doorstep with cameras and recorders. Seems the word is out that you and Johnny—''

"I just read about it in the paper."

"Well, so has the rest of the state, apparently. They're swarming over this place like a bunch of locusts. I've had to lock the windows and doors. I swear to God someone tried to shimmy down the chimney a few minutes ago."

"Have you heard from Johnny?"

"Not yet. If they're this bad here I can only imagine what they're like at his place. Oh, your father called. Three times. He didn't sound happy."

"I'll get there as soon as possible."

"Don't bother. If I were you I'd find a place to ride this one out. Let Johnny's people handle it. They're equipped for this sort of thing."

"What cave do you propose I hide in?"

"A very dark one. Gotta go. I think someone just fell off the roof."

"Great." Leah slammed down the phone. "I suppose this means I'll get sued."

"Problems?"

She looked around as Jake stepped into the office, closing the door behind him. "Problems, you ask? I'd say that's an understatement."

"No." He shook his head. "I'm telling you you've got problems. Two television crews just arrived. Unless you want your pretty face plastered all over *Inside Edition* tonight, I'd suggest you use that door and get the hell out of here." He pointed to the back entrance. "I'll stall them as long as I can."

"Mind telling me where I'm supposed to go? They're swarming all over my house. If I show up at Johnny's it's only going to add fuel to the fire."

He reached into his jeans pocket, pulled out a set of keys, and tossed them to her. "Casa Grande Apartments on Grand Avenue. Apartment two ten. It's not fancy but it'll give you a place to crash until Johnny can get the situation under control."

Grinning, Leah shook her head. "This is crazy."

"Did you think a relationship with Johnny Whitehorse would be anything else?"

"I didn't think. Period. Johnny's just Johnny to me. I have to remind myself that he's . . . not the same guy I fell in love with a lifetime ago."

"You could have done worse. You could have hooked up with a guy like me who's generally pissed off at the world, hasn't voted since I was twenty-two, and would rather spend Sunday afternoons with my arm up horses' asses than with family or friends. Now get outta here before I change my mind and toss you to the sharks."

Edwin Fullerman calmly adjusted his glasses and cleared his throat as Johnny paced to the window, peered through the curtains at the swarm of reporters gathered over the grounds, then turned on Edwin again.

"I swear to you, Johnny. I didn't leak the news of you and Leah. I wouldn't do that even if I was pissed because you fired me. Hell, you've fired me a dozen times over the last five years. I don't take those tantrums seriously. You calm down after a few days and I get my job back. You fire me. I kiss your ass. We shake hands and make up and that's that. Christ, if I went around blabbing my clients' confidences to the media there wouldn't be an entertainer in the business who would return my phone calls.''

Johnny kicked a chair as hard as he could. It bounced off the wall and tumbled across the floor.

Jack entered the library from the adjoining office. ''Leah's line is busy. The operator says it's off the hook. I tried the track and got hold of Jake Graham. He told me to, and I quote, 'Stick the phone up your butt, fella. The lady isn't here.' I identified myself as your employee, but seems he's gotten two dozen such 'employee' phone calls in the last hour.''

Edwin sat on the edge of the desk and crossed his arms. ''I suspect this marriage thing is going to open up a very big can of worms regarding the issue with the senator and his involvement with Formation Media.''

''Not to mention Dolores's death, if, indeed, he was involved with her death.''

''The papers this morning were already rehashing the casino fiasco and the fact that you won't let it die. If, as you say, you located Rainwater's source, proving that Foster is up to his earlobes in dealings with Formation, then he or she better get the guns ready.''

The phone rang. Jack left the room to answer it. He returned shortly, his face white. ''Better turn on the television. The DA is making a statement.''

The walls of Jake's apartment were stark white—not a solitary object to break the monotony of being surrounded by bright glare. The furnishings, however, were as plush as money could buy: rich brown leather wraparound sofa and chairs with ottoman; marble-top credenza with carved mahogany legs—eighteenth-century French antique, Leah surmised—Oriental carpets, a scattering of bronzes, and a few potted tropical plants. There were unpacked boxes stacked in a kitchen that looked as if it had rarely, if ever, been used. Curious, Leah peeked inside the refrigerator to discover a quart of milk, a six-pack of Mexican beer, and a molding chunk of sharp cheddar cheese from a cheese store at the local mall. The freezer was totally empty.

Leah paced the immaculate apartment, checking her watch every few minutes and attempting to call Shamika, then Johnny, to no avail. The lines were constantly busy. She flopped on the sofa with a huff of exasperation, and closed her eyes.

So much for work.

So much for spending a lazy Sunday afternoon on a hammock with her son, or binging on popcorn and laughing at a black-and-white Godzilla with Oriental eyes that had apparently attained its black belt in karate.

So much for harboring the slightest inkling that she could marry Johnny Whitehorse and walk off into the sunset like any other blushing bride who had married the love of her entire life. Johnny was not just any Joe Blow. They would not live happily ever after in a little white cottage surrounded by a picket fence. Not if the media had anything to do with it.

And not if her father had anything to do with it.

When she opened her eyes again, the room had turned semidark. A small lamp glowed on a nearby end table. The smell of food and the rattle of pans in the kitchen made her sit up and frown in confusion.

Jake exited the kitchen in that moment, a glass of Zinfandel in each hand. "It's about time you woke up." He placed the sweating glass of wine on the table beside her. "Hope you like Chinese and tofu. I don't eat meat." He grinned. "I took a chance that you would still be here and figured you'd be as hungry as I am. I'm afraid my fridge doesn't offer much in the way of nutritional supplementation, unless you like cheese two months beyond its expiration date."

She gave him a sleepy smile and tried to read her watch.

"Eight-thirty," Jake said, dropping into a chair. "Food's ready when you are."

"I should call home."

"I already have. Your friend Shamika says things have quieted down, though she won't guarantee there's not someone still stuck in the chimney."

Leah relaxed back on the sofa and reached for the wine. "I probably shouldn't on an empty stomach. One glass of this and I might be tap dancing on your eighteenth-century French credenza."

"Ah, a fellow antiques enthusiast."

"I learned a great deal from my mother. On summer breaks she would take me to New Orleans to visit her parents and we'd scour the antiques shops looking for certain collector's pieces." She sipped the chilled wine, then grinned. "You don't strike me as a man who gets his thrills from stumbling over bargains in musty old antiques shops."

"My parents owned an antiques shop. My summers were spent abroad, mostly in England, going from estate sale to estate sale buying up antiques and bringing them back to sell in the States. It's how I got into veterinary medicine, as a matter of fact. Our summer home was right down the road from a racetrack. While my folks were bargaining for deals I was tagging along behind the track vet, driving him crazy with questions."

She studied her surroundings. "Nice apartment. I take it you haven't been here long."

"A year."

Leah raised her eyebrows and glanced again at the blank walls.

Jake laughed. "Okay, I admit to a certain hesitance over hanging pictures and cluttering furniture with dust catchers. All that shouts too much of permanence. As my ex-wife will attest, I'm not a permanent kind of guy.

Must be the gypsy in me. Stay in one place too long and I get itchy feet.''

"I suppose you could pass as a gypsy. Tie a bandanna around your brow and wear a large hoop earring in your left ear.''

"Been there and done it already on the Harley I bought after the wife decided I was too mercurial in my moods. I think she called it my mid-life crisis.''

"Was it?''

"I think it was more the old I-don't-think-I-love-you-anymore-so-I'm-going-to-act-like-a-child-and-make-you-run-not-walk-to-the-nearest-divorce-lawyer.'' He shrugged. "It was civil. No kids involved, so that helped.''

"Regrets?''

"No.'' He shook his head and finished his wine. "I didn't love her anymore, so how could there be regrets? Ready for food?''

"I'm starved.''

Leah smiled and Jake headed for the kitchen.

The doorbell rang.

Jake yelled, "You wanna get that?''

Leah set her wine aside and walked to the door.

Johnny stood in the dark, hands in his jeans pockets. "Hi,'' he said simply, and stepped into the apartment.

Jake stuck his head around the corner and grinned. "You're just in time for tofu and sprouts. Want wine or beer?''

"Beer.'' Johnny bent and kissed Leah's mouth. "Hi,'' he repeated, giving her a wink.

"I've been calling you all day.''

"You and fifty thousand other people.'' Catching her hand, he walked to the sofa and dropped onto it, pulling her down on his lap. "I finally called Jake myself and he told me you were here. We thought it best for you to stay until all the dust settled.''

"I was just about to call Shamika.''

"You won't get her.'' He kissed her again. "She and

Val are at my place, making themselves at home by now I suspect, being waited on hand and foot. I get the feeling Shamika approves. Val thinks he's at a hotel. He keeps asking if they can get room service."

Jake handed Johnny a beer, then picked up Leah's glass of wine and put it in her hand. "I think this calls for a celebration. To Johnny's good news, and to your impending marriage."

Leah laughed and shook her head. "Why am I getting the feeling that I'm missing some vital information here. What's your good news?"

Johnny drank deeply of his beer before answering. "The DA announced that my blood tests were clean."

"And? What about the negligence issue?"

Jake retreated to the kitchen and Johnny considered his answer a long moment before replying. "There are other aspects of the accident they're looking into, of course." He kissed her hand and looked hard into her eyes. "The only thing that matters to me right now is you and Val, and our spending the rest of our lives together."

TWENTY-ONE

"I know this sounds crazy, and a month ago if somebody had told me I'd be bored enough of being waited on hand and foot to tear out my hair I would have: one, suggested they were on drugs; two, insisted they were out of their minds; and three, told 'em to their face that they were simply jealous and to *get a life.*"

Her hands on her hips as she watched one of Johnny's many housekeepers haul away Shamika's dirty laundry, Shamika shook her head. "Is that all that woman ever does? Everytime I change my underwear she snatches them up and washes them. I'm starting to get a complex."

Shamika looked around at Leah where she lay across Val's massive bed, coloring within the black lines of the crayon book her son had been scribbling in the night before. "If Professor Carlisle could just see you now," Shamika laughed.

Leah tossed aside the red crayon and rolled to her back, sighed heavily, and shook her head. "How did my mother do it? No wonder she couldn't get through the day without drinking. I can't believe I once looked at

this indulgence as commonplace, something to be expected in life.''

"Val seems to be enjoying it.''

Leah smiled. "Val is enjoying Johnny. He thinks it's
very awesome—*his* new word, not mine—to be driven
to school by a chauffeur.''

"Call it what it is, girlfriend. *Bodyguard.* Not a bad-
looking one at that. I hear he played for the Broncos for
a couple of seasons, until his back was injured. Divorced. Two kids. Thirty-two years old and makes
nearly fifty grand a year.''

Leah laughed. "So when are the two of you going
out?''

"Saturday night. Dinner at seven. I got my eye on a
little red number with spaghetti straps and a neckline cut
down to here.'' Shamika sat down beside Leah and
stared at the wall. "Seriously . . .''

"Yes, let's be serious.''

"I think it's wonderful what Johnny is doing for you
and Val, and me too for that matter. But especially Val.
I've never seen him happier. Every day is like Christmas. Johnny's there when Val eats his breakfast. Johnny
makes sure he gets off to school on time. Johnny reads
to him at night—''

"And you're feeling as if you're not needed anymore.''

Shamika shrugged and grinned. "I confess; I'm missing the little guy.'' She flopped back on the bed and the
two of them stared at the ceiling. "I don't know what
it is about Johnny, but Val is thriving and that's all that
matters. How about you, Leah? How are you doing with
all this?''

"I feel like Cinderella.''

"So why are you still holding out on the marriage
proposal?''

"I married Richard for the wrong reasons: security,
money, fear of surviving on my own. Probably all the
reasons why most women get married. I don't think I

ever really loved him. He was simply a means to an end.''

"But you love Johnny."

"Yes." She smiled dreamily.

"So you've got your cake and can eat it too."

"But I can't give up *me* again. I worked hard to get through school, to become the finest vet I'm capable of being. Not simply to survive, but because I love doing it. I don't want to be like my mother, a fixture to take out and show off occasionally. I have to have a purpose.''

"Spoken like a true modern woman." Shamika rolled from the bed. "But from one modern woman to another, life is gonna suck real bad when you get to be fifty or sixty and you look up one day and find yourself alone. Think back over the last few years and your regret over having walked out on Johnny the first time—the love you felt like you missed out on.''

"I failed once, Shamika."

"Get over it. Get over this fear you've got of having more children. Get over this hang-up you've developed over failure. Get over this absurd need for your father's approval.''

"Now *that* is absurd."

"Is it?" Shamika walked to the door. "He's never going to change, Leah. He is what he is. Senator Foster is a machine. Cold, hard steel. So what if he offered you a job? You know as well as I do why he did it. To buy you over to his side. To woo you away from Johnny. To assure your loyalty when the caca hits the fan. Look at it this way, Cinderella. How many people in life actually get a second chance to recapture the greatest love of their life?''

As Shamika left the room, Leah got up and walked to the window. Below, men milled about the manicured grounds, most dressed casually in jeans and tee shirts, the telltale bulges of their hidden guns the only evidence that they were anything more than gardeners. Not that she wasn't accustomed to men lurking around their home with guns tucked under their belts; since her father had won his seat in the Senate, weapon-toting companions had become the norm.

Certainly, that had been a half a lifetime ago; she'd been a teenager who thought it was cool to be driven to school by bodyguards. And this was now. She was an adult with a career; she thrived on fresh air and sunshine, her independence, and her privacy, of which she had become obsessive since Val's birth. How would she learn to deal with living their lives in a fishbowl, unable to curl up under her blanket of denial whenever life threw her a curve she did not want to acknowledge?

But she also thrived on Johnny Whitehorse. Since he'd moved her into his house a week ago she had never felt so alive or happy . . . or in love. At times she felt positively delirious . . . so why couldn't she shake this sense of impending doom, as if the sky would open up at any moment and rain catastrophe on her head?

At nine-forty that night Leah said goodnight to Roy Moon, patted the Arabian stallion she had ridden the last hour in the indoor arena, and headed for the house. Hopefully the meeting between Johnny and his staff would be ended. She wanted to talk to him again about her returning to work now that the media had backed off in the attempts to wrangle interviews and photos from them. Not that she was worried that she would lose her job; Johnny was one of the bosses, after all. In fact, the entire board of trustees had given their approval of her taking as much time as she needed for the media storm to subside, as they all knew it eventually would. Until the recent accident with Dolores, Johnny had managed to maintain his privacy in Ruidoso. To most of the locals he was simply Johnny, hometown boy made good. Had it not been for Dolores's death and the frantic scramble to cover it in the media, life would have remained relatively normal at Whitehorse Farm except for the occasional out-of-towners who cruised by in their rent-a-car to snap photos of Johnny's front gate.

Ed, Roger, and Jack filed out of the house and streamed down the front steps, briefcases in hand, faces somber as they marched toward their cars. They barely glanced at Leah, as if intentionally ignoring her existence. Robert Anderson tarried on the porch, the light overhead casting sharp shadows on his face.

"Everyone looks very serious," she commented as she mounted the front steps.

Robert didn't smile. "It wasn't much of a meeting. My client's thoughts appear to be elsewhere."

Val's laughter erupted from the house, bringing a smile to Leah's face.

Anderson shook his head and with a muttered curse headed for his car. Watching him go, Leah yelled, "Robert, I take it you don't have kids."

"No!" he shouted back.

"I didn't think so," she replied, then said to herself, "Lucky kids."

Johnny met her in the foyer, pushing Val in his wheelchair. Shamika followed, the ex-Bronco football player at her side. He peeled away from the others and said, "I'll bring the car up."

"Are we going someplace?" Leah asked.

"Johnny has surprise for Val," Val announced very clearly, looking up at Johnny and grinning.

"Oh?" She kissed Val on the cheek and smiled at Johnny. "Is it bigger than a breadbox?"

"Definitely," Johnny replied.

"Bigger than . . . a twenty-one-inch television?"

"Absolutely."

"A . . . six stack of hay bales?"

"Much bigger."

She feigned a frown and narrowed her eyes. Val's grin grew wider and Shamika shrugged as Leah glanced at her for a hint. "Is it on the premises?" she asked.

"Nope," Johnny said.

The car stopped at the foot of the steps and Johnny eased Val's chair down each stair as the driver opened the car doors, then hurried over to help put Val in the backseat.

"Am I invited?" Leah asked.

Johnny turned and lifted his hand to her. "Would I go anywhere without you?"

"I don't know. Would you?"

"Not unless I felt it would be detrimental to your life and happiness."

"You are such a smooth talker, Johnny."

"And you love it."

"Oh, yes." She took his hand. "I most definitely love it."

The lights of the Big Top Carnival and Circus lit up the night sky in a bloom of red, green, gold, and blue twinklers. The glowing marquee out front read:

WELCOME VALENTINO STARR!

There was a scattering of cars and vans in the parking lot, each showing handicapped license plates. As the driver parked the limo among them, Leah looked at Johnny, then Shamika, who had begun to grin. "What's going on?"

"Johnny rented the carnival for tonight, for Val and his friends."

Leah sank back in the seat, glad for the darkness that hid the look of raw emotion she was certain was etched in her face. She couldn't speak. She did not dare look at Johnny or she would burst out in tears.

Johnny took her hand. "I trust you remember this place."

She nodded and swallowed. "You brought me here on our first real date. I got a stomachache eating corn dogs and cotton candy. You won a giant walrus playing Skee-Ball. I still have it, by the way. And at closing time you got your friend who operated the Ferris wheel to stop us at the top so we could watch the fireworks exploding all around us. I think we ended up making out more than we watched the fireworks.''

"We made our own fireworks.'' Johnny wiggled his eyebrows, making Shamika laugh and Leah blush.

Both children and adults rode the rides; played the games—all of which had obviously been rigged to allow the children to win—ate cotton candy, popcorn, and ice cream; and watched the circus of trained elephants, tigers, and horses, not to mention the lithe trapeze artists flying through the air with the greatest of ease.

Val rode the merry-go-round twelve times, Johnny and Leah at his side, coaxing him to hold fast to the rising and falling steed with arched neck and flaring nostrils. By the eighth ride he was gripping the pole with his own hands, his legs locked around the animal's body, whooping and laughing and shouting to Shamika, who waved each time they flew by her: "Val flying now, Mika!''

Just before midnight everyone climbed aboard the Ferris wheel. It slowly rotated high into the night sky, allowing them to look out over the grounds of bright, vibrant lights the color of rainbows. With Val sitting between her and Johnny, Leah held her son's hand and pointed to the distant glow of downtown Ruidoso; then they counted the stars overhead and watched a meteorite streak across the universe in a burst of fiery light.

At straight-up midnight, the Ferris wheel stopped, leaving Leah, Johnny, and Val swinging at the very top. Then the first streaks of fireworks whirred into the sky above their heads and exploded, sending red and green sparks mushrooming to what seemed to be forever. Then more, popping, banging, inundating the night with light, until the shapes of words formed before Leah's eyes.

MARRY ME

Smiling, laughing, ackowledging the applause and whistles of approval from Val's guests, Leah turned her tear-filled eyes to Johnny's and nodded. "Of course I'll marry you. Of course."

The phone rang at three A.M. Johnny fumbled for it, glancing at Leah to see if it had disturbed her.

"Johnny? Johnny, it's Savanah. Are you alone?"

He sat up, shook his head in an attempt to clear his mind of its grogginess, then leaned slightly over Leah to see if she was really asleep. "Good as," he finally replied in a slightly slurred voice.

"What is that supposed to mean?"

"Exactly what it sounds like."

"Leah is there, isn't she?"

"So what?"

"Tell me the rumors aren't true. Are you marrying her or not?"

"What's that got to do with anything?"

"Everything, considering what I'm holding in my hand."

He glanced back at Leah and partially covered the phone with one hand. "You got them."

"Those and more. Seems I'm not the only one who sneaks the occasional forbidden photo."

There came a muffled voice, then a loud, "Hello?"

Johnny jerked the phone from his ear.

"Hello? Hello? I don't think there's anyone there. Hello? Mr. Whitehorse? Is that really you?"

Lowering his voice even more, Johnny whispered, "Who the hell is this?"

"Maude Elliot, Mr. Whitehorse. This is really Mr. Whitehorse, isn't it? The guy on Fifth Avenue? The one with his jeans unzipped?"

He rolled his eyes and left the bed, tucked the phone under one arm and walked to the bathroom, closed the door, eased the lid down on the toilet and sat down in the dark.

"Hello? Is anyone there?" Maude Elliot seemed to scream.

"Obviously Savanah has a good reason for this," he finally replied, more to himself than to Maude Elliot.

"I'm a photographer, Mr. Whitehorse. I've worked for Formation Media for oh, golly, five years or so. Well, I really don't work for FM. I'm freelance. I move around a lot. Sometimes the resorts contract me to, you know, take pictures of their guests or do promotional shots for brochures or ads or postcards. I work mostly with the island resorts: Barbados, Aruba—"

"What are you telling me, Ms. Elliot?"

"Oh please, call me Maude."

He nodded and took a deep breath.

"I met Savanah last year when I came up to Toronto for the opening of the Crystal Casino. We sort of hit it off. She's a darn good photographer—"

"Get to the point . . . Maude."

"Oh. Sure. I guess you're wanting to get back to bed, huh? Heck, I'm used to these kind of hours—"

"Maude."

"Oh. Ah . . . Savanah has filled me in with what's going on, you're trying to nail that senator? Good for you. They're all a lot of sleazebuckets you know, would sell their blind grannies if they thought it would buy them a few votes. Anyway, what she's got here, the photos, they're good, a little grainy, but . . . what I've got are better."

Johnny frowned. "Are you saying you have photographs of Foster—"

"Aruba, three years ago. You see, Formation never holds their meetings in the same place; for obvious reasons they wish to keep their anonymity. Just so happens I was there doing a shoot for one of their competitors, the Hilton I think, or maybe it was Holiday Inn. I wandered over to the Rama Rio Resort with the thought of knocking on a few doors, handing out a few business cards, drum up a little business. The place was swarming

with bigwigs; I mean these cats were dripping the di-
nero, know what I mean? Major big shots we're talkin',
and pretty damn creepy lookin' if you ask me. I thought
I'd fallen into a friggin' United Nations powwow. Japanese, Mexicans, Middle Easterners. And right there
among them was these familiar faces."

"Foster."

"Among others. Ever heard of Gary Taylor?"

"Elected governor of Nevada the last election."

"Bingo. How about Mark Schwin?"

"Minnesota senator."

"And last but not least, Harry Johnston."

"Just announced his intentions of running for governor of New Jersey the next election." Johnny closed his
eyes. "Jesus. You have their photographs?"

"Not with me, of course. They're in my files. Shoot,
at the time it just never occurred to me that there was
any kind of shenanigans going on. I just happen to collect photos of the rich and famous; occasionally I can
make a buck or two on them if the right opportunity
comes along."

"Where are your files, Maude?"

"Home."

"Where is home?" he said through his teeth.

"The Caymans."

"Put Savanah on the phone, please."

Savanah got back on the phone.

"Is she a nut or what?" Johnny asked.

"Not at all."

"Where are you now?"

"Atlanta. On my way to the Caymans."

"Once you get your hands on those photographs, stay
put. I'm flying down to get you myself."

"What about Leah, Johnny? What do you intend to
do about her?"

"I don't know," he said in the dark.

• • •

When Leah awoke, she reached for Johnny. He wasn't there. She sighed and closed her eyes, smiling as she thought of the night before, of fireworks and falling stars, and the happiness in her son's face. It was a dream. A wonderful, beautiful dream. Too romantic to be real. Too miraculous to be believable.

The door opened and Shamika, grinning ear to ear, walked in pushing a wheelchair.

Leah sat up and rubbed her eyes.

"Well? What do you think?" Shamika parked the chair by the bed. "It arrived this morning. Top of the line, honey. This baby is good for a hundred thousand miles at least. And get a load of this." She dropped into it and touched a button. The chair moved forward. She touched another and it rolled back.

Leah slid from the bed and moved slowly around the chair, her throat beginning to hurt. "Am I really seeing what I think I'm seeing?"

"This sweetheart must have put Johnny-boy back a good twelve grand. And not only that. I just got a call from a Jolene Carrington at Albuquerque Medical Research Institute. She spoke to Johnny three days ago. He's arranged for us to take Val in to be evaluated for Botox treatments. If he's considered a good candidate they can begin the treatments immediately. Like that day."

Leah pulled off her nightgown and grabbed for a tee shirt, then her jeans. She began to laugh so hard she stumbled around with one leg in her pants, the other out.

A maid appeared at the door, and Shamika, laughing too, cried, "Hold on to your drawers, Leah, the panty snatcher is back."

Grabbing up the panties Johnny had pulled off her the night before, Leah tossed them to the wide-eyed servant. "You may have my panties. You may have all of my panties. I may never wear panties again, for that matter." At last she wiggled the jeans up over her naked hips and snapped them. "Where is Johnny?" Barefoot, she ran from the room.

"Haven't seen him this morning," Shamika yelled after her.

She took the stairs two at a time, barely managing to contain her outrageous desire to slide like a mischievous kid down the winding banister. On tiptoe she moved to the office door, which was slightly ajar; hearing someone speaking quietly, she nudged the door open.

Edwin Fullerman sat behind Johnny's desk, his back to Leah as he spoke on the phone.

"Look, Ted. We are not prepared at this time to go on record with any public accusations. What good would it do either of us? Until we have proof positive in our hands we keep our mouths closed. All I can tell you now is that Johnny is on his way to some undisclosed location to pick up the evidence to nail that son-of-a-bitch. I can appreciate your position. District Attorney Singer has been more than patient. You know and I know Johnny didn't drive himself off that road and intentionally kill Dolores Rainwater. He was purposefully rammed off that road by another car. Your forensics experts have verified that beyond a shadow of a doubt. But until we've established a motive . . . exactly. We'll be faced with another scandal that will end up hurting a lot of people and damaging Johnny's reputation."

Ed tapped on the desk with the end of a pencil as he nodded and sighed into the phone. "I've attempted to call Robert Anderson this morning. No luck so far. But I'm sure Johnny will want you to discuss your plans to publicly make a statement regarding the accident and the investigation with Bobby before you go on the air. Yes, I realize both the DA's office and the police are getting a lot of heat over this. It looks as if you're protecting Johnny.

"What? You can tell Singer to kiss our ass. No way is Johnny going to turn himself in to the frigging police for questioning. I don't care if this makes the police and

DA's office look like a bunch of dunces. Fine. Make your goddamn statement. Someone ran Johnny and Dolores off the road that night in an obvious attempt to kill them. The police are investigating the evidence. At this time Johnny makes no further comment on the matter."

Ed slammed the phone down and swung around in the chair. His eyes widened to find Leah standing in the door.

"Oops," he said, and dropped the pencil to the desk.

"What's going on?" Leah asked, her stomach feeling queasy all of a sudden. "What are you saying? That someone attempted to murder Johnny and Dolores?"

He rocked back and forth in the chair and drummed his fingers on the desk. "Yes," he replied carefully.

"Why wasn't I told about this?"

"Johnny didn't want to overly alarm you."

She walked slowly toward the desk, her eyes locked on Ed's. "Why are the police keeping so hush-hush about it?"

"You know the press and the wild public speculation. The last thing we want to do is throw open a can of worms."

"Then you have an idea who's behind it?"

Ed looked away. "Nothing definite."

"You just told Ted Weir that Johnny is off someplace gathering evidence. Obviously you think you know who did it."

Mouth pressed, Ed considered his words. "First and foremost, Ms. Starr, we must protect Johnny. It's our job. He didn't get to where he is by dumb luck. He never made a move in his career that wasn't orchestrated beforehand. He's methodical and goal oriented. He's surrounded himself with people as brilliant and motivated as he is. You know as well as I do that Johnny has no intention of spending his life in front of a camera. He has far greater aspirations, not to mention brains."

"You're not answering my question, Ed. Who would want to murder Johnny and Dolores?"

"Someone who considers Johnny a threat, I suppose."

She stared at Ed and watched as a red flush crept up his face, making his green eyes look greener behind their wire-rimmed spectacles. The sick feeling in her stomach spread through her body like icy tentacles as she backed to the door.

"You bastards," she said, shaking her head. "You're going to accuse my father of this, aren't you?"

"I think you'd better talk to Johnny—"

"My father might be a machine but he's not a monster. He's not a murderer."

Leah turned for the door.

Edwin jumped from his chair. "Leah, wait—"

"Go to hell," she shouted. "All of you."

Savanah finished spreading the collection of photographs out over the table as Johnny leaned over her shoulder, inspecting each picture. There were images of sea birds and waves crashing against craggy shores, sunbathers frolicking in the surf, smiling seaside waiters serving guests icy drinks. There were others of plush hotels with brass ceiling fans, cool marble floors, and lush tropical trees growing in the foyers, and restaurant shots of buffet tables laden with passion fruits, mangoes, and papayas.

But it was the last dozen photos that Savanah laid down that grabbed his attention.

Maude Elliot picked up one of the three-by-fives and waved it at him. "Got this with a telephoto lens. That sweetheart could define a nose hair at half a mile."

Johnny took it and walked to a light.

Maude chuckled and elbowed Savanah. "He's damn pretty, ain't he? If I wasn't sixty-five and gray-headed I might put a move or two on him. Always did like the tall dark surly kind."

Savanah smiled and reached for a photograph.

"He don't say much, does he?"

"He's simply very careful with his words."

"Guess he'd have to be, being who he is and all."
She reached for the vodka and Seven she had put down
earlier. "Sure you two don't want a drink? By the looks
of those clouds I suspect you're going to be here a while.
Storms predicted for all night. I'd think real hard about
taking that Cessna up in these winds. You guys care for
a sandwich? I've got goose liver and pimiento cheese.
Don't know about you, but I'm starving."

Maude moved to the kitchen as Johnny shifted
through the many photographs of well-suited businessmen, among them the familiar faces belonging to Foster,
Taylor, Harry Johnston, and Schwin.

"It's the same group that came to Toronto last fall,"
Savanah said. "They blocked off an entire wing of the
hotel to assure their privacy from the guests."

Johnny took other photographs and studied them as
intently, then joined Maude in the kitchen.

"You do all your own developing?" he asked.

"Sure do."

"Can you enlarge this photograph to bring out these
faces a little more clearly?" He pointed to the slightly
blurred image of a man standing behind Senator Foster.

"Sure. No problem." Putting aside her sandwich,
Maude headed for the darkroom.

Johnny walked to the plate-glass door and looked out
on the distant horizon, where the gray rainclouds met
the wind-whipped ocean. Maude was right. No way was
he taking his plane through those clouds.

"I expected more enthusiasm." Savanah moved up
beside him. "It's Leah, isn't it? You know this will destroy her. More important, it will undoubtedly destroy
the two of you."

"She'll see reason. She has to."

Savanah laid her hand on Johnny's arm. "For your
sake, I hope you're right. Me? The bastard killed my
sister. I'm going to make sure he goes to prison for the
rest of his life."

"Maybe."

Frowning, Savanah shook her head in confusion. "Maybe? Are you telling me that you question whether Foster was behind the attempt to kill you and Dolores?"

Johnny turned away. "I think I'll have that sandwich now."

Savanah paced as Johnny stood at the glass door, ate his goose-liver sandwich and watched the rain slam against the coast. Lightning danced above the waves and thunder vibrated the walls of the condominium.

Finally, Maude emerged wearing an apron and rubber gloves. She handed the still damp photograph to Johnny. He moved to the lamp and turned the eight-by-ten into the light.

"Ah God," he groaned. "That son-of-a-bitch."

TWENTY-TWO

"Johnny's in Albuquerque," Shamika explained. "He asks that you not come to any rash decisions. He'll explain everything to you when he gets home."

"Did you tell him what I told you to tell him? Shall I repeat it for you in case you forgot?" Leah replied, her attention fixed on the hotel lobby's front entrance as she gripped the phone receiver to her ear.

"Honey, I don't use language like that in mixed company."

The lobby doors opened and a group of laughing tourists entered, their hair and clothes dripping water. Behind them, rain streaked like knives against the pavement.

"I take it you've not seen your father yet."

"I've been waiting since eleven. No one seems to know when he'll return, or where he is for that matter."

"If he's smart he's gotten the heck out of Dodge before the you-know-what hits the fan."

"You know as well as I that my father backs down from nothing."

"Neither does Godzilla. If something or someone gets

in his way he just stomps the bejesus out of it. In fact, that's probably where he is now, preparing to launch a full-scale attack against Johnny. Your office phone is ringing again. Shall I answer it?''

''No.'' She glanced at the elevator, the front doors, the entrance to the coffeeshop.

''I know you don't want to hear this now, but I got another call from the school. Sandra Howard is extremely concerned over Val. Leah, he's not taking this situation well. He's confused and showing signs of his old depression. He keeps asking for Johnny.''

''He'll get over it. There was life before Johnny Whitehorse—''

''Apparently not for Val, and if you'll be honest with yourself for once, not for you either.''

Leah looked at her watch. Sandra Howard would be loading up the kids into the bus about now. The trip from the school to home normally took thirty minutes, but in this rain would take longer. If she left now she would make it home in time for Val's arrival.

Shamika sighed. ''Why, exactly, are you trying to see your father, Leah? What will it accomplish? Do you think by looking him in the eye and asking if he was in any way involved with Rainwater's death you're going to determine if he's lying or not? Where have you been for thirty years? The man is a United States senator, for God's sake. They *invented* the lie. In fact, I think I read someplace that the serpent in the Garden of Eden went on to become the first elected politician.''

The lobby door opened again and a man entered, his attention focused on the umbrella he was struggling to close.

''Leah, are you there?'' Shamika said in her ear.

''Yes.'' She nodded. ''I have to go now. I want to be home when Val gets there.''

''That's the first sensible thing you've said today.''

Leah hit the End key on the mobile phone, then the Power button, her gaze still locked on the man who finally turned toward her, mopping his damp face with a handkerchief. He looked directly at her, and froze.

"Hello, Robert." Leah tucked the phone into her pocket and moved across the lobby. "I thought you were staying at the Inn of the Mountain Gods."

"Right." He nodded and folded the handkerchief. "Just here on business. And you?"

"I came to see my father."

His eyebrows raised and he glanced toward the elevator. "I didn't realize the senator was in town." He tapped the end of his umbrella on the floor to dislodge the remaining rain. "What's Johnny up to these days?"

Leah frowned. "Haven't been by the ranch in the last couple of days?"

"I spoke with Ed and Jack a couple of times. Ed tells me that you and Johnny have been holed up like lovebirds making plans for your marriage."

"So you haven't spoken with Johnny personally."

"Can't seem to get through to him." He gave her a thin smile. "You can't keep him all to yourself, you know. The man's got responsibilities. Tell him to give me a call. We have issues to discuss."

"I'll bet."

They stared at one another a silent moment, then Leah looked away. "I have to go. Val will be on his way home."

"Good seeing you again, Oh, and drive safely. We wouldn't want another of Johnny's girlfriends to end up like Dolores . . . would we?"

"Why do I get the impression you would like nothing better, Mr. Anderson?"

Turning her back on Anderson, Leah exited the hotel, glancing back briefly before running through the rain to her truck. With water running down her cheeks, she stared out through the rain-spattered window, watching as Anderson left the hotel and headed for his rented car.

Odd that Anderson would know nothing about Johnny's being out of town, or the fact that she, Shamika, and Val had moved out of the ranch and back home two days ago. Why hadn't Ed informed him that Johnny was after evidence to prove her father was somehow involved with Dolores's death? Johnny never made a move or a statement without first consulting the consequences with Anderson.

The truck shimmied, coughed, sputtered, and died three times before the engine finally turned over. The wipers scratched across the windshield, doing little to alleviate the torrent washing down over the truck. Leah drove as slowly as possible through the downtown traffic, revving the engine to keep it from dying when she was forced to stop at red lights.

She turned on the radio just as the news came on, then turned it off. She wasn't in the mood to listen to more discussion about Johnny and her father and the investigation of Formation Media and Dolores's death, or the speculation on whether or not she, the senator's daughter, would marry Johnny Whitehorse.

Turning on to Highway 249, she left the heavy traffic behind her. The rain, however, fell harder, forcing her to a crawl as she did her best to make out the broken yellow lines on one side, the shoulder of the road on the other. Cars moved up behind her and, growing impatient, whipped around her regardless of the slippery highway and the fact that visibility was virtually nil, their tires sending water spraying in a blinding curtain over her windshield.

Again, a car moved up behind her, close, its bright lights like two staring eyes in the thick gray rain. It did not move around her, just inched closer, until it seemed to Leah to be inches from her bumper. If she was forced to brake suddenly, especially in this rain, no way would the driver avoid rear-ending her.

Carefully, she eased over to the shoulder, allowing him room to pass. The car crept by her, its driver waving his thanks before speeding off into the haze.

Tense, her hands gripping the steering wheel almost

painfully, Leah did her best to breathe evenly as she
moved back onto the road, dropping her speed even
more as she came to a bend in the highway.

Through the deluge came a flash of colored lights. The
cars that had passed her moments before were braking
and pulling off the highway as police in rain slickers
waved them aside to allow one of the many emergency
vehicles through. Sirens screaming and beacons blinking
red and yellow lights, first one ambulance streaked by
Leah, then another, on their way to Ruidoso Hospital.

From her position she could just make out the jackknifed cab and trailer of an eighteen-wheeler that had
obviously failed in its attempt to avoid hitting another
vehicle. Leah turned off the engine and jumped from the
truck, catching her breath as the rain speared into her
face like little needles. She ran along the highway shoulder, shielding her eyes with one hand, nudging her way
through the onlookers in hopes of offering her medical
expertise in any way possible.

A cop shouted at her and she yelled back, "I have a
medical background! Perhaps I can help . . ."

Behind the policeman emerged the accident, the
smashed truck cab pinning a vehicle to the ground.
Blinking rain from her eyes, Leah moved toward the
scene, glass shards crunching under her feet, the squawk
of walkie-talkies and the shouts of paramedics assaulting
her ears. Sirens shrieked as another ambulance eased
through the growing crowd and headed for town.

"No, no," she said aloud, shaking her head as her
heart crawled out of her chest and up her throat, each
beat as deafening as the thunder crashing overhead. A
pressure centered behind her eyes, and she could not
blink, or breathe, or move as she focused on the crushed
and twisted remains of a school bus.

"That's my son's bus," she choked, pointing to the
crumpled mass and turning to the officer who walked
toward her through the rain. "That's . . . Oh, God. Oh
my God."

• • •

Ed stood by his car near the runway as Johnny and Savanah walked away from the Cessna.

"You both look like hell," Ed remarked as Johnny
opened the passenger door.

"That good, huh?" Johnny dropped into the front seat
as Savanah crawled into the back. She lay down on the
seat with a groan.

"Don't anyone wake me until this time tomorrow,"
Savanah said as she closed her eyes.

"So are either of you going to let me in on where
you've been and what you were doing? Mind telling me
why I've had to make up excuses why you could not or
would not take or return phone calls? All hell has broken
loose while you've been off gallivanting around the
country."

Johnny reached into his pocket and pulled out a candy
bar. He glanced back at Savanah, who appeared to be
sleeping already, then ripped open the Butterfinger and
began to eat.

"I haven't eaten since yesterday at noon. Stop at the
first drive-through you come to," Johnny replied.

Ed rolled his eyes. "The senator has publicly chal-
lenged you, Johnny. He went on the six o'clock news
last night and confronted you, the district attorney's office, and the police department to put up or shut up.
Why, you ask? Because the word has finally come down
from Washington: an investigation of the good senator
and Formation Media is being launched. The district attorney finally admitted too that they believe the senator
and Formation Media might have links to the accident
that killed Dolores. Why, the media asked? Because, according to Johnny Whitehorse, at the time of Dolores's
death she had evidence of Foster's affiliation with Formation Media, thereby establishing motive for the senator and/or Formation to kill you both."

"What about Leah? How is she taking it?"

Ed eased his foot off the gas and looked at Johnny,

his normally ruddy complexion drained of color. "Oh, man. I forgot. You don't know. There was an accident yesterday. I would have called you but I didn't know how to reach you. I thought you might have heard about it on the news or something."

"What accident?" Johnny crushed the Butterfinger in his hand as he stared at Ed, waiting.

"Val's bus was hit by a truck yesterday afternoon during a storm. Five were killed, Johnny: the driver, a Sandra Howard, and three kids. The driver lived long enough to tell authorities that the brakes went out on the bus and he couldn't stop. They ran through a stop sign, directly in front of an eighteen-wheeler. No way could the truck's driver avoid hitting them. Val is critical, Johnny. According to Shamika, the doctors don't offer much hope."

A slender blond man with a deep tan stood outside Val's hospital room door, smoking a cigarette and staring at his feet. He looked up and frowned at Johnny as Johnny moved by him, headed for Val's room.

The man grabbed Johnny's arm. "Hey, buddy, where the hell do you think you're going?"

Once Johnny had believed Val to have his mother's eyes, but looking down into Richard Starr's eyes, he realized he had been wrong. He bit back his urge to wrap his hands around Val's father's throat and crush it, not just because he had abandoned Leah and Val, but because he'd married Leah in the first place.

"Nobody goes in there except family," Starr said.

Johnny jerked his arm away and turned for the door.

Richard grabbed him again. "I know who you are, Whitehorse. You might muscle your way around Hollywood or Washington, but not here. You're going to leave my kid and my wife alone."

"*Ex*-wife."

"*My* kid."

Johnny replied with a short laugh, put his hand on

Richard's chest, and shoved him against the wall. He then pointed his finger in Starr's face. "Be nice. Be very nice, Dickie, or I'm liable to do something I'll later regret. I'm in a particularly sore mood right now, and anyone who has known me for any length of time knows my patience has its endurance. Backed into a corner, I come out swinging."

"Are you threatening me, Whitehorse?"

"Definitely."

"I'll get the cops."

"You do that." Twisting his fingers in Richard's shirt, Johnny pushed him toward a nurse and orderly, who caught him before he fell on his face. The pair stared at Johnny as if a unicorn had suddenly materialized before them.

Johnny eased open the door.

Leah sat at Val's bedside, her head resting on the bed, eyes closed, her hand holding her son's as the monitors beeped frighteningly weakly in the quiet.

Johnny sank against the wall, unable to speak.

First Dolores. Now this. But this was worse, so much worse. This was a child. A very special child. Who might have, if things had gone differently those years ago, been his and Leah's. A young soul, a broken spirit that ached to fly. Johnny had wanted so desperately to teach him how.

Leah opened her swollen red eyes and raised her head slowly. For the briefest instant a look of desperate relief wiped the lines from her brow, and her lips trembled. Then, just as swiftly, it was gone, replaced by an outrage that hit Johnny with a sickening punch.

"Get out," her lips whispered.

"Please—"

"How dare you."

"Don't do this, Leah."

"If you don't leave this minute—"

"I have to see him."

"Haven't you done enough? You've destroyed my

father and, thanks to your subterfuge regarding your feelings for us, you've broken Val's heart. If you don't leave here now I'm calling the police. I'll file charges on you for harassment.''

"I love you. I love Val.''

Looking as if she might crumble into a thousand pieces, Leah sagged against the bed. "I so wanted it to be true. That you loved us. I can't tell you how often I fantasized of our finding one another again, of your coming to love my son like I do.

"I think, if I really want to be honest with myself for a change, that my real reason for returning to Ruidoso was in hopes of your forgiving me for my stupidity years ago. How infantile to believe you would come to care for us more than you care to remedy an injustice perpetrated against your people. Very selfish on my part to think you would give up half a lifetime of struggle for love. Johnny Whitehorse never turned his back on a fight. He always saw his obligations through. Funny. One of the very attributes that made me fall in love with you in the first place is the same one that breaks my heart now.''

Johnny shoved away from the wall. This time as he moved toward the bed Leah did not stop him.

Johnny touched Val's cold brow. "Hey, pal. It's Johnny. I've brought you something.'' Reaching into his shirt pocket, he withdrew the small trinket that had been carved into the shape of a human form. "It's called a *tzi-daltai*. A very long time ago I made it for your mother. I never got around to giving it to her. The *tzi-daltai* is carved of wood that has been struck by lightning, and therefore considered powerful and with much energy to ward off evil and illness. My grandfather gave me this wood when I was your age. Now I give it to you.'' He laid the talisman on Val's chest over his heart.

Turning again to Leah, he did his best to smile as he touched her face. "*Sons-ee-ah-ray*. My morning star. I told you once that I would not lose you again. I meant it."

Pressing a kiss to her brow, Johnny held Leah briefly before turning for the door.

Richard Starr stood with Shamika in the waiting area outside Val's room. Shamika hurried over to Johnny and threw her arms around him. He hugged her close as she wept against his shoulder.

"Where is her father?" Johnny asked.

"With his attorneys," she replied, wiping her face with a tissue. "Would you believe he hasn't even been up here yet? Sent word last night that as soon as his meetings were over he'd come up."

"Call me if anything changes. I'll be at the ranch."

She nodded as Johnny walked over to Richard, who ground out his cigarette in an ashtray.

"You and I will meet again," Johnny told him, the tone of his voice enough threat that Richard looked nervously toward the nearest exit.

Searching his pocket for coins, Johnny moved to a pay phone on the wall. He punched in the ranch number and waited as the phone rang. Ed answered.

"Is the meeting arranged?" Johnny asked.

"One hour from now."

"Did you reach Inspector Parker?"

"Everything's arranged. How's Val?"

"He's going to be fine," Johnny replied in as strong and positive a voice as he could manage, then he added, "But I'm not so sure about his mother."

Savanah paced as Roy Moon, Ed, Jack, and Johnny drank their hot coffee in silence. Inspector Parker, District Attorney Singer, and Ted Weir chatted quietly in the corner of the office, laughing occasionally, as if arresting someone on suspicion of murder and attempted murder was nothing out of the ordinary.

The door opened suddenly and Robert walked in. "Sorry I'm late. I was on an overseas call when I got your message." He stopped short upon seeing Parker, Singer, and Weir. "This looks serious."

"Very," Johnny said. "Sit down, Bobby."

Robert cleared his throat and sat down, placed his briefcase beside his feet, and took a deep breath. "Should I get my recorder for this?"

Johnny shrugged. "Why not?"

Robert dug into the briefcase for the recorder, his gaze moving over the law officials in the back of the room. "I hope you haven't discussed anything with them that might prejudice your rights."

"Wouldn't think of it, Bobby. You've taught me better than that." Johnny grinned as Robert hit the On button, then sat back in the chair.

"So what's up?" Robert asked.

Savanah moved up behind Johnny. "I work for the Crystal Casino in Toronto. I'm Dolores's sister."

"Really. My condolences to your family." He crossed his legs and looked from Savanah back to Johnny, then to Ed and Jack.

"Where were you the night of my accident?" Johnny asked.

"That's a very odd question."

"Did you have a conversation with Dolores two days before her death?"

He shrugged. "Maybe. You know Dolores. She was always calling me or Ed, asking our advice on one thing or another."

"What was her reason for calling you that day?"

"I . . . don't recall."

"I'll tell you why she called you." Savanah moved around the desk. "To ask legal advice regarding evidence I supplied her of Senator Foster's association with Formation Media. She thought way too much of her career to jeopardize it in any way. Although she didn't mention you by name, she told me when we spoke on the phone that she intended to contact an attorney just to be on the safe side."

Savanah sat on the desk before Robert, her knee touching his. "Aside from me, Johnny, and Dolores, you're the only other person who knew about those photographs, Mr. Anderson."

Johnny opened the desk drawer and retrieved several papers. He handed them to Robert, remaining silent as Robert shifted through them, his brow beginning to sweat.

"Would you like to explain what you were doing in Albuquerque before my accident? Why you rented a car at the airport that afternoon and returned it early the next morning, apologizing for the fact that you were in a slight accident but the insurance you took out on the car would take care of it."

"After the accident, I phoned your home," Roy stated. "It was around one o'clock here. I got your answering service and left a message that was urgent. You called me back an hour later and said that you would be on the first flight available."

"At two A.M., after turning in the car you used to run me and Dolores off the road, you went over to another rental company and hired another car. The one sitting in my driveway right now. You grabbed a few hours' sleep at the Best Western near the airport, then you drove back to Ruidoso, arriving at the ranch around seven."

Robert swallowed. "You've been busy the last few days, Johnny."

"You taught me to make sure all my *i*'s were dotted and my *t*'s were crossed, Bobby."

The district attorney stood up. "The big question is: Did you perpetrate this crime on your own?"

Averting his eyes, his lower lip starting to tremble, Robert shook his head. "Neither Foster nor Formation were involved in this in any way. I acted totally on my own. Jesus, Johnny, I didn't mean for anybody to get killed. I just thought that if I scared her enough she'd think twice before pressing on with her investigation. I'd been working for Formation for several years. I knew if

WHITEHORSE   323

Dolores began uncovering too much, my association
with them would come out and I'd fry right along with
them."

"Who, exactly, is 'them'?" Ted Weir asked.

Laughing dryly, Robert raised his eyebrows. "Oh, no.
The only way you're going to get that kind of information out of me is going to be with a promise of wit-
ness protection."

Singer picked up the tape recorder and hit the Off
button. He slid the machine into his pocket before turning to Johnny. "I take it you got the evidence you
needed on Senator Foster and Formation."

Johnny looked past the DA, into Savanah's eyes.
"No," he replied.

"But you said—"

"I lied."

Silence filled up the room briefly, then Ted said, "It
won't end here, Johnny. Photographs or not. You realize
that don't you? At some point you're going to have to
tell what you know to the committee."

Johnny did not respond as Robert was escorted out of
the office between Parker and Singer. Roy, Ed, and Jack
followed, leaving Savanah and Johnny alone. She closed
the door and leaned against it, her face aflame with
color.

"You bastard, Johnny. What do you think you're doing? You're going to let Foster get away with it, aren't
you. All because of her. Because of Leah and the boy.
My God, I never believed you would turn your back on
your people."

"We all must make choices in life—"

"And you choose her."

"I can't destroy her. I would rather destroy myself."

"You're going to do just that, Johnny. You won't be
able to live with the guilt. Every time you look in the face
of one of our people's children you'll know unimaginable

shame. No matter how deeply you love this woman, you are who you are, and *what* you are. That will never change.''

Johnny withdrew the envelope of photographs and tossed them across the desk.

''Fine,'' Savanah cried, grabbing up the package. ''I'll do it. For Dolores—''

''Do you think Dolores's intent to blow Foster and Formation to hell had anything to do with loyalty to our people? If you think that, then you are more naïve than I thought. Dolores wanted a network job. She couldn't give a damn about the People.''

Savanah marched toward the door, yanked it open, then stopped, slowly turned, her eyes filled with tears. ''You know if I do this and Foster is destroyed, she will still blame you.''

''Perhaps.''

''You love her that much?'' She shook her head. ''Damn you, Johnny Whitehorse.''

Leah smiled into her son's drowsy eyes as the doctor in charge quietly relayed orders to the attending nurses. He then placed a comforting hand on Leah's shoulder. ''We're over the worst, I think.''

Shamika moved to the bed and took Val's hand. She held it to her cheek and did her best not to cry as Leah pressed a kiss to his brow. His lips curved into his familiar smile, and light flickered in his eyes.

''Johnny?'' he whispered.

''Johnny was here to see you this morning. He brought you a gift.'' She held up the amulet. ''He made it himself, just for you.''

''Johnny still love Val?''

''Oh, yes, my darling. He loves you very, very much.''

''Val, Mama, and Mika go home with Johnny?''

Leah looked up at Shamika before responding. ''We'll see. First you have to get well.''

His eyes drifted closed. Leah and Shamika continued

to hold his hands as the doctor completed his chart, then set it aside.

"His condition has stabilized, Mrs. Starr. The best thing you could do right now is to go home and get some sleep. If there's any change we'll call you."

Shamika nodded. "I'll stay with him."

Leah took a weary breath and nodded. "Maybe for a while."

Upon leaving the room, Leah found Richard in the waiting area, asleep on a sofa. She had been angry with Shamika at first over contacting Richard's parents about Val, then thankful. Richard had arrived in a few hours, had donated blood just in case Val needed it. Thank God, he hadn't.

"Leah?"

She turned.

Savanah Rainwater moved out of the shadows. "I'm happy that your son has improved."

"I thought you left Ruidoso days ago."

"I did. But I had some unfinished business."

Leah looked beyond her, scanned the hospital corridor.

"If it's Johnny you're looking for, he isn't here. I left him back at the ranch. I assume he's still there."

"If you came here to defend Johnny—"

"I guess you haven't heard."

Leah frowned, uncertain if she could handle any more bad news at the moment.

"Johnny has just cleared your father of my sister's death."

Sinking back against the wall, Leah closed her eyes.

"That's where Johnny's been the last few days, gathering proof that Robert Anderson is the one who ran Johnny and Dolores off the road that night. You see, Robert is involved with Formation Media. Very much involved. Along with a number of senators and governors, all of whom are making it very easy for a great many very powerful men to control the gambling in this and other countries.''

Savanah reached into her purse and withdrew a package. She placed it in Leah's hands. ''Johnny gave these to me to do what I want with them. They're photos I and another photographer took at the Crystal Casino in Toronto and the Rama Rio Resort in Aruba.

''If I use those photographs . . .'' She looked away. ''Let's just say I've always considered Johnny Whitehorse a gift to our people, one, I'm sorry to say, who isn't appreciated by the People as he should be. Sometimes we stand so close to a good thing we can't see it distinctly enough to recognize its worth. I've known Johnny to love only one thing greater than the People, and that was you. Until today I simply didn't realize just how much he loves you, that he would sacrifice all that he believes in and has worked for to protect your heart.

''At this very moment your father is preparing to go on television to make a statement regarding the fact that he has been cleared of Dolores's murder, and the fact that Johnny has publicly stated that he will no longer pursue the senator's affiliation with Formation Media, that as far as he knows no evidence exists that could link your father to Formation.

''I feel sick when I think of what this will do to Johnny. His reputation, his political future, his . . . pride. When at last he has found a voice to speak to the world against injustice, who will listen to him now? And believe him?''

Savanah turned and walked down the corridor.

Leah opened the package and withdrew the photographs.

Senator Foster adjusted his tie as a young man blotted his nose with powder and another smoothed down a few gray hairs on the top of his head. His speechwriter shoved several papers into his hands as a KRXR producer barked orders into a headset and nodded to Foster.

"Whenever you're ready, Senator."

Foster stepped through the door, waving at the mob
of reporters who filled the room with the harsh glare of
videocamera lights. He carefully moved over the tangle
of electrical cords, gingerly mounted the dais, and
stepped up to the mike.

The cameras whirred and clicked. Foster posed, smiling, both hands raised, thumbs up as the din of reporters
began to shout for his attention. He waited for the noise
to subside, smiling, laughing, shrugging and mugging
for the dozen cameras zooming in for a closeup of his
face.

"Senator, how are you feeling?" someone shouted.

"Relieved. The accusations hurled at me by Whitehorse the last few years took their toll, of course."

"What about the Senate investigative committee? Do
you think they'll be satisfied with Whitehorse's statement that he doesn't plan to further pursue this case?"

"I don't anticipate there being any problem with that.
My attorneys are with them now."

"What about your plans regarding Whitehorse? You
stated previously that you intended to bring a civil case
against him for slander."

"I fully intend to do just that. What that man has put
me and my family through the last few years is unspeak-
able."

"Senator, any truth to the rumor that you will now
make a bid for the presidency?"

"Before the senator responds to that question," Leah
said as she stood up, "perhaps he would like to explain
what business would take him to the Crystal Casino in
Toronto as well as the Rama Rio Casino in Aruba—both
owned by Formation Media—both times corresponding
with meetings of the very powerful and questionable Formation consortium."

The room fell silent as Leah moved from her chair
and toward the dais where her father stared down at her,
squinting from the lights, his jaw working and his face

turning red. He glanced at the cameras and the reporters, and cleared his throat.

"Leah? What the hell are you doing?"

"I asked you a question, Senator. Will you stand there and deny you were ever at those casinos?"

"I might have visited them. Hey, even senators are allowed to have a little fun now and again." He laughed into the mike, his eyes narrowing as Leah stepped up onto the dais beside him and laid down the photographs. She covered the mike with her hand and looked into his eyes.

"I was wrong, Senator. You *are* a monster. I'm just sorry it's taken me so damn long to admit it."

Leah turned her back on her father and jumped from the dais. The room full of shocked reporters came alive, swarming over one another in an effort to thrust their microphones at her face.

"I have no comment regarding my father's crimes or his impending resignation. The evidence in my possession will be turned over to the proper authorities as soon as I leave here. You may discuss the issue with them."

"Ms. Starr, what about the rumor that you intend to marry Johnny Whitehorse?"

"True," she replied, smiling.